DIVIDED

BEN ANDREWS

Edited by Eden Editorial.

Cover art by Tithi Luadthong

ISBN: 978-1-9192367-0-4

In a world that seems full of darkness, this story is here to shed some light and hope.

* * *

Part One

"In the heart of democracy's embrace, the vote bears all power, uniting families or driving them apart. Let the tapestry of a nation be woven not with the threads of falsehoods, but with the enduring fabric of transparency and unity."

Chapter One

Freedom Day

The crowds flocked like sheep to the stands, adorned in the colours of 'freedom', the blues and purples that cover the country's flag. The cracked streets and litter-strewn roads seemed like a distant memory as they drew nearer to the imposing capital building, where the wall stood at its thinnest. Cheers roared through the crowd, infusing the district with an energy it hadn't experienced in years. Maya kept a close eye on her mother while guiding her through the throngs of people in time for the Freedom Day speech. Brass bands blasted music from atop the metal wall, a song Maya did not recognise.

Her brother Liam glanced back and smiled at both of them, forging a path toward the wooden barrier that served as yet another wall to separate them from the civilians on the other side. Guards stood, lined up in rows beyond, the grey towering wall as their backdrop.

The band concluded its performance, followed by a chorus of cheers. Atop the grey metal wall, the governor of New Albion approached the stand. Maya quickly glanced at her mother, whose opposition to the divide was well known, although her wide smile contradicted this as Governor Granswick began his address.

"Esteemed citizens of Albion! Today we gather to celebrate Freedom Day. A momentous occasion marking the triumph of progress and unity in our beloved country," Granswick proclaimed. "As the governor of New Albion, I stand before you with a heart filled with pride and hope for our shared future."

Cheers from the other side of the wall momentarily drowned out his words. The governor turned toward the crowd surrounding Maya and raised his arms into the air as if embracing the entire nation. The people celebrated, lifting mugs of bitter ale and applauding the Governor fiercely. Liam joined them, clapping together with the crowd like an eager seal, and although Maya expected as much from him, she couldn't help feeling disappointed by her mother's willingness to play along with this facade. The sight forced Maya to close her eyes.

"Twenty years ago, our nation reached a crossroads," Granswick continued, projecting above the jubilant noise. "The vote incited fears and uncertainties in all our lives, but today, we stand here as living proof that embracing innovation and change was, indeed, the right decision. A decision we continue to uphold today."

Maya's mother wiped away a tear, and Liam put his arm around her shoulder in a hug Maya had been denied. Suppressing a shout, she bit her lip, asking above the crowd's clamour, "What truly lies behind this so-called 'freedom,' Governor?"

As his speech ended, the governor pressed a button atop a small podium, where the country's flag dropped along the wall, covering the cold exterior in bright blue and purple. The crowd became even more boisterous, and Maya braced herself for the inevitable surge of noise. It was moments like these where Maya couldn't help but yearn for her father's presence. Fixated on the flags swaying against the cold metal wall, she wondered if he was on the other side, cheering along with a different family without sparing a second thought for her or Liam.

"Today marks a new day for us to come together and share our knowledge and push forward for a brighter future together. Freedom Day has opened the way between the city and our people," the governor declared.

Maya forced a smile at Liam, who bowed his head; it was as if the governor was addressing him personally.

The pageantry continued for hours, and Maya's feet throbbed from having stood in the same spot on the cracked concrete. The crowd gradually thinned until only the most devout supporters lingered, eager for another glimpse of the handsome and charismatic governor from the new world who remained beyond their reach. Those who stayed raised their hands in the air, hanging onto the governor's every word. Maya watched them all now. An elderly lady closed her eyes and swayed to the band's music; they played an old anthem, a song of solidarity that had existed long before the divide.

"I'm going to the Old Vic to celebrate with the dock gang," Liam announced, turning swiftly to head back toward the district.

Their mother tapped Maya's shoulder. "You seeing Carla

there tonight?" She asked, swaying to the rhythm.

Maya narrowed her eyes, sensing what her mother's unspoken expectations were. Was this a last-minute test? "Want me to keep an eye on him?"

Nodding, her mother offered a sympathetic look. "Please. He has a lot going on over the next few days, and I don't want him suffering with a poor head."

"Will you be okay here?" Maya asked as her mother leaned against an old friend, or perhaps a stranger. She wasn't sure. "Take care of yourself, Mum. Don't overdo it either." Maya kissed her mother on the cheek and left the parade.

Strolling so close to the wall, Maya peered around the streets she had traversed her entire life. The stark contrast between the two sides became even clearer. Faint cracks in the concrete connected the roads, yet the fractures were insignificant compared to the scene before her only a mere few feet away.

Maya had always taken pride in her side of the nation, where people stood steadfast in their beliefs and voted with their hearts. But in this moment, she couldn't escape a sense of being cheated. The government forced over half the population to move to one side of the country, resulting in fewer homes and less land compared to the other, an unjust disparity. Sighing, Maya gazed up at the crumbling buildings lining the narrow pathway. People converted many houses into makeshift flats to accommodate multiple families, including Maya's. But if the rumours were true, the other side of the wall boasted ample space for every person, with clean streets and immaculate homes. Such inequality weighed heavily on her shoulders, while one question played on repeat in her mind: why was this allowed to happen?

The raucous atmosphere of The Old Vic surrounded her, where drunken men and women gathered outside to revel in the newfound promises of Freedom Day. Maya wasn't yet twenty-five, which meant she had, fortunately, avoided being part of the first batch of people able to venture across the wall. The thought of such a leap terrified her, as did the prospect of Liam working for New Albion. Would she lose him to them? She couldn't contemplate that now.

The Old Vic's neon signs illuminated Maya's face in the country's vibrant colours. Ripped banners and flags hung on the roof, remnants of past movements that no longer existed. Maya gently patted the shoulder of a stumbling man, who belted "Freedom Day for all!" at the top of his lungs. Pushing through the creaking wooden doors, Maya left the drunkenness of the outside world behind and stepped into the electric atmosphere that was The Old Vic.

Inside, timber beams reinforced the ceiling, lined with dusty relics from long-forgotten voyages and distant lands that now lay underwater. Weather-beaten flags and tattered sails adorned the walls, each telling a tale of the world's storied past. From how many years past? Maya did not know for certain. People did not share the history of this country, of the world beyond, as greatly as they once did. She could retell stories from school, from her father about her home, but these items, with their faded colours and dented metal, told stories of bloodshed and difficulties that the government would not relate.

Maya searched for Liam, ignoring the aged games of truth or dare and the marks from drunken stories. Instead, she found Carla behind the bar. With a headband holding back her blonde hair and flushed cheeks, she poured drinks and took orders from thirsty punters.

"Need a hand?" Maya shouted over the music.

Carla shook her head, unable to reply over the cacophony. Instead, she passed a glass to Maya, who joined her beside the bar. "This one's on the house," she said. "Bloody hectic here tonight. Too much dancing for my liking. It hasn't stopped! They'll regret it in the morning, mind." Maya raised an eyebrow. "I heard the other side is getting three days of celebration. It must be easy for them to carry on into the night with sore heads, unlike us. I mean, look at Gil!" Maya glanced at Gil slumped down on a table. Carla shook her head and turned away to tend to another customer.

Maya looked towards Gil again, who slept with his hand still wrapped around his drink, before squinting through the smoke-screen to search the mismatched tables. Still, there was no sign of Liam.

As night descended, Maya considered going home. She assumed Liam had made a wiser choice and retired early, too. Swirling her drink around the glass, she winced at the bitter taste lingering on her tongue. Carla leaned over the bar to rest her chin in her hand, seeming to eavesdrop on the intoxicated argument taking place beside her.

"We should never have agreed to this in the first place! But now it's here, we need to grab it!" slurred a man, slamming his fist onto the worn bar. It was George, Maya realised, and so she joined them, patting her coworker on the back.

Smiling at the woman opposite him, Maya gestured with her glass towards Carla before turning back to face her. "Part of the late-night crew?" she asked. "What are you arguing about now?"

The slender woman turned her head. She scraped her

black hair back into a tight ponytail. "About Freedom Day, and the utter hypocrisy that comes with it, name and all."

George shifted his attention to the woman. "It isn't that at all. We've waited years for something like this, a chance for us finally to catch up to those on the other side."

"And you believe everything you're fed?" The woman asked, sipping from her glass.

"Of course. They have no reason to lie," George said confidently, prompting a stifled laugh from Maya. "Got something to add? Your own brother is on his way over there, ain't he?" George said, pointing at Maya.

Maya narrowed her eyes, feeling embarrassed beneath the woman's judgemental gaze. "Yeah, well, I told him not to apply for that. But I'm not his keeper. I'm staying here, this side of the wall. That's all I can do."

The woman smiled. "I don't blame anyone. The apprenticeship scheme is tempting. It's designed to be. But my gran has told me too many things about life before the divide. They're all liars, both sides. It's better off this way. Keep them apart from us."

Carla handed Maya another drink and kept one for herself. "It'll be interesting to hear from everyone who goes over to see what life's really like over there," Carla said, swinging her right arm in the air; she had her left arm removed from below the elbow when she was young.

"You hear so many things about how wonderful and clean it is. Might not all be true," Maya added, sipping her drink. The bitterness still stung her throat. "Liam said that they are forbidden from discussing their work on the other side. Once they come back over after work, that's it. Says so in the contract. Loads of rules! Pages and pages of them."

The woman raised an eyebrow. "Who's going to stop

them?"

George stopped Maya from answering. "They'll know. Over there, they have all that stuff: trackers, IDs, cameras in every corner. They know everything about everyone on that side. I've heard all about it," George explained. "It's like another world over there. They have kept most of it secret from the rest of us so far, ain't they? It'll stay that way. Mark my words."

Maya pushed her drink away, not in the mood to argue with George, especially while intoxicated. She didn't want to face him tomorrow with no recollection of what she'd said. "I'm going to leave you guys to put the world to rights. I should head back home, anyway."

Maya returned along the narrow streets, a mismatch of makeshift extensions attached to the side of buildings, now used as extra bedrooms for families, and market stalls closed for the night. More litter than usual blew across the roads in the night winds, scattered remnants of the Freedom Day celebrations, posters, food cartons, and flags, all meant to create a sense of unity in the country. She passed by a small group of huddled individuals, who whispered with their hoods up, holding tight to the carefully folded banners beneath their arms. Protesters. It was strange not having seen them during today's event. Perhaps New Albion had sent additional guards over the divide to keep things in check, Maya thought.

As Maya reached her home, she found Liam leaning against the faded and chipped brick walls with a cigarette burning away in his hand. Embers floated off in the wind, carrying the weight of his thoughts. Liam seemed oblivious to Maya's approach. Only when she stood a few inches away did he finally react.

"Mum know you're out here smoking?" Maya asked.

Liam rolled his eyes and tapped the end of the cigarette into the air. "I'm old enough."

"Then tell her," Maya said with a closed smile.

"Nah, don't want to upset her." Liam puffed his chest out, the skin showing between the buttons of his shirt.

"She wanted you to have an early night, you know."

"She wanted you to come home sober, but here we are."

Maya pushed Liam's arm playfully and leaned against the wall beside him. "Can't sleep?"

"Why'd you ask?"

"Come on. It's okay to be nervous. It's a big deal," Maya said.

"What is?" Liam blew smoke into the air with a smile as Maya glared at him. "I'm just messing with ya, sis. To be honest, I'm shitting myself. All I've ever known is the dock, the lads, and trading. I'm going to stand out the second I step foot over there."

Maya took the cigarette from his grip and placed it between her lips, inhaling the smoke until she felt the heat fill her chest. "I've heard it's paradise over there, but I've also heard… other things. It's not too late to say no. If you really don't want to go, no one will mind."

Liam raised an eyebrow, his eyes flicking towards the flat. "What about her?"

"Yeah, good point. Mum's counting on the extra money. Guess we all are."

"You'll be taking up my old job, too, sis. How are you feeling about it?"

Maya glanced in the direction of the dock in the distance, across the city and toward the ocean, a world she didn't know. Liam accepting the apprenticeship scheme in New

Albion meant she got to fill his role here, while also continuing her delivery job. "It'll be fine," Maya said, trying to reassure herself as much as him. "I'll do what I have to."

"Won't we all." Liam flicked the cigarette butt on the ground before stubbing it out with his shoe. "They're a talented group down at the dock. Just keep your wits about you. Listen to their orders and do what they say." He turned to open the door. "Gil will keep an eye on you."

"But who will keep an eye on you?" Maya asked. "No one knows what it's like over that wall or the world they have created there. Please, Liam. Be careful. If it's too much, leave and come home. There's no shame in it."

Alone, Maya looked up at the sky. The glow from New Albion made the stars difficult to spot now; she used to see so many as a child. Her earliest memory was sitting on her father's knee, gazing up at the night sky as he pointed out different constellations to her. She glanced toward the blue radiance of life emanating from the other side of the wall, a stark contrast to the darkness enveloping hers. She thought of her father again, wondering why he had lied, why he voted the way he did. A choice that tore their family apart and split the country into two. Now, all these years later, her brother was stepping over the line, venturing to see what else the world could offer. Maya squeezed her fingers tightly, hoping she wouldn't lose him to the divide as well.

Chapter Two

A New Beginning

The taste of salt lingered on Liam's tongue as the sea breeze grazed his cheeks; he breathed in the familiar scents of the docks and glanced at his surroundings. Weathered ropes dangled from the towering cranes, hoisting heavy containers from the ground to waiting ships. Those vessels, which were once grand vessels, now bore the marks of time, their hulls rusted, and paint flaky under the relentless assault of the waves.

The crew moved in sync like a dance of thieves. Sweat dripped from their brows as they skilfully manoeuvred the cargo onto the docked ship, while Gil stood nearby with a cigar dangling from his mouth, watching their every move. Liam licked his lips, savouring the taste of sea salt. He wondered if he should stay, forget the scheme, and continue to work in the world he knew, and with the people he admired.

Striding along the dock, he glanced at the missing nails in the wood beneath him, remembering all the places and times he had stumbled and tripped as the new boy on site. Yet navigating these well-worn paths now felt like second nature. He skilfully skipped the loose boards on his way over to Gil, who blew smoke from his cigar.

Liam clutched the papers his mother had given him, overcome with a mix of excitement and nerves. His mother had insisted he double-check everything, but he hadn't. Instead, he folded the documents and trusted that she knew what she was doing.

Gil's gravelly voice broke through his thoughts. "Still got time for us, boy?" he asked, a hint of amusement in his eyes. "There's still time for you to haul a few containers up there."

Liam glanced down at his clothes, hoping to keep them clean for his upcoming meeting. With wide eyes, he looked at Gil, silently pleading. A knowing smile crept along Gil's lips, concealed partly by his white beard. Liam playfully pushed his shoulder. "Don't do that, Gil. I'm already nervous as it is."

Gil chuckled and rested the cigar in the ashtray. "I remember you said the same on your first day here," he replied. "But you got over it, and you'll do the same over there."

Liam had spent years on the docks with Gil. He looked towards Gil's shack, the place he called an office, and thought of the photo he came across long ago. "Seeing as it's my last time here, you ready to tell me about the woman you have shut away in your desk draw?"

Liam smiled. Gil refused to speak of the woman in the photo, and it had almost become an inside joke between the men who'd worked here the longest. He'd blown his top when he first caught Liam looking at it. Ever since, Liam always wondered who she was.

Gil narrowed his eyes. "She's a memory, boy. That's all you need to know about the matter." His eyes fell on the stack of papers in Liam's hand. "What you got there?"

"Papers," Liam replied, swinging them into the air. "ID, certificates, stuff like that... I think."

Gil raised an eyebrow and patted Liam on the shoulder, knocking him forward. Liam rubbed his arm and knew that Gil's gesture was supposed to be encouraging, even if it stung a little. "Well, I best get on board. That shipment won't sail itself to the west." Gil made to step away.

"But..." Liam trailed off, and Gil's stern look told him to keep any objections to himself. Gil ingrained his mantra, "No moaning, no complaining, no worries," in every dock worker's mind. They were a team, like cogs in a clock, and everyone had to pull their weight to maintain the place smoothly.

Liam stepped back into the makeshift shelter. During work hours, Gil often stood there, watchfully overseeing operations to ensure every second was accounted for and up to date. As Gil's stony expression relaxed into raised cheeks, a wry smile crept onto his weathered face. He playfully slapped Liam on the shoulder again, causing another surge of pain to move to his spine. "I'm only messing with you, lad. Couldn't help but give you one last go," Gil chuckled, his gruff laugh resonating in the air. "So, who's coming over then to see me? Not the governor himself?"

Liam shook his head, a hint of excitement in his voice. "No, it's a woman. Someone in charge of the freedom scheme. I'm not sure of her name; Mum said it should be written there... somewhere." He glanced over Gil's shoulder at the endless words printed on the pages, and his heart raced as he tried to locate any information.

Gil's thick finger paused on a line about halfway down the page. "Here it is. A Miss Abigail Thorn," he declared, his tone tinged with curiosity. He turned to address the crew working alongside the ship. "Listen up, lads! We've got an unmarried woman here today. So, you best look smart. Can't have you lot showing up our Liam now!"

Liam couldn't help but grin at Gil's remark, grateful for his mentor's support. He brushed off his uniform; it was unusual for him to wear such formal clothes at the dock. Feeling the heat under the morning sun, and he wiped his brow, trying to cool down before Miss Thorn's arrival. The nerves crept back in then, and he fidgeted with his collar.

"I hope she's nice. What do you think she'll want to ask me?" Liam asked, hoping for some reassurance.

"Don't worry about it, lad. Leave it to Gil," he said, with a reassuring grin.

The sun hung low on the horizon and burned through the clouds as Liam anxiously awaited the woman's arrival. When the patter of approaching footsteps reached his ears, he turned to find a woman in a crisp black suit striding toward him in high heels. She had neatly tied back her dark hair and scanned her surroundings with sharp eyes. He swallowed hard, feeling a sudden wave of anxiety wash over him. He quickly tapped Gil on the shoulder. "That's her. It's got to be."

Gil turned and licked both of his palms before flattening Liam's hair. He sized Liam up. "Stand up straight, boy. Let her see that chest of yours and those big shoulders. It'll impress her, show you're strong." He gave Liam's stomach a friendly pat, prompting him to straighten in his seat. "Good Afternoon, Miss Thorn. It's a pleasure to meet you on such a bright day." Gil put out his hand to greet her, but Miss Thorn merely glanced at it, refusing to return the gesture.

"Miss, I'm Liam. I think you're here to see me," Liam said, extending his hand to mimic Gil's greeting. "It's an honour to meet you and for you to see my place of work."

Liam nervously handed over the documents he had been clutching all morning, his palms already sweating from the tension in the air. Miss Thorn nodded and began flicking through them. "Paperwork. Of course," she remarked before pulling out a small device to scan the documents. "I still can't get my head around you lot over here not using these. Still, needs must." She placed the papers along the table beside Liam, meticulously scanning each one. Her gaze shifted to Gil. "And you are the Dock Master?"

"That's right, ma'am. I've worked these docks my whole life, even before the divide," Gil replied proudly.

She handed the papers back to Liam, returning her attention to him. "And Liam, you've worked with Gil for a while now. What made you want to join the program?"

Liam glanced at the floor, noting how polished her shoes looked compared to his worn-out boots. Gil's gentle cough prompted Liam to gather his thoughts and glance back up to meet her stern face. "Well," he began, scratching his head and squinting against the beam of the sun. "I didn't want to let the opportunity pass. It's my chance to explore new possibilities and make a difference, I suppose. Plus, my mother was really keen on it."

Stepping forward, Gil said, "The boy is a brilliant worker, one of my best. He'll do you right, work hard, and do anything you ask of him without questions. Fast learner too, as long as you explain things clearly to him." Liam tried to hide the smile creeping along his lips. "To tell you the truth, I'll be sad to see him go. But he's a bright lad when given the chance. I know working over there will do him good. Seeing a new world."

Miss Thorn continued tapping away on her device as Gil spoke, apparently engrossed in whatever information she was gathering. "I'll send some paperwork to your address, Liam. I'll need you to fill the forms in: size, measurements for uniforms, stuff like that. Orientation is in four days. We expect all apprentices to be at the government building at ten a.m. sharp. New Albion side, not old. We will send you all the information, so until then, consider which role you'd like to apply for."

When she turned away. Liam stared at Gil, who shrugged. "Is that all, Miss? Am I in?"

Spinning on her heel, she said, "Yes. It was only a brief meeting to gather paperwork, meet your place of work, and check you were who you say you were. Our side usually completes such things in seconds." She looked Liam up and down. "Things take so much longer here. Good day."

With that, Miss Thorn bid him farewell and made her way back through the bustling docks. As she disappeared, Liam let out a sigh of relief and turned to Gil, who watched him with pride. "Well done, lad," he said, clapping Liam on the back once more.

"Thanks Gil." Liam let out a breath, then laughed. "You're like a pussycat compared to her."

"Lots of change coming to this country. It'll be good for you to be at the front of it."

Liam leaned against the wooden table. "There are changes going on here, too. You'll look out for Maya, won't ya? Working the dock will be tough for her."

Gil lit another cigar. "She's tougher than you give her credit for, son. I looked out for you, didn't I?" Liam nodded. "Well then, I'll do the same for her too. Get her doing the same shifts you did. She'll soon learn."

Liam stood up. "What? The exact same?" Gil blew a puff of smoke into the hot air. "You're not sending her over to No Man's Land, are you? To do trades?"

"That's right. She's taking your role on, ain't she?"

Liam narrowed his eyes and wafted the smoke from his face. He'd just about been able to cope doing the trades, whereas Maya had never set foot in No Man's Land. He remembered his first time there, how out of place he felt, and how tricky it was to navigate the rules. "Gil, it'll be too much for her. Let her settle in first."

Gil shook his head. "Sorry, lad. My dock, my rules. I'll train her; I'll teach her what to do, and more importantly, what not to do. She'll be okay. I'll look out for her, like I always have with your family."

Liam scuffed his foot along the wooden dock. He couldn't fault Gil there. He had always been there, offering Liam and his family work opportunities for years. "Okay. I trust you. After all, you turned me around."

Gil smiled and rested a hand on Liam's shoulder. "Was a pleasure lad."

"I never thanked you for taking me on and teaching me… everything. It meant a lot to me."

A puff of smoke escaped the side of Gil's mouth as he said, "Come on now. Enough of that. You ain't leaving forever, and I ain't dying. So cut that out. The other guys will start talking." With that, Gil set off towards the boat to shout commands to the lads, the orange sun setting in the sky behind them. The sound of waves crashing made Liam feel nostalgic, making his eyes water. He quickly swiped at the tear rolling down his cheek as he got up, dusted off his clothes, and made his way home, leaving the docks behind him.

In the small, grimy mirror in his family's apartment, Liam's reflection stared back at him, except he looked different in his crisp navy-blue uniform. The fabric seemed foreign against his skin, and the pristine white shirt felt stiff and formal, and he self-consciously tugged at his collar, trying to get used to the feeling. With a deep breath, he collected his leather bag, another item sent from the other side, and checked inside it, ensuring that the device they had supplied him was there and undamaged.

"You ready, love?" His mother's voice echoed from the hallway, and he turned to face her, mustering up a confident smile, despite the anxious flutter in his chest. He took one last look in the mirror and nodded. His mother paused behind him with two bags under her arms. "I need to pop out and see a few clients. The summer heat is really making people struggle. Good luck today," she said, leaning in to kiss him goodbye. "And remember, once you're back here, on this side, no talk of that place. I'm happy for you, but I don't want to hear about it, and I don't want you getting into any trouble." She glanced towards his bag, as if suspicious of the device they'd supplied him with.

Liam knocked on Maya's door on the other side of the hall and entered. She'd drawn her tattered curtains, and the morning heat blazed through her small window, demanding entry. She turned her head, her hair a mess. "I'm off," Liam said gently as she opened her eyes a crack. "Gil's expecting you later today. You remember that, right?"

Maya let out a groan. "Yes," she managed, and Liam smiled, turning to close the door. "Wait, Liam!" she shouted, shifting herself up and wrapping the blanket around her. "Have a good day, yeah?"

He nodded. "I'll be fine," though he couldn't escape the nerves gnawing at his insides.

Maya laughed.

"Just be yourself. Any advice for work? Anything Gil doesn't like?"

Liam stepped into Maya's room, the wooden floor creaking beneath his footsteps. He pulled open the curtain and unlatched the window, allowing fresh air to circulate. "Yeah. Don't be late. Do what he asks and don't do anything he doesn't."

Maya rolled her eyes, pulling on a pair of jeans. "Yeah, yeah, all the normal stuff a boss says, got ya." She saluted playfully.

"I'm serious. It's a big deal. You'll be doing trade runs for the dock. So, keep your wits about you."

Maya's narrow eyes lit up. "Trade runs? Me?" She scrambled towards him on her knees, yanking at his trousers. "What do I have to do? Isn't that stuff dangerous?"

"And illegal, yeah," Liam replied, "But it pays well, so you got no choice. Plus, he trusts this family." He gently removed her grip from his uniform. "It'll mean going into No Man's Land. Just listen to what he says, listen to whoever it is you have to deal with, and do not question the way of things. Get in and get out. No messing around."

"Okay," Maya whispered, sitting on the edge of her bed. "Sounds like you have nothing to worry about, then. It's me who should be panicking." She fell back and pulled her pillow over her head.

Liam surveyed the room, now bathed in an orange glow. An empty bottle sat on the floor, where remnants of the liquid dripped from the end. She'd left a paper box of half-eaten food on the cabinet. "I'm going to be away a lot more going forward, Maya. I'm going to need you to step up."

She pulled the pillow from her head. "What does that mean?"

"Mum can't do as much as she could before. She does what she can for the community and visits people just as weak as her, truth be told. This heat, it's getting worse every summer. The winters are harsher too. She can't cope like she used to. Just try to mature a bit, like me," Liam said, pulling his shoulders back.

Maya rolled her eyes and chuckled. "Yeah, you're simply a brute, mate, but I hear you. I can do this. Don't spend your time worrying about me."

Liam walked towards the government building. The stages and celebrations from Freedom Day were now gone, leaving the place deserted except for a few recruits making their way inside. Following the wall, he noticed how the divide merged seamlessly into the towering building, leading to an entrance he never thought he'd step through. Shielding his eyes from the sun, he looked up at the tall pillars on either side of the entrance, their tiles laid out in intricate patterns, and the brickwork immaculately maintained. It was one of the few buildings on this side of the wall kept in such esteem.

Taking a deep breath, Liam stepped forward to join the line of recruits forming at the entrance. A mix of excitement and nervousness bubbled inside him as he waited. He tightened his grip on the strap of his bag, which provided only a small sense of reassurance. One step at a time, the line slowly advanced until he finally made it inside the building. The abrupt change in temperature took him by surprise, as if he'd stepped straight into a freezer.

Five lines continued into the vast hall, each leading to a scanner. The white marble floor reflected his image as he walked along, trying to find the right spot. Beside the scanner was a screen, and he rummaged through his bag, trying to remember his mother's advice, the order of what he needed to do. He pulled out the device, looked at it to turn it on, and placed it against the scanner. Green lines flashed along the screen, moving up and down. He glanced around to see if any workers could help when the screen flashed green and the barrier lifted. Liam hurried through, glancing back as it closed behind him, sealing off the path for the next person. He lifted his head as the cold air brushed against his forehead. Breathing it in, he allowed the air to fill his chest. He stepped forward and began walking along the long, vast hall towards the door that led to the other side. To New Albion.

Chapter Three

Crossing the Divide

On the unfamiliar streets of New Albion, Liam followed the line of fellow recruits, his eyes wide with wonder. The city was a stark contrast to the bustling chaos of Old Albion; here, the sandstone-coloured pavements were pristine, and manicured green bushes laid the path ahead. The silence surprised him. Back home, the streets resonated with the constant hum of activity, but here, he could hear birds chirping, the gentle rustle of the wind, and the rhythmic patter of his own footsteps.

Like him, the only souls braving the roads were those en route to the orientation, all clad in the same navy-blue uniform he had received, an air of camaraderie among strangers.

Adding to his fascination was an intriguing sight: a dark, box-like machine, smaller than a car, that glided along the road, sweeping away dirt and dropped leaves. Such a scene was beyond anything he had ever seen back home, where members of the community took turns sweeping up the rubbish. The advanced technology here truly made New Albion feel like another world. Lost in thought, Liam realised he'd fallen behind the others. He pulled out the map he'd drawn with his mother's help, using the instructions documented in his paperwork. A red line showed what streets and paths he needed to take. His eyes lifted, locking onto a bell tower in the distance with a clock beneath it. That was the landmark his mother had mentioned.

As Liam continued along the path, engrossed in his map, he collided with someone and dropped it. He glanced up to apologise.

Before him stood a young man with an air of regal elegance, tall and lean, with dark blonde hair neatly tucked behind his ears. The man wore a uniform like Liam's, but he exuded a certain authority and experience that set him apart. Liam straightened, feeling suddenly self-conscious about his own stiff attire. "Sorry about that, sir," he stammered, unsure of how to act around this well-kept gentleman.

The man kindly handed Liam his map. "Don't be silly. Here, you dropped this. I assume you're here for the orientation?"

Liam nodded. His cheeks flushed, worried that the man might judge his simple drawing as he folded the map and tucked it into his bag. "Yes, that's right. I got a bit distracted. New Albion really lives up to the rumours."

"I'm Alexander," the man chuckled. "But you can call me Alex. Orientation begins shortly. Follow me, and I will show you the way. It'll give you a chance to look around without having to keep your eyes glued to that map." With that, Alex set off at a brisk pace with long strides that covered more ground, forcing Liam to not fall behind.

As they walked, Alex pointed out the different districts. "This is District 1-A, where the government buildings are. All the buildings you'll need are in this area. And over there in 2-A, you'll find the historical buildings, if you ever wish to explore them and learn a bit about our history."

Liam nodded, trying to make sense of the districts. "Not very imaginative names," he remarked.

"No, well. It's easier that way," Alex smirked, explaining that the AI works best with simple numbers and letters. "Because District A is closest to the divide, they sort most official business into that district. Understand?"

Liam nodded again, and though he didn't completely understand the intricacies of it all, he didn't want to seem ignorant. Instead, he said, "Yeah, I think so."

As they continued their walk, Liam tried to fill the silence with small talk. "I saw a machine just now, cleaning the street. Quite amazing."

Alex raised an eyebrow. "A street cleaner? Well, they are some of the more basic help we have here." He laughed.

"What's so funny?" Liam asked, scratching his head.

"Oh, nothing. Just your innocence," Alex replied with a warm smile before stopping at the street corner and pointing ahead. "Okay, follow the road to that building over there. That's where you need to be. I'll let you venture on your own. I can't have people thinking I have favourites." He chuckled.

Liam walked toward the grand glass building, its towering walls reflecting the glint of sunlight. Inside, a buzz of people stood in lines, and he joined one as it slowly inched forward. Each person reached a scanner, like the one he had used to enter New Albion. Fishing out his ID, Liam scanned in, relieved when the green light flashed to grant him access.

As he stepped through, he spotted Miss Thorn making her way in his direction, holding a device in her hand. "Liam, I'm glad you made it. Your device please?" she asked, glancing at his bag.

Liam's mind momentarily blanked as he tried to process what she was asking for. "Device? Oh, *my* device, sorry." Panic set in as he put his bag onto the floor and crouched to rummage through it. He felt her eyes burning into the back of his head, even more so when he couldn't find it amidst the endless paperwork. He felt a pen, one his mother told him to bring, but no device.

"Having trouble?" She asked, tapping her foot.

Liam stood. "Well..." he said, patting his uniform. There it was, in his pocket. He sighed and pulled it out. "Here you go."

She reached out her other hand. "ID? The certificate that was sent to you."

"Oh right, yeah." Liam felt panic run through him again as he pulled the paper from his bag and flipped through, looking up at her and then the paper. The words were a jumble of backward symbols and letters. He smiled at her and picked a page. "Is this the one?" he asked, handing it over.

"Give that to me." She snatched the pile of papers and thumbed through, pulling one page out before handing the rest back to Liam with a sigh. "Right, all those papers you have there are not needed. Your ID will now be linked to this device." She waved the device in front of his face. "Going forward, all you need is this. Everything will be stored on there. Any idea on what role you would like to explore, or would you prefer to let the AI choose for you?"

Liam furrowed his brows, trying to grasp the options presented to him. "Chosen for me? What do you mean?" he asked.

Miss Thorn sighed again, seeming slightly exasperated. "There are two options. First, you can enter your information through the system, allowing the AI database to determine the best role suited for your strengths. Or second, we have an option for Old Albion citizens like you, where you can select a role on your own. Judging by your swiftness in finding your paperwork and device, I would suggest allowing the AI to select a role for you."

"I see," Liam replied, glancing around the bustling hall. People were beginning to form into groups and heading off in various directions, holding devices that showed they had chosen their roles. "What do I need to do?"

Miss Thorn tapped Liam's device and pulled out a small box from her pocket. "Place this on the right side of your head, just above your ear," she instructed, showing him a tiny white circle. Liam looked at her, confused. "It's perfectly safe, see." She turned her head to reveal a small circle placed on her own head.

Liam picked up the device, dangling it between his fingertips. "What does it do?" he asked, glancing around at the others.

"It connects to the device here," Miss Thorn explained, gesturing to Liam's device. "It feeds back information about your location, health, and other relevant data. You'll take it off when you finish for the day." She gently guided his hand to place the device above his ear, where it stuck like a magnet to the skin. "This was all written in your original contract. You read it, didn't you?"

Liam nodded, though he hadn't read the contract, not one bit. His mother had assured him it was fine. "Okay, what now?" he asked, wanting to move past the subject.

Miss Thorn continued tapping his device. "Now, you'll hear a slight ringing in your ear for a few seconds. After that, it's all done. Ready?" Before Liam could respond, a ringing pierced his right ear. He closed his eyes and clenched his jaw, waiting for it to stop. When it finally did, he opened his eyes to find Alex in the background, assisting another person with a similar device. Alex seemed to be in the same role as Miss Thorn. Liam looked at Miss Thorn's cold narrow face, and then over at Alex, who patted the recruit kindly on the shoulder.

"So, what does it say?" Liam asked.

Miss Thorn looked up with a smile. "Guard duty," she replied. "Alexander!"

Liam felt his heart race as Alex finished his conversation and walked towards them. "Meet Liam. He's been appointed guard duty. Can I leave him with you to show him the ropes and go over things? That section is now full. So, if you can take Liam, that would be great." Miss Thorn walked off, without another look at either of them, to approach another recruit. Liam did not know what guard duty entailed, but he enjoyed how important it sounded.

Alex smiled at Liam and handed him his device back. "We meet again, and so soon."

"Yeah, small world," Liam replied, trying to make light of the situation.

Alex chuckled. "Guard duty, huh? Lucky governor." He looked Liam up and down. "Is that what you expected?"

Liam shrugged. "I didn't know what to expect, really."

Alex nodded. "None of us did. This is all new to us as well, remember? It's exciting, though, having some fresh blood in the system. Beats us sitting around speaking to the screens all day, anyway."

Liam followed Alex as they walked through a narrow hall; the architecture bore a resemblance to the government building he'd gone through to get here. Elaborate designs along the pillars and complicated tiles on the ceiling. "So... guard duty? What exactly is that?" Liam asked. "Are you a guard?"

Alex chuckled again. "No, not precisely. I'm in charge of the new recruits. Now, guard duty! It's a simple role; it's more of a name, really. You won't be expected to rush into battle or protect the governor, if that's what you're thinking."

Outside, a vibrant courtyard greeted Liam with an array of intoxicating colours: bright reds, blues, and yellows, all shimmering in the midday heat. They followed a gravel path that cut through the pristine grass, neatly guarded by short picket fences. To the side, Liam noticed another small box, like the one cleaning the streets, except this one was clear white, gently spraying water on the flowers. On the opposite side, a second machine cut the grass, trimming each blade to precision.

Alex stopped, seeming to notice Liam's wonder. "What, not going to tell me you're surprised by lawn engineers now, are you? You are so funny."

Liam glanced at his shoulder, where Alex now rested his hand, leaning over him. "No, of course not." Liam straightened. "It's just that we don't have these kinds of things in Old Albion. It's strange, it's only a few miles away, but it's so different."

They continued their walk. "This route is one you'll follow as part of your duty. Your device will have everything mapped out for you, right there in red, see?" Alex pointed to the screen, displaying a map of the government building with a red line running across it. He tapped it, and a list of times appeared. "You'll follow the route to the time. It's easy, really."

"So, lots of walking, then?" Liam asked, grateful that his job involved being outside.

"I'm sure a strapping man like you can manage that," Alex teased, laughing. "It's not all walking routes, though. Eventually, you'll be expected to stand in on meetings, events, things like that. Important work."

"Events? Like Freedom Day?" Liam asked, recalling the recent celebration.

"Exactly. It's mainly all show. When we have special visitors, you'll stand in the room on the Governor's side, with your arms behind your back, and face forward. It makes people feel uneasy and benefits us during negotiations."

Liam nodded, taking it all in. "It sounds like there's a lot more to guard duty than I initially thought."

"Oh, there is, eventually. But don't worry, you'll get the hang of it soon enough, and I'll be here to help you along the way," Alex assured him with a smile. "Let's continue our tour."

Once they passed through the courtyard, Liam entered a more clinically decorated area, stripped down to cold white partitions and bright lights.

They entered an elevator, and Liam's ears popped as the doors opened onto a different floor. They walked through hallways with glass walls showing empty rooms and unoccupied desks. Slowing down, Liam tried to take everything in. "What are these rooms used for?"

Alex stopped and opened a door, gesturing for Liam to enter first. "Offices, or at least they were, once. Not so much anymore. Most staff work from home now. These rooms are being changed bit by bit. We'll eventually hold servers in here; it'll allow more power for the AI database, allowing it to do more around the country."

A wry smile appeared on Liam's face. "Ha, so it ended up taking jobs then, like they warned?" He turned to Alex and crossed his arms.

"Well, no. The government's latest report shows that jobs are up by twenty percent, except many more work from home and stay in their allocated areas." Alex wrapped his arm around Liam's back and guided him towards a window. From here, Liam could see the entire city, past the tall buildings that towered over green fields, homes, and parks. Alex traced a path on the window with his fingers. "See, following the lines of the roads, you can see how the city and houses are arranged into blocks."

Liam stepped back, suddenly dizzy from the height. "So, people don't leave their area?"

"Not so much anymore; there's no need. That's why the street was so empty when you arrived this morning."

Liam turned back to the door and stepped into an office on the opposite side. "Can you see Old Albion from this side?" he asked, rushing towards the window. Outside, he saw the divide, just as grey and cold as it looked on his side. He had never realised how high it was raised above the ground. He followed it with his eyes, every curve and slight bend until it faded away in the distance. It truly seemed never-ending. Across the wall were the houses of his district, each house roof painted sky blue to blend into the surroundings.

"Come on. Enough looking at the scenes. Let's carry on." Alex led Liam back to the hallway and to the doors at the end. Inside, there were other guards. Liam counted twelve before losing track. Some were clearly new, like him, while others' uniforms had faded, showing they had been in the job for a while. Alex clapped his hands together to capture the room's attention. Liam joined the other guards, who straightened and lined up against the wall at the first sight of Alex. Liam positioned himself on the far end, and Alex stood beside him, joining the line. "I thought you were in charge," Liam whispered.

Alex shook his head and placed his finger on his lips. "The manager of this building is the boss. There's one for each department. He'll be here in a second to introduce himself, and then we can relax a bit."

Liam faced forward, staring at the blank wall before him. A man entered from the glass double doors at the end of the room, his steps echoing along the floor before coming to a halt. "Welcome, recruits. It is truly an honour to have you all here today," he announced bluntly. "This time has been long in the making. All of you here today are the first, the ones who will decide if this scheme works or not." The man began walking along the line. His deep voice was commanding. When Liam first heard him speak, something in his head recognised it, the tone of it. "I want you to understand how important it is for us to get this right. The people of Old Albion voted against the use of AI, a choice some later regretted, while others stood by it. Either way, today, we begin the first steps into allowing each other back into our lives. I want this to work. We can offer each other so much. So, as we get through your trial, be patient, ask questions, and *learn*." Liam held in stomach. Could it be him? "All recruits will be given a hand, someone more experienced to guide you. You will follow them for the first few weeks, and after that, if things work out, we will offer you permanent contracts."

Liam felt Alex's finger press into his arm, and he turned to peek at him, finding a smile on Alex's lips. Liam smiled back before facing forward. The manager continued to step along the line until meeting Liam's eyes. Liam held his stare before focusing on the opposite wall. A bead of sweat appeared on his forehead as his heart raced. Liam's eyes darted back to the man in a flash, wanting to confirm what he had seen, yet the man walked past and gave Liam one last look before returning to the centre of the line. He was still speaking, talking about responsibility and the importance of duty, but Liam couldn't hear the words any longer. Thoughts rushed through his mind; he couldn't believe it. He turned his head again, with a desire to look at him one more time. It was him, he thought, except with less hair, and more lines along his eyes. But it was him. Liam clenched his fists.

His father.

Obviously, his father didn't recognise Liam; how could he? It had been twenty years. Liam was just a boy when they last saw each other. Had Liam really changed that much? He shook his head, trying to process the overwhelming emotions surging within him. His father finished his speech and returned to the room he came from. The entire lineup of guards let out a sigh of relief and finally relaxed their shoulders. Alex turned to Liam. "So, are you ready to do everything I say?" He jabbed Liam in the side. "What's up? Don't let Robert scare you. He's as gentle as can be."

Liam bit his lip. Robert. His father's name. It was him. The man who lied, who said he sided with his family yet voted against them. The public release of the votes tore the man from his home and sent him to live in New Albion. Liam looked at the doors to where his father had been and wondered if he knew his son had stood right before him or if he had forgotten that life and moved on to make a new one.

Chapter Four

Navigating the Unknown

Maya's trusty ancient moped soared through the air like a bullet as she navigated the streets with ease. With wind-kissed cheeks and hair whipping around her face, Maya embraced the speed, the freedom. She closed her eyes for a moment, approaching the main street, savouring the rush of adrenaline before opening them again to focus on the road ahead. The bustling market stalls and pedestrians blurred into a colourful collage while the vibrant life of the district unfolded beside her.

Maya weaved through the crowd on her moped, dancing between the dusty crossings and counting the side alleys that intersected with the main road. She knew every twist and bend by heart. Tightening her grip on the handlebars, she prepared for a sharp turn down Rust Avenue and gradually slowed.

She halted at an unexpected obstacle in her path. A lazy cat sprawled over the road, basking in the scarce shade provided by a nearby market stall. Irritation flickered across Maya's face. "Stupid cat, move!" she yelled. She couldn't slow down on her shift, not now. She felt a tinge of guilt for getting irritated. The cat merely lifted its head, unimpressed, before promptly returning to its slumber. Sighing with exasperation, Maya swung her leg off the moped and pushed it forward, glancing around. New posters adorned the walls with fresh plaster. "Oh god," she muttered under her breath. "Lottery Day coming back around already." She ripped the poster from the wall and threw it to the ground.

She scanned the address again. She hated doing a run in this area of the district, where the homes and businesses were so close to the divide. It was always the topic of any conversation.

Above the rusted metal gate was a sign which read 'The Serpent's Lounge' in faded green paint. With her head still pounding from the night before, she pushed open the creaking door and descended into the dimly lit cellar. She had one last delivery to make before her shift was over, though she still had to face another one at the docks later. Maya gave a weary sigh and stepped into the smoky room.

The Serpent's Lounge was an underground bar housing rebellious youth with nothing better to do than chat, listen to music, and discuss the world's troubles. The air was thick with smoke, yet even then, you could discern the neon lights on each table, casting a glow that danced on the ceiling in vibrant strips of colours. Navigating through the clusters of teenagers, Maya shouted, "Delivery for Kong!" She double-checked the name on the package to ensure she said it right, yet the conversations continued.

Maya walked up to the bar, where a server with long

dreadlocks blew a puff of smoke into the air. The server forced a smile, her tight leather outfit reflecting the diffused neon colours in their surroundings.

"Got a parcel here for Kong. I'll leave it on the bar," Maya announced, placing the package on the side.

"You Liam's sister, ain't ya?" asked the server; her dreadlocks cascaded around her face.

Maya bit her lip and briefly closed her eyes before turning to face the woman. "What's it to you?" she asked, her voice guarded.

The server scrutinised Maya from head to toe. "Used to work the docks. Came in here a few times. He's gone to the other side today, ain't he?"

Feeling the attention of more eyes on her, Maya shifted on her feet. "What he does has nothing to do with me," she said, striding towards the exit.

The server's voice followed her, yet it now held a bitter edge. "Tell him he ain't welcome here no more. No one who goes over there to work for *them* is welcome here."

Maya's jaw clenched tighter, her frustration mounting as she watched the woman rip open the parcel. She couldn't simply walk away from this. She turned back to face her with narrowed eyes. "We are all just trying to survive. If he must go over there for work, to provide for his family, then *I'll* welcome him. It's not like you lot down here don't use tech, searching for any scraps you can," she retorted, her voice firm. Maya couldn't help but smile as she glanced back at the package she'd just delivered. It likely contained some electronic device. Items that were strictly prohibited on this side of the divide yet still used behind closed doors. Raising an eyebrow, Maya goaded, "Wanna show me what's in that?" She left a pause. This woman, she was Kong, the parcel was for her.

Kong rolled her eyes, snatching the package and placing it behind the bar. "Yeah, well, we don't go over there or accept their money. What your brother is doing goes against every rule we have here. Like I said, he or anyone else who steps over that line ain't welcome."

Maya seized a handful of Kong's vibrant dreadlocks, woven with colourful strips of cloth, and yanked the woman's face down onto the bar. She spat, "No one with any taste wants to be down here, anyway." She cracked Kong's face into the bar before releasing her hair and brushing her hands together.

Maya stepped away and walked towards the steps, sensing the intense gaze of the patrons tracing her every move. Groups of partygoers leaned forward in their chairs, preparing to pounce if needed. Maya's heart pounded as she made her way outside, her mind abuzz with conflicting emotions.

She jumped onto her moped and sped off, heading for the docks, with dust billowing up behind her. When she glanced back, she glimpsed Kong appearing in the doorway. Her gaze filled with disapproval as she wiped the blood from her nose.

As Maya pulled up, she heard the pounding water. Across from the road, and down the wooden steps, were the docks where Liam worked. She peered out towards the sea and made her way down to where the waves crashed into the shore. The blue ocean covered land that once formed part of this country, and Maya tried to picture what the district would look like were it not submerged beneath the waves, with so many homes and memories hidden in its depths. How many more years until the sea also buried the dock where Maya stood?

Through all the shouting, Maya spotted Gil sitting beside a makeshift shack. He welcomed her with a warm smile. She had known him for years, ever since she was a child, but they had never formed a close bond like the one he had with Liam. A sense of trust existed between them that went beyond words. She waved to him and tucked her hair tight into a band as the wind picked up around her ears.

"Maya, love. Come in," Gil said, pushing open the door to the disused boat hold. Weathered timber formed the walls, and gaps between the slates offered glimpses of the outside. At least inside the shack, she could hear him better without the breeze. He still shouted, though; after years of sitting on the dock, it was no surprise his hearing was so poor. "Did the boy get off okay this morning?" he asked, settling on top of a wooden box.

Maya nodded. "That's why I'm here."

Gil wiped his forehead. "Good lad. Right, so you've come to take the baton then. Think you're up for it?"

"If my brother could do it, I'm sure I'll cope," Maya said, trying to hide the slight quiver in her voice. She didn't want to show any signs of fear to Gil, despite spending all night thinking about her shift, while knowing it could end with a visit No Man's Land.

"Got a supply shipment due anytime now. Need you to pass a message on for me," Gil said, leaning forward and lowering his voice for the first time. "It needs to be kept... *discreet,* you get me? I've always trusted your family. Hope I can keep saying the same to you?"

"Whatever you need, Gil. I've been told by Liam and Mum to do what you say to the letter."

Gil let out a chuckle and smacked his thigh. "God love

your mother! Right, serious stuff now." He pulled a small note from his pocket. "Pass this over to a woman named Nic. It's the details on the shipment and what we also expect her to hand over. You drive, right?"

Maya nodded. "I've got my moped," Maya bit her lip, hoping Gil wouldn't question her further.

"Good. Go on your bike today to keep things quiet. You'll be going through the divide; you know that, don't ya?"

"No Man's Land, right?"

"That's right. You been there before? Liam given you the lowdown?"

Liam had only said to do what she was told and keep her wits about her. Maya bit her lip and shook her head. "Only a brief warning. Nothing else."

A sly smile crept onto Gil's face. "I trained him well. I want the same from you. Speak of this to no one. Getting caught will mean the end for all of us."

Maya took the note and tucked it into her pocket. "Okay, I have the message. What do I do with it?"

"Go along to the outskirts, beyond the city walls. There, you'll be out of sight from anyone watching from the wall. Right out, on the border of the countryside, is where you'll find the entrance to No Man's Land. I'm sure you've heard of it before."

"Only in stories," Maya said.

"You can head in there," Gil tapped a map of the city he'd unfolded in his hand. "Go through the entrance, but go *slow*. Ask to speak to Nic and do not, under any circumstances, speak to or hand that letter to anyone but her. You get me?"

"Does she know I'm coming and not Liam?"

Gil shrugged. "I sent word, but blast knows if it got there. You'll have to make sure she knows. Make sure not to mention my name to anyone apart from Nic." He smiled. "This means a lot to me, girl. To all the crew. Plenty of work for you if this goes well. Plenty of cash too."

"What is it we're trading, exactly?"

"Your brother never asked these kinds of questions." Gil laughed again. "This one is simple. It's fresh water coming from overseas. Easy trade for us and them."

Maya tapped her pocket to make sure the note was secure. She never thought the trades would include things so basic as water. "What do they offer for that? Surely there isn't much they have to trade with?"

Gil stood and moved towards the door, his figure silhouetted by beams of light shining through the shack. "They have a deal with some members of New Albion to sneak stuff over from there and across the wall through No Man's Land to us. Other countries want their stuff, even if us lot here don't."

"Right, well. I best make a move." Maya stepped past Gil, the breeze stinging her ears.

"Wait until the sun goes down. Easier to get around unseen then."

Maya leant on her arm, swilling the last remains of her drink around the glass. She peered up. The Old Vic was getting busier, with men and women filling in after a day's work. "You going to sit with that all night, or will I finally see you break your wallet open and buy a drink?" asked Carla, placing some coins into the till. "Need another?"

Maya shook her head and tucked her hair behind her ear. "No. I'm still on the clock. Is the sun down yet?" she asked, placing her finger around the rim of the glass.

Carla glanced behind Maya as the door swung open,

shaking her head. "The sky is orange out there. Won't be long now. Why, what you got planned for the night?"

"Doing that shift for Liam, ain't I? Never noticed how late he worked before. All I want to do is go home and sleep." Maya rubbed at her temples. "Guess my days of drinking into the early hours are behind me."

Carla laughed and pulled Maya's glass away from her. "What's he got you doing, anyway?"

Maya looked around to make sure no one was listening. Gil had specifically told Maya not to mention it to anyone, but Carla wasn't anyone. Maya trusted her. "Some trade stuff, boring really, except for where it takes place." Carla raised an eyebrow. "No Man's Land," Maya whispered.

Carla stepped back, clattering some bottles behind her. "What? You're going over *there*? Maya!" Carla leaned forward, lowering her voice into a whisper. "You know how awful it is over there, right? I mean, look at me. My parents gave me up to stop me from being sent there with them. Are you sure you know what you're doing?"

Maya leaned in closer, her voice barely audible above the chatter in the bar. "I know. I've heard the stories and saw the fear in people's eyes whenever it's brought up, but Gil asked me to do this, and it means a lot to him and the crew. Plus, I need the extra cash, and I trust Gil, you know that."

Carla's concern was obvious as she whispered, "But it's dangerous. No Man's Land is no place to mess around. I've heard rumours of people disappearing over there, never to be seen again."

"I know, I know," Maya replied, her tone uncertain. "But what choice do I have? My family needs the money, and this is the only way I can help."

Carla sighed. "Just promise me you'll be careful. And if

things get too sketchy, get the hell out of there, okay? No job is worth risking your life."

Maya nodded, appreciating Carla's concern. "I promise. I'll be cautious; Do what I need to and get back home as soon as possible."

Carla gave her a tight-lipped smile. "Alright then. Just be safe, Maya. And remember, you've got friends here who care about you."

"Thanks, Carla," Maya said. "I'll see you later. Hopefully, in one piece."

Maya stepped outside, where the vibrant orange sky was now a faded memory, hidden behind a blanket of grey clouds. The dust had settled with the quieting wind. She checked her pocket to ensure the note was still secure before starting up her moped. With night falling, the once bustling streets had emptied. Maya sped through Main Street, passing closed market stalls and glimpses of warm, dimly lit family homes.

While speeding through the city, the familiar sounds of the district faded. The desolate ruins and overgrown parks on the outskirts of New Albion approached. The wind howled in Maya's ears, and her heart raced as her mind drifted to all the stories she'd heard about No Man's Land. Whispered tales that made even the bravest shudder. Despite her resolve to help her family, doubt gnawed at her insides, and she questioned whether she was truly prepared for what lay ahead.

Her body jolted as she navigated cracked streets and uneven terrain, pushing her moped further towards the unmapped countryside, where few dared to venture.

Rolling hills and forgotten landscapes unfolded before her, like a realm lost in time, bathed in silky moonlight. Even the youngest children in Old Albion knew better than to explore these parts.

Turning down another road, Maya headed for the imposing great divide. In the distance, closer to the city, Maya saw a faint glimmer of light atop the wall. Where vigilant guards kept watch to ensure no one dared to cross the border.

As Maya pulled up, she spotted the entrance. Broken metal protruded like sharp shards of glass, and long, pale grass and creeping vines covered the makeshift hole. Maya scanned her surroundings, surprised to find no guards keeping watch. The eerie silence seeped into her bones as she cautiously approached. Turning to gaze at the outskirts, she couldn't help but question what was worse? The unknown dangers lurking beyond the parameter of the city, or the forbidden territory of No Man's Land. Since childhood, people warned her against both places, yet here she was.

Maya's heart pounded in her chest as she approached the entrance. The silence only seemed to amplify her heartbeat, and she couldn't shake the feeling of being watched. Her mind raced with thoughts of the stories she'd heard, the disappearances, and unknown dangers that awaited her beyond those vines and leaves. Biting her lip, she pressed on and stepped into the darkness.

Chapter Five

Into the Shadows

With each step, Maya ventured deeper into No Man's Land. She squinted, attempting to adapt to the surrounding darkness, while feeling the cold, wet earth beneath her feet. She wrinkled her nose at the stagnant smell of mud, left to fester in the space between worlds. Gazing up, she could make out the inside of the great dividing wall. A metal shell with pillars holding the imposing structure together.

With courage, Maya continued, passing through the metal divide to the other side, where the moonlight illuminated the vast, empty expanse. Miles of unused land stretched out before her, an empty canvas painted in silver. Surveying her surroundings, Maya glimpsed a faint glow in the distance, a beacon in the dark expanse. She glanced back at her moped, only a few feet away. The noise of its engine would draw unwanted attention, so with a resigned sigh, she began walking toward the distant light.

Maya had heard countless stories throughout her life about No Man's Land. A place created as retribution for those who dared to spoil their votes, where people lived and died, cut off from everything. Inhabitants of a lawless world, abandoned and forgotten: an emblem of punishment for anyone refusing to pick a side in the conflict that had long divided the nation.

Maya felt isolated in the desolate landscape; even the wind that had accompanied her journey seemed to have abandoned her in this forsaken place. As she approached the source of the faint glow, more details came into focus until a small group of makeshift buildings appeared, their roofs and walls fashioned from reclaimed metals and scavenged parts. Maya's heart pounded in her chest when she spotted a man waiting outside; he immediately lifted a gun, pointing it at her face. She froze and raised her arms instinctively in surrender. She locked her wide eyes onto his, fear mingling with determination.

"Who goes there?" the man asked, his grip on the gun unwavering.

"I come from the dock in Old Albion," Maya replied, keeping her voice steady. Gil's warning echoed in her mind—*speak only to Nic*—and one look of this young man said he wasn't Nic.

He squinted and glanced behind her to check if anyone else accompanied her. "You alone?"

Maya nodded, her heart pounding against her ribs. "I'm here to speak with Nic. No one else," she asserted, trying to steady her breathing as her chest heaved with nerves. "Can you take me to her?"

The guard chuckled, amusement dancing in his eyes. "I

ain't your keeper. Make your own way. Start any trouble, though, and you'll see the end of this." He smirked, waving his gun towards her.

"I understand." Maya swallowed the dry lump in her throat and mustered the courage to walk past him, her eyes never leaving his gun.

In the shantytown was a narrow main road, flanked by small one-story buildings on either side. The place made Old Albion seem like a palace in comparison. Passing through the desolate road, she noticed faces peering at her through broken glass windows and quickly averted her gaze, not wishing to draw any unnecessary attention. Along the street, she spotted a slightly taller building, which stood more stable than the rest. She assumed it was the main structure where she would find Nic.

Approaching the building, Maya halted at a grim sight above the doorway: a human skeleton, tied up and hanging, no doubt as a warning. She winced, sensing a shiver crawl down her spine. Liam must have faced true dangers in this lawless place, and her respect for him grew, knowing he had walked these darkened streets, facing the threat of guns and violence without ever uttering a word. It cast her brother in a new light, and she admired his courage.

Maya paused outside the building to watch a woman smoking leisurely nearby. The letter in Maya's pocket felt both heavy and tempting. A part of her wished to read it to gain an advantage before speaking to Nic. Unlike Liam, she couldn't rely on physical intimidation to protect her. She needed information to stay ahead of the game.

She locked eyes with the woman, who seemed to notice the letter Maya now held in her grip. The woman's gaze was sharp, sizing her up. "Got a problem?" Maya asked, narrowing her eyes to project confidence. She stubbed her cigarette out on the wall and walked away without a word.

Maya stole a glance at their surroundings to ensure they were free from prying eyes. She turned her attention to a small lamp hanging nearby, its flame flickering in the darkness. An idea struck her then, and she took a calculated risk. Holding the letter above the gentle flame, she let it hover just long enough to melt the seal. She removed the letter from the heat and carefully opened the envelope.

Gil laid out his instructions clearly on the page, and Maya attentively read each line, despite her unfamiliarity with some details. It was about the water supplies, as expected. However, what caught her attention was the trading item. They were exchanging two hundred and fifty bottles of fresh water in exchange for twenty PC-I Devices. Her heart skipped a beat. Because of its advanced AI technology, Old Albion banned PC-I Devices. Possessing one was a serious offence, and anyone caught with a device faced severe consequences from the government. Carefully folding the note back into its envelope, Maya sealed the wax once again and gripped it with a trembling hand. Maya took a deep breath, preparing herself for the encounter with Nic. She pushed the heavy doors open and stepped in.

Inside, the intense aroma of lavender hit Maya first, making her eyes water as they adjusted to the light. Then she absorbed the rest of her surroundings. Sporadically placed oil lanterns along the walls created flickering flames that cast dancing shadows throughout the room. While closing the door behind her, a gentle breeze brushed against her ankles as a reminder of the world outside. Maya took a moment to appreciate her vicinity. The place was unlike anything she had seen before.

Thick materials covered the walls, with embroidered colours and shapes patched onto the fabric. It gave the room a rugged appearance. Faces of men and women, dressed in torn yet thick clothes, turned to look at her. Maya offered a small smile to those watching, trying to appear as confident as possible.

In the back of the large room was a remarkable ebony wooden table, skilfully carved from a thick tree trunk; various items adorned it—papers, trinkets, and jewellery. The table seemed to hold an air of authority, as if it were the centrepiece of the entire room.

Maya took measured steps toward it, feeling the weight of stares tracking her movements. The tables, made from metal off-cuts bolted together with large, rusted screws, served as seats for the others in the room. As her eyes further adjusted to the light, she saw that various salvaged materials; pipes, metal sheets, mismatched doors, and window frames made up the entire building. It was a testament to the resourcefulness of those living in No Man's Land.

A man jutted out his leg, blocking Maya's path and stopping her in her tracks. Black dust coated his face, and he had tied his oil-dark hair into a low knot. Maya withdrew, and the room fell silent at the impending confrontation. His eyes locked onto the note in her hand. He reached for it, but Maya instinctively pulled it away and clasped her hands behind her back. "Hand it over," he demanded, resting his hand on his belt. Maya glanced down at the hilt of his gun, similar in design to the man she encountered at the entrance.

Unfazed, Maya stood her ground, trying to maintain her composure. "I'm here to see Nic. I've already had a long day," she replied firmly, stepping forward. "So, move."

The man put out his arm to stop her. "What's your name?" he asked, his voice gruff.

Maya matched his defiance with her own. "What's yours?" she shot back. A faint smile crept onto her face, trying to mask her nervousness.

"Lucas. Who sent you?" he questioned, clearly not backing down.

"I'm here to see Nic," Maya repeated, refusing to reveal any more information. "I'll only speak with her."

Her gaze darted to his gun, her gulp betraying her fear. She wanted to be strong, but the weapon unnerved her. She took a deep breath to steady herself. "Either take me to her or get out of my way." She stared into his intense blue eyes, which looked strangely familiar.

Lucas stood his ground, his body tensing. Clearly, he would not budge. Maya's legs felt like jelly, and her heart raced. She considered retreating and running back home, forgetting this dangerous endeavour. But that wasn't an option if she wanted this job. She needed to provide for her family. Maya bit her lip again, summoning enough courage to take another step. He still didn't move. Maya had to break through.

With a rush of adrenaline, she shoved against him, yet Lucas merely chuckled at her attempt. Gritting her teeth, she clenched her arms and pushed harder. The room watched in silence, and no one moved to intervene. Lucas maintained his stance, unyielding, while Maya's frustration grew. She impulsively raised her foot and kicked him in the shin. He finally stepped back, releasing his hold on her as she stumbled past him.

"You little bitch," he spat, reaching for the gun at his belt.

Amid the tension, a woman in the back of the room stood and clapped her hands to capture everyone's attention. “Enough!” she shouted, her tone laced with unmistakable authority. The room fell silent, and all eyes turned to her. "Leave her, Lucas. Why don't you go rest your leg? Poor darling," she said, a mix of annoyance and affection lacing her voice.

Maya returned Lucas's scowl with one of her own, yet maintained her composure as she approached the table where the woman stood. The room seemed to hold its breath as Maya handed over the letter with a determined look. "I assume you are the famous Nic? Gil sent me," she said firmly, her voice steady as the woman nodded. "Here are his instructions for the trade."

Nic took the note from Maya's fingers, examining it intensely. "How do I know I can trust you?" she questioned, raising an eyebrow. "Where is the boy?" Her eyes bore into Maya, searching for any signs of deception.

Maya held Nic's gaze with no sign of faltering; "It's me who's here now. That's all you need to know," she said. "Do you accept the terms listed? Or do you not have the PC-I devices?" A faint smile tugged at the corners of her lips. Maya wanted Nic to understand that she was aware of the trade's details. A risky move, but one she hoped would demonstrate her knowledge and competence. Maybe even gain her trust.

A flicker of surprise crossed Nic's eyes for a moment, her guard slipping slightly. "The boy never read the letters," she admitted, leaning towards Maya. "I think I'm going to have to keep an eye on you." Nic turned her attention to the letter, swiftly signing it, before folding it back up. "Tell Gil that I only want you to do the delivery run, no one else. We'll see what you're really made of." She handed the letter back to Maya. "You've impressed me so far. Few make it to this building without opening their mouths."

When Nic's demeanour softened, the atmosphere in the room eased, and the people resumed their activities. Maya felt the weight of their gazes lift, and she took a deep breath, trying to relax. "Lucas!" Nic shouted. "Please return our guest back to the border. Fill her in on what she needs to know, and... be nice." She smiled before returning to her seat with folded arms.

Lucas appeared, a face of stone as he glared at Maya. "Come on then." He pointed towards the door, and Maya nodded one final time at Nic and trailed behind him. She hoped Lucas wouldn't shoot her once they were out in the open.

Maya followed behind Lucas, keeping a few paces between them. He had said nothing to her; in fact, he barely looked her in the eye while guiding her back to the wall. "Are you going to tell me anything, then?" she asked, noticing his limp. "I'm sorry about hurting you, by the way."

He stopped and turned. "You didn't hurt me."

Maya stifled a laugh. "Yeah? Then why are you limping?" She circled him, stirring up dust around their feet.

He shook his leg, the one Maya had kicked. "I'm not. Anyway, I've had a long couple of days. If you tried that move during my peak, you'd have had no chance." He smiled.

"Well, let me know when you want round two."

Maya peered up at the sky, where the stars twinkled against the dark backdrop. A clear horizon at night meant unbearable heat for the morning. "What's it like living out here, then? We hear so many things back home, about how dangerous it is, with people going missing and getting killed."

"What do *you* think of it?" Lucas asked. "That's what's important."

Maya tapped her chin. "It doesn't seem so bad, well, for what it is. It's pretty empty here. No more dangerous than Old Albion." Her gaze fell on the gun holstered on Lucas's belt. "Well, apart from those. Then there are all the reports of missing people who have travelled over here."

"People don't go missing out here, at least not without good reason."

"Are you sure about that? There have been reports of people from both sides of the wall vanishing."

Lucas kicked a rock with his foot. "People who come here, who see No Man's Land for what it is, choose to stay and fight alongside us. They don't disappear or get killed. They join us."

Maya continued walking with her hands clasped behind her back. "What do you mean, fighting?"

Lucas scratched the palms of his hand.

"Nothing. It's just a saying we have here. Anyway, Nic wanted me to tell you about the trade." Lucas pointed towards the divide. "There is another entrance, a more spacious one further down in the outskirts. That's where we trade larger items."

"The outskirts? God, I thought coming here was bad enough."

"It'll be fine. It's empty there, completely abandoned by the guards. Gil will give you a truck; you arrive at a set time and make the trade." He glanced at Maya's arms. "Though I don't know how helpful you'll be. The water shipments are heavy. It was never a problem when Liam did it. He helped move the stuff and got it done in quick time."

"Well, I guess you'll have to rest your legs extra hard that day." Maya stopped; the divide was only a short walk away now. "Can I ask what stops you from leaving? The entrance is right there, and the outskirts are huge. Why not escape?"

A smile played along the corner of his lips.

"This is my home. I could ask you the same thing. No

sane person would venture deep into the outskirts, anyway. Now that really is a place people don't return from."

Maya looked down at her feet, realising her naivety. She had grown up thinking of No Man's Land as an awful place, existing only for punishment. People told her things, and they made her believe them without seeing it herself. "Have you always lived here?"

"My whole life." Lucas nodded. "My parents were sent here when the vote happened."

"Are they… still around?"

Lucas shook his head. "No. People don't tend to live long out here. It's why you need to make the most of every day." Tears filled his eyes. "These lands are harsh, Maya. That much is true. They're wild and cruel, but they're home. We've made a life here and have plans for change. We want to make things better and fair."

"Is that to do with the *fight*?" Maya asked.

"I've said too much. You know what you need to do next: do the trade, show you can be trusted. You've already won over Nic, so you're ahead on that front already. If you can do that, then maybe we can talk more later on." Lucas turned to walk back to the small village. "Maybe I'll take you up on round two as well."

Chapter Six

Unraveling Truths

Liam slammed his fist onto the table, knocking water from his mother's cup to splash across the surface. She glared at him and pulled the cloth from her shoulder to wipe up the spill. "What's wrong with you now?" she asked.

Liam looked at the payslip again, scanning the numbers and words written beside them. "This," he said, handing it to his mother. "Why have they deducted so much?" He searched his mother's eyes to gauge her reaction and wiped his brow. He glanced toward the cracked-open window next to the sink, where the non-existent breeze offered no relief from the stifling heat inside the flat. "It's barely more than I used to get at the dock!"

His mother tapped her fingers along the table's edge. "Darling, it's the tax. Look here," she said, tracing her finger slowly across the paper. "Tax A is taken from New Albion."

Liam studied the word above his mother's fingertip. T... A... X... he repeated in his head. He looked underneath to find the same word again. "What's that then?" he asked.

"That's Tax B. It's the percentage Old Albion takes when they transfer the money from the account to coins," she explained.

"*Two* lots of tax? The pay gets reduced to practically nothing after that! Why did that useless mayor Lewis agree to this scheme if it isn't even helpful to us over here?" Liam pushed the payslip away and crossed his arms.

Liam's mother patted him on the shoulder and returned to the sink, leaning her hands across the cracked porcelain. "I know, love. He did what he could, I suppose. Once the month is up, you'll still be far better off from what Gil offered you." She turned, offering a weak smile. The orange haze from the window made her glow; her brown hair, now faded, glinted a red hue in the light, yet wrinkles were now more apparent beneath her eyes, her skin paler than he remembered from a few months ago. He wanted to ask about his father and admit to having seen him on orientation day. But he kept it to himself for the time being. He hoped to come across his father again and speak to him first before mentioning anything to his family.

Liam forced a smile, hoping it would brighten his mother's day. "Okay, if you think it's worth it, Mum, then I'll continue." Liam turned toward Maya's bedroom. "Is she still knocked out in there?" Emma, his mother, nodded. "She can't carry on like this with those extra shifts Gil has her on. She'll end up burning out if she keeps drinking all night." He stood up and collected his bag. "Want me to speak to her?"

"No, I'll do it... gently," she replied with a soft laugh. "I have a few things she needs to help me with, anyway."

***

Liam rushed through the district to get to New Albion. More so than before, he noticed the dust-clogged air clinging to his throat, the cracks along every wall, and the weeds growing in every corner. As he made his way through the gates, his world became cleaner and brighter as he stepped onto the freshly cleaned streets, shining beneath the early morning sun.

He checked his device; he'd been assigned the same duty this week. Guard the courtyard. Follow The Governor to lunch. Break. Courtyard. Governor meeting. Liam sighed and went to his post. He nodded at Jake, the other recruit, beside him. "How are you finding it?" Liam whispered.

Jake shrugged. "Better than sitting at home."

Liam rolled his eyes. He looked down the corridor, a spark of hope that his father would appear. "Hey, have you seen that guy since the first day? The one who came in, gave a talk, and walked off?"

Jake gave another shrug. "Don't think so. Most of those posh folk look the same to me. I just stand and do my job." He yawned. "Why'd you ask?"

"No reason," Liam replied. He hated staying still in the same spot for hours. He leaned against the brick wall and watched the shadows move. A statue stood in the middle of the courtyard. Having observed it for the past few days, Liam knew that when the statue's shadow reached the flower bed, important workers would march through. He counted in his head. One, two, three—like clockwork, a handful of people walked through, dressed in blue. Trailing behind them was Alexander. Liam stepped forward and joined him, falling in line with the group as he moved to his next guard duty.

"Settling in okay?" Alex asked, slowing his pace slightly to create distance between the group.

"It's alright," Liam said eventually, earning a raised eyebrow from Alex. "It's repetitive. Kind of... well, slow." Liam hesitated. He felt a connection with Alex, someone who seemed far more approachable than the other officials. "But I'm grateful. Really, I am. I just don't see the point in it all."

Alex laughed. "Welcome to the boring world of work. Maybe you'd be happier back on the docks?"

"How did you know I worked on the docks?"

Alex smiled. "I'm responsible for all the new recruits in this work district. They gave me a large document all about you." Alex winked, and Liam couldn't tell if he was serious or not. "They'll post you and Jake outside the Governor's office again today. Are you both getting along with each other?"

Liam nodded and kept quiet, instead of admitting that Jake was more boring than the job itself. Yet he found Alex's playful eyes comforting, and a part of Liam wanted to confide in him about seeing his father. "Will I always be guarding Governor Granswick, or will there be others someday?" Liam asked, trying to sound casual.

Alex seemed puzzled. "Others?"

"Yeah, like Robert. The man who spoke to us all the other day."

Alex laugh. "Robert? I'd be lucky if he spoke to me out of choice. No, he keeps himself to himself. Only did that speech because he had to. Just keep focused on your work and your shifts." With that, Alex left, and Liam rejoined Jake to guard another door to meetings taking place on the other side. Liam sighed; he felt trapped within these dull white walls that offered little to his imagination. He strained to hear muffled voices from inside, trying to pick out words he couldn't quite decipher, before giving up and slumping back against the wall, counting the hours until his shift ended.

Liam checked out through the scanners and placed the small device attached to the side of his head in his locker. He'd only been working on the scheme for a week, but was already bored. He didn't fancy speaking to Miss Thorn about his schedule, either. Instead, he scrolled through his hand-held device until Alex's profile showed up on the list. A green circle glowed around a photo of his face, and when Liam tapped it, a chat box appeared, along with three dots. Liam's heart raced. He glanced around, desperate to see if Alex was nearby. A message popped up, and Liam stared at it just as three more dots appeared. He waited, scanning the message to see if any words stuck out, but none did. He closed the device and looked up to find Alex walking towards him with a smile plastered on his face. "Liam, so glad I caught you before you left. Come on, I have a task for you."

Liam rushed after Alex, quickening his pace as he walked outside the building. "Wait, what are we doing?" He ran, trying to catch his breath. "I've finished for the day."

"Did you not read my message? I'm taking you out. Spark your mind a bit." Alex winked.

Liam followed Alex, still dressed in his usual royal blue uniform. His attire was much more casual than Liam's; he had his sleeves rolled up, and the top button on his vicar's shirt undone. He'd even brushed his regular pristine blonde hair forward. As they circled the perimeter of the government building, Liam's device vibrated in his pocket. He pulled it out and glanced at the bright red message displayed on the screen. "What does this mean?" he asked.

Alex tapped the screen and placed his own device beside

it. "Oh, nothing. Just a warning to say you're leaving the designated area. I've disabled it for you now."

Alex led Liam across the road, past where Liam had gone before, and through a single alley until they emerged into a new district. A short and simple sign hung above. B-1. Even Liam could work that out. "You've taken me to another district during work? Don't I need to head back home? I can't stay in New Albion after hours." Liam looked around. It was against the rules for Old Albion civilians to be seen outside of District A, let alone be here after work hours. "Won't I get into trouble?" he asked, pulling on Alex's wrist.

Alex turned around, peering at Liam's firm grip on his arm. He smiled. "Not at all. I've been told to *stimulate* you to find out what's going on up there." Alex tapped Liam's head.

"Stimulate me?" Liam felt his cheeks burn. "What do you mean?"

Alex laughed again as a car appeared beside them and the door opened. Liam peered inside. No driver. He glanced at Alex, who had already shuffled into the back seat. "Come on then, you silly boy." He patted the seat.

Liam's legs trembled as he took a step forward. "Is it safe?"

"Get in."

Far too many tales and rumours about the strange things occurring in New Albion spread back home. Cars that drove themselves, food prepared by AI and machines that clean the air around. When Liam got into the car that immediately sped away, he thought of all the men he'd spoken to, who laughed at the thought of a self-driving car. Liam joked for years that he'd never use one, yet now he found himself in one, on the other side.

"What's this about? Where are you taking me?" Liam

asked, trying to sound relaxed.

"Just on a brief visit in my district. It's the only place I'm allowed to travel to. Them the rules, even for me."

Watching the world through the window, Liam pinched himself as he scanned the mostly empty roads, if not for the driver-less cars speeding by. Blocks and blocks of houses mirrored both sides of the road, all the same design. A staleness lingered inside the car. What was this trip about? Had Liam done something wrong? Was he being fired? He looked up at Alex, who smiled back at him. Maybe he'd arranged this day out just for them, Liam wondered.

The car came to a stop, and Liam got out, shaking his numb leg to circulate the blood through it. "This is district D, my home," Alex said. Liam looked before him at the people chatting in groups, standing in front of a street full of shops, bars, and restaurants. Every building around had clean sharp lines, metal structures painting bold shapes along their outline. Vending machines adorned each shop front, with screens displaying buttons and words Liam could not read. "Did you want to sit in or out?" Alex asked, bringing Liam back to earth.

"Out. I like the clean air over here."

Alex walked towards what Liam assumed was a restaurant and tapped the screen before glancing at his device. "I'll put it on the work account," he said, entering through the doors with Liam following behind.

Inside, the restaurant looked like a palace: gold-plated ornate walls, moving images in picture frames. Within, more of those machines—the ones that cut the grass and cleaned the streets—served food from the kitchen to the couples at their tables. "Don't worry about them. They won't bump into you. Come out, our table is over here," said Alex.

Liam followed Alex's footsteps like a lost child. They sat down on a balcony overlooking a large body of crystal-clear water that sparkled in the evening sun. The breeze blew gently along Liam's face as he peered over at Alex, whose wild hair swayed in the wind. "So, are you ready to tell me why you've taken me out for dinner?" Liam asked.

"I can tell there's no point skirting around the subject with you," Alex said. "My superiors wanted me to check in on you to see why one of my apprentices is unhappy. To say I was shocked when they told me it was you... well, that's an understatement."

Liam blushed, nodding and staring at the floor. "Who said I wasn't happy? I didn't mean anything when I said the work was boring earlier, honest." The usual playfulness in Alex's eyes had vanished.

"It isn't what you said, more of what your body told us... or them, I should say."

"My body?" Liam lifted his arms, looking over them. He flexed his bicep and noticed the shirt grow tight around his upper arms.

Alex let out a laugh as a machine arrived, presenting two plates to the table. Liam collected them both and handed one to Alex. "That device you wear all day, the one stuck to the side of your head?" Liam rubbed his temple, where the device always was. "It tracks your movements at work, but also keeps a log of your heart rate and blood pressure to provide us with an overall picture of your mood and health during different times of the workday. The bosses noticed you were low, and after only a week, it rang alarm bells."

Liam looked at the device attached to the side of Alex's head. "I didn't know they'd be taking such notice." Liam glanced down, pushing the food around his plate with a fork.

"I can't lose this job, Alex, not so soon. It's too important to me and my family."

"Don't worry, you won't be going anywhere. I wanted to ask what we could do to make it better." Alex speared a piece of fish and put it in his mouth. "I noticed you're most bored when still, like when guarding a door or entryway. Maybe I could get you to shadow me for a while? Get you in on the real action."

Liam's eyes widened. "You could do that? I mean, I don't know too much. I never really finished school, but I'm strong, and I learn on my feet. Shadowing you… it could work."

"My own protector." Alex dabbed the corner of his mouth, smiling. "It's quite the offer. I notice your heart rate fluctuates frequently at certain times."

Liam looked away again to stare at the view beyond, glimpsing the blue roofs of Old Albion in the distance. "Why did they create that law?" Liam asked, hoping to change the subject. "They give us no funding or anything, but are happy to supply us with paint to paint the tiles blue."

Alex tapped his chin and turned to look out at Old Albion in the distance. He sighed. "Yes, well. Some decisions made here weren't all good," he whispered. "The official reason is the paint helps keep homes cool in the new temperatures we've found ourselves in. Although, off the record, it's purely for show. People who live in the towers, penthouses, and the offices in district A want an unspoiled view. When leaders from other countries visit, they don't want to see what little the other side offers."

Liam narrowed his eyes. "It isn't that bad, you know. It only fell apart because of the wall. Because of *your* government."

"Who are also *your* employers, so watch what you say."

Liam folded his arms. "What exactly do you think it's like over there? Most of us didn't even choose this, you know."

"Neither did I, but you can't be angry with me because I'm on this side and not the other. It isn't my fault my family voted to side with the use of AI."

"Full of broken promises and lies, though, wasn't it? The whole thing. Look around. You're told where to live, how and where to work. Jobs are vanishing from every corner with these machines running around for you. I don't think it's right, and I can't believe you do."

Alex sighed. "Liam, where has this burst of anger come from? I thought we were having a lovely time."

"We were, but I don't agree with your answers to my questions."

Alex smiled and rested his cutlery on the side of his plate. "But look what AI has allowed us to do. In such a short time, we've changed the way everything works! Look at the sky; smell the air. It's clean, no rubbish or litter anywhere. These rules work. Whether you agree with them or not."

"Only because you took everything for this half and left Old Albion to rot. Where do you think all that rubbish goes? Where do those machines take it? Do you even know?" Liam slammed his hand on the table, capturing the attention of the other guests.

"I don't know? Sent to burn somewhere, probably." Alex raised his hands. "I can file a request form and find out for you, if you like? The country is 98% fully recyclable, you know. I read a recent report on it."

Liam laughed. "What, like the one that told you employment was up twenty percent? Yeah, right! Like you can really trust those things." Liam crossed his arms again, trying to contain his anger. "I can tell you where it goes. It's piled over the wall and left to rot in No Man's Land for them to deal with. You think that's right?"

Alex rolled his eyes. "Please, the people there are nothing but convicts and murderers. People banished."

Liam got up. "I want to go back to District A. I need to get home." He turned to walk off and said over his shoulder, "I wouldn't want to break the rules and get banished into No Man's Land now, would I?"

Liam felt all eyes on him as he stormed through the restaurant; he froze when Alex grabbed his hand. "Liam, please, slow down. I don't want us to fight like this." Alex turned to face him, the sun setting in the sky as he looked around. Liam wanted to leave but didn't know how. "Please, what can I do? I want to learn from you; I want to learn about the other side. Obviously, I have my view on things, and you have yours."

"Your view has been fed to you. Mine comes from experience." Alex looked at him, puzzled, and Liam feared he'd said too much. He'd ruined both his chance of having a career and a friendship with Alex.

Alex removed his device from the side of his head and switched it off. "Liam, you can trust me. Please believe that. I was sent here to reassure you, but I wanted to help you because I *care*." After looking around, Alex grabbed Liam by the hand and walked along the street until stopping at a junction. Alex pulled Liam down a small alleyway. Following his steps, Liam turned, facing him. The alley was thin; there was hardly enough room for both of them. "This is off the book now. Ask me what you want; I'll try my best to answer if it means you'll stay."

Alex was so close that Liam felt his chest beating. He wanted to trust Alex, despite knowing him for so little time.

Something told him he had his best interests in mind. "Robert. I want you to tell me about him."

Alex frowned. "Robert? Why?"

"I just do, alright? Tell me about him; tell me how long he's worked there, what he does, and how I can speak to him."

Alex smiled. "Thought he'd be a bit old for your tastes."

Liam pushed his shoulder. "Not like that. Please, I'm serious."

"There isn't much to say. He works with the higher-ups and runs in the same circles as Governor Granswick. He's a nice guy, hard working. Like I said, he keeps himself to himself."

"Does he have a family?" Liam asked, ignoring most of what Alex had just said.

"Family? No, I don't think so. He's a loner. Liam, why the fascination?"

"No reason." Liam looked towards the alley entrance. "Should we go? I can't be here past eleven."

Alex looked up at the sky, still orange. "You have hours yet. Come on. Open up, tell me. Why is Robert so important?"

"How do I know I can trust you?"

"Well, you can't, I guess."

"Huh?" Liam tried to step back.

"But you have my word."

Liam stared at the ground. "That isn't enough."

Alex looked around and took Liam's hand in his. "You can trust me," he said again, his grip firm on Liam's hand. Liam stared into his eyes, a forest of deep green: crystal clear and full of truth. He squeezed Alex's hand, relishing the warmth radiating from him.

"Okay, but if you go behind my back, I'll never forgive

you," said Liam, and Alex smiled. "When the vote happened, and the failed attempt to stop all the fighting and arguing, they announced the divide out of the blue, right?" Alex nodded. "Well, when they announced everyone's vote publicly, it tore my family apart. My father lied to us. He told us he voted against the use of AI, like my whole family did, but when they announced the vote, and we saw his name listed, we knew he was going to be taken away. It broke us; my mother was in bits, and our family was left with nothing when we were moved to Old Albion."

"I'm sorry Liam. I've always heard stories about how upset people were, but I've never heard it firsthand."

"For my entire life, I gazed at that wall, questioning my father's absence and wondering why he never reached out."

"He might not have been able to. Getting across the divide is no straightforward task, even now. When it was new, there was no chance of any contact. The government was so strict back then; everything had to be done by the book for years. I guess we have Freedom Day to thank for the somewhat relaxation now."

"It's easy enough, though. It is doable. I've travelled through No Man's Land plenty. If he wanted to, he would have."

"What does all this have to do with Robert, though?"

Liam wiped away a tear and released his grip on Alex's hand. "Don't you get it? I thought you were the smart one," Liam chuckled. "Robert is my father, and when I saw him the other day, he didn't even look twice at me."

"I see." Alex lowered his arm. "So, you want to speak to him in private? Ask why he never tried to see you again?" Liam nodded, his chest feeling tight. He felt so relieved to have finally told someone. "Crossing the divide and breaking rules... It isn't easy over here. We are watched and monitored at every turn. Robert is high up; it would be even more difficult for him." Alex placed his device back on his head and turned it on with a tap. "I'm not excusing him. Maybe there was more he could have done to see you all, but death is a gigantic risk no matter the prize."

Liam looked at Alex, his heart pounding. "What are you doing? I thought you said I could trust you."

Alex glanced up and smiled the same smile he always gave Liam. "You can. Get the car back to the gate and go home." Liam turned his head to find a car parked just outside the alleyway. "When you come to work, act normal and try to keep your heart rate and mood levels up, even when you see me," Alex laughed. "I'll arrange a meeting. One with me and Robert, and I'll bring you along. Is that okay?"

Liam beamed and turned towards Alex. "Really? It'll be that easy?" he asked, stepping closer, his hand brushing against Alex's fingertips.

Alex replied with a wink. "Go home. I'll see you in the morning."

Chapter Seven

Connected Bounds

Maya welcomed taking refuge indoors after incessantly itching her wrists from the humidity that had plagued them for the past month. But as always, the weather had unpredictably shifted, and now rain came down in torrents from the sky, transforming the streets into a shallow pool. Homes, once safe havens, have become prone to leaks, and dampness cloaked the air.

Ascending the darkened steps, Maya carefully followed her mother down the corridor, keeping close behind her in case she stumbled. Carla came after them. As they approached the apartment door, a dim, yellow light flickered, highlighting the peeling, stained white paint that adorned the walls.

Maya's mother had requested Maya's company for some morning visits, a request she would have normally turned down to nurse her hangover in bed. However, today was different; Maya wanted to catch up with Carla, and the only way to do so was by accompanying the visit to Carla's grandmother.

Inside, a constant buzz of static emanated from an old radio in the lounge. Maya tried to hide her distaste for it as she entered. The apartment bore many marks of neglect, with black mould marring one entire wall beside the kitchen. The musty smell permeated the air, making each breath a struggle as Carla closed the door behind them, enclosing them in the stagnant space. "You two clean up the kitchen a bit. I'll see how she's feeling," Maya's mother commanded.

As Maya made her way through the open-plan room, the photographs hanging on the wall drew her attention; each picture offered a glimpse into a world that no longer existed - a world forever altered by the divide. Among the family photos was one of Carla as a baby, cradled in the arms of her parents. In the vibrant city, before anyone imagined the divide. The sight brought a smile to Maya's lips, and Carla moved to stand beside her, gazing at the photo too. "Don't stare too long or you'll see how much of an ugly baby I was," Carla teased, stepping into the kitchen.

"So, we meeting at The Old Vic tonight?" Maya grabbed a sponge from the sink and soaked it to clean the kitchen counter.

Carla responded with her familiar grin. "You know me. I earn my money there and spend it there too. It's a vicious circle."

Maya chuckled and sprayed cleaner along the countertop, struggling to get the last few drops from the bottle. She had to broach the subject of No Man's Land with Carla. Maya was responsible for delivering the shipment of water to the meeting point tonight, and in a moment of foolishness, she'd promised Gil and Nic that she would drive. "Don't fancy an early night to come help me, do you?" she asked, trying to sound nonchalant.

Carla stopped in her tracks and turned to Maya. "Really? What other job you got now? Is two not enough for you?" she joked, waving her one arm in the air.

"It's for Gil. I said I could drive... well, didn't say I couldn't..." Maya hesitated, feeling her cheeks flush.

"You didn't! Why?" Carla interrupted.

"I didn't want to make a bad first impression! How was I meant to know he'd get me doing a delivery on my first week?" Maya explained, her voice trailing.

Carla raised an eyebrow. "Where is it going?"

Maya glanced away, drying the side of the counter with a rag. "Well, about that," she hesitated. "It's outside of the city."

"How far?" Carla asked, her brow furrowing with concern.

"Near the outskirts - well, more *into* the outskirts." Maya confessed, and Carla stepped back. "But listen," Maya said, reaching out to grab Carla's shoulders. "It's safe. Quick, in and out. All I need you to do is drive. I'll do the rest."

"I don't know. Let me think about it." Carla let out a sigh. "Come on, let's go help your mother."

They joined Maya's mother, Emma in the dimly lit lounge, where Carla's grandmother lifted her head and coughed into a handkerchief. She greeted them with a warm smile. "My darlings," she said, raising her hands to urge them closer. Carla leaned in to embrace her grandmother, while Maya merely crossed her arms and offered a warm expression. She soon noticed her mother with a ticket in her hand. Emma's expression shifted from a beaming smile to a slight frown when Maya asked, "Mum, what have you got there? I hope that's not what I think it is."

Emma rolled her eyes and glanced apologetically at Carla's grandmother. "Olive gave it to me as a thank you," she explained.

Maya laughed and squinted at Olive before snatching the ticket from her mother's grip. "Really? You're taking part in The Lottery now? What's gotten into you? Ever since Freedom Day, you've been waving that flag like you're from the other side."

Carla sat down between Maya and her grandmother, looking warily up at them both. "Maya, why don't we talk about this later?" Her mother suggested, reaching to retrieve the ticket from Maya's grasp.

"No. Let's do this now," Maya insisted. "It's bad enough Liam has trotted over there to work, and now you're getting a ticket in the hopes you can move over! Why?"

"Don't think I haven't heard the whispers when I walk, the gossip and chattering about how my son is one of them, a scab who's stepped across the line." Emma's cheeks glowed with emotion. "If we win using this ticket, and that is a big *if* - then we can give Liam a home and residency in New Albion full time, where he can work, live, and have a better life. Don't you think it's worth it?"

"Liam can work there if he wants and bring their money back to this side. I have no problem with that," Maya said firmly. "But I draw the line at us entering the lottery to scramble for a chance to live there. I expected more from you, Mum." She softened her tone as she glanced at Carla's grandmother. "Just look around at what this country has turned into. People falling sick and dying in their homes with no hope of reaching old age. This is what the divide has done to us. *We* are being punished for choices made by your generation." Maya's gaze returned to her mother. "And we're left to make a life for ourselves. Surely you can see the damage they've done here. Look at all the people you care for, Mum, who have died unnecessarily! If Carla was in New Albion, she would've had the care she needed when she was younger. She would have two arms and maybe be a teacher or a judge or something. But they've left us here to survive the best we can."

Carla wrapped her arm around herself, avoiding direct eye contact with anyone in the room. Sensing the weight of the moment, Maya gently placed her hand on Carla's grandmother's shoulder, who had started coughing again. "Maya, get her pills from the bedroom," Emma snapped. Maya rushed into the bedroom, where she quickly retrieved the faded boxes of pills lining the bedside table. She handed them to Carla, who brought a glass of water from the sink to help her grandmother. Emma leaned over Olive and glanced back at her daughter. "I think you've said enough. I can take it from here, girls."

Carla gave Maya the cold shoulder as they walked towards The Old Vic, refusing to say more than a few words until they joined George and a few friends already a few rounds deep, judging by the abundance of empty glasses littering the seating area. George laughed heartily and held his side. Perhaps nursing an injury, Maya thought.

"The face on you, Carla! Anyone would think you were working a shift tonight," George teased, playfully jabbing her arm. Carla scowled at him and turned away, seeking the attention of the barman.

"We had a few words, that's all. Nothing we won't forget about in a few minutes, ain't that right?" Maya interjected, attempting to ease the tension. She smiled at Carla, who purposefully shifted her head to speak with another member of the group. "What's happened to you two?" Maya asked, glancing at one of George's friends, a young man she didn't know, with a bandage wrapped around his head and covering one eye.

They exchanged glances before shame flashed across their faces. They took a sip of their bitter ale. "Bit of quick cash, that's all," George admitted, seeming to downplay their situation.

"Quick cash?" Carla repeated, focusing her attention on the group again as a tray of drinks arrived. "What did you guys do?"

George offered a tired smile, underwritten with a deep sense of foreboding. Maya observed how they held themselves with no visible bruises or cuts. The bandages appeared professionally wrapped, like medical wraps, rather than a hasty remedy from a paid fight. "What have you two done?" Maya whispered. She turned to Carla, wide-eyed.

Carla seemed confused by Maya's reaction. "What? What have they done?"

Maya raised her eyebrows at the boys. "Come on, just tell us."

"We had no choice," George admitted. "We needed the cash, alright? I ain't proud of it. Rent was due and our bills were mounting up."

Carla took a sip of her drink and leaned forward on the table. "Will someone tell me what the fuck is going on?"

Maya pursed her lips and narrowed her eyes at George. "You've sold something, haven't you? You bloody idiots."

"Sold? What do you mean?" Carla locked eyes on the bandage wrapped around George's friend. Her hand instinctively moved to her mouth. "No. What did you do?"

"I sold my eye, alright?" he blurted.

Maya watched as Carla rolled her eyes. "You haven't sold your eye, you idiot."

"Well, you know what I mean. I'm blind either way. They offered me a few years' worth of pay for it in one lump sum. It wasn't a choice; I *had* to do it."

Maya's heart pounded. Desperation drove them to such extremes. She turned to look at George. "What about you?"

"A kidney," he replied matter-of-factly. "We did it a week or so ago. Only just feel good enough now to come out."

Carla's grip on Maya's arm tightened, her eyes wide with disbelief. "You *willingly* did this to yourselves? Really?" She glanced at the stump where her arm once was, a reminder of the sacrifice she'd made for survival. "You chose this? You chose to cut years from your life for money?" Carla abruptly stood and stormed from the table, disappearing into the crowd behind them.

Undeterred, George proudly displayed a lottery ticket between his fingers. "Got enough to get one of these, though," he said, as if to justify their choices.

Maya's anger intensified. "You fools," she snapped, her mind racing. She rose and pushed her way through the inebriated patrons to catch up with Carla. She made her way towards the stairs leading to Carla's room above the bar.

The creaky wooden steps protested under Maya's weight as she ascended to the attic, prompting dust to rain from the hatch as she pushed it open and stepped into Carla's room. Carla sat on the bed, staring into the small circular stained-glass window. Maya offered a reassuring smile and joined her on the mattress.

"Don't worry about those guys. They're fucking idiots,"

Maya said, trying to lift Carla's spirits.

Carla gave a weary sigh. "I know. I shouldn't let their stupidity get to me, but it's just so bloody senseless. Such a waste." She wiped her face with her hand and then gestured to the scar on her arm, where the rest of it used to be. "I've never allowed this to hold me back, but seeing them willingly cut up their bodies for cash, it just... infuriates me."

Maya couldn't help but laugh, finding a sliver of humour despite the serious conversation. "You won't believe what they splurged on with the money," she said, a playful glint in her eyes.

Carla looked up, curious. "What?"

"A bloody lottery ticket." Maya shook her head in disbelief.

"Jesus, *fuck me*!" Carla shouted, falling until her face landed on the pillow. "Those bloody tickets, honestly." Carla laughed with Maya before bolting upright up again. "You know what really annoys me? That people here *have* to do that. Struggle their whole lives, cutting off bits of themselves to get by. Then you turn your head, look towards the divide, and know they're all living the best possible life, just a stone's throw away."

Maya nodded. "Yeah. Seeing No Man's Land, and how those people were treated - thrown away like..." Maya trailed off at the look on Carla's face. Her parents. "Sorry, I didn't mean them... I should shut up."

"No." Carla said, grabbing Maya's arm. "You're right. My parents were thrown away and punished for not following orders, the same as us lot were. Punished for not voting. Those in the generations before us voted no, and because they didn't believe the lies, they did this to us." Carla waved towards the window, the world outside.

"Please come with me tonight to the drop off. Come see the people. They might know your parents and be able to tell you something."

Carla eyed Maya up and down. "We both know people out there don't last long. You think they'll still be going, after all this time?"

Maya shrugged. "If not, someone there might know them and can tell you about them, about why they did what they did." Maya held Carla's hand. "Come on. You drive, I'll get some snacks. It'll be a road trip."

"A road trip to hell, yeah. You're really selling it for me." Carla laughed.

"When I was there, it wasn't like the stories. They were a community." Maya looked towards her lap. "I think there's more going on there than we know. If you mean what you say, about how unfair this place is, maybe we'll find some answers there. A way to... change things."

Carla narrowed her brows. "You really want me to come, don't you?"

Maya nodded. "It's either that, or join those two idiots downstairs again."

Carla rolled her eyes and stood up. "Fine. Let's go before I change my mind"

The docks crackled with electricity as Maya and Carla approached the wooden beams, where the violet dance of crashing waves lay beyond, coating the air in sea salt. The hustle and bustle of shouting men and women from a docked ship joined the clash of the sea. Maya pulled her hood tighter over her head, gripping Carla's hand as they navigated through the commotion, with Gil standing at the centre of it all. "Is it always this hectic?" Carla shouted, struggling against the wind.

"Gil!" Maya's voice pierced through the chaos, causing the workers to scatter in different directions. Uncharacteristic panic filled the air - a rare sight in the otherwise controlled environment overseen by Gil. Maya hurried to his side as he strode towards the docked ship.

"Why is she here?" Gil asked bluntly, wiping the rain from his face.

"I needed a driver, and she's capable. She can handle herself." Maya shouted, trying to project her voice through the heavy rain. He narrowed his eyes, stopping beside a wooden container. "Did the shipment arrive on time?"

"You're damn lucky it arrived at all. I'd be questioning her presence more if my mind wasn't preoccupied," Gil retorted, pointing a thick finger at Carla. "Suppose you'll be offering me a week of free booze at The Vic, though?"

Carla nodded firmly. "Of course. Call it a gesture of solidarity."

Gil groaned, then turned his attention to the frantic men, shouting and waving. Beside Maya was an old black van, which she assumed would be her and Carla's vehicle for the drop-off. "What's happening here? Why are we lucky to have the shipment?"

Gil cleared his throat. "The West Country, across the sea, is experiencing a spike in heat, unbearable temperatures, and wildfires."

Maya knew little of the West Country's situation; she barely knew what her own country had been doing for the past twenty years, let alone them. However, she knew that people from overseas sought refuge here often, and her mother had provided shelter and aid to countless individuals over the years.

"Aren't they used to such heat by now? Hasn't the west dealt with similar situations for years?" Carla shouted.

"They have, but this time some fringe government added a bloody civil war to the mix. Fighting and chaos, coupled with the fires, its desperate times for everyone," Gil explained, gazing at the distant divide. "No matter what we face, someone somewhere else will always have it worse," he sighed. "You two need to get this shipment over to No Man's Land. It might be the last water they'll see for a while, especially from the west," Gil instructed.

"Is it a safe route there?" Carla's eyes widened with concern.

"Don't worry; the papers are in the van's cab. Just keep quiet, and you'll get past the checkpoint guards," Gil assured her, handing Carla the van keys. His eyes fell towards her arm. "Are you sure you can handle this?"

She snatched the keys with determination. "I'll be fine," she declared, striding towards the van.

"Feisty one, isn't she?" Gil remarked, smiling. "You better get going before this place turns into chaos, and that van gets hijacked."

Maya nodded and hurriedly rushed to the van, the relentless rain pelting her body like a barrage of bullets. "And remember," Gil called. "Keep Nic on your side. Rumour has it, she already admires you."

The howling wind carried away his words as Maya prepared for another uncertain journey to the outskirts.

Chapter Eight

Hidden Alliances

The van rocked from side to side as Carla skilfully navigated the darkened, desolate roads. Maya glanced in the wing mirror at the faint glow of lights behind them. She clasped her hands together to seek warmth from the icy wind seeping through the gaps in the aged vehicle. The outside world echoed the harsh reality of the world they lived in today - trees loomed like ghosts, with skeletal branches and rotten trunks surrounded by overgrown weeds obscuring any signs of past human life. It was a barren land, where forgotten fields and villages lay as silent reminders of vanished communities.

The city's outskirts were strictly off-limits, guarded fiercely by the city watch, where miles of untamed wilderness lay beyond. Only a few brave or desperate souls, it was rumoured, inhabited these forsaken territories, eking out a harsh existence in the lands known for winter floods and summer fires. Stories of treachery, betrayal, and murder circulated about those who risked crossing over, making it a place forever veiled in darkness. A place you dared not step.

Maya glanced at Carla in the driver's seat, her face now etched with stress as they ventured deeper into the outskirts, far from the city's safety. Maya couldn't help but be in awe of Carla, who had never allowed her missing limb to hinder her from anything in life.

"What way, Maya? Are you looking?" Carla shouted, snapping Maya back to the present.

Maya refocused on a fork on the road ahead. "Right. Keep going towards the divide to the East!" Carla expertly turned the wheel, flooring the brake. The van rumbled as they made the sharp turn, the bottles of water sliding and rattling in the rear.

"So much for you saying Gil wouldn't mind me coming along," Carla grumbled, adjusting the wing mirror. "The look on his face when he saw me. I could have killed you."

Maya chuckled and popped open a bottle of ale. "It was nothing. As soon as you offered him a week's worth of free booze, it was water under the bridge. Anyway, I told him we come as a pair."

"I'm starting to think I've undervalued myself," Carla retorted, narrowing her eyes. "We're coming up to the checkpoint. You sure about this?"

"It'll be fine. Gil's sorted it for us," Maya reassured her, winding down her window as Carla brought the van to a halt. "Evening," Maya said casually, resting her elbow on the open window.

"What are you two girls doing out here?" The man's face remained obscured in shadows, the only light emanating from a lamp behind him. His hat concealed any discernible features as he leaned into the car window, forcing Maya deeper into her seat. "Who are you working for? This van is Gil's."

Maya cleared her throat and presented the paperwork Gil had given her. "That's right. It's all here. We've taken over from Liam."

"The boy's dead then? Not surprised by how often he roamed these parts." The man licked his finger and flipped through the paperwork. Maya flinched. The flyaway comment about her brother being dead struck a chord, despite knowing he was far from it.

"He was a good man, you know."

"What's that?" the man grunted, seemingly disinterested.

"Liam. He was a good man," Maya repeated.

"Yeah, I'm sure someone will miss him. Okay, on you go." He waved his hand, wafting smoke throughout the cab as Maya rolled up the window. "And tell Gil the price has gone up."

"What a jerk," Maya muttered as Carla drove the van forward.

"So, what do we do now? Is it much further?" Carla asked with a touch of anxiety in her voice. She tapped her finger against the steering wheel.

"Gil said it would be just a few minutes or so down this straight path, and then we'll see a turning for the drop-off point." She peered out the window into the darkness, trying to catch any glimpse of the world beyond. "By the way, do you have any idea why your gran gave my mother that lottery ticket?"

Carla sighed, and Maya didn't miss her eye roll. "Maya, please, can we not get into that ticket again now?"

"It's only... they're so expensive, and there's such a slim chance of winning. It's a once-a-year opportunity. Why would your gran just give it away like that?"

"Maybe she doesn't think she'll last till the drawing day," Carla replied bluntly. "You've seen her, Maya. She's old. Not many make it much further, especially not in this heat."

Maya turned away to peer outside again, desperate to see any signs of their destination. She said too much and had once again upset her friend. Carla was right; her gran probably didn't have long left, not even a few weeks. No one ever did once the coughing started. Once it was in the lungs, that was it.

"There's the sign by the road!" Maya shouted suddenly, pointing towards the windscreen. "Turn in there by that red piece of metal."

Carla pressed down on the brake, jolting Maya's body forward. She pulled the hair from her face as the van turned into a narrow path flanked by bare trees, with logs laid on either side of it. Illuminated by the van's headlights was Lucas. Waving at them.

Outside, the cold air wrapped around Maya, who pulled her coat tightly around her waist and nodded at Lucas. She extended a hand to help Carla from the van. "Lucas, the shipment is here. Do you have the devices?" She blurted. "Sorry. This is my friend Carla; she's the one who got us here."

Carla waved, staying beside the vehicle door.

"You shy or something?" Lucas shouted back. He turned to wave the others toward the van. "Get the back open for us," he said to Carla. Her eyes widened at the people emerging from the shadows. She pulled a small handle to release the back doors of the van, and with a click, they swung open, and one by one, the people formed a line, passing the containers of water along it. It wasn't long before the rain started again, pounding on their shoulders and adding to the work.

Maya observed the scene and noticed Nic standing at the back with her hands on her hips. Maya whispered to Carla, "You alright? You seem unusually quiet."

"I'm fine. Just a bit of a shock, that's all."

"Shock? To see that the people out here aren't scary monsters, but just like us? Yeah, I felt the same way," Maya chuckled, but stopped when Carla's face dropped.

Nic moved to stand beside them. "Who's this? Thought I said I wanted you - and you only to do the drop-off," Nic said, her gaze fixed on Carla.

"Yeah, well, if you wanted just her, you wouldn't have gotten a drop-off at all," Carla retorted, shooting Maya a smile. Carla hesitated under Nic's penetrating stare.

"This is Carla. No one stronger or more loyal," Maya said.

"Carla?" Nic grabbed Carla's chin, tilting it to meet her gaze. "Nice name."

Carla gulped, but nodded. "Yes, Ma'am."

Nic's eyes roamed Carla's body, and she leaned in closer to her face. "Well, I'll be damned. You two, follow me," Nic said, turning back towards the divide.

"Where are we going?" Maya asked, glancing back at Carla.

"I said follow me," Nic replied, already marching towards the wall.

"Nic, there are a few things you need to know," Maya said, trying to keep pace. "Gil wanted me to say that this might be the last shipment from the west for a while."

"Trouble?" Nic looked back at Maya, who nodded. "It's

okay. We can find other routes. We always do." Nic stopped at the divide and gestured for Carla and Maya to step in.

They had carved out a small shelter in the space between the walls of the divide. Maya looked around, tracing the metallic scaffolding above them. Workers set wooden planks along each level, disappearing into the darkness. The rain pounded, echoing through the space, and the metal sang a song as the raindrops hit all sides. Nic stood by a makeshift lift crafted from reclaimed wood and attached by thick ropes. "Come on. You two, in here with me," Nic said, turning to the man holding the ropes. "It's okay, they're welcome." She assured him with a look of commanding authority.

Maya and Carla stepped into the lift, and when the small gate closed behind them, the man pulled the lever. Ropes tightened around the box, which shook as it lifted them into the air, passing levels of scaffolding built like a tower block. "Where are we going?" Maya asked, turning to face Nic.

"The meeting room, somewhere private. It's been a challenging day for us," Nic replied.

"Excuse me, Nic, was it?" Carla said. "I was told I'd be in and out for the drop-off. I don't mean to sound rude, but what are we doing up here?"

The lift came to a halt, and Nic pulled open the gate before leading them to a table. "I'm going to be honest with you girls. There's been an attack tonight; guards have captured members of our group and taken them over to New Albion," Nic said, sitting down in the chair as if her legs had collapsed beneath her. "News of the war across the seas seems to have only aggravated them more, but we carry on." She leaned forward on her elbows. "Carla, such wonderful eyes you have. Quite captivating."

Maya looked at Carla, confused why Nic wanted to

speak about her eyes. What was Nic's plan, bringing them up here with no one else around?

"Thank you. They're somewhat of a family trait, so my gran tells me." Carla replied, her cheeks turning a faint shade of pink.

The raindrops fell harder up here near the top of the wall, creating a cacophony of metal clangs that added to the storm outside. "Tell me," Nic said, sitting back in the chair and interlacing her fingers. "What history do you have with No Man's Land?" She smiled. "It's clear you don't want to be here, but yet, here you stand. There must be a reason."

Carla bit her lip and glanced towards Maya. "I wanted to help, that's all."

Nic's gaze shifted to Maya. "Loyal friends are scarce. Loyalty is what we look for here."

"I'm not moving here, if that's what you're asking," Carla replied, stepping back from the table. "This place has taken too much away from me already." She turned to Maya. "I'm going to wait by the lift. If you're not out in a few minutes, I'll go without you."

Maya watched Carla vanish into the shadowy hallway before turning her attention back to Nic, who was still watching Carla's departure. She couldn't understand Nic's fascination with her friend, and then she realised - the connection to Carla's parents. Maya glared at Nic. "Are Carla's parents still alive? Are they still here?" She asked, sitting on the corner of the table.

Nic smiled. "Quite observant. The boy never asked such questions. I could rely on him to take letters and not snoop around them too," Nic laughed. "He never invited his friends along, either."

"Yeah, well, I'm not Liam. Answer me. What do you

know about Carla's parents?"

"They're dead, if that's what you are asking." Nic rose and turned to the back wall, where posters, old maps, and plans were stapled. "Do you know who decorated this office? Who chose the plans you see on this table?"

"You? You're the leader of this place, after all."

"These trade plans here, the ones from five years ago. Those were the plans made three *leaders* ago. Still pinned up with paper as fresh as the plans I've made today," Nic said, pulling a cigarette from the drawer. "Every time we begin to make plans to change people's minds, we're killed, taken out, and another replaces us. I've only been here a year or so in the top job, and it feels like decades."

"What's that got to do with Carla's parents? Were they leaders here once?" Maya asked, trying to make sense of Nic's revelation.

"No," Nic blew a puff of smoke into the air. "They were warriors. Fighters for the cause. People who were fed up with their lives and wanted to make a difference. I see that spirit in you and in her." Nic tapped the ash into a tray, and Maya searched the room, trying to piece together what Nic wanted. Was she asking her to join the group? To fight against the government?

"The lift is coming up!" Carla shouted from outside. "I'm going once it's here."

Maya turned to Nic with endless questions on her tongue, including a request for more time. "What do you want me to say? I'm not a warrior. I'm none of those things."

"Time is rare. It isn't something I have a lot of. We are down people, and the offer is there for both of you."

"What do we get from it?"

Nic's eyes glossed over Maya, from her face down to her

boots. "The chance to make a difference. To join a rebellion to stop this world from going to shit. There is so much you don't know, so much both sides keep hidden. Think about it. Discuss it with Carla. It's in her blood to fight."

"Maya, you coming?" Carla shouted.

Maya smiled at Nic and nodded. "When you next hear from me, you'll have your answer."

As they made their way down the lift and back towards the exit of the hideaway, Maya spotted Lucas dragging a container of bottles past them. He flashed her a smile, which Carla appeared to miss, lost in her own thoughts. But something caught Maya's attention when she looked back at Lucas. His eyes pierced through the darkness as lamps flickered around him - those blue eyes, like the ocean. The ones that felt so familiar to her before, a beauty that could only be passed down through family.

Chapter Nine

Bloodlines

Liam wiped the beads of sweat from his brow as the driverless car dropped Liam off, alone, in front of the towering skyscraper. The building's glass exterior gleamed, pristine and unblemished. He stepped over the threshold to enter the reception, his footsteps echoing across the empty, marble expanse. Liam's gaze drifted toward the elevator on his right, recalling Alex's precise instructions. Seventh floor, apartment B. With a decisive motion, he approached the lift and pressed the corresponding button. The doors slid shut, enclosing him in a gold-plated chamber adorned with mirrors, multiplying his image on an infinite scale. He stood a little taller to correct his posture, as if the very environment demanded it.

The elevator ascended, and the pressure in Liam's ears popped upon arrival as the doors glided open. He stepped into a corridor of the same white marble, its polished surface almost reflecting his image. He rapped his knuckles lightly against the door - three succinct knocks that echoed in the quiet space. His fingers danced over his device, like Alex had instructed, to ensure no trail led back to him.

The door swung open, and Alex greeted him with a welcoming smile. He gestured for Liam to enter. Inside, the air seemed to hold a hint of moisture. Alex's attire was different today - a crisp white vest, loose fitted cotton trousers. Not a thread out of place, and his hair was still slightly damp. Liam glanced at the clock on the wall, realising he had arrived early. "Don't worry about the time," Alex said apologetically, shutting the door behind them. "These past few days have been a whirlwind, and I'm a bit delayed. Just give me a moment to change, and we'll get started."

Liam's gaze roamed the pristine white lines of his apartment, as sterile as a corporate office and devoid of any character. The absence of photographs on the walls made it feel more like a transactional space than a home. Liam offered a small smile before strolling towards the balcony to slide open the glass door, allowing the gentle morning breeze to caress his skin. The skies had cleared, replacing the previous gloom with a serene expanse of blue. He peered out over the districts of New Albion and beyond the imposing divide toward the western sea. Liam tried to envision the hardships experienced by those on the other side. He had caught wind of a war brewing; his mother was occupied with finding refuge from the influx of displaced people. A pang of guilt tugged at him for his absence from the docks and inability to assist Gil.

A chill danced along his neck, and Liam's eyes fluttered open. A faint buzzing sound drew his attention to the thin vent above the door, where, through the glass, he spotted Alex, his hair now dry and neatly tucked behind his ears. Clad in a deep blue uniform, Alex seemed to come alive against the monochromatic backdrop. "Better step inside. We don't want any prying eyes, even this high up." Alex suggested, guiding Liam into the apartment and shutting the door behind him. "How's things back home? I've heard rumours about countless refugees washing up on shore."

Remaining on his feet, Liam glanced again at the apartment - clean, cold, and impersonal, like a museum exhibit. "Things are okay," he said. "Mum's been working non-stop. I used to pitch in with the shipments overseas whenever stuff like this went on. But it seems worse this time." Liam smiled at Alex, happy to see him again. "I haven't spotted you around work lately. Everything been okay?"

Alex gave a weary sigh. "Mum fell ill and needed a transplant. Out of the blue, they found a donor. Another AI advantage. I don't even know why I worried."

Concern creased Liam's brow. "Is she getting better?"

With a nod, Alex confirmed her progress before asking, "Care for some coffee?"

Liam shook his head. "Nah, coffee's not my thing. Never much of it around back home, so never grew a taste for it." He tapped his fingers on his thighs, his impatience beginning to show. "Hey, about those cameras in the hallway? They won't raise any alarms about me being here, right?"

Alex leaned back thoughtfully, his gaze contemplative. "The cameras don't capture actual footage, just monitor movement, body heat, and device locations. Stuff like that. We found AI handled data more efficiently than visuals. If you've followed the steps I gave you, we're in the clear."

"So, have you arranged the meeting with Dad... I mean,

Robert. Has he accepted it?"

"That's why I wanted to talk here." Alex moved toward the kitchen, staring at his device before returning with a steaming mug of coffee. "I had an idea, you see. Confronting him directly might not be the best approach."

"No?"

Alex smiled. "No. I've secured a small promotion for you under my direct recommendation."

"And they accepted it? Just like that?"

"I know it seems sudden, but... they tasked me with making you happier, more driven." Alex tapped his chin. "Let me explain. Remember how they gave me your personal file?"

"Yeah, the one you glanced through."

"Yes," Alex said. "After getting to understand you better, it didn't seem fitting. Besides, the person they described didn't match the Liam I've come to know."

Liam furrowed his brow and leaned closer to Alex. "Why? What did it say about me?"

Alex took a sip of his coffee. "Do you know why they initiated this Freedom Day program? Why they sought people from Old Albion to work here?"

"Well, the idea was to bridge the gap between us, right? That's what we were told."

"Exactly." Alex strolled toward the balcony door, his gaze lost in the distance. "I've always accepted the narrative I was fed. We all have, living here. Never questioning the status quo." He turned to face Liam. "We get housing, employment, leisure activities - it's all part of the job, and better yet, it's free. Except it's not. It clearly comes at a price." He stepped closer to Liam and set his coffee on the table. "Now, I don't know what to trust. I don't know whether to believe the files they had on you or any of the files kept on everyone else in this program." Alex hesitated, grappling for the right words. "They portrayed you all as... uneducated, friendly, and blindly loyal individuals. When I read about you and got to know you better, when I saw the fire in your heart at the restaurant, it just didn't... add up."

Liam's gaze shifted to his lap. The government accepted Liam for the programme because they saw him as mouldable and easily manipulated. "So, what do *you* think of me now?" he asked, locking eyes with Alex.

Alex drew nearer until he settled beside him on the sofa. "Liam, I think you're quite amazing. I don't have a clear understanding of what's happening here, the divide, or how everything came to this, but I'm wondering if maybe I should begin asking questions. Maybe even attempt to uncover some of it with you."

"And you think Robert has some answers?"

"It's a possibility. I can grant you access to most places, and with you serving as his guard, we can gather information." Alex took Liam's hand in his own. "Part of this promotion means you work alongside him instead of me; you could take part in meetings and significant events. Now, there's something I want to discuss, and I need you to know that there's no need to be embarrassed or upset, all right?"

"Upset?" Liam stood, freeing his hand from Alex's grip. "About what?"

"Please understand that I don't mean to belittle you, but am I right to say you can't read? I saw you didn't finish school or pursue any higher education."

Liam's cheeks flushed with warmth. He couldn't bring himself to meet Alex's gaze. "I'm not dumb, if that's what you're saying. I didn't complete school because I didn't have the luxury of choices. We had no options. I had to work as soon as I could to support my family, to support my sister in actually finishing school."

Alex rose to his feet and took Liam's hands in his own again. "I understand that now." He glanced down, a bashful smile touching his lips. "They fed us a false narrative about your side; they said you had the same opportunities as us, but now it's clear that wasn't the truth." Alex met Liam's eyes, his gentle smile easing the tension. "They won't be monitoring you closely; they've already dismissed you as insignificant and uninformed. If I tailor the report to reinforce the image they want, you can gain access to places and conversations you otherwise wouldn't without their watchful eye on you. What do you think? Can we both do this? Can you do this?"

"What, play the fool?" Liam grinned. "Sure, I can manage that. If it brings me closer to the truth and to my father, then I'm in."

A few days had passed since Alex had requested Liam to keep his distance before beginning his new role. Liam felt somewhat apprehensive as he strode through a part of the government building he had yet to explore. The people bustling around him exuded formality, all dressed in stiff suits and avoiding eye contact like it was key to their survival. Following the location indicated on his device, Liam arrived at the designated spot and waited for his father. A thumbs-up image from Alex flashed on his screen as a silent reassurance.

Footsteps reached his ears, causing Liam to glance upward. The double doors leading into the office swung open, revealing his father. Robert's gaze lingered on Liam; he appeared to assess him more intently than he had during their initial encounter on initiation day. Liam offered a tentative smile and held his breath. He desperately hoped that a trace of recognition would manifest in Robert's eyes.

"You have to be the new boy." Robert's voice broke the silence, drawing Liam's attention. He turned away from Liam and strode toward his desk. "I must admit, the notion of having someone to train took me aback, especially this early on. But now that you're here, I understand the reasoning behind it."

"Thank you, sir. I'll do my best to quickly catch on," Liam replied earnestly.

Robert regarded Liam with a genial smile. "I have no doubt about that, lad. I've been informed that you'll be acting as my personal guard during your training. I assume you might have some inquiries before we start?"

Liam scratched his head. He had hundreds of questions, though none of them were appropriate to ask. "What is it you do here, exactly?"

Robert laughed and turned on his monitor. "Well, I'd thought you'd have already known that. I suppose they're sending you lot off to anyone now. Always the trouble when you start a new scheme, nothing but guinea pigs." Liam stepped towards the desk, looking over Robert's shoulder. "This is what I spend most of the time doing, just scrolling through numbers and endless amounts of data."

Liam leaned in to peer at the screen. Rows upon rows of endless figures. "I thought that was what AI was for?" Liam replied, pulling out a chair to sit beside Robert.

"Yeah, well. That stuff worked a little too well. Now everyone has practically the same role. AI took over everything, so now all people do is work off one of these screens. It's pointless work, checking what the AI has done."

"The people who work from their homes now, right? I heard most of them do data work."

"That's right. They became so used to it that no one wants to do anything else." He looked Liam in the eyes, examining them for longer than what felt normal. "Why do you think that lot up there wanted to drag you guys in from over the wall? Get you doing the jobs us lot don't want to do." He rested a hand on Liam's shoulder. "I mean, you got bored with guard duty after a few weeks. Hardly surprising, is it?" A faint buzz emanated from Robert's device. "Ah, come along, young man. We have a meeting to attend. An ideal occasion for you to sit in and glean insights from some of the brightest minds within our society."

Liam trailed behind his father, maintaining a respectful two-step distance. He keenly observed Robert's air of authority within the building. The respect his father garnered from his colleagues was palpable, clear in the nods and bows he received from his fellow guards as they passed. They entered the office on the top floor of the tower, and Liam's gaze swept across the assembly of men and women in formal suits. The panoramic expanse of glass that formed an entire wall showcased the sprawling cityscape of New Albion behind them, illuminated beneath the sun's brilliance. Liam acknowledged the three other guards on duty with a subtle nod before mirroring their actions, adopting an upright posture, and folding his hands behind his back. He positioned himself to the left of his father.

"Ladies and gentlemen, I extend my gratitude to all of you for joining us today." The governor's voice resounded through the room, commanding attention. "As you are undoubtedly aware, the situation in the western region has undergone a significant escalation in recent days.

Consequently, we must deliberate on our strategic path forward. Furthermore, our ongoing surveillance efforts have yielded positive results, culminating in the apprehension of several members of the No Man's Land faction, and thereby weakening their resistance."

A jolt of recognition stunned Liam upon hearing the mention of the No Man's Land rebellion. His thoughts involuntarily turned to Nic and her comrades, yet he silently reminded himself to remain composed despite the waves of concern threatening to engulf him. Nic was too resourceful and cunning to be captured; still, the news of lives lost cast a sombre shadow over his thoughts.

Robert leaned back in his chair, a subtle yet noticeable shift in his posture. Liam noted the telltale twitch of Robert's right foot beneath the table - a gesture betraying his father's restlessness. "We were told the west wouldn't be reaching this point of conflict for months yet. Are we still working towards the same deadline as before or has this moved things forward?" he asked.

"Our communication channels with President Alma remain intact, and our dialogue shows that he is effectively holding the line. His intention to visit our nation in the near future remains unchanged. Therefore, I emphasise the need for timely submission of the feedback reports from participants in the new scheme, as previously outlined."

A voice belonging to a blonde woman sat across the table captured the room's focus. "Sir Granswick, if I may interject," she began. "Considering the influx of refugees from the west into Old Albion, will our decision to accept civilians under the Freedom Day initiative not inadvertently align us with the western aggressors?"

Liam peered around the room. He wasn't sure if the other guards were from Old Albion like he was. In fact, he wondered if anyone present was. He made certain to look forward and keep his face still and unreactive to anything being said.

"It will not pose a challenge; their perceptions of our allegiance will be duly clarified once the feedback from our endeavours is presented. Until then, our primary focus remains directed toward curtailing the No Man's Land resistance group - a force that presents the most significant threat to stability within our domain," Granswick replied. "Old Albion's attention is aptly diverted by the ongoing refugee influx, ensuring that our actions remain largely unnoticed. Intelligence indicates that the resistance group's supplies will dwindle in the imminent weeks, leaving them vulnerable and prone to capture. As long as the western conflict persists, we shall wield this as a strategic advantage."

The governor pivoted his gaze toward Liam, and the room's attention converged upon him. It was an unexpected spotlight that took Liam by surprise. "Considering recent developments, the outcomes of the Freedom Day initiative have exceeded our expectations. Notably, the shift in sentiment toward New Albion has been marked, with a growing acceptance of technological integration and heightened job satisfaction." The governor's extended hand toward Liam signalled his approval. "We are proud to announce the promotion of Liam here, who will now be under the guidance of Robert. He has quickly earned resounding endorsements from his previous hand. He stands as a show of our trial phase and is a testament to the efficacy of our strategic endeavours." A modest smile tugged at Liam's lips, yet he instinctively turned his head. "Now, we are all up to date. The plan is to stay focused and deliver the results as soon as we can." He nodded as the group stood.

"Now please, return back to work."

Back in Robert's office, Liam watched his father produce a bottle of brandy from his bottom desk drawer. Two glasses landed on the table with a gentle clink, followed by the cascade of amber liquid filling each glass. He nudged one tumbler closer to Liam. "Drink up. You survived your first meeting." His lips brushed the rim of the glass as he took a sip.

Liam's eyes never left the glass. "But won't the device pick up the reading?" he asked, tapping the small circular attachment on his head.

A trace of exasperation passed across Robert's face. He leaned forward and deftly removed the device. "There you go, problem solved. Now, drink up, boy."

Liam shook his head as a ringing echoed in his ears. He lifted the glass to breathe in the scent of liquor. It was potent, far richer than anything he had ever encountered at The Old Vic. He took a cautious sip, the fiery liquid singing over his tongue and throat. He coughed, shaking his head. "Man, that's some powerful stuff."

"Changed your mind?" Robert asked. Without waiting for a response, he poured Liam another glass, who now found himself better prepared for the sharp burn that followed, along with a spreading warmth in his chest. "Good lad." Robert joined Liam and finished his measure in one smooth motion. "So, you heard what the boss said about all of us enjoying this place and the AI. What's your real take on it?" Robert tapped the device he'd removed from Liam's head. "And I want the truth."

Liam stared into his glass, absently turning it in his hands. "I'm not sure. When I first got here, it felt strange. I'd grown up with the notion that AI was bad, like a kind of cheat. Going against that notion feels like betraying my family."

Robert regarded Liam for another moment before pouring more brandy. "And now, after using and seeing it in action, what do you think?"

"Well, I've gotta admit, it seems to work from what I've seen. The city's clean. People have homes and jobs, but I haven't seen how people live beyond work. I can't help but wonder if they feel trapped, confined to their zones, with no freedom to roam."

"In Old Albion, you're free to go wherever, right?" Liam nodded. "It wasn't always like that here. These rules came about slowly. The method we have now works better. Splitting things up into living districts makes it easier for the AI and prevents mistakes."

"I have one question, though." Liam said, taking another sip. "If you don't mind."

"Go on, speak your thoughts. This is a place for open discussion - no judgement, just learning," Robert encouraged.

"The state of Old Albion is mainly because of lack of funding. New Albion almost completely cut us off," Liam stated.

"That's the reality. We can only provide what our country produces. Once AI took off here, there was no comparing the two sides," Robert responded. "Remember, the divide may only separate us by a few meters in parts, but we are two different countries, with different laws."

"The mayor of Old Albion tells a different story."

Robert chuckled. "Don't pay much heed to his words. The man lives in a luxurious mansion, well away from prying eyes. If things have gone awry in Old Albion, it's because of the ones in power over there, not here."

"I find that hard to believe. He wouldn't take it all for himself. The disparity between the sides is too vast for it to be one man's doing."

"Listen. Nowhere is perfect, not here or anywhere else. But you can witness the difference firsthand. Healthcare has improved significantly with the tracking device, something that was only made workable with the application of AI. Entrust that same task to be carried out by humans, and the country would be financially ruined within a year."

Leaning back, Liam contemplated Robert's words with a deep breath. His lungs had felt much better since he began working here. Old Albion's streets and the gruelling hours of labour filled his mind. Perhaps his people made an error by being so resistant to change. Lifting his gaze, he caught Robert's smirk once more. "You keep watching me," he said.

Robert tapped his foot lightly. "Just waiting."

"For what?"

"For you to ask if I remembered you."

The glass slipped from Liam's hand and clattered onto the table. "So, you did recognise me."

A small smile tugged at the corners of Robert's mouth. "Naturally. Why else would I accept someone to shadow me?" He laughed, extending his arms. "Come here, son," he beckoned, drawing Liam into a warm embrace.

Liam raised his gaze to his father, who studied him from head to toe. "Why did it take you so long? So many years went by without a word."

Slowly, Robert nodded. "I know. It's not something I'm proud of. Everything happened so swiftly when they announced the votes. Seeing your mother's reaction to finding my name on the wrong side... It filled me with self-loathing, deep to my core."

"Why lie? Why not just be upfront in the first place? It was just a vote."

Robert stood to pour himself another drink. "It's hard to convey the atmosphere in the country at that time. It was like a volcano about to erupt, with tensions escalating by the day. People were getting angrier and angrier." He glanced at Liam. "You had to choose a side. The media were pushing for conflict, one side or the other. I had to lie, to agree with my wife, family, and friends. How could I have foreseen that my votes would be made public a few years later?"

Liam picked up the bottle, replenishing his glass. "That might be the explanation. But all these years... I took jobs across No Man's Land, trying to get closer to you."

"I'm sorry. I was a government employee. Anyone caught gaining unauthorised access to Old Albion faced a grim fate in the early days."

"You could have sent a message! Anything to let us know you were still there."

Robert sighed. "You're right, of course, but it didn't seem fair. It was better for me to fade into obscurity. I've been alone since then, throwing myself into work and nothing else."

"Do others know about me? Who I am?"

"No. Nobody here does. But we can make up for lost time now. Work together, get to know each other," Robert suggested. "And Maya, my dear Maya. Did Emma ever move on? Remarry?"

Liam laughed softly and finished his drink. "No. Love and marriage aren't exactly priorities over there. If you're wondering, Mum's unwell. She won't admit it, but I can tell."

"Sick?"

"Everyone eventually falls ill. If it's not the dire living

conditions, it's the hours of work that wear you down." Liam rubbed his eyes, stung by the drink's aroma. "Don't pretend you're unaware of the situation. You hold an influential position here; you're aware of what's happening."

"You're giving me too much credit, son. I don't know as much as you think," Robert admitted, stepping forward to place a hand on Liam's shoulder. "I want to assist you in any way I can. I can send money now to your account and you can exchange it for coins for your mother. Anything you need. Just don't leave. Let me train you and show you the opportunities here."

Liam turned away, his gaze settling on the door. A part of him wanted to escape. The plan wasn't meant to speed up this quickly. He was supposed to remain inconspicuous, report back to Alex, join forces, and bring down the entire regime. But now, he was caught between conflicting choices. Had he prematurely judged New Albion? He faced his father again, the worry clear in his bloodshot eyes. "I won't tell Mum and Maya about you, not yet. It would be too painful." Liam shifted his stance. "I'll stay under your watch, but I need to witness the reality here, Dad, not just the curated version. Will that be possible?"

Robert stepped closer, a genuine smile forming on his lips. "I'll do whatever it takes to keep you by my side, son." He pulled Liam into another embrace.

Liam closed his eyes, exhaling slowly as he surrendered to his father's firm hold. It was as though years of tension had shed from his body as he relaxed, resting his head against Robert's shoulder. But worry still held him tighter.

Chapter Ten

Ripples of Rebellion

The battle cry of hard labour reverberated, like a rallying call that carried the weight of determination with it. Maya stared at the scene before her. She released the rope alongside five others, slowly lowering a box into the hull of a ship worn down by the ravages of war. The midday sun cast warm rays upon their work, a welcome relief after the recent downpour in the last few days. A breeze from the west swept in, carrying a mixture of dust and ash from the country on the brink of collapse.

As the container settled into place, Maya wiped the sweat from her brow, feeling the satisfying ache in her muscles. The group shared a collective moment of respite, their chests heaving as they knelt on the ground to catch their breath. Maya's lips curled into a weary but triumphant smile, mirroring the others, whom each carried the weight of their labour with an exhausted yet determined air.

Maya unscrewed the cap off her glass bottle and glugged it, closing her eyes at the cool water cascading down her throat. The momentary pause allowed her to reflect. The ship, now prepared for its journey homeward, held more than just cargo; it bore the hopes of their endeavours, a lifeline to those waiting on the other side.

With the container secure and her thirst quenched, Maya turned to gaze at the horizon, the expanse of sea stretching endlessly before her. She took another swig of water and envisioned a family, not unlike her own, eagerly expecting their latest shipment - a vital commodity that could offer them a few extra weeks of sustenance from the harsh realities of their existence.

Maya observed the procession of weary dock workers filing past her. Their camaraderie was clear in their pats on her shoulder as they headed to clock out for the day. Swiftly rising to her feet, Maya continued on her way and passed by Gil's office, who she found engrossed in a solitary game of cards. "You planning to be at the Old Vic tonight, Gil?" she asked with a touch of playful curiosity.

Gil glanced up, cupping one hand around his ear in confusion. "What was that, lass?"

Maya rolled her eyes and sidled up beside him, grateful for the shade the office provided. "I asked if you'll be down at the pub tonight."

"Aye, you bet. Half days call for a pint or two. It's the only way to survive 'em," he chuckled. Maya turned to leave when his voice caught her attention again. "Hold on a tick, lass. Before you dash off, how's it all treating you so far?"

Maya hadn't yet confided in Gil about her encounters with Nic or the invitation to Maya and Carla to join the rebellion group. She took a moment to collect her thoughts. "It's been a whirlwind. I won't lie. But the team's been great, and you certainly haven't given me any time to stop and think."

A faint smile tugged at the corners of Gil's lips. "Glad to hear it. I've been keeping an eye on your energy levels, and I must say, you've been impressively resilient. Not every newcomer adapts so quickly. How'd the trade with Nic's lot go? You haven't said much about it."

"It went smoothly," Maya commented, her tone casual. "Lucas and his group collected the water and handed over the package. Just wrapped it up and sent it off now."

"And Nic herself? Was she overseeing things?" Maya nodded. "Did she have much to say to you?"

Maya's thoughts danced on the edge of the truth, but she tread carefully. "Not too much, really. More of a stern look than anything else. She intimidated Carla. I mostly focused on keeping her at ease so we could get away quickly."

"Nic built herself a reputation as a formidable leader, turning No Man's Land into a place to survive rather than perish, but don't let her facade fool you. I'll tell you the same as I told Liam. Be cautious when dealing with her, unless I give the green light. She's not above taking advantage of people, including sacrificing her own."

Maya offered a reassuring smile, stepping back another step as she prepared to take her leave. "Don't worry, Gil. I have no intentions of making deals with anyone else but you. You mean a lot to me and my family. I won't forget your advice." When Maya stepped away, she couldn't help but feel a pang of concern at the sight of Gil alone, engrossed in cards, but her own responsibilities urged her onward. "See you at the pub, Gil. We can set the world to rights then."

Gil nodded, returning his attention to the cards as he flipped one over to make his move. "Aye, just remember what I said. Your family's important to me, too. Don't want to see you caught up in something you can't escape."

At an abandoned park in the district, Maya watched Carla, who crouched with the sunlight setting her golden hair aglow. A small cat emerged from beneath the bench, drawn by whatever Carla held in her hand. As Maya approached, her gaze met the creature's. It looked up at her, its matted fur and protruding ribs revealing the harshness of its existence. Smiling gently, Maya extended an empty hand as a gesture of trust. The cat, however, retreated, seeking refuge once again under the bench.

"Suit yourself," Maya mused, rising to her feet. She playfully brushed off her clothes and turned her attention to Carla, wrapping her in a quick hug. "So, how long have you been waiting here? And why this meeting spot?"

The park, once a vibrant children's playground, was now an ad hoc shelter for animals. Beneath the worn concrete floors and broken remnants of plastic shelters, rows of benches had been ingeniously woven together. Maya could almost glimpse the park's former glory, recalling Liam's childhood stories of places such as this, compared to its current state.

Carla revealed a bag of cat biscuits from her backpack. "How about we walk and chat?" she suggested, giving the bag a little shake before moving toward the next makeshift cat shelter tucked beneath a bench.

"Are we going to discuss Nic's offer, then?" Maya asked, following Carla's lead.

Carla appeared to ignore the question and instead,

marvelled, "Isn't this place something? Despite everything that's been happening and all the disruptions. People still find time and resources to come here and care for these animals." She grinned at Maya before helping her to her feet. "Here, you feed the next one."

Taking the bag of treats, Maya approached another bowl and peered down into two eyes, gleaming like reflective mirrors from beneath a bush. "Carla, what's your take on Nic's proposal?" she asked.

"Maya, keep your voice down." Carla cautioned, crouching beside her. "Just give the food. Little Albert gets scared by noise."

Maya suppressed an eye roll, shaking some biscuits into the bowl. Carla gently pulled her back and settled down near her. As Maya watched, she tried to hold her breath to quiet her movements. A cat emerged then, cautiously extending a paw before more of it materialised, a black cat with eyes brimming with sorrow. Maya held the cat's gaze for what felt like an eternity before it mustered the courage to emerge. Its tail hung low as it snatched a single biscuit before darting back into the shadows. Maya glanced at Carla, whose smile had blossomed into full-blown joy. "Should we decline?" Maya whispered.

Carla's grin faded. "I'm not sure," she murmured back as Albert took another bite. "It's risky. Even with the knowledge we've gained about that place, it still feels daunting. Those tales about No Man's Land are hard to shake."

"We grew up on those stories. It's only natural they'd stick in your mind." Albert inched closer, brushing against Maya's knee. She looked at Carla again, who gave her a nod of approval. Slowly, Maya lowered her hand to the cat's back to offer soothing strokes. "But what about the chance to make a difference? Isn't that worth the gamble?"

Carla stood and stepped out of the shelter into the sunlight. "How much can two people really achieve? I don't want to follow my parents into an early grave."

Maya continued to scratch Albert under his chin before rising to her feet. "Nic saw something in your family. She said they were fighters and recognised that spirit in you, too. Just look around," Maya gestured toward the animal shelter. "You're already channelling it to help these cats. Why not take it a step further?"

"So, you've made up your mind," Carla challenged. "You're joining no matter what I say?"

Maya hesitated. "I don't have all the answers, but I want us to make this decision together. Think about it, we could find answers about your family, your parents. If I were in your shoes, I'd want to know."

If the opportunity presented itself, Maya would grab at the chance to find her father and ask him the questions that had burdened her ever since he left.

Carla turned away and began heading toward the bustling streets of the district, with Maya following close behind. They passed through the rusty gates of the park and into the lively city surroundings. "Liam has been to New Albion," Carla mused, proceeding to the division. "Why not ask him to help locate your father and find answers for you?"

"I wish it were that simple. Over there, things aren't easy. They have rules for everything."

Carla's laughter echoed as they made a sharp turn and stepped over a tattered poster left behind from Freedom Day. As they emerged from the narrow alleyway, they passed the imposing government building, where Maya had stood to witness the governor's speech, and where Liam crossed to the other side every day. Maya slowed her pace as she caught sight of a small cluster of individuals, all donned in dark, hooded jumpers as they hurriedly unpacked items from their bags. A sense of urgency marked their movements as they unfolded posters one by one and hoisted them high above their heads. Then they started chanting.

Carla's grip tightened on Maya's arm, and she tugged it to get her attention. "Let's go before things escalate."

Maya shook her head and continued watching. The group cheered, their voices echoing throughout the square. Onlookers on the opposite side of the plaza had paused, turning their heads to listen.

"Power to the people, rise and fight, our voices united, breaking the night!" the chant rang out on repeat, each rendition gaining more volume and momentum. Maya couldn't help but smile, sensing Carla's tightening grip.

"You see, they don't need us," Carla remarked. "They seem to have it all under control."

Maya glanced at the entrance of the building as a contingent of about ten men arrived, some clad in black guard uniforms and others in blue, like Liam's uniform. They approached the group of protesters. While she had heard of such demonstrations before, she'd never witnessed one firsthand. A thrill coursed through her as one demonstrator shoved back a man in blue, who stumbled to his knees. "That's right!" Maya couldn't help but shout, overcome with a sense of exhilaration. "Speak your truth!"

Carla yanked Maya's arm down. "You're going to get us in trouble."

"Good," Maya retorted, an unyielding determination in her eyes. "Isn't that the whole point? To stand on the sidelines and witness those who are actually making a difference?" Carla's gaze shifted toward the growing crowd.

"Even if we're not joining them, we can at least show our support," Maya added, lifting her arm once more in an emphatic gesture of solidarity.

The man on the pavement regained his footing and turned to the others in blue, spurring them into action. Maya's gaze narrowed, and a shiver of unease ran through her. Could Liam be among them, tasked with quelling any hint of free speech? Her heart pounded as she watched the scene unfold. The men encircled the protectors and yanked them to the ground, their fists flying, dust swirling, and their voices echoing in a defiant chorus. Maya's pulse quickened.

Instinctively, she stepped forward, her voice primed to shout at the men to demand they cease their brutal assault, but Carla's firm grip pulled her back. The officers in blue and black uniforms brandished their weapons - sticks, tasers, batons, and launched an unrelenting barrage against the protesters. Agonised screams ripped through the air, accompanied by the thuds of blunt force and the sickening crack of impact. Posters and banners dropped to the dust-covered ground as the men mercilessly pummelled the protesters. Maya's eyes widened in horror as one protester struggled to sit up, his bloodied face contorted as he locked eyes with her for a fleeting moment before another blow struck him down. Crimson stained the ground beneath him as he collapsed.

"We can't just stand here!" Maya's voice trembled, and she tried to move forward - to intervene and put a stop to this senseless violence. However, Carla's arm remained, her grip unyielding. "You can't think this is right," Maya implored, her eyes locking onto Carla's.

Carla bowed her head, her grasp on Maya's arm the only sign of her own struggle. "I don't want to see you get hurt."

Maya wrenched her shoulder free. The men in blue were

now securing the protesters and binding their arms behind their backs before forcibly dragging them towards New Albion. Maya pondered the fate that awaited them - bereft families left forever to wonder about their loved ones' mysterious disappearance.

Tears welled in Maya's eyes as she turned to face Carla. She took a hesitant step back, surprised by the emotion that had overcome her. Yet, Carla's resolute stance remained unshaken. Wiping her own eyes, Carla's voice wavered as she said, "This... this wasn't how it used to be, was it? Is it getting worse?"

Their eyes stayed locked on one another. Maya nodded. "It's getting worse, and we can't ignore it."

Carla turned her gaze towards the government building, her fist clenched. "We can't turn a blind eye anymore. Let's go. Right now."

Maya's heart swelled. "Right now? You mean it?" she asked, her voice quivering.

In a surprisingly even tone, Carla nodded, "I mean it. Let's do something about it."

Maya led Carla across the divide and through the desolate expanse of No Man's Land. The shanty town came into view, its ramshackle structures a testament to its resilience over the years. Maya's heart quickened as they drew nearer.

The familiar guard stationed on the outskirts acknowledged Maya's presence with a nod, granting them passage without the need for questioning. A skeleton hung pinned together above the entrance, the sight of which stirred an involuntary shiver in Maya's spine. She glanced at Carla, anticipating a similar reaction, but found her focus unbroken, ignited by a fiery determination that still burned fiercely ever since the protest.

They stepped inside the main hall of the shantytown, and their entrance prompted the quiet conversations to falter. The room directed their attention to the newcomers. Familiar faces and strangers alike turned to observe their arrival. Nic, seated at a table, looked up. She seemed weary; fatigue lingered in the lines of her face, her eyes betraying the weight of her responsibilities. Maya, having not noticed the shift in atmosphere before, now sensed the palpable tension hanging in the air.

"Girls, welcome." Nic said, her voice tinged with warmth. She extended her arms to pull them into an embrace. "I'm pleased to see you both. We have much to discuss, and time is of the essence. Please, follow me." With a sweep of her hand, Nic pushed aside a heavy maroon curtain, which concealed a hidden doorway. Carla followed her lead without hesitation, and Maya strode behind her, wondering what had happened here. The atmosphere was tough on her first visit, but something felt different this time. Loss and fear weighed heavily on them all, more than she'd ever noticed before.

Before the shadows closed around her, Maya caught sight of Lucas in a corner, surrounded by a small circle of companions. A smile graced her lips, and she waved at him before they made their way deeper into the heart of the enclave. The weight of their decision settled upon her shoulders. She wanted this.

"You've arrived during a tumultuous time. I apologise for the lack of a warmer reception." Nic's words sliced through the tension as Maya and Carla quickened their steps to catch up with her as they hurried through a narrow hallway into the outside.

"What's been happening here?" Maya asked.

Nic came to a halt beside a weathered jeep; Carla wasted no time climbing into the passenger seat, with Maya scrambling up after her. The engine roared to life with a sputter, and Nic slammed her foot on the accelerator. The expanse of dust-covered land stretched out before them, illuminated by the pale silver of the moon. As Maya's eyes adjusted to the darkness, she made out the scattered piles of disused metal.

She recalled the official explanation for this place's creation. Two miles of barren land, torn apart between Old and New Albion for the people in No Man's Land to die, but they lived, and survive. The wall narrowed the closer you got to the capital, but out here, near the outskirts, the free and empty territory spread for miles.

Maya gripped the jeep's frame, the wind whipping against her cheeks as they sped along. The journey was brief, yet the sight that greeted them was unexpected - they were at the wall. Except, it was not the wall in which Maya had entered No Man's Land before; it was from the opposite side, facing New Albion.

Without delay, Nic hopped out of the jeep, her boots stirring up clouds of dust. "We're close to New Albion," she stated, her voice low yet commanding. "You're safe, as long as you keep quiet. Stay behind me and let me do the talking."

Recently, Maya had a habit of going against the advice of her mentors, but something in her stomach told her to follow Nic's word this time.

Carla and Maya followed Nic to a makeshift entrance by the wall, reminiscent of the one they had used on their side. Two guards stood beside the doorway, clad in royal blue and armed to the teeth with weapons. "Nic, is that you?" one guard called.

Nic stood firm and addressed them directly with her hands on her hips. "I've no time for bullshit. Where are my people? I've lost twelve in just a matter of days."

The guards' stony expressions shifted to a mix of embarrassment and apprehension. *What were they hiding?* Maya thought.

"Why are you looking so sheepish? Where are they?" Nic demanded.

Maya glanced between Nic and the guards, a growing sense of unease settling in her chest. Her mind raced, connecting dots and drawing conclusions about what she'd seen earlier. Were these the men responsible for the brutal treatment of the protesters? Were they involved in the disappearances? Or just allies from another side?

Nic clenched her fists until her knuckles went white. "Are there any survivors? Any at all? Give me something to hope for."

Then, the guards shook their heads and downcast their eyes, revealing the grim truth without saying it. A lump formed in Maya's throat.

"They're gripped by fear, so at least we have that," Nic muttered. She turned to retrieve a box from the jeep before handing it to the guards. "This is for you. It's not much, but we can't spare more right now. Can we expect anything next week?"

The guards hesitated, and they exchanged a wide-eyed look.

"We're uncertain," one guard mumbled. "The situation is becoming more complicated. Defying the rules doesn't just mean fines or imprisonment. If you think the restrictions are tightening for Old Albion, just wait. They will soon extend here to us as well. We can't risk these meetings anymore."

Nic tapped the box held by one guard and sighed. "I'll be back next week. If I see you, I'll consider it a small victory. You two," she turned to Maya and Carla. "Let's head back. Time to return home."

Once they were in the jeep, Nic eased off the accelerator, so the rush of air was now more of a gentle caress against their cheeks. "So, girls, you've witnessed the reality of how things unfold and the dangers of change. Carla, what's running through your mind?"

Carla turned her head, staring into the horizon. "I'm not entirely certain what to think, truth be told. But one thing I am clear on - I'm furious. Hearing about the fate of your men only worsens my anger. All those innocent lives, gone without a trace. Like they meant nothing." Her gaze shifted to Maya, her voice heavy with sadness. "It's just unbearable."

Maya nodded, looking into her lap. Stories were often told of those who vanished when entering the restricted areas or the outskirts. Was it all fake? Were the government behind these missing people all along? Maya tried to recall the faces of the men who were dragged away; she wanted to keep their image alive, in case no one else could.

"Carla," Nic's voice was steady. "We don't dwell on the sorrow here. Loss is a sad thing, yes, but there's no room for it in this world, not like there use to be. Instead, remember the principles they stood for and the legacy they left behind. What this group is truly about. Understood? That's what needs your focus."

Nic brought the jeep to a halt, and Maya and Carla disembarked to follow her lead. "I'm going to be frank with you two. Our numbers have dwindled recently, and both of you have impressed me. If you're here to answer the question I posed earlier, I hope you're now more aware of what you're signing up for."

Carla's grip on Maya's hand tightened, and it was as if Maya could almost feel Carla's resolve emanating from her skin. Carla wanted this. Ever since the vote, ever since they erected the divide. Maya had no say in the world she grew up in. Money was tight, her home was a mess, people around her were sick, and the stifling oppression had only grown each year. She turned to Carla, and a grin threatened her friend's lips. A fire burned in her eyes. Maya knew what she wanted to say, and she knew Carla agreed.

"We want to join," Carla affirmed. "That's why we're here."

A smile touched Nic's lips. "I welcome you with open arms. Follow me inside," she commanded, leading them to another section of the building, which was dimly lit by the lanterns, casting a glow on the thick rugs covering the floor. Fabric adorned the walls, and in the centre, a pile of burning coal glowed like molten lava. Nic clapped her hands, and a crowd gathered, encircling Maya and Carla as they stood beside Nic. "Today, we welcome two new members to our cause. We also bid farewell to those who've made the ultimate sacrifice in our battle for freedom. We won't shed tears for them, not until this is over, but we'll cry out in defiance to honour their sacrifice."

Nic extended her arms and clasped Maya and Carla's hands with her own. "Will you stand with us: fight for truth, vanquish the shadows, and pledge yourselves to the cause?"

Maya's throat felt dry. This was serious now. It wasn't a dream or a whim. Maya watched the steaming metal before her. There was no going back. Was she sure she wanted this? Was her future even worth anything if she didn't at least try? She met Carla's determined gaze and nodded. "We do," she affirmed.

Nic released their hands. "Place your right foot on the

stool." As Maya and Carla complied, Nic turned, a red-hot iron poker in her grasp, before handing another rod to Lucas. Nic locked eyes with Maya, and then the iron descended. A searing pain shot through Maya's body. She stifled a scream and held Nic's gaze, refusing to break eye contact. She wanted Nic to know she meant this and that no agony or fear would stop her. Maya and Carla endured the pain with resolve as Lucas branded Carla, too. Maya clutched Carla's hand, intertwining their fingers.

As the iron withdrew, the ache slowly subsided, revealing a smouldering burn, a permanent mark on their skin. "Well done," Nic said, full of respect. "You are now members of our ranks. Your mission is clear - to topple the government, ruling our land, eradicate the divide, and reunite our fractured nation."

Maya glanced down at her branded ankle, the fiery symbol of their commitment. Despite the pain, a surge of pride welled within her. She was a part of something larger now, a force for change. Determination coursed through her veins. She was here to reshape history, to leave her mark, and being part of Nic's rebellion meant she finally had the chance to stand up and do something that counted.

Part Two

"In the shadows of despair, where hope seems distant and walls close in, humanity finds its hidden strength, and from the depths of desperation, the fiercest flames of resistance are born."

Chapter Eleven

The Divide's Gaze

Liam's stride grew more confident over the passing weeks until he glided through the corridors, head held high, and acknowledged the smiles and nods from those he passed. He had initially questioned the legitimacy of the respect he received, wondering if his connection to his father had got out, but he had only confided in Alex about it, and he could trust him. Liam told himself that every night.

But gradually, Liam embraced this new role. Attending meetings alongside Robert opened his eyes to a new world of knowledge and a fresh perspective on what New Albion offered.

Passing Alex in the corridors became a daily highlight - a cherished moment in Liam's day. The limited time spent together was precious. They sat side-by-side during breaks, sharing food and stories about their day. Yet, over time, Liam shared less. The power and influence that came with being by his father's side overshadowed the access Alex could provide. Alex's role wasn't as high up as Liam first thought when they met. In fact, when it boiled down to it, Alex was relatively normal and low down in the pecking order. Their relationship seemed to shift slowly, and Liam grew more guarded about what he shared, especially moments with his father.

Together, they discovered a secluded courtyard shaded by a towering fruit tree, which became their personal sanctuary. New Albion's climate control systems helped ensure the heat never burdened Liam as much as it did when he was home. Instead, the gentle cool breeze purified the surrounding air, providing a tranquil setting in the scorching midday temperatures.

Alex unwrapped a sandwich and offered half to Liam with a warm smile on his face. "Today, we have something new. Give it a try," he said. Liam examined the crisp brown bread, which smelled of fish. "It's salmon, a rarity these days. Taste it and let me know what you think."

Liam took a bite, savouring the rich flavours caressing his tongue. The delicate blend of salmon and the tangy white sauce left a lasting impression. He couldn't help but think of the brave fishermen risking their lives to catch such precious fish, and he made a mental note to never take such meals for granted, remembering Gil's stories.

Liam's device buzzed, signalling the end of their break. "Already?" he sighed. "It never feels like enough."

Alex offered a reassuring smile and carefully wrapped the sandwich. "If you have a few hours to spare before you clock out, why don't you join me tonight? There's a show on, and I'd love to introduce you to another side of New Albion, beyond the stuffy office spaces and work."

Liam hesitated. "Am I allowed?"

"Of course!" Alex stood and placed a hand on Liam's shoulder. "Just ask your father to assign you a few hours of free time. I'm sure he'd do anything for his son."

Liam reclined beneath the tree, soaking up the sun's warmth as Alex walked away. He closed his eyes, a contented smile on his face, as he cherished Alex's lingering scent. When his device buzzed once more, Liam groaned and rose from his seat. He brushed grass off his clothing and headed to meet his father.

Liam stood before Robert, who idly scratched his stubble, and another man stood nearby. Robert greeted Liam with a warm smile, gesturing toward a circular pedestal beside him. Adjusting his uniform, Liam regarded the unfamiliar surroundings. The room was impeccably pristine, with a large mirror front and centre. No natural light entered, only the bright white from above. Rows of clothes hung on a silver metal rack. Blues, reds, yellows. All colours Liam had seen others in the government building wear.

"What's happening?" Liam asked, searching the room.

Robert leaned in, his expression serious. "There have been some developments. The government now knows that you're my son, and, well, I've taken the liberty of arranging a proper uniform fitting for you."

"They know?" Liam asked, incredulous. "But how?"

"I informed them," Robert said, resting a reassuring hand on Liam's shoulder. "It was a necessary step, especially considering the work you'll be doing alongside me. Not to mention, this opens up unprecedented opportunities for you."

Liam furrowed his brow, recalling the sudden change in

people's treatment of him. Was it all because of his newfound status as Robert's son? "So, does this mean I can finally tell Mum and Maya about you? I could explain everything to them."

Robert's grip on Liam's shoulder tightened. "Not yet, Liam. It wouldn't be safe at this stage. Let's get you trained, integrated into our system, and then we can consider broadening our... efforts."

With a reassuring smile, Robert released Liam's shoulder. Standing tall, Liam felt rigid and stiff as the man beside them started taking measurements of his body. He tried to hold his breath, fearing that even the slightest exhalation might skew the readings.

"Make sure the fit is snug, accentuating his stature," Robert instructed the tailor. "He'll be positioned beside the governor on official duty."

Liam blushed at the pride in his father's words. After all these years, hearing his father was proud of him meant the world.

"I'm surprised you don't have a machine doing this stuff over here." Liam said, looking the tailor up and down.

"Granswick wants only the best for the uniforms on those standing beside him. Don't you worry; AI will still play its part."

Once the tailor had taken Liam's measurements and entered the data into a device, the sounds of machinery starting filling the air, accompanied by the occasional clinks of metal and rustling fabric. Robert lifted his chin. "Go ahead, boy. Collect your uniform and try it on."

Liam found the outfit neatly displayed inside the room. The tailor had diligently trimmed any loose threads, leaving the remnants scattered on the polished marble floor. "Please, sir, try it. If there are any issues, we can make adjustments and print out a new one," the tailor said, bowing before heading toward the door.

Liam hesitated, uncertain of where to undress. The room was empty, except for the machine to the left of him. He gingerly removed his shirt, glancing back at the man to make sure he wasn't watching. It felt odd to be so self-conscious. Back at the docks, he'd undressed countless times among fellow workers at the end of every day, so why did this feel different?

He slipped the newly tailored clothes over his body; each piece fit perfectly. The golden buttons on the top were stiff, making it a bit of a challenge for Liam to thread them through the freshly sewn buttonholes, especially with his broad fingers. When returning to the other room, Liam turned to inspect himself in the mirror, straightening himself up as best he could. His brown eyes stood out vividly against the light blue fabric, and his once unruly hair seemed tamed and proper. Liam smoothed down his attire and ran his fingers along his neatly groomed stubble. He hadn't noticed how much he'd changed or the neatness and smartness of his appearance since he started working here.

His father wore a proud smile and asked, "Do you know what this uniform represents?" He handed Liam a black leather band to be worn across his shoulder and waist. "Confidence, presence, and loyalty, my boy," he continued with a hint of nostalgia. "This uniform has roots stretching back centuries, back to when the royal family ruled. While they may be long gone, some royal traditions remain in our country, and this uniform is one such symbol."

Robert then presented Liam with a slender sword. Confused, Liam examined the lightweight weapon and tapped the end with his free hand, jolting at the pain in his fingertip.

"What am I supposed to do with this?" Liam asked, still assessing the thin rapier.

"Like I said, it's mostly for show in ceremonies and pageantry. This sword won't ever need to draw blood, Liam, so you needn't worry about that," Robert explained. "But it will command respect, respect that I want you to earn and relish."

With that, Robert turned towards the exit. "Come along, boy. We have a meeting to attend, and I want you front and centre beside the governor."

The top-floor office boasted glass walls, revealing a breathtaking panorama of the entire city and the sprawling lands beyond. Liam shadowed his father as he led them to the gathered officials at the room's rear, who each stood in a neat line, their figures silhouetted against the city's skyline. He halted behind his father as Robert extended his hand to greet a distinguished guest.

"Liam," Robert whispered. "Please meet our esteemed visitor, President Alma, from the West Country. He's here on a special visit to see how our country is progressing."

Liam wiped his clammy palm on his trousers before firmly shaking the president's hand. "Hello, Mr President. I hope you're experiencing a warm Albion welcome."

Robert cleared his throat and corrected him. "New Albion, of course. My son misspoke."

A bead of sweat formed on Liam's brow. Though his new uniform looked impeccable, its thick fabric and snug fit left him feeling somewhat confined. He turned, only to recoil at the sudden presence of Governor Granswick. He instinctively took a step back. "S-sir," he stammered, extending his hand.

"Sir Granswick." The governor shook Liam's hand with enthusiasm.

"This is my son, Liam. He's your additional guard, one of the recent transfers from the Freedom Day scheme," said Robert.

Granswick's gaze met Liam's then with a nod.

Liam still couldn't believe it. He had crossed paths with Governor Granswick multiple times since working alongside Robert, yet this was the first time the governor had truly acknowledged him.

Governor Granswick's eyes brightened, appraising Liam as if he were a prized catch from a market. "A strapping lad from the district, you say? Why, you should've told me earlier! Come closer, lad," he commanded, grabbing Liam's hand again for another firm handshake. The governor studied Liam from head to toe, sizing him up. "My gosh, you look just like him." Granswick muttered. "Made of sturdy stuff from over there. President Alma, come here!" Granswick shouted, looping an arm around the president's back and directing him toward Liam.

Robert leaned forward to whisper in Liam's ear, "Just nod, smile, and be yourself. Understand?"

Liam couldn't muster a reply. His stomach was so tightly knotted that he couldn't have spoken even if he'd wanted to.

"This is Robert's son, Liam," Governor Granswick declared. "He hails from the district on the other side of the wall and is an integral part of the new integration initiative you've come here to witness."

President Alma leaned in until his face was inches from Liam's. "How are you finding it here? Are you enjoying your time in New Albion?" The president asked softly.

Liam glanced over at his father, who gave a subtle nod of encouragement. "Yes, sir, Mr President. I've had the privilege of being paired with an exceptional guide since I joined the program, and I've learned a great deal about the use of AI."

Robert took a step forward, proudly stating, "My son is being modest. He has recently been promoted to the position of a Governor's guard, and he's actively involved in the data checking system alongside me, too. Several others from the program are progressing ahead of schedule as well."

"And the devices," President Alma inquired, "are they proving useful to you?"

Robert interjected before Liam could reply, "My son can't remember life without one. He's already formed a connection with another New Albion resident, and the data from their interactions provides invaluable insights into the differences between civilians from both sides of the country."

Liam maintained his composure, careful not to betray any emotions on his face. Alex. They were talking about Alex and the bond they had formed. But why would President Alma be interested in such a mundane thing?

"I see," President Alma remarked, turning his attention back to the governor. "The program's achievements have impressed me thus far. Shall we proceed with the photograph now and then continue our discussion in private?"

Everyone got into position, forming a line along the glass wall. Liam stood beside his father and the governor. Leaning closer to his father, Liam whispered, "Dad, what was that all about? Were you talking about Alex just then?"

"Not now," his father whispered, flashing him a stern look. "Concentrate on the task, smile for the photo, and I'll grant you a few hours of leave tonight."

"Tonight?"

His father's grin widened. "Didn't someone invite you to a play?"

Liam felt his cheeks flush with embarrassment. "Who told you?"

"Focus on the camera and smile, my boy," Robert said. "Alex made a request for you to extend your stay beyond working hours, and I've approved it. Now, face the camera, and show the world who you are."

Liam followed the path on his device toward the theatre and waited for Alex to join him. He kept his gaze averted as groups of elegantly dressed people flowed into the grand, golden entrance. He couldn't escape a sense of unease, as if he didn't quite belong. Liam half-expected a message on his device to appear and declare his invitation a mistake. Liam fidgeted on the spot, only glancing up occasionally to see if Alex was approaching.

Behind him was a digital poster along the entire wall, showcasing the play. Though he couldn't decipher the words or the title, the central figure was a dark-haired man in a suit, standing beside a strikingly dressed woman in red, with the backdrop of the city behind them. Before he could examine it further, the poster shifted into a different image, accompanied by scrolling text he couldn't read.

An arm draped over Liam's shoulder, and he jumped as a familiar voice chimed, "Well, well, don't you look dashing?"

Startled, Liam turned to face Alex, who had stepped back to assess his appearance.

Liam patted down his new uniform. "I received this today, and I didn't have time to find anything else. I thought it might help me blend in better here."

Alex grinned. "My own personal royal guard accompanying me to a play? I'll be the envy of everyone, won't I?" He peered down at his own attire: a simple plain shirt, a tight maroon blazer, and black trousers. "Although, now I feel somewhat under dressed. Come on, the show will start soon."

Various scents of wine, oak, and history greeted them upon entering the theatre. Liam was momentarily awe-struck in the presence of it all as he settled into a plush, red velvet chair.

"What's this all about, then?" he asked, taking in his surroundings. "I've never been to a play before." Liam thought back to The Old Vic. Bands had played music there, stationed between the tables. In fact, years ago, there were speakers, poets and entertainment. But as the years passed, money didn't allow for the arts to prosper in Old Albion.

"It's called 'The Galleon,'" Alex explained. "It's a love story about a passenger from a ship discovering a new land and those in the unknown country embracing him. I've seen it ten times already."

Liam raised an eyebrow. "Ten times? Why?"

Alex chuckled. "Each instance, there's something new. The play was written centuries ago, but now it's rewritten annually by AI, which introduces fresh scenes, characters, and twists with each new showing. I come to see it every time there's an updated version, and it never disappoints."

"Are the two people from the poster the main characters, then?"

"Yes," Alex confirmed. "Anita and Theodore. They always fall in love by the end."

"Why is it always them?" Liam questioned. "Shouldn't

the AI mix it up a bit? How about Theodore and Rupert?"

Alex playfully nudged Liam's shoulder. "Maybe that wouldn't have the broad appeal of the program aims for in its rewrites, but that's beside the point. It's the excitement of the changes that matter. Perhaps this year, they'll surprise us with a different love story."

The man sitting beside them leaned closer to Liam. "Are you placing any drink orders? Need something?"

Liam glanced over to see a small wheeled box in the aisle beside them. "Sure," Alex replied. "I'll have a Gin Gimlet. Liam, what would you like?"

Liam raised an eyebrow, his mouth watering. "A cold lager sounds good."

The man scoffed. "Lager, is it? Are you certain that uniform belongs to you?"

Liam turned to Alex, confusion on his face. "What's wrong with a lager?" he asked, narrowing his eyes.

The man swiftly lifted his hands in a placating gesture. "Nothing at all, my friend. I meant nothing by the comment." He punched in the drink orders on the machine, and it glided away. Yet as the man turned towards his female partner, Liam heard him whisper, "That's an Old Albion folk, no question. You can hear it in his voice, the way he speaks. Guess they're even invading our theatres now."

Liam clenched his fists involuntarily, but he resisted the urge to make a scene, especially as Alex's guest. Instead, he gritted his teeth and focused on the play, waiting for it to begin.

As the lights dimmed and the actors took the stage, Liam struggled to follow the unfamiliar dialogue. The words used were unlike any he'd heard before. He yearned for the female character to retaliate, and for the male lead to stop talking so incessantly. Gradually, his eyelids grew heavy, and Liam sank deeper into his seat. Whenever he felt himself drifting off, he jolted back to attention and glanced at Alex. The warm, gentle glow on his cheeks made the discomfort seem worth it. Alex's eyes followed the actors' every move until he hung onto their every word.

Liam couldn't grasp the intricacies of the plot or discern the hidden meanings beneath the declarations of love, but as the play reached its conclusion, he had discovered a new side of Alex, a tender one. Flushed, Alex wiped a tear falling from his face and flashed Liam a smile that stretched as wide as his face allowed.

"So," Alex said, gently resting a hand on Liam's leg. "What did you think? You're lucky. That was the best version I've seen yet."

Meeting Alex's hands with his own, Liam smiled back. "It was great."

Outside, the air was humid, and there was an added awkwardness to the pair's parting. Moments like these would be so much simpler if they lived on the same side. Liam had to leave and head home. He removed his jacket, tossing it over his shoulder. "Hot tonight, eh?" he said, unbuttoning the top of his shirt. "Guess it hits you more with that cold air constantly pumped inside." He wiped his brow, longing to lean closer to Alex and whisper secrets in his ear. Others left around them, wandering off into the night together.

"You never explained what the uniform was all about," Alex said. "Are you being promoted above me already?"

"This?" Liam looked down at the stiff attire. "Yeah, I feel ridiculous in it."

"But you look great, Liam."

"Do I? I feel suffocated. I'm starting to miss my vest and shorts from the docks more every day."

"Is this down to your father?"

Liam nodded. "Yeah. He told the government about me being his son. Everyone had been treating me differently, and now I know why."

"At least it's out there now." Alex tapped on his device. "I've ordered you a car. It should take you right up to the gate."

"Thanks for tonight. Although, I'm not sure I really fit in with New Albion's nightlife."

Alex leaned against a brick wall, smiling. "You did just fine. I was impressed with how you handled that guy who dared to question your excellent choice of beverage."

"You overheard that, huh? What's wrong with a lager, anyway? It's the only thing in the district that doesn't taste terrible."

"I can only imagine."

"One night, I'll take you over to Old Albion to show you a proper night out. That'll put some hair on your chest."

Alex glanced at Liam's open shirt. "That must explain yours," he said, laughing and pushing himself from the wall with his foot. "It's a shame you have to leave. The night is still so young."

"Those are the rules, at least for us Old Albion folk."

Liam reached for Alex's hand, intertwining their fingers briefly before letting go.

"You know, with the news of your father being out in the open, we could make a case for you moving over here to this side."

The car pulled up beside them. "No way, they'll never allow that."

"They seem keen on experimenting, to see what works and what doesn't. Look at your uniform, your role. They might be open to the idea." Liam furrowed his brow as the car door opened behind him. He had to go. "Think about all the things you could experience. Consider it, Liam. Discuss it with your father, perhaps? He seems quite amenable to your wishes already. I'm sure you could persuade him."

Chapter Twelve

Scattered Lives

Maya stared at the empty glass, her head throbbing from the bitter taste of ale lingering in her mouth. She rubbed her tired eyes. Sacrifices had to be made. Balancing the gruelling work at the docks with her deliveries and her commitment to the rebellion group was physically draining her. She sniffed at the remnants in the glass, jolting upright at the acrid scent, and when the last drops touched her tongue, it sealed her decision. The delivery job had to go. She couldn't give up the solace that came with a drink.

The kitchen was quiet, with her mother already having left for the day. Liam leaned against the counter, spooning oats into his mouth. Their relationship had shifted since he'd joined the other side, as if a distance had settled between them. Maya scratched her ear and reached for some bread. "Working again today, I see? And a new uniform, too."

Liam paused, glancing down at his outfit. "This thing? Yeah, it looks fancy, but it doesn't mean much." He lifted his arm, studying the sleeve. "Hey, do you think I'm losing weight? These sleeves feel loose."

Maya couldn't help but smirk. "That's what happens when you spend all day in those tower block offices with the other half."

She'd noticed her own body changing recently, too. The extra hours at the docks had altered the fit of her clothes until her shirt sleeves now snugly fit her arms. Now, looking at her brother, it was clear he'd slimmed down. "They've promoted you already, then? They must really like you over there."

Liam continued to chew his food. "I can't talk about it, sis. I'll be back late tonight, so please tell Mum I'm sorry. But there will be an extra payment in our family account."

Maya gritted her teeth, wanting to shout at him for not being there for their mother. But she knew the additional income was worth it. The only reason Liam was doing any of this was for a better life here. "What are they like over there? Made any friends?"

"They're just people like us. Not much else to report."

Maya had come to the same conclusion about the people in No Man's Land. With that, Liam slung his bag over his shoulder, wiped his mouth, and left.

The house was quiet once more, affording Maya a moment for her thoughts to surface in the silence. It wasn't long before a faded note appeared beneath the door. Maya knelt to retrieve it, the loose seal barely containing its contents. Inside, the note read, *'Meeting this afternoon. Assistance needed for a drop-off. Come alone.'*

* * *

As the sun dipped low in the horizon, casting a crimson hue across the landscape, Maya revved up her moped to journey into No Man's Land. The guards at the checkpoint had become familiar faces to her, yet she resisted the urge to wave or smile. After all, they weren't her allies. Only men who turned a blind eye to her passing through.

Beyond the divide, Nic stood waiting beside the entrance to the base, with one arm folded across her chest, and the other poised around a lit cigarette. Wisps of smoke escaped her mouth, spiralling into the wind. She casually flicked the cigarette to the ground as Maya approached and stamped it out beneath her leather boot. "First one to arrive. I appreciate punctuality," she remarked, turning to enter.

Maya followed Nic inside, where Lucas awaited, donned in a vibrant red coat and goggles, preparing for some sort of journey. On a nearby table, Nic deftly folded a piece of paper and discreetly slipped it into her pocket. "The letter mentioned a drop-off. What exactly are we doing?" Maya asked.

Nic's eyes met Maya's. "You can partner up with Lucas. He's in charge of distributing supplies and water to various sections here. It's an excellent opportunity for you to become better acquainted with our community and make a positive impression."

Maya furrowed her brow. She had always assumed this small shanty town was the entirety of No Man's Land. "Are there different districts out here too? I thought this was all there was."

Nic circled the table to where a few crew members sat. "No Man's Land is home to a diverse array of people. Some have been here since the day of the Divide, and others have been banished to this place for various reasons over the years. We don't discriminate, Maya. Our mission is to welcome and unite."

"Banished?" Maya repeated, her voice tinged with curiosity. "From Albion?"

Nic nodded. "Primarily from New Albion. This place serves as punishment for those who step out of line over there. Saying that, we have seen less arrive recently. Perhaps they have found an additional punishment." She rolled her eyes at that. "Anyway, there don't seem to be many laws in Old Albion to break, at least none that force them here, so be thankful for that."

Maya's tone turned hostile. "And you accept them, even from over *there*?"

Nic halted and whirled toward Maya, their faces inches apart. She leaned closer until Maya felt the brush of her warm breath. "The only ones we judge are the ones perched in those towers high above us. As a leader, it's my duty to establish the rules. We *don't* divide; do you understand?"

Maya nodded, chastened by Nic's piercing gaze.

Nic proceeded to the various tables, distributing pieces of paper to the groups, who acknowledged their assignments. "Your brother," Nic said, seemingly out of nowhere. "He did some work for us in the past before moving over, correct?"

Maya nodded. "He was loyal to you and Gil, but he's over there for the money and security. Nothing else."

Nic raised an eyebrow. "Are you certain? I've been informed that he's been rapidly rising through the ranks."

Maya immediately thought of Liam's new pristine uniform.

"I need you to do something for the cause," Nic continued, her expression serious. "It's a task that must be carried out. You can't overthink it."

Maya's mind raced. What was Nic about to ask of her? Was it going to be a test of loyalty? Did Maya have to say yes, no matter the request? What if she asked Maya to go behind her brother's back, to hurt or hinder his career? Was that something she could do for the greater good?

Maya braced herself. "What is it?"

Nic placed a small device on the table and slid it toward Maya. "Attach this to your brother's uniform. If he's in the position we suspect, he'll have access to information and conversations we desperately need. Plant it discreetly; don't warn him or let him discover it. We'll handle the rest."

Maya glanced at the tiny device, a weight forming in her chest. How far was she willing to go to prove her loyalty to the group if it meant sacrificing her relationship with her brother? "Liam won't be in any danger, right?"

Nic smiled, resting a chilly hand on Maya's shoulder. "No one will harm him. Nobody will even notice if you do it correctly. Are you ready to head out?"

Maya looked over at Lucas sitting at the corner table, his face illuminated by the flames, his sharp features darkened by the dancing shadows. "I wanted to ask you something while we're alone, and it seems like now is the best opportunity."

"Go ahead. There are no secrets here."

Maya scratched her neck. "It's about Lucas and Carla," she whispered. "You mentioned how her parents died here. That they were fighters for your cause."

A smile tugged at Nic's lips. "You have hours to spend with the boy. Any questions you have for me, ask him instead." Nic clicked her fingers. "Lucas!" she called. "Get some goggles and gear for Maya; she'll be joining you on the run."

* * *

Maya gripped Lucas's hips firmly, the icy wind whipping through her hair. Her gloved hands adjusted to their new fit as she tightened her fingertips against the cold. Lucas turned, a white smile visible through the fabric and goggles covering his face. "Just hold on, and check the connection now and then, got it?" he shouted above the wind. Maya nodded, stealing one last glance behind her. They rode a quad bike and towed a large trailer loaded with supplies. "Is the connection stable?" he shouted again, revving the bike with his right hand.

Maya examined the thick metal pin securely in place and nodded. Without warning, Lucas sped up, kicking dust up from the ground. She turned her head to see the trail they left behind and gripped Lucas even tighter. The empty landscape around them became a blur until there was nothing but open space and sky ahead. "How far to the first stop?" she asked, struggling to speak over the roaring wind.

"Why? Do you already grow tired?" Lucas teased.

Maya laughed, readjusting her goggles. "Not at all. I'm excited to see where you're taking me."

Lucas chuckled while the world whizzed by. Maya bounced in her seat as Lucas sped across dunes and small hills, each bump sending butterflies through her stomach. The angry crimson of the daytime sky gradually gave way to a serene darkness as Maya opened her eyes to wipe the dust from her goggles. A warm glow in the distance came into view.

Lucas slowly decreased his speed, although his spirits remained high as he slowed to a stop. Maya removed her goggles and wiped her face with her sleeve to rid the gritty dust clinging to her skin. "Grab a bag of supplies," Lucas said, hefting a water barrel over his shoulder. "We'll take them to the door."

Maya leaned over the trailer and chose a supply bag before following Lucas. He stopped a short distance from a ramshackle dwelling that hardly deserved to be called a house. Someone constructed it from rusty sheets of metal and bits of slate to form a makeshift roof, making Nic's hideaway seem like a luxury. Lucas knocked on the door and then turned to Maya. "Miss Green lives here. She's sweet, but she'll probably want to ask you a hundred-and-one questions."

"Of course." Maya straightened and patted down her hair.

The metal door swung open with a creak, and behind it stood a fragile-looking woman with wild white hair and lines etched deeper than crow's feet into her skin. "Lucas, my love. Are these supplies from Nic?"

Lucas wrapped an arm around the woman and planted a gentle kiss on her forehead. "We brought three bags and a barrel for you all."

Maya smiled, feeling self-conscious as she raised the lone bag she had chosen from the back. "Here you go, Miss... uh, Green."

"Oh, please, call me Lydia," said the woman. "We're not used to seeing such young and beautiful faces out here."

Maya felt her cheeks redden as she shuffled her feet in the dirt. Accepting compliments was never her strong suit. She glanced at Lucas, stricken by their oddly intense bond. "Are you sure about that, Lydia? Lucas is standing right here, you know." Maya offered a forced chuckle, hoping her humour would land.

Lydia waved her hand dismissively. "My boy always

was a looker." She pinched Lucas's cheek, tilting his face toward her. "Now go fetch the rest while I get to know the new girl."

Lucas looked away, and all Maya could think of was *'my boy'*.

"Are you going to be okay here, Maya?" Lucas asked with a mischievous grin.

"Go on, shoo." Lydia waved him away. "Come inside, love. He can do the rest."

Lydia's home on the inside resembled the outside, with a single wood fire crackling in the front room. Two dogs slept on red woven rugs that hid the dirty floor beneath. "How long have you lived here?" Maya asked, searching for questions that wouldn't come across as insensitive.

"Since the divide. We were among the first to be banished here and gradually built this place up over time," Lydia replied, yet Maya didn't miss the trembling of her lip. "It's not much, I know. But these walls, everything in here, owe itself to the resistance group, the leaders before Nic."

"It's wonderfully cosy," Maya offered.

Lydia chuckled. "You sound like an estate agent. Gosh, remember them?" Lydia gave a small chuckle. "It's cramped, but it's home. We've raised all our kids here and watched Lucas grow up. It's served us well."

"Oh, Lucas lived here?"

"You're very new here, aren't you, dear? Lucas lived here ever since he was a little boy. He's carried a heavy load on those young shoulders. Always has." Lydia placed a kettle on the fire. "He gets it from his father. Could never let anything go and would do anything for anyone, even if he was a stubborn so and so."

Aloud, Maya wondered, "How long ago did he...?" She

searched for a gentler word, "Pass?"

"Lucas was just a little boy, only 2 or 3, I think, when he lost them both. They didn't last long out here."

"Did everyone sent here spoil their vote?" Maya asked, smiling as she accepted the warm drink.

"Who's to say? Even to this day, some still deny spoiling their vote. Lucas's parents both claimed they voted in favour of AI, but the official records said otherwise when they were released, and that's how they ended up here." Lydia took a sip of her beverage. "There was no time back then to question anything. We were forced into groups the second it was announced; we were lined up and told exactly where we'd be moving to. The entire country changed in a single moment. We made plans between us; everyone did what they thought was right. At that moment, there was no telling what was a good choice or a bad one. You just had to go with your gut and hope it was the right thing to do."

Maya nodded, remembering the day her father left, and how he promised he'd be back soon. Even though she'd been young, she recalled it clearly, still feeling the terror and panic of that day.

"I can't imagine what it was like for you all. Even I struggle to remember the world before the divide. I can remember flashes of things, but it's hard to know if those memories are real, or just things we were told."

Maya thought back to the day her father vanished and wondered how many other families the wall had torn apart.

"Many lives were toyed with for political gain, my dear. It was a truly desperate time. Lucas' parents spoke of a child before him, one they gave up for a chance at a life outside of No Man's Land. People were terrified, and all sorts of horror stories circulated when the announcement was made. They thought they'd be dead within a week and wanted their child to have a chance at a better life."

"But then they went on to have Lucas? It seems like a strange choice."

Lydia shot Maya a look, one that made her realise she'd said something foolish. "Things happen, dear. Life continues on. You don't always get to choose the outcome."

Maya gripped the mug in her hand and took another sip of water, noting the faint taste of lemon. She seemed to be good at saying the wrong thing today. It was hard to work out how life here worked, discerning what tales were true about No Man's Land and what were lies to frighten the people into submission. She felt ignorant after what she had said to Nic and now Lydia.

Lucas broke the awkward silence as soon as he re-entered. The dogs stirred by the fire and greeted him with excited pants and wagging tails. "Are you two all caught up now? Have you gotten to know each other?" asked Lucas.

Lydia answered before Maya could. "She's been asking me all the questions. Maybe next time, we can switch and get to know her a bit better."

"We should get going. Nic wants us to make a few more deliveries before heading back."

Lydia rose from her seat and pulled Lucas into a hug. "Perhaps pay your parents a visit. It's been a while, and the visit might be a good history lesson for Maya here." Lydia shot a meaningful glance in Maya's direction as she took the mug from her hand.

They continued their drop-offs, visiting three small hamlets, each the same as the other, all populated by survivors desperately seeking peace. Every individual they met was caring and welcoming, each with their own unique story to share.

A clear view of stars and a full moon marked the night sky as they neared completion. Maya detached the trailer from the quad bike, pulling it into a shelter at their final drop-off point. Sighing, Lucas wiped his brow. "Ready to head home, then?"

"Don't you have one more stop to do?" Maya asked.

"My parents? Yeah. I'll tell Lydia I visited, but no harm in a white lie."

"Come on. I need to see these places and learn as much as I can if I'm ever going to stop putting my foot in it."

"Said the wrong thing to Lydia?" chuckled Lucas. "Come on then. We'll do a quick tour and then it's time to head home."

Maya tugged on Lucas's jacket to keep him from getting onto the bike. She snatched the keys from his fingers. "You can give me directions," she said, jumping into the driver's seat.

It was only a quick ride before they parked near a small hill beside a set of steps carved into the mound. Maya followed the trail up to the make-shift fence, which was formed of wooden planks of all different shapes and sizes. She glanced at Lucas; he had removed his scarf and goggles and now ruffled up his hair, his eyes moistening.

"What is this place?" Maya asked, walking towards the entrance. Lucas followed her as she led the way up the shallow steps until reaching a solitary tree at the top with a bench beneath its branches. Maya gaped at the panoramic view spreading out for miles - still and silent land, dotted with signs of life and the places she knew well, some she'd visited today, and others she might never see.

Lucas slumped onto the bench, and Maya sat beside him,

pulling her knees up to her chin. She gazed ahead at the endless rows of graves; some were stones carved with names she couldn't make out, and others were marked with rotting wood and pieces of used metal. Each one represented another's beloved, yet to her, they were all strangers. She turned her head to Lucas, who kept his eyes fixed on one point. "Your parents are here, then? Where are they?"

"Somewhere there," Lucas pointed, squinting with one eye.

Maya tried to see where he was pointing, but the exact location didn't matter much. She smiled and nodded. "Is this graveyard where everyone is?"

"We bury only those who die for the cause here. Those who were branded, like the one on your ankle."

Maya's eyes widened. She had assumed that this cemetery contained all the people from No Man's Land, not only those in the group. "So many people in such a short time."

"Most people out here dream of joining the movement. Gives them a glimmer of hope that they will help to bring change and open up the world to give their loved ones a better future." Lucas narrowed his eyes. "My parents gave their lives, hoping I'd be saved."

"Do you think they'd be happy that you're a part of it now?"

Lucas laughed. "My mum would probably say I'm a fool, no doubt. Maybe she's right."

"Then aren't we all fools?"

"Can't argue with that." Lucas turned to Maya. "I want to make a change, though." He waved his hand toward the graves. "So all of this doesn't feel so pointless."

Maya toyed with the box Nic had given her, realising the

power it held to ignite a revolution in the world. "What happened to your parents? Lydia said she brought you up from a young age."

"They died."

"Yeah, I got that far."

Lucas rubbed his arm, smiling slightly. "When I was a few years old, they left me with Lydia and were called to help the group. New Albion sent people to attack parts of No Man's Land, worried that news was getting around about us. That night, hundreds died, all for nothing. My parents happened to be in that number."

"So, the deaths came from New Albion? From the Governor Granswick's command?" Maya thought of Liam's new uniform and rumours of him posing alongside officials. Knowing he could be part of something so sinister left a bitter taste in her mouth.

Lucas nodded. "My parents didn't have time to finish the job they signed up for. I joined Nic's group when I could. I guess I thought that if they couldn't see it to the end, maybe I could."

Maya peered out at the cemetery again, unable to comprehend the scale of deaths. Would she one day be peering out at Lucas's grave? Perhaps she would also be buried here. She looked into his eyes, now grey beneath the moonlight. She wanted to ask him about his family and question what Lydia had said. "Have you ever heard rumours?" Maya began. "About a sibling?"

Lucas met her eyes, his thick brows raised. "Yes, though I've always tried not to think about it. I heard things when I was growing up. I suppose Lydia was waiting for me to ask, and well, I never did." Maya glanced away. "You know something? I know you do. Your eyes give it away."

Maya shifted her gaze to the ground. "It might not be my place, but I know how much she'd want to know. Maybe if I run it past you first, I'll know whether it'll break her heart."

Lucas leaned back on the bench, lifting both arms to support the back of his head.

"I think it's Carla. Your sister. You have the same eyes and you're both stubborn."

Lucas turned his neck slightly and grunted with a laugh. "That so?"

Maya settled back, too, the tightness in her chest easing. "Well, I've said what I needed to. It's up to you now. Want me to tell her?"

"No." Lucas kept his head up, peering at the sky. "I'll see to it. Are you sure, though?"

Maya thought back to the photo of Carla's parents in her grandmother's home. They were both so young. The spitting image of Lucas now.

"I've had plenty of hints, not just from Lydia, but Nic as well. I'm sure."

"Nic's really opening up to you, then. Makes a change."

Maya toyed with confiding in Lucas, though she hadn't known him long, and they hadn't exactly gotten off on the best foot. But there was an aspect about him she liked. A trust had formed between them. She felt like she could tell him anything, and he would keep her thoughts safe.

"She's asked me to do something. To go behind Liam's back."

Lucas sat up, resting an elbow on his knee to look at her. "Your brother? He's a good guy. What does she want you to do?"

Maya played with the device in her pocket, flicking it between her fingers. "Bug his clothes so they can listen in on his conversations at work."

"I see." He scratched his head. "I saw that photo of him. He's got friends in high places."

Maya twisted her neck. "You've seen it? Is it bad? Does he look like… one of them?"

Lucas laughed. "A bit, yeah. But he also looks totally lost. You going to do it?"

Maya shrugged. "I don't know. I already feel so guilty."

"I think you should," Lucas said. "If he finds out, he'll get over it. But gaining that access could lead to all of this ending. Isn't that risk worth it?"

Maya returned to her position and looked away from Lucas, instead peering at the night sky as thoughts spun around her head about every fight and argument that could come from this. But the graves in front of her offered a fresh perspective. After all, there was nothing worse than a wasted life. If Maya held even a bit of power to end this mess, she'd be a fool to let feelings get in the way.

Chapter Thirteen

Closed Doors

Liam stood guard in New Albion, despite arriving earlier than usual. His shift didn't start for another hour, but he wanted some moments to observe the world before life began, before work. Yet the streets were empty, as they so often were. All he could think about was Alex's question after the theatre show, and the possibility of living here, alongside his father, and spending time out of work with Alex. It seemed like a fantasy before, yet one that could now be his reality.

He turned away from the government tower, which shone beneath the sun, the darkened glass reflecting life around it while hiding all that went on inside. Instead, Liam strode towards the historical building in District 2-A, with its pillars and detailed stone markings distinguishing itself from the straight lines mirrored by the rest of the country's architecture.

Liam stepped in and gaped in wonder. The room was vast, with a reflective marble floor and stained-glass windows overhead, creating a mosaic of colours along the walls beneath the early morning sun. On the day he met Alex, he'd told Liam about this building, and how it housed the world's history. A subject Liam had never been fond of. History meant learning, and learning meant reading, a mix Liam could never work with.

Each step echoed as he strode past the podiums, glass cabinets, and boxes lining the wall. He peered into the first one that housed a map of the world. He'd never seen a world map before, not one as detailed as this. It must have been the old world. It was huge and spilt into different sections, with oceans thousands of miles wide. He remembered from stories as a child that the planet had not looked like this for many years. Beside the map was a wall of text, yet he couldn't discern the words. How would his life have differed if he had grown up here with his father? He would have received an education and a government job working alongside his father. Who knows how high up he'd be, or how much smarter.

Liam clutched the rapier strapped to his hip and traced a finger along his new uniform with a smile. He continued to walk around the exhibit, taking in as many details as he could. Fine bone china plates, crowns, rings, and gold were on display on the shelves. Hanging on the wall above was a painted timeline ranging from decades ago to today. Underneath certain years, the artist depicted images of erupting volcanoes, floods, disappearing land, and vanishing people. screaming while fleeing the disasters. The present day showed computers and AI, highlighting the success and happiness of the population. Liam looked at the date.

Twenty-five years ago. The vote. The results were practically an even spilt between the country. He had vague memories of that time. He was only young, but the arguments and fighting persisted long after they held the vote. That split the country in two, tearing his family apart. Then in the five years after that, the wall went up and the life he knew changed forever. Liam looked at the end of the timeline and wondered what other images would be added to this wall. He didn't have the answers, but smiled. Soon, Freedom Day might be added. Maybe one day, someone could paint the end of the division there too.

Liam checked his device; he'd been inside longer than he thought and was now late for work. He left the building and rushed towards the tower. People were already within. He darted through the scanners, collected the device from his locker, and placed it on the side of his head. He glanced at his device again, unsure where his father would be. Liam walked the corridors, a white labyrinth where every turn looked the same as the last.

He kept moving, checking his device. A wall of text flashed as a notification, but he couldn't read the words. Sweat dripped from his forehead as he turned a corner and stopped at a door that stood out from the white walls. The door was crimson. No one else was nearby. Heart thumping, Liam pushed the entrance open. He didn't know what he expected to find, yet his head buzzed with history, and the excitement of this new world he desperately wanted to explore to escape the mundane.

Inside, the air was damp. The door opened to stone steps descending in spirals. He followed the steps for what felt like forever until he heard the clatter of metal and the low moans of men. He pushed past the door that met him at the end, allowing his eyes to adjust to the surrounding darkness.

Gliding his hand along the rock wall, he withdrew his fingers to find them coated in wet slime. The stairs ended in a narrow room, with a lone wooden stool and metal grated doors. He was inside a prison; he realised. Designed like the ones abandoned in Old Albion, ones he used to play in as a child. Liam looked around, wide-eyed. He couldn't believe a place existed like this in New Albion; everything he knew about this side of the country contradicted the sight before him. He stepped past the metal door, finding rows of cells lit by flame torches on the wall. He didn't dare step any further. Screams of pain tore through the corridor, with men begging for help, water, or their lives to be ended. A cold rushed through him; he backed away when a man shouted. "Guard, are you back?" his gruff voice echoed. "Please. Some water. It's been days now. Please, I need water."

Liam bit his lip. There was a bucket beside the stool with a few wooden mugs on it. Liam filled the cup and stepped towards the cell, leaning down to where the man huddled on the ground, his face beaten black and blue. The injuries didn't look new. Smiling, Liam passed the mug across. "Here you go. Drink it up."

The man swallowed the entire contents. "Thank you. I have been here for weeks, and they never feed us."

"Why are you here?"

The man let out a chuckle and then gripped his ribs. "I take it you rarely work in this area. Maybe I've said too much."

Liam raised his hand. "Please. I am only here for information. I can get another mug of water for you if it'll loosen your tongue." Liam turned to fill the mug again and handed it back to the man.

"I'm here for the same reason most others are. For...

speaking out."

Liam's brow furrowed. "About what?"

"The truth about New Albion. A bunch of guards stopped our protest in Old Albion and took us away." The man wiped his lips. "I thought the two sides were separate, you know. Two different countries, that's what we were told, wasn't it? But I don't think they are. How could New Albion hold us all here like this while Old Albion do nothing to get us back?"

Liam accepted the empty cup from the man. "They will let you out; they have to." Liam looked around. The opposite cell was empty. "That one's empty, see. You just need to wait." He pushed himself back onto his feet, turning to leave.

"There are ones who leave, that's true, but they're not sent to their freedom."

Liam turned to give a half smile to the man. He needed to leave. The guard who was supposed to be here could return any second. Seeing this place and the treatment people suffered chilled Liam to the bone. But he had to question why these people were here. Did they deserve this punishment, or was it just the cost a country had to pay to make it safe for everyone else?

After work, Liam slowly made his way towards the scanners. He slowed his pace, knowing Alex would soon join him. Within a few steps, he did exactly that. Liam turned to him, yet kept his face averted. "Are you okay?"

Alex nodded. "Yes, sorry. Feeling a bit low, I suppose. Although I was scared to admit it, in case the people upstairs monitor my mood, too." He chuckled.

"Do they do that? I thought that was just for us new lot."

"Maybe." Alex's eyes darted around before he whispered,

"Sometimes, if people call in sick for the day, they check their health report to see if they're truly sick or not."

Liam scuffed his feet on the ground. "What got you feeling low, then? Maybe talking about it will help disguise it from them."

"I don't know, really. I mean, we had such a fun time the other night, watching the play and spending time together. I'm sad we can't do it again like now or tomorrow, every night, in fact." Alex cleared his throat. "Well, maybe not *every night*, of course. I don't want you thinking I'm obsessed, but well, what I'm trying to say is. It was fun, right?"

Liam smiled, nudging Alex's shoulder with his as they strode beside each other. He rested a hand along his device and peered out the window at the divide towering above, keeping them apart. "Have you ever done something adventurous, something against the rules?"

Alex narrowed his eyes. "Me? I couldn't possibly say. What do you have in mind?"

Liam shrugged. "Not sure, but that play. It was full of adventure, right?" It was the only part he could follow, Liam thought. "The man on the ship who sailed to new land. I want that kind of buzz again. It's one I get sometimes when I'm with you. Seeing this new world for the first time... every new corner feels like an adventure. I want you to be able to feel that, too."

"It's a pleasant idea," Alex said. "But the option for adventure isn't one you'll be able to find easily in New Albion."

"But if I knew a way, one for us to feel free, would you do it?"

Alex smiled. "You're worrying me; what are you talking about exactly?"

Liam stopped and removed the device from the side of his head, placing it into his lock box. "Can you turn that thing off? You must know how it all works."

"My device?" Alex lowered his voice and leaned in closer. "Well, technically, yes. There is a way to hide some of the up-to-date information, but why would I?"

Liam grabbed Alex's hand and pulled him close. "Will you let me take you on an adventure, Alex?" Alex's fingers tightened around Liam, and he felt the warmth emanating from his chest and the exhilaration dancing in his gaze.

"What has got into you?"

"I've had quite the day; my mind has been racing, and I want to do something, something unplanned and exciting, and I want you to experience it with me. Do you trust me?"

Alex glanced down at their entwined hands. His eyes appeared to smile as he nodded. Liam turned to pass through the scanners, Alex following behind. He didn't look back. He knew this was risky, stupid, and reckless; if he wasn't careful, he could end up where that man was earlier, but he also felt alive and knew Alex needed to feel the same.

Chapter Fourteen

Under the Stars

Liam's heart thundered as they raced through the streets, their hands tightly entwined. Liam led Alex past the city, leaving the surveillance cameras behind. As they slipped through narrow alleyways and twisting roads, Alex's smile widened, the wind rushing past him. The city disappeared from view until a wild expanse greeted them instead. As they approached the checkpoint along the divide, the realisation of their plan sank in. Were they really about to do this?

Liam matched Alex's pace as they walked side by side. He noticed the control gates ahead and worry etched on Alex's face.

"Are you sure this is safe?" Alex asked, coming to a halt.

Liam smiled and released Alex's hand. He stole a glance at the gate, checked the time, and ran through the plan again in his mind. "He's on this shift. It'll be fine. I'll talk to him, and he'll let us pass."

Alex nodded and inspected his device. "It's still locked off. No tracks or notifications." Alex laid an arm over Liam's shoulder. "Okay, take me across the divide. I want to see your world."

Liam puffed out his chest and knocked on the gate, craning his neck to check for guards atop the wall. He tried to steady his breathing while they waited for the footsteps from behind the door to finally reach them. With a groan, the rusted metal hinges creaked open, and a man's face appeared between the narrow gap.

"What is your business here?" the man asked lowly.

Liam smiled, his neck twitching nervously. "It's me. I used to do some work for Gil. For Nic."

The guard looked past Liam and toward Alex. "Who's that?"

"We need to get to the other side. Come on, you know me."

The guard narrowed his eyes. "I don't know... I don't remember you." Liam glanced back at Alex, who glared at him beneath the hood. His stomach tightened. He faced the guard again, the dim light illuminating enough of his face to reveal the hint of a smile slowly forming on his lips. He stepped closer to them and slung an arm around Liam before opening the gate. "Get in quickly; you're lucky you caught me. I'm off this shift next week."

Liam pulled Alex nearer as they passed through the doorway. "Thank you. You had me worried for a moment there."

The guard laughed and patted them both on the back. "How could I forget you, mate? We spent many hours out here, staring into the wilderness, waiting for supplies." Liam paused just short of the other side to where the door led to No Man's Land. "Things are changing around here. Seems to me you got out at the right time."

Liam's world had changed. He'd seen enough of it in his new role, but knowing the same was being said out here made him worry for his sister. He hoped she was coping, too.

"Is that why your shifts are changing?" Liam asked.

"I can't stomach it anymore, especially when they want us to open fire, to kill. That work isn't for me."

Alex stepped forward, his eyes the only visible part of his face. "Open fire? Who's given that order? What's their district number?"

The guard chuckled, and then his mouth dropped open. "District number, is it? Who are you, anyway?" He narrowed his eyes, his gaze shifting between Liam and Alex. "You haven't brought him here to set me up, have you?"

Liam noticed the guard tense and the curl of his fingers into fists. "No, we both work for the council now, but we're not here to cause trouble. We just needed a way through, together."

Alex unwrapped the scarf covering his face, and Liam stepped in front of him. "Being ordered to kill must be against the law. Right?" Liam asked.

The guard shrugged. "Well, what's prohibited officially and what goes on in practice are two different stories."

A voice echoed from above, and the guard grinned, gesturing for Alex and Liam to pass. "Be on your way. You should find one of Nic's bikes here; leave it at the Old Albion entrance for us. Try to keep her happy, and I'll keep the old man above distracted while you go."

"Thank you, sir," Alex whispered, extending his hand.

"I'll look into those orders and see if I can make a change."

The guard ignored Alex and strode off, leaving them alone. Liam had already uncovered the bike. "Let's go, then. It's not too late to change your mind." Liam smiled and patted the leather seat.

With dust swirling in the sky, Liam sped towards the entrance to Old Albion, a path he'd traversed countless times. It was a direct route, avoiding Nic's hideout. Distant lights signalled the hidden life out here. He pondered Maya's choice: had she joined the rebellion group?

Alex's arms tightened around him, while the stars and moonlight guided them toward the dividing wall. Liam turned his head slightly and shouted, "So, what are you expecting from tonight?"

"My expectations are low, but my excitement is high," Alex replied.

Liam laughed. Alex always had a way of words. "And the devices, are you sure they won't detect your absence?"

"Do you doubt my brilliant skills? We're safe, but let's not make a habit of this!"

On the other side of the wall, Alex's steps drew nearer to Liam's, yet his usual bravado had waned as they approached Old Albion. Liam guided him past the crumbling walls of abandoned homes and cracked streets, wrinkling his nose at the smoky air filled with the stench of burning debris. Liam peered around the place he'd called home for years, his cheeks reddening as he watched Alex take it in for the first time. His silence spoke louder than any insult about the city ever could. Liam kept pace with Alex, breathing in his rich cologne.

They stopped just short of the city, where loud cheers

and music spilled into the streets, an orange glow lighting the district. As they strolled closer, a street vendor called out to them to sell his bottled beer.

"So, are you ready to experience the real Albion?" Liam asked. He turned to the vendor to purchase two bottles, tossing some coins at him in thanks. He handed a bottle to Alex. "Let's start easy. We'll have a few drinks at The Old Vic and see where the night takes us."

Alex smiled and sipped his beer; his face scrunched up. "When is the curfew? How much time do we have?"

"Curfew?" The vendor chuckled. "I think you're in the wrong place."

"Ignore him," Liam said, guiding Alex toward the main street. "We don't have curfews here. We work and live as we please."

Alex looked puzzled and took another sip from the bottle. "Really? We were always told that the law was uniform across the country. Interesting."

Exiting the alleyway, the lights of the city's main road welcomed them, along with the blur of bustling people. The heat trapped in the narrow streets filled the air with a warm, familiar scent that stirred memories for Liam. Alex stood dazed amid the traffic of people, watching men returning from work in their dirt-smudged vests and cargos. Sweat trickled down his forehead when he turned towards Liam, who patted him on the back and guided him toward The Old Vic.

Outside, smoke veiled the bar as groups of men gathered, laughing and cheering, with cigarettes burning in their free hands, with ale spilling from their free hand. "Will I be safe here?" Alex whispered.

"Of course. There's no safer place than with the

workingmen of Old Albion," Liam assured him, stepping toward the door.

A hand grasped Liam's shoulder, bringing him to a halt. He turned, blinking at the smoke stinging his eyes. "So, you finally show your face?"

Liam waved the smoke away to find George smiling at him.

"Are you all right, sir? You're bleeding," Alex pointed at the dark red stain on George's white vest.

George laughed and patted Alex on the back with a thud. "Who's this, then? Not your usual type, Liam. Where did you find this posh bit?" he boomed, turning to the other men.

Alex's eyes widened. "Not his usual type, eh? Is that so? Please, tell me more."

Liam gritted his teeth. Though he was used to the banter from the docks and bars, Liam didn't want Alex to misjudge him, not yet. "Ignore him; he never could handle his drink. Come on, we'll head inside." Liam said.

The heat from outside followed them into the pub, where the ground creaked under the weight of closely packed patrons, the floor sticky from spilled drinks. A lively band played at the far end, and Liam led Alex to the wooden bar, wiping his brow. "Is it usually this... vibrant?" Alex asked, clutching Liam's back.

Liam chuckled and ruffled Alex's hair. "Most nights. We like to celebrate this side. No harm done."

"So, tell me about your usual taste in men, then," Alex probed.

Rolling his eyes, Liam tried to get Carla's attention. "Ignore him. George likes to play the big man."

"Did you see? He's wounded, smoking, and drinking. Shouldn't he be home recovering?"

"He'll recover here with a drink in his hand like the rest of us," Liam replied. "He's been a fool, selling pieces of himself for quick cash. Let the man drown his sorrows if he wishes; he's earned it."

Alex nodded as Carla approached. "Hello, handsome," she said, studying Alex. "Haven't seen your face around here before. A friend of yours, Liam?"

"Two ales, Carla. Is Maya out tonight?" Liam asked.

Carla fetched two bottles from behind the bar and handed them to Alex. "Your sister doesn't know life outside of work anymore. Much like you, I might add."

Liam smiled, glad that Maya wouldn't be here this evening. He wasn't ready for her to meet Alex.

Time passed, and after several bottles, Liam found himself beside the band at the front of the crowd. Alex had left his jacket somewhere, probably on someone else by now, and danced to the music. Sweat poured from them both, their hair plastered to their faces as they moved with the other dancers. Alex swayed and held onto Liam for support, a huge smile etched on his lips. "I may stink," he began, "and this whole place may stink." Alex hiccuped and gripped Liam's arm. "But I've never seen or had a better time than this."

Liam smiled, noticing Carla stop behind them. She leaned in to Liam's ear. "I think you should get some fresh air; not sure he can quite handle a proper night out."

Draping his arm over Alex's shoulder, Liam brought him closer. "Come on, we have more of the district to see before you call it a night." He shouted over the music, taking one step at a time toward the door.

They stepped outside into the crisp air, leaving the warmth of the pub behind. Alex spun in a circle, and Liam held his shoulders, trying to steady him as he accidentally bumped into a man and knocked his drink over him. "I'm sorry, my fellow patron. Please, allow me to pay for the cleaning." Alex fumbled to retrieve a handkerchief from his pocket and began dabbing the spilled ale on the man's shirt.

The man took a step back, looking Alex up and down, his face flushing. "Who the hell is this?" he asked, shifting his eyes to Liam.

"He's had a bit too much, Gary. No harm intended." Liam smiled. While Gary was calm on the docks, a few drinks of bitter turned him into another beast.

"I didn't mean any offence, sir," Alex slurred, swaying. "Let me send you some credits. I'll pay for new silk." He laughed and dropped his device on the ground before bending to pick it up. "Oops."

Liam bit his lip, watching Gary's temper flare as he eyed not only Alex, but the device, too. Alex swayed and clutched the device, meeting Gary's eyes again. Gary clenched his fists as Liam pulled Alex closer, trying to defuse the situation. "Please, let's not make a scene."

Gary plucked the burning cigarette from his mouth and flicked it to the ground. Before Liam could intervene, he landed a swift kick to his stomach, leaving him gasping for breath. When Liam stood upright, Alex was on his knees. Another blow to the cheek met Liam as he turned to face Gary. A click echoed in his head, and the world spun as Gary raised his fist for another punch. Liam dodged it, landing a shot on Gary's jaw, knocking him backward onto the table, scattering ash from an ashtray into the air.

Liam brushed off the pain, then moved to help Alex to his feet. He dusted Alex off before assisting Gary, who chuckled and lit another cigarette, blowing smoke in their direction.

"Nice to know if there was ever a war, our side would win," he mumbled between breaths.

Liam looked at Alex's dusty face, who approached Gary. Though his hair obscured his face, his gaze was intense beneath it. "I don't need someone fighting my battles for me," Alex said, and, without warning, landed a punch squarely on Gary's nose. Liam was sure he heard a crack that time as Gary's nose jolted left. Liam pulled Alex back, who swayed in the toxic fresh air. "Come on, show me the other sights of this wonderful place," Alex said, wiping his bloody hands on his top.

They spent countless hours travelling the streets of the district, sampling the late-night market stalls and drinking spirits from bars and clubs. Stepping from one location to the next, the world soon became a blur of colour and motion.

"I think I've lost my jacket." Alex slurred. "The air here is much closer than back home. How on earth do you manage?" Alex undid the top few buttons on his shirt.

"We manage by drinking and working the sweat off. Come on, the pubs are closed; the birds will be up before long." Liam pulled Alex beside him, their clammy hands clasped together as they journeyed towards the outskirts, away from the noise of the district.

They crossed broken rubble, and then what was once a sports field back before the divide. Liam hauled Alex up a set of concrete steps before sitting beside a broken swing overlooking the district. The dim light of dawn brought the world to life. The hum of people echoed across the open land as the pair slumped together, with Liam leaning against a fragment from the past. Whatever it was, it served no use now. Liam tried to focus on Alex, yet the world was a blur. He smiled, running a finger along his face. "You comfy there?" he asked, placing himself above Alex, who now lay on his back.

"It's the best view I've ever seen." He chuckled, his eyes half open.

"You're drunk." Liam felt his cheeks warm as he leant closer to Alex until their breaths intertwined. They stared into each other's eyes. Liam's arms tightened, losing himself in the details of Alex's face and those emerald eyes.

Alex craned his neck until his lips met Liam's. He closed his eyes, relishing the moment and the bitter taste on one another's lips.

He hadn't planned for things to turn out this way when he joined the other side. Their ploy to unite and end the injustice faded to a wild memory as they laid together in a drunken embrace. Liam opened his eyes and smiled before meeting Alex's mouth yet again. Liam didn't want to think about business now. He wanted to let go. He desired to do something he knew he was good at and worry about the consequences later.

In moments, their shirts were off. The dirt, gritty and hard beneath them, scratched as they twisted and rolled in each other's arms. When dawn broke, the sky came alive in a beautiful orange whirl and only when the birds sang did Liam fall asleep, wrapped in Alex's arms. Their moment of passion lead into the morning, no one around except themselves.

Liam lay beside Alex, watching the cloudless sky above, deep in thought. The hiding, the secrets; all he wanted was to stay in his arms forever, but they'd have to return to New Albion soon. He shifted to loosen Alex's arms before pulling his jacket tighter around Alex's shoulders and stroking his hair into place. Alex slowly opened his eyes before shielding them from the sun. "Is it morning?" he croaked.

Liam nodded. "We need to get back, though I'm not sure how we'll manage it."

Alex shifted himself until sitting. "You look sad. You're not regretting things, are you?"

"No. Why would I?" Liam puffed his chest. "Just sad that a good night has to end." Liam pushed himself up and offered Alex his hand. "You look a mess." He said, brushing the dirt from his back.

"Well, your breath stinks." Alex replied, grinning. "Come on. We should get back over before the rest of the world wakes up."

Liam ran up the stairs. The lights flickered in the hallways as he approached the door. He'd left Alex below on the street, unable to stomach the thought of showing him where he and his family lived. It made his heart sink. He stepped into the kitchen, where the black mould now covered the entire back wall along the window. His mother stood before the sink, inclining her head towards the view. She turned to him, crossing her arms. "Who's that you've left down there all alone?"

Liam rolled his eyes, reaching to collect his folded uniform on the side. "A work friend. I just need to change." Liam removed his top and then cupped his hands below the sink to splash his face with water. The icy chill made his head spin.

"You should have brought him up and introduced us."

Liam shook his head. He wasn't sure if Alex would speak to him after today, not after last night. He knew they'd complicated things.

"Is Maya in? Carla said she was working too much. Is she?" Liam asked.

"If she is, she's crashed out in there." Emma pointed to the bedroom door. "So, your work friend?"

Liam sighed, chucking on his clean uniform. "Mum, please."

"Is he from the other side? I thought you weren't supposed to cross over with them?"

"Yeah, so keep quiet about it then. It was a one-off." Liam glanced towards the window. Was it a one-off? Or was there a world where they could be together?

Emma opened a draw to retrieve a piece of paper. "If I can, I'll try to do something about it. New Albion is the future; everyone says it. We've all come to admit that now." She clutched the paper in her hands and showed Liam the ticket. "If luck is on our side, lottery day might have an answer for you."

He scrunched his face, trying to control his breathing. He needed to get back to Alex. "A lottery ticket? For residence on the other side?" Liam leaned in for a closer look. The writing was a usual mess of letters. "They cost so much. How did…"

"Never you mind. It isn't a guarantee, but it's all I can offer you."

"What about you? And Maya?" Liam asked, thinking of his father. There could be another way. He bit his tongue, deciding to stay silent about him. Guilt crept along his body as the words stuck in his throat.

"We'll be okay. As time passes, they may loosen up the rules for us." Emma tucked the ticket away with a shake of her head. "It's only a dream, anyway. No point us getting worked up over something that might not happen." She smiled and brushed the dust from his top. "You go. Keep your friend company."

* * *

Liam and Alex journeyed back through No Man's Land in silence, though Liam wasn't sure if the silence was because of last night, or Alex's regrets about it. His head pounded against his skull and worsened with every bump beneath his feet. He assumed Alex felt the same, if not worse. The morning heat was humid, and Liam already felt dirty in his new uniform. He turned to smile at Alex, who returned it. It was only then Liam noticed how pale he was and the dark rings under his eyes.

They pulled up at the same gate from last night, returned the bike back under the sheet and crept towards the entrance. "Your mate still working, you think?" Alex croaked.

Liam shrugged. He hoped they'd arrived during exchange and there was no guard on duty at all. He noticed the door was ajar as they approached, and Alex pointed towards the handle.

It dripped with blood. There was more on the floor as Liam nudged the door open with his foot. Alex's face paled even more so, if that was even possible. Liam stepped forward, with Alex following behind him, device in hand. "Let me get back online to see if there was any alert."

Liam yanked the device from his hand. "No, they'll track you the second it's on. I ain't having them take you away, Alex. Come on. It doesn't look like anyone is still here."

Liam peered inside the camp built into the wall. No sign of struggle, and no sign of a captain either. He followed the drops of dried blood in the dirt until finally finding a body. Gunshot to the head.

"It's the guard from last night," Alex said, stepping closer. He crouched down, touching the man's wrist. "He's cold. Been dead for hours, I'd say." Alex rose and turned to Liam. "Is this because of us? Does someone know we went through here?"

Liam couldn't pry his eyes away. The body. The blood. An empty vessel now lying in the dirt. "Come on; let's get back. Go to work as if nothing happened."

"Really? Pretend this didn't happen?" Alex asked, rushing after Liam, who made his way to the other side.

"Yes. You heard him last night. He refused the new orders and wanted to quit. Guess that was the answer."

"You know," Alex panted, already breathless. "I knew this government wasn't all roses, I wasn't that blind, but seeing all this firsthand and hearing the rumours... it feels like New Albion is being played as much as Old Albion."

"Maybe we need to question things more. It's not like we don't have access."

"If you want a bullet in your head, then go ahead. We can't take these risks anymore, Liam. Last night was..." Alex paused. "*Fun*, but we can't do it again. My mother relies on my work more than ever since her operation."

Liam nodded, clenching his jaw as they made their way back into the city.

They had lived in a fantasy, deluding themselves with a plan to gather information and confide in each other in secret. In reality, it was a child-like dream. An excuse to be together. But now, with blood and death only a stone's throw away, that fantasy needed to end. They had to get a grip on reality; this was real life, and it had *real* consequences.

"I'll see what I can find out. We don't both need to be at risk." Liam stopped and grabbed Alex's hand. He wondered how he'd react, but he didn't pull away. "Take a step back. Keep your head down. We should go back to how it was before. If I come across anything major, then I'll let you know."

Alex tightened his grip. "As long as you'll be safe, too." He looked at his device. "No messages. If they knew about last night, they haven't said anything."

Alex released his hands and faced the city. He turned back after a few steps, a smile stretching along his cheeks. "For the record, it was worth it. Last night." He laughed. "Hopefully we can do it again."

Liam scratched the back of his head to stay calm and not react, but inside, he felt like crumbling.

Chapter Fifteen

Sending Help

Guilt was something Maya was increasingly accustomed to as she listened to the thudding footsteps from the above apartment echoing through the kitchen. Liam had left for work early - a new habit he'd picked up, and standing by the sink, her mother clutched bags, coughing as she stepped towards the door.

Maya shot up, catching one bag before it fell to the ground. "Mum, let me take that for you." She leaned closer, studying her mother's clammy skin. "Are you okay? I don't think you should go to work today."

Emma rolled her eyes and tutted. "I am perfectly fine, Maya." She reached with her spare hand for the bag, and Maya hesitated, glaring at her mother's pallid complexion and sunken eyes. Maya shook her head. "I have a few free hours. Let me give you a hand."

Outside, the heat was relentless. The air was still, and a layer of red dust covered every surface. "Gosh, it's getting worse," Emma said, blowing loose hair from her eyes. "I swear it wasn't like this when I was younger."

Maya tried to remember her childhood. Before the divide went up, she had just been a toddler; she could hardly recall what it was like then, let alone how hot the summers were. She tried to picture her mother as a young woman, and then her father, too, yet his face and memory were becoming more and more distant.

They journeyed across the cracked streets, with the early morning rush still to begin. Maya kicked up dirt with each step while clutching the bags in her hands. "How many stops you got today?"

"Not a lot. There's a nasty cough going around, and lots of my patients aren't up for visits right now. The resident refuge needs some supplies, so we'll head that way." Emma let a small smile grace her lips, though only for a second. "I worry how many will make it through this summer if it carries on like this. I don't even want to think about what the winter will bring."

Maya looked at her mother, about to reply until a crash sounded, followed by a scream. Maya spun towards the noise and rushed to the woman on the floor. She reached for her hand as the dust settled. "Are you alright?"

The lady wore a long, patterned garment made from a thick wool that covered her entire body. She brushed herself off with a chuckle, though one from embarrassment, Maya realised. "I am sorry. Thank you for helping me," she said with a western accent.

Emma stepped forward to drape her arm around her. "You must be from West Country."

"Yes. I came over a few days ago with some relatives, although we've become separated."

"Come on, follow us. I know of a refuge. We can hopefully find out about your family there." Emma turned and led her in the right direction with her arm still wrapped around the woman. Maya was in awe of her mother. It was like the pair had been friends for decades with the ease in which she helped this stranger.

"What's going on in the west?" Maya asked, trying to keep pace while holding Emma's bags.

The woman glanced back, her blue ocean eyes taking Maya by surprise. "Terrible things: arguments, fires, and what we think is the beginnings of a war. It won't be long until the news reaches here. Some of us had the chance to leave early."

Maya bowed her head. She knew the west was struggling. Gil had informed the workers at the dock about bringing in refugees on some boats and shipments, speaking of a civil war and frightened residents. The fear seemed to grow more each day.

"Did you come by boat?" Maya asked. "I work on the docks."

The woman glanced at the floor. "Yes. It was our only option. I am sorry if it's a burden."

"Not at all." Emma stepped in. "The dock master, Gil, has helped many people from all over the country to come in and find help. We can't offer much here right now, but if it's safer than home, then you are welcome."

"Thank you." The woman cupped Emma's hand in hers. "We heard stories of what happened to your country. When I was a little girl, we would visit often, but when the planes stopped and travel was restricted... well, you soon forget, don't you? The freedoms you once had, ones you took for granted."

Maya's mother nodded. A flash of spark spread across her face. Maya wondered if perhaps her mother was remembering the world as it once was. "I must say your English is outstanding... sorry, I didn't even ask your name."

"Mithra."

"Emma, and this is my daughter, Maya."

Mithra smiled, stretching her wrinkle-covered face. "English is the language of the world now, dear. No escaping it. We were all forced to learn it in school when I was a young girl." She sighed. "As time went on, it became the language of the west. Not many still know our original tongue, but at least our accents remain as a little reminder of our history, I suppose."

Maya's cheeks reddened, as though the decades of imposed change upon other nations were her fault. It all stemmed from the people in charge, those who ran this country and then divided it. "My friend Carla is from the West Country. Isn't that right, Mum?"

Emma nodded, stopping to push open a door to what was once a white building, now covered in red dust. "That's right. Well, her mother's family was from the west, but she was born here." Emma opened her arm for Mithra to step inside, and Maya followed, welcoming the shade. "Right, if you wait here, I'll go check some information for you."

Maya trailed her mother in, placing the heavy bags onto the floor before the desk. She wanted to stay with Mithra to learn about her history, her life, and the world outside the divide, but she wasn't as natural as her mother was. She couldn't speak and chat to a stranger as though they were family.

"Did you ever go to West Country, you and... Dad?" Maya asked her mother.

Emma frowned. "No; we never made it over. Travel by boat never sat well with me, and there were so many restrictions and tales of dangerous waters, waves ten feet tall and ships crashing into sunken land... I never wanted to risk it." Emma paused. "It's the main reason the travel limitations never had much push back all those years ago. The world was changing every month, becoming more and more unsafe. Even our own country was flooding in parts. No, it was safer this way, better for the future generations. Everyone agreed."

Maya tried her hardest not to roll her eyes. 'Safety' was the same excuse for the divide going up all those years ago when they cast the vote. Making choices about the world for people like Maya, who never had a say in the first place.

She watched as Emma ran her finger along the pages on the desk. "What are you looking for?"

"Mithra's name. If her family registered, they would have written each person they arrived here with. Hopefully, one of them made it already."

The pages contained hundreds of names, some scratched out in black ink. Had those people returned home or had they not survived the place where they'd sought help? Behind them, Mithra screamed, but this time it was a scream of joy. Maya spun along with her mother to find two people embracing Mithra: a younger man and a woman. Maya stood awkwardly beside Emma while they hugged and fussed over each other. The gentleman with long dark hair turned towards them first, a wide smile across his face. "This is Emma and her daughter Maya," Mithra announced with open arms. "They brought me here, and look! Here you all are."

Maya looked at her mother, who beamed, banishing all traces of her sickly look from this morning. "I take it this is the family you arrived here with?" Emma asked.

The man nodded. "Yes. This is my sister, Urwin, and you already know our mother."

Urwin stepped forward to clutch Maya's hand the same way Mithra had held her mother's on the walk over. "Thank you for helping. My brother and I were so worried. When we got split up, we heard nothing for days, and, well, we thought the worst."

Watching the family rally around each other made the feeling hit Maya again. Her chest was tight; she wanted to keel over and vomit on the floor. That bond between the siblings was clear for all to see. She reflected on Liam and what she'd done, betraying not only him but her mother, too. She hoped her actions were right, and that Nic knew what she was doing. But it didn't stop Maya's constant worry about tearing her family apart more than ever before.

Chapter Sixteen

From Within

The sterile white walls and bright lights amplified Liam's exhaustion. He stood on duty, listening only to the rhythmic tapping of a keyboard that made him struggle to keep his eyes open. Governor Granswick sat behind his desk, engrossed in work; Liam felt a world away from the previous night's passion and freedom, but also the haunting reminder of death.

The blood splattered across the dirt, the waste of human life, was what Liam thought of.

"Liam, come here." Granswick's low, gruff voice broke through his thoughts. "How are you finding the work, the shifts, the city?"

"Wonderful, sir," Liam replied almost instinctively.

Granswick chuckled. "We can keep this between us, no one else. You are Robert's son, correct?"

"That's correct, sir," Liam admitted. "It has been... very special, getting to know him again."

Granswick raised his bushy eyebrows. "He is a good man, loyal to me and the council. I'm sure we can count on your loyalty as well. You impressed me when you met President Alma; you said all the right things. But when I ask you questions in private, I expect the truth."

Liam's heart fluttered, and the rush of anxiety was akin to the feeling of Alex's lips against his, though not quite the same. "Well, sir, it's been eye-opening," he admitted, darting his gaze around the room to sense any hidden cameras.

"You're safe here," Granswick assured him, watching him closely. "No need to worry about surveillance."

Liam took a deep breath. He could be honest, but could he trust Granswick? How much honesty would he allow before putting a bullet in him? Liam smiled. He could tell the truth, but it needn't be completely free of lies. "People in the district have used many names for New Albion for years now, names I won't repeat. But the opportunity to come over and make a living... it was like winning lottery day. This place is clearly the future."

"But you still question it, even now you have seen it?"

"No, sir. There's no doubt this place represents the future in many ways. However, in Old Albion, there's a sense of... freedom. Choice seems somewhat limited for the residents here."

Granswick smiled. "Isn't it worth sacrificing some freedoms for a better life, an improved future?"

Liam hesitated; he didn't want to anger the governor. "I can't say for certain, sir. If people are presented with a choice of having a future with no freedom or freedom with no future, I'm not sure what they would choose."

Granswick stroked his chin. "What freedoms, in your opinion, are lacking here?"

"I don't live here, sir," Liam admitted, clearing his throat. "But from what I've seen, everyone appears to have the same roles, the same income. Little variety."

Granswick clasped his fingers. "The universal income is a direct result of AI, boy. You see, AI cannot think; it cannot create new ideas. All it can do is pull from creations already made. Do you understand?" Liam nodded. "Listen. All the information that AI uses comes from us - our textbooks, artwork, research. In a way, AI has taken *everything* from us, including work from our people. But also, the information used by AI comes from our minds, our ancestors. So, I made sure to pay our people fairly for the AI's usage of our shared knowledge. A set fee for the use of all the art and literature in the world. It's a fair deal."

Liam nodded, biting his lip. "Okay, but what about telling people where to shop, live, and who to interact with? Splitting them up into districts. Is that needed?"

"It's efficient. Crime is practically non-existent thanks to the districts."

Liam couldn't help but recall the guard with a bullet in his brain, and the men locked up in the cells. Was crime really that low, or just hidden? "Does every crime get reported?" he asked.

"The database is meticulous. I can assure you that nothing goes unnoticed."

"May I ask you something else, sir?" Liam questioned softly.

Granswick nodded. "Nothing I'd want more."

"Is permanent residency in New Albion a possibility for people in the Freedom Day program?"

A wry smile curved up Granswick's lips. "People, or you?"

"Me, sir."

"If that's the case, it can't be too bad here," Granswick chuckled. "As I mentioned earlier, your father has done a lot for us." He shifted his attention to his computer screen, sifting through various windows of information. "Eventually, we plan to pilot a merger; we will begin with a select few to assess how well the integration goes. I heard about an incident during a theatre performance involving one of our residents and yourself."

"You did?" Liam asked. How did Granswick know about that? Had Alex told him?

"The database doesn't miss a thing, remember," Granswick smirked. "We warned the man in question, and we've had no problems since."

"Is he okay?" Liam inquired as an image of the dead guard resurfaced in his mind.

"He received a fine; it's nothing he won't be able to recover from." Granswick glanced at his fingernails. "Would you like to submit a request to move over? Of course, your father will need to be informed, and I'd expect you to live in his residence until we can arrange a more permanent living situation for yourself."

Liam's mind raced as he considered the implications of Granswick's offer. He had a lot to explain to his mother, and Robert, too. And then there was Alex.

"Can I think about it?" Liam replied at last, shifting his gaze from his boots to Granswick.

Granswick closed the tabs on his computer. "Of course. You were the one asking."

Liam steered the conversation back to safer territory,

away from his personal dilemmas. "Has President Alma returned to West Country safely?"

Granswick nodded. "He has. It was only a brief visit."

"Will he succeed in the war over there? Many people have arrived in Old Albion by boat; they tell gruesome tales about the conditions in West Country. The ash from the fires is even affecting our air."

"Yes, the dust is causing some issues with our air purification systems, too. However, we remain hopeful that President Alma can control both the natural fires and those ignited by the state's enemies."

Liam scrutinised Granswick's expression, which remained inscrutable. "But how many people will survive for him to rule over? My mother helps house people from the west; she's told me all sorts about the devastating fires, and the rising tides consuming the land. It paints a bleak picture."

Granswick's tone hardened as he said, "You truly inherit your father's inquisitive mind. West Country isn't your concern, lad. Concentrate on the tasks at hand here. Focus on the opportunities New Albion offers, and once you decide, I'll put forward your request for relocation."

"Before I go, sir," Liam hesitated, noticing a slight twitch in the governor's neck. "You spoke of a plan for the Freedom Day program during President Alma's visit. I can't help but feel like I'm part of that."

He sighed. "The divide was a concept created by men in power before me. It served its purpose back then, when the country reached a point of no return. But what worked then doesn't apply today. As much as it pains me to say it, the division of our people gave each side struggles. Freedom Day took a lot of work, Liam. To get things right." Granswick slowly rose and walked towards the window, clasping his hands behind his back. "Society works in one way. You need cogs from both ends for it to work; otherwise, things come to a halt." He turned to face Liam again. "I'm not sure we will ever be able to get rid of the divide, not truly, but Freedom Day is the first step. New Albion is the future; it's something you will want to be a part of. But in order for us to find success in this endeavour, we need to take the best we can from Old Albion."

Liam furrowed his brows. "It sounds like you are speaking of something beyond New Albion."

Granswick shifted his gaze from the window to Liam. "This world is fragile," he admitted. "Lives are being lost worldwide. The global population is at its lowest in decades. We must have a plan for every outcome. This opportunity ensures people are not left behind."

"Are people like me part of that future you speak of?"

Granswick smiled, his eyes glinting. "How much do you know of the past, boy? Of the ancient world?"

Liam shrugged. "I didn't attend much school, sir. History isn't wildly known in Old Albion like it is here." Liam thought back to the map in the historical building, and the timeline of events painted along its wall.

"You have heard of the great deserts, the land that was once an ocean, and oceans that were once land, yes?" Liam nodded. "What we know about those ancient civilisations is not from the information gathered by everyday people, but from the leaders - the Kings and Queens. Great minds, writers, and poets. They are the ones who made history and wrote it down in stone. That is what we are doing here." Granswick unlaced his fingers and relaxed his arms. "We are at a unique point in the world, lad. Where we can be the ones to write history that will be remembered for centuries. I want to offer you the chance to be a part of that scripture. To mould it."

Liam tried to keep up, his head spinning with images of the greater world. Granswick's words painted pictures in his mind. He'd never realised how smart the governor was until now, much smarter than Liam gave him credit for. He seemed to know such a vast wealth of facts and could pull information from nowhere. Maybe he should listen more to learn all he could from this great mind before him. But why was Granswick opening up to Liam so easily? Offering him so much so freely?

"Why me? I am not special, sir. Not really."

Granswick bowed his head. "You are the spitting image of someone. The same face, broad frame, kind mind. I need someone like you going forward. I need history to be... correct."

Liam felt somewhat lost in Granswick's cryptic words, sensing that he was veiling important details. He wanted to ask more and delve deeper, but he feared pushing boundaries, the implications of which he couldn't fully comprehend. Fortunately, his device beeped, breaking the silence.

"I need to get to my next shift, sir," Liam said, relieved. "Thank you for taking the time to speak with me so honestly and allowing me to be honest, too."

Granswick nodded. "Remember, this stays between us, boy. Don't make me regret trusting you."

"Of course, sir. Thank you for your time."

Liam's hand gripped the door handle just as Granswick called him again, "Boy. Your education, your reading and writing... It needs to be improved." Liam looked to the ground; shame flashed across his face. "You will attend lessons with Alexander, whom I know you attended the theatre show with. He is an excellent teacher and a smart man. You'll need a wide set of skills going forward. Understand?" Liam nodded, leaving the office with a smile plastered on his face.

Robert hunched over his station, repairing a miniature machine. *One job AI couldn't do*, Liam thought. Robert turned as Liam entered; goggles covered his face, and a small screw hung out of the corner of his mouth. "Liam, pass me that screwdriver on the desk, will you?"

Liam handed it to his father. "Who broke it?"

"What?"

"The machine. Who broke it?"

"No one," Robert replied sharply. "Things just break sometimes."

"Yeah, suppose they do," Liam replied, watching the door in case Alex passed by.

"How was your shift with Governor Granswick? I often get reports about how dull they can be," Robert asked.

"Not for me. He seems to like me today." Liam crossed his arms, perching on the side of the desk.

Robert dropped the screwdriver and turned to face Liam. He narrowed his eyes. "What do you mean by that?"

"He asked me to speak honestly."

"And did you?"

Liam felt his collar tighten around his neck. Had he been too open? He had intended to mostly guard his thoughts, but as he reflected on their conversation, he realised he'd allowed too much truth to seep out.

"Yes, eventually."

Robert sighed and turned back to his work. "What did he

speak about?"

"Not much," Liam replied. "Things about the Freedom Day program, my thoughts on New Albion, the future, you."

"Me?"

Liam laughed. "Yes. He told me how loyal you were. He really admires you."

Robert let out another heavy sigh while tightening a screw. "Well, loyalty doesn't always get rewarded, and one doesn't always have a choice."

Liam clenched his jaw. "What do you mean by that? Everyone in this building is so bloody cryptic."

"It means from now on, don't be so honest when he asks you questions."

Robert may not want Liam to be truthful with Granswick, yet still expected him to lie to his mother and sister. If they found out about Robert, they'd have every right to disown him. "I want to tell Mum about you. She's been making plans, and if I don't say something, she's going to waste everything she owns on a stupid dream." Liam blurted, not knowing where his anger came from. It felt good to say it.

"What is she doing?"

"She wants me to live here. She bought a lottery day ticket and is pinning all her hopes on getting me residency."

Robert rolled his eyes and wiped his hands with a cloth. "She won't win, so there's no harm."

"But she's got the ticket. The money is already gone. If I make arrangements, she can sell it before the lottery day."

"Arrangements?" Robert raised a brow.

"I spoke to Governor Granswick."

"About moving here? What did he say?"

"He agreed. Said it could be an excellent test for the

integration program he's working on."

Robert sighed again, his frustration becoming more evident. He stormed towards the office door and locked it. "Liam, why do you want to move here?"

"Because it's the future. There's nothing in Old Albion for me - for anyone! Everyone knows that. It's already been run into the ground. There is no growth there, no opportunities."

Settling into his desk chair, Robert ran his hand along his prickly chin. "Freedom Day was a mistake. The only good it's brought is..." Robert paused. "Well, you know what good it's done for us. But it isn't as simple as you think it is."

"Whatever it is, it doesn't change the fact I'd have a better life here. It would give Mum and Maya a better chance at coming over too."

"I don't know what fantasy you're living in." Robert tapped the side of Liam's head. "But it will not end in a happy ever after." He peered around the room, paused as two people walked past the door. "Give me your device; remove it from the side of your head too," Robert said, removing his own.

Liam's hand hovered beside his device. "I'm not meant to take it off until I finish my shift."

"Just do it!" Robert yelled. He tapped something into Liam's device, shutting the screen down until it appeared like a black mirror. "Tell me: Why do you think President Alma arrived here amid a war in his own country?"

"Support?" Liam scratched his head. "To gain arms?"

"The world isn't straightforward anymore, Liam. Each play involves a multitude of reasons." He picked up Liam's device, shaking it before his eyes. "These things are government-made and handed to every civilian. Every worker, child, parent. They track your every move."

"It's how AI works. Alex explained it to me when I first arrived."

"That is one use, yes, but like I said, every move has more than one reason behind it."

Liam crossed his arms. "What is the other, then?"

"This country has gained vast amounts of wealth, Liam. How do you think we expanded the technology so fast?"

Liam turned his head. "You cut off the supply for Old Albion, left us to fend for ourselves, and then reaped the rewards."

Robert shook his head. "No. We supply more to Old Albion than you know. The mayor has been in Governor Granswick's pocket since day one of the wall. The real money comes from here." Robert shook the device again. "Do you know how much one person's information can be sold for? Let alone every resident of a country?"

The device mirrored Liam's image: his crisp uniform, short haircut, the council symbols branded on his chest. Behind him was his father, with his grey hair and strained eyes, cracking around the corners. Liam shook his head.

"What else do you know? How much is being kept secret?"

Robert brought another seat at his desk. "I don't know it all, but the state visit from President Alma was to show off the concept of the divide. Freedom Day is the next step and will eventually be the merger between us all. It was all planned years ago. When I was a child, floods swept the world. They tried to rebuild, yet every day new reports emerged about counties and islands wiped out completely. Times were bleak, and the government saw an opening." Robert ran his hands through his hair. "They attempted to find anything that would divide us, any reason that would stick, anything that caused arguments and division. The media, newspapers, and the old social platforms sought to create a divide any way they could." Robert caught his breath. "This was a way to sort the population and keep everyone in line. It could have been anything, but AI was a big talking point and that so happens to be what they focused on."

"Divide and conquer," Liam whispered.

"In a sense, yes. It worked too."

"So, what is with the devices, the data?"

"Money. Control. The government knows every detail of your life down to when you wake up and go to sleep. Your health, mood, diet, what makes you feel good or bad. Everything."

"And Freedom Day?"

"They need the other half of the puzzle. They know how people act and live with this life, under this control. Now they need to collect data from the rest of society to compare, so creating another divide in the future will be even easier for them. A flawless design of control."

"And this is what President Alma wants? A blueprint to do the same in West Country?"

"From what I understand, yes. West Country is fighting with themselves, and thus President Alma wants to gain control. With the wildfires wiping everything out, it's the perfect time for him to do that. Being at war means there will be no election. He can hold on to power for as long as it continues. It isn't too dissimilar to how Granswick held on to his role for so many years here."

"And we, the government - can sell that plan to him, and any other country who wants it?"

"Exactly." Robert looked up at Liam, his eyes piercing.

"When I arrived here, split apart from all of you, I had a choice. I could either fight against it or give in and fit in. I worked my way up from the bottom and did what I was told every step of the way."

"You want me to feel sorry for you, Dad? We were left to struggle back home."

"I know," Robert dropped his gaze. "It haunted me, but I wasn't converted here. I've kept things - documents, information, things I shouldn't know, and things I've stored along the way."

"About President Alma, and the plan to sell personal data?"

"Exactly. I didn't want to inform you of this because it's dangerous. But if Granswick is sniffing around you, I need you to be aware of what's truly going on here."

Liam looked at the files on his father's screen, and the odd words sticking out every few lines; it was nothing he could decipher or remember. "Why not leak the information? Get it out there?"

"No. It would be too risky. I'd be..."

"Killed?"

Robert swallowed. "Killed?"

"I know the government does it to people. Workers from this side."

"You stay quiet about such things. No matter what we know of this place, you'll want to be on this side of the soil in the next few years." Robert closed the computer. "You keep your head down and don't mention a word of this to anyone. Try to get on with your life. Happiness is scarce, and I don't want you getting ideas about changing the world when you can have a quiet life. Leave that for someone else, for another generation."

Liam thought of Alex, wondering if that life his father described was with Alex. While it might be easier to sit back and enjoy the good, it didn't stop Liam from thinking about the bad: Gil on the dock, Carla behind the bar, his sister, leaving everyone behind. He looked back at his father then and wondered if that was the reason he hadn't tried harder to contact them. All these years, he relied on playing the easier game: gathering information and keeping notes, creating an exposé ready to detonate to make himself feel better.

"I'm on the side of good, son. But in this world, you need to know when to show your hand and when to keep your secrets to yourself. You understand, don't you?" Liam nodded. "Keep a distance from Granswick, but try to use what you know as an advantage. You can have a good life. Let others fight the battle later when you have lived."

Liam nodded, peering back into his father's eyes. He brushed down his uniform and gripped the hilt of the sword at his side. Liam had gotten good at pretending, he could do it for a while longer.

Chapter Seventeen

Untied Bonds

Maya stumbled into the kitchen, momentarily blinded by the morning light pouring in. Two figures stood amidst the brightness. Shielding her eyes, she blinked away the remnants of last night until she clearly saw her mother. Emma paused in her conversation, hands on hips. Facing her was Gil, announced by not only his appearance but the sudden aroma of sea salt. Maya offered a tentative smile. Her mother's expression felt like an anchor slowly dragging her under, while Gil conveyed a sense of sorrow. He gave a subtle shake of his head.

Maya fought the urge to scratch her ankle where the burn, now a scar, lived. Had someone informed Gil? Or had her mother noticed the mark? Her gaze darted to the door, half-expecting a sudden incursion of New Albion guards to seize and drag her away, perhaps with Liam among them.

"What's going on?" she finally blurted. "Why did you both suddenly stop talking when I entered the room?"

Emma briefly looked at Gil. She gave a faint smile, yet the sorrow in Gil's eyes spoke volumes. "Maya, I've been worried," her mother began. "I was discussing your work hours with Gil. You've been exhausting yourself, working relentlessly."

Maya glanced at Gil.

"The hours you've reported to your mother... She's right to be concerned."

Maya held her breath and grappled for words. She'd used her job at the dock to obscure her activities in No Man's Land. "I..."

"I've assured Emma that I'll reduce your workload. Sometimes having a dedicated worker can be both a curse and a blessing," Gil chuckled. "That said, we've got an early shipment today and I could use your help if you're up to it?"

Maya nodded, puzzled by Gil's cover-up. She turned to her mother, whose face illuminated with pride.

Outside the apartment, Gil matched Maya's pace. She offered a polite smile, thankful for his help. "You didn't have to cover for me, you know," she said.

Gil raised an eyebrow. "Your mother does what she can to keep you lot safe. I do what I can for the same reason. I did it for your brother, and I plan to do the same for you."

"I'm grateful, Gil. I appreciate all you've done for my family over the years. But we both know I wasn't spending all those hours working for you."

"She doesn't need to know that. As long as you're not getting into anything reckless." Gil paused. "That place, Maya, it enticed your brother; they pulled him with ideas to change the world, but he declined their offers. I hope you've done the same. If such an offer was made at all, that is."

Maya stopped at the corner, aware that Carla was waiting for her. "I handle the drop-offs there. I don't interact with anyone in No Man's Land. Liam advised me that was the best approach, as have you."

Maya turned to leave, yet clenched her jaw at Gil's hand on her shoulder. "If there's anything you need to discuss, Maya, you can always talk to me. Please remember that."

She offered a half-smile and a nod. Gil had been a constant support for the family all these years, employing Liam and enabling her mother to assist those in need. She was grateful for his concern, and though it pained her to hide the truth from him, Nic had stressed the importance of discretion. Maya remained silent, hoping she'd made the right choice.

The weight of guilt sapped Maya's energy on her venture toward No Man's Land with Carla, rendering their journey a slow, laborious trudge. She wished to tell Carla about Lucas to prepare her before their encounter, but Lucas had asked her to keep quiet.

"What do you reckon is the big deal about tonight?" Carla broke the silence as they crept through the wall.

Maya merely shrugged. Since planting the bug on Liam, the sleepless nights had worn her down, ensnaring and suffocating her within a web of secrets.

"It must be something major, calling everyone in like this," Carla said, kicking at the dust as she walked.

Maya rubbed her forehead to ease some of the tension pounding in her skull. She took a swig from her water bottle, the heat akin to needle pricks against her skin. She spotted Lucas as they approached the gate, leaning against the rusted metal wall in the distance.

While she cared for them both in different ways, her loyalty was always to Carla. They had years of history. If Carla were to find out Maya had kept this information to herself, she risked losing her longest friend.

Maya grasped Carla's wrist, halting. "Hold on a second. Lucas is there, and he wants to talk to you—to us—about something," Maya blurted. With a deep breath, she stared at the ground before peering up at Carla, her eyes pleading. "I'm sorry, mate. Trust is vital, and I don't want you to walk into this blindly."

Carla furrowed her brow. "What is it?"

Maya didn't wish to hurt anyone, but if this was the other way around, she would want to know the truth. "I overheard some rumours about Lucas... about your parents," Maya sighed. "During a recent job with him, I discovered your mum and dad had another child before they died."

"What? Maya, what are you talking about?"

Carla yanked her arm free from Maya's grip and whirled to face the camp, spotting Lucas by the wall. She glanced back at Maya, her deep blue eyes glistening with tears.

"I wanted to tell you," Maya said, reaching for her.

Shaking her head, Carla stepped back. "Why would my parents give me up only to have another child? That doesn't make any sense."

"Nothing in this world makes sense, Carla. I didn't believe it at first either, which is why I never said anything."

"But now you have all the answers," Carla said. "Does he want to speak about it? Does he want to give his sister a hug?" Carla gestured at Lucas in the distance.

Lucas advanced toward them, likely seeing Carla's

reaction. "He's a good guy. A connection to your parents."

Carla glanced back at him as he approached. "I can't believe you kept this from me. Didn't I deserve to know before I turned up here?"

Maya winced. She'd completely messed this up, and now she risked angering them both.

"He wanted to be the one to tell you. I didn't want to betray his trust."

Carla chuckled. "*His* trust? So I guess our fifteen-year friendship means nothing?"

Maya bit her lip; everything was coming out all wrong. "I didn't mean it like that. I only wanted you to be happy and confirm it was true before telling you."

Maya had run out of time. Lucas had arrived, the wind playing with the frayed edges of his clothes as he drew closer. He pushed his hair back and pulled up his goggles, offering a gentle wave. "Hello," he whispered. "I assume by the body language that Maya has filled you in?"

Carla stood rigid, surveying Lucas from head to toe. "How do you know?"

"Well… I don't. Not officially. But my parents have a story similar to yours," Lucas replied. "It's not too different from many stories out here, but I've heard whispers about a sister who was given a better chance than I was. I often wondered why that better opportunity wasn't granted for me."

Maya reached for Carla, who shrugged her off and observed Lucas intently, seeming to scrutinise his face. Gusts of wind picked up around them, kicking up clouds of dust; Maya could have sworn amid the obscurity that Carla wiped away a tear. "I'm not ready to embrace a family I never knew," Carla stammered, her words punctuated by heavy breaths. "We need to get to the camp. Nic has a meeting planned, doesn't she?" Carla didn't wait for a response. Instead, she strode off, imprinting the earth in her wake, while the dust whirled in angry spirals behind her.

Walking alongside each other, Lucas and Maya shared an uncomfortable silence. "I had to tell her. The guilt was too much," Maya admitted. "I've been keeping too many secrets recently."

"It's alright. I suppose this and the situation with your brother was a lot to handle all at once," Lucas sympathised. "It could have gone worse; she didn't hit me or run away, did she?"

Maya chuckled, noting the distance Carla had created between them. "She kind of did run away," Maya said, patting Lucas on the back.

Passing through the gate to the hideaway, Maya glanced above them at the swaying skeleton affixed to the arch. "I don't know if I ever asked, but what's the deal with that thing, anyway?"

Lucas chuckled. "Him? Oh, that's a story. Nic tells it better than I do, though."

"Well, Nic's not here."

Lucas sighed. "His name was Theodore Lockhart. Ever heard of him?" Maya shook her head. "He was a big name a while back—way before our time—but your parents would probably know the name."

"What did he do to end up displayed like that?"

"Remember that when the divide went up, this place was like the wild west, even more so than it is now. They sent people here to die as punishment for not voting. They didn't design it to be a home for anyone."

"Yeah, but why single him out?"

"He was a media personality; he worked with the government and was the *'man of the people.'* He had supporters from both sides of the argument."

"And he ended up here?" Maya asked.

"Exactly. He campaigned for the use of AI and swayed a lot of votes from the opposition. Promised and said whatever he could to win support. But when the government announced they would make everyone's votes public, his name was on the list of non-voters. Well, you can imagine that it didn't go down well with anyone."

"Was he truly that influential? Just one man? I'm surprised the government didn't save him."

"When people were forced out here, left to survive, it didn't take long for a leader to emerge. Every place needs someone in charge. The first leader of No Man's Land wanted to make a statement and prove they meant what they said, so Theodore was hunted down, killed." Lucas paused and rubbed his neck, letting the information hang in the air for a second. "People blamed him solely for the divide, you know. He was despised for spoiling his vote and refusing to back up his own claims. People felt cheated and lied to; they were angry. When he died, it was agreed to leave his body on display as a warning or a reminder of what occurred."

Had Theodore influenced her father? He had voted for AI and concealed his vote from his family. She questioned how much damage one person could cause. Was it genuinely his fault, or were the people who blindly followed him equally to blame?

"The first leader sounds like quite the tough guy," Maya commented.

"Don't let Nic hear you say that," Lucas said, pushing the door open for Maya.

Inside the room, a bustling crowd enveloped Maya, who scanned the area, searching for Carla. It didn't take long to spot her. She stood behind the makeshift bar, juggling between serving drinks and sipping her own. Her face, shadowed and closed off, warned Maya not to intervene.

Maya proceeded toward the front to where Nic sat at a table, her attention fixed on the documents and devices splayed across it. Several individuals clustered around her, equally engrossed. When Nic's gaze met Maya's, a mix of emotions flashed between them. Nic seemed almost sympathetic, her eyes softening as Maya advanced. She froze at the photographs on the table: images of the governor with her brother Liam in uniform. Seeing him captured in black and white made her feel like a traitor.

"Maya, I'm glad you could make it. Any issues at the checkpoint?" Nic inquired.

"No, it was quiet. Strangely so."

"Next time, I'll need you to use a different route. Things are changing; New Albion is getting wise to our trade points. They've cut us off from their side. I fear Old Albion will be next."

"Understood. I assume today's meeting is significant, then?"

"Yes, it might be the last one for a while, depending on how things go."

Maya observed how a hush consumed the room at Nic's words. It was almost easy to forget the space was brimming with people. Nic moved aside to lift a rug, revealing an entrance to the back room. "I need a word with you in private."

Maya ducked her head and stepped inside. The room was compact, every inch covered with fur rugs and carpets.

Confidential words with Nic were never a good thing; Maya had learned that much already. Whatever Nic wanted to say, it wasn't likely to be good. "I planted the bug, did what you asked," Maya said.

"I'm aware, thank you." Nic poured a drink with steam billowing from the teapot. "Things progressed faster than we expected. It seems young Liam is better connected than even we thought."

Maya's heart sank. Was her brother now an enemy? "So, he's working alongside the governor?"

"Not exactly, and not maliciously, either. But I wanted to warn you before you hear the rest of what we've discovered."

Nic displayed a calm and caring side that Maya wasn't accustomed to. "What did you find? Is my brother okay?"

"Yes, he's fine. The information we've obtained came from a man who is training him. The bug you planted didn't just record speech; it also allowed us to access files from the computers within range." Nic offered a cup to Maya, who accepted. "This won't be easy to hear, Maya, but we suspect Liam is working alongside his father—your father."

Maya could barely hold the cup as the words hit her like a blow to the stomach. Her father was alive—not just alive, but employed by the government, and Liam knew all along. The room spun, and warmth flushed her cheeks. Maya had spent sleepless nights worrying about betraying her brother, only to find out he'd been working alongside their father the whole time.

Maya rested the cup on the table, her strength crumbling. She sank to her knees, reeling from the revelation, and Nic hurried toward her, crouching to her level. Gently, Nic clasped her shoulders. "You don't need to despise him.

Your brother is powerless over there, Maya. He wouldn't have kept this from you if he didn't have to." Nic peered into Maya's eyes. "Liam is a good man. I truly believe that. He's given us the tools to fight this, perhaps even enough to end it. Remember that."

"What have you found?" Maya stammered, her thoughts in disarray.

"Follow me. We need to proceed as normal. We can't let these things change us. Understand?" Nic hoisted Maya to her feet and snapped her fingers in front of Maya's face. "Come on."

Maya located an unoccupied seat in the room and turned to find all eyes on Nic, who dominated the space with a single glance. "Thank you all for coming today. I know the journeys here are hard, and they try to sever our ties at every opportunity. We've endured years of torment, and yet we stand firm with the possibility of change on the horizon," Nic declared. "A new member has played a significant role in our movement. They've provided access to information we never had before, and we're now at the brink of a new era. The fight to end this begins now."

The room erupted with cheers and a chorus of stomping feet and clinking glasses. Crowds hung on Nic's every word. Maya scanned the area, observing the relief but also the fires of determination burning bright in the eyes of the people. Despite the celebration, Maya felt a deep sense of regret, unable to shake the guilt of betraying her brother.

Nic turned and played a recording. It was the governor, her brother's voice, and then, unexpectedly, her father's, piercing through her like a forgotten memory, a voice she never thought she'd hear again. Her father's unmistakable gruff tones played on the speaker, discussing the divide and detailing years of planning. He spoke of personal data, selling concepts to the West Country, and strategies to divide and control a nation—details that echoed out in the room, while a smile crept across Nic's face.

Elation consumed those around Maya, but she couldn't share in their joy. If this recording came out, she had no idea what would happen to her brother or father.

"We've decided. Lottery Day is when both sides come together. We will stage an intervention. We will unveil New Albion and the government for their misdeeds, and once the truth's known to the people, their power will be no more," Nic proclaimed to the room, stirring another round of cheers. "We will storm Lottery Day and mark the beginning of the end of the divide! Who is with me?"

Nic didn't need a response as the room was buzzing, alive with renewed hope. It was what Maya had wanted all along—to dismantle the government. Yet, the thrill of victory felt hollow. Knowing what it meant for her family and the people she cherished cast a shadow over the jubilation.

The charged atmosphere persisted long after Nic's speech, but Maya couldn't escape her father's words.

Behind the bar, Carla clutched a drink and flashed a smile at Maya. Maya nodded back, finding it amusing how quickly friends could get over arguments. Lucas remained seated in his familiar spot in the corner. "How did that feel?" he asked. "Hearing Liam's voice. Feels like it's been ages since he was around."

"It's not been that long. Would you miss me that quickly?" Maya retorted with a playful smirk.

Lucas chuckled as Carla joined them, placing a glass in front of Maya. "This one's for you. Not sure what you drink," she said, gesturing towards Lucas.

"If it's wet, I'll drink it," he replied.

"Noted." Carla turned to Maya. "How are you feeling? That was your father's voice, right? That's what everyone is muttering."

Maya nodded and held the glass. She tried to suppress a smile. Even after lying to Carla, her friend took no time at all to forget what had happened. In the blink of an eye, it felt like they were back to normal. "I'm more concerned about *what* was said. I think everyone suspected the government of terrible things, but the extent of this deception is sickening, and to think that my father is involved."

"Liam too," Carla added, taking a sip of her drink. "I saw him the other night; he was out in the district with some posh guy. He seemed like he was from New Albion, now I think about it."

Maya felt sick. She'd only found out her father was alive and working for New Albion's government. But if the plan went ahead, would he even live to see another week? Maybe he'd follow the same fate as Theodore Lockhart, if the government didn't get to him first.

Maya pushed her chair back and stood. "I don't care. After Lottery Day, it sounds like there won't be a New Albion left."

Lucas laughed, flicking a rolled-up piece of paper across the table. "You think this will be the end? That we'll expose this big secret, and everything will come to a close? Just like that?"

"Don't you?" Carla interjected before Maya could respond.

"You're both new here. I've been a part of this group for years now, and I've seen three leaders. Events like this pop up all the time. We get our hopes up, celebrate the thoughts of a new world, and then something happens, which, more often than not, ends in death," Lucas said, looking at Carla. "Our parents are evidence enough of that."

Carla dropped her head, and Maya returned to her seat. She was seething and wished for nothing more than to vent and let it all out, but she couldn't. "What will playing the audio do? They'll figure out it came from one of our own, right? We've seen New Albion's guards before. They're not to be taken lightly when rules are broken."

A hand settled on Maya's shoulder. "It's heartening to see family reunite in such trying times," Nic remarked, glancing at Carla and Lucas. "Reconciliation and unity are the cornerstones of our society, given all we've been through." Nic turned to face Maya. "I understand your concern, Maya. Joining our group and receiving our mark solidified your commitment. You both were aware of this when you joined us. We'll do everything in our power to ensure your brother's safe exit. He'll most likely be in Old Albion during the Lottery Day draw, on the side of his home and people. If things unfold as planned, he'll be with his family when he needs to be."

Maya nodded. She wanted Nic to know she was fully committed to the group.

"I can't assure the same outcome for your father, however." Nic's grip on Maya's shoulder tightened. "I won't sugarcoat it. He holds a prominent position and will face consequences for the leak. Sacrifice is a necessary part of change. Keep that in mind as we move forward."

"I feel like I've had to give up so much in a short time," Maya replied.

"It shows strength, a trait you possess in abundance," Nic said, releasing her hold. "The road might grow darker before we see the light. The next stages of your lives will be a test. Mine will come on Lottery Day. As the leader, I'll stand on stage and reveal the truth to the world. It's something I'm ready to do. All I ask is that you attend, support the group, and be on alert. Maya, I need you to keep this from Liam. Don't breathe a word until the time is right. Can you do that? We cannot afford for word to get out."

Maya met Nic's eyes, sensing Carla beside her, and Lucas lurking behind them in the shadows. She nodded without hesitation, consenting to something she hadn't fully processed. But what choice did she have? Maintaining silence ensured Liam's safety and kept her family intact. Even after the divide ends, that's the best she could hope for.

Chapter Eighteen

Untold Truths

He ran a finger down Alex's bare back. Their time together felt like a secret, hidden behind closed doors. In stolen moments before and after work, they tried to see each other. Liam leaned into the feather pillows as a smile crept along his face. The humming of the air filter wafted the chilly breeze throughout the room. He propped himself up on his elbows, looking at the notebook he'd abandoned on the table, containing the words Alex had tried to teach him. Reading lines and turning letters into words could not occupy them for long. He got out of bed and found his clothes on the floor. Alex turned, his hair a wild mess. "As much as I enjoy this, we really need to stop."

Liam hopped on one leg to pull his trousers on. He knew things couldn't last, but he wanted to savour these moments while he could.

"You came over here to learn," Alex said, passing Liam his shirt. "But your passion gets the better of you. Don't think our lessons will stop because of this."

Chuckling, Alex leaned over to connect his device. His face dropped.

"What?" Liam asked. He pulled his top on, struggling with the buttons. "Has something happened?"

Alex glanced at Liam before shutting his device and tucking it into his pocket. "Nothing, just work. I'm needed there early. You smarten up here and head off after me. We don't want people to see us leaving at the same time." Alex ran his hand over Liam's stubble. "Remember to take your notes with you. Your reading is coming along so fast; I'd hate for you to fall behind."

Liam caught a separate car to work. He hated sneaking around when all he desired was to spend his time freely with whomever he wanted. Liam tapped away at his device as the outside world rushed past him. Clean streets and green parks surrounded the newly built apartment building. He thought back to his mother and sister, and the flat he'd called home for most of his life, with the flaking paint, broken windows, and complexes that housed double or triple what they should. People stuffed into tiny boxes, expected to survive. Thinking of a better existence for himself made Liam feel guilty, but what was so bad about bettering his existence if he could?

He looked up once more at the government building behind him. The car continued past his work. Liam glanced at his device again, wondering why it had taken him back to the entrance to Old Albion. He swiped the device to find a message from Alex. He stared at it and made out a few words, but nothing he could make sense of. Beside the text was an audio icon. *'Liam, I've re-directed your transport. Take today off; stay home. I've explained to them how sick you are. I will explain more when I can.'*

Liam closed his device, his heart racing. What would force Alex to lie for him? Had someone found out about them spending the night in the district together? Liam scanned out of New Albion and handed in the circular device attached to his head before heading home.

Thoughts filled Liam's mind as he trudged through the district while panic gnawed at his insides. Why had Alex told him to leave? Inside his apartment block, the sound of footsteps resounded above, he froze when reaching his floor. A hooded figure crouched outside his front door, slipping a note through the gap beneath the floor and the door frame. The person rose and turned to leave, but Liam stood in their path. The dimly lit hallway partly obscured the person's face, the hood draped over their head did the rest. "What are you doing here? Who are you?" Liam asked, attempting to peer under the hood.

The person froze, their hand edging towards their pocket. Liam watched with anticipation, waiting for their next move. "Let me pass, and I won't hurt you."

The voice was that of a young girl, barely older than fifteen. Liam raised his hands in a pacifying gesture. "I live in this block. Up a few flights," he lied.

"I said let me leave. Step aside," she insisted. Her tone shook as she brandished a small gun, her finger trembling on the trigger. Memories flooded back to Liam of the guard at the gate, the blood on the floor. He didn't want to die, not like this. Reluctantly, he stepped away, keeping his arms still. She hurried past him. Liam desperately wanted to say something, but fear locked the words in his throat.

Liam waited a few moments until her footsteps faded

and the front door slammed shut before approaching his own door. He pushed it open and searched the floor for the note, but found nothing. Looking up, he spotted Maya in the kitchen, filling a glass at the sink with her hand tucked in her pocket. Dark circles ringed her eyes as she attempted to tame her unruly hair in the window's reflection.

"Is Mum home?" Liam asked, already knowing the answer.

Maya shook her head and moved towards her room, taking a sip from her glass. "No work today? Does your boss not need you around?"

"Did a letter arrive just now?" Liam asked, dodging the question. He suspected Maya was hiding something and wanted her to tell the truth.

"For you? No, I don't think so," Maya said, avoiding eye contact.

Liam squinted. "Are you okay, sis? Are you safe?"

Her shoulders tensed. "I'm fine. No need to worry about me. I'd ask about your work, but I think I know the answer."

"If I could say, I would."

His lies gnawed at his insides. He wanted nothing more than to tell Maya about their father, but it wouldn't be right. If he was to tell anyone, it should be their mother first. He needed to keep his father's whereabouts hidden for the time being.

"Yeah, sure you would. I'm going to lie down, try to catch up on my sleep."

Maya shut her door while Liam slumped into an armchair, suffocated by the heavy weight of deceit. He despised lying to his sister, and he couldn't shake the notion that she, too, was being untruthful. That girl at the door just now—whoever she was—was dangerous. No rational person carries a gun to deliver a letter. Liam paced the kitchen for what felt like forever, observing the sun's journey across the sky. Maya must be asleep now, he thought, nudging open her door with his foot. Maya was indeed in a deep sleep, with an unfinished drink by her bedside, and her bag sprawled on the floor. It appeared she had packed, ready for departure. He tiptoed around her and scanned the room. The letter was there, peeking from the pocket of her trousers. Stretching cautiously, he plucked it from her person and unfolded the note. Of course, he couldn't decipher all of it, so he opened his device and snapped a photo before deftly slipping it back into her pocket.

Liam returned to the kitchen, pulling down the blind to shield himself from the relentless sun. He examined the photo, willing the jumbled letters to coalesce into words he could understand. Maybe he should have paid more attention to Alex's teachings, rather than his body.

Tapping the image on his device, he pulled up a menu. There had to be a way for AI to read this for him. He noticed the icon again, the one that played back Alex's message, and pressed it. *'Routes closed. Come through The Serpent's Lounge. Files and data compromised. Need all eyes and ears. Nic.'*

Liam's heart raced. He clenched his fists and punched the chair beside him. Maya had joined the rebellion. That explained her long hours and frequent absences. His device beeped once more with a message from his father. *'Come in now. No questions asked.'* His gaze flickered towards Maya's room. He could stay and persuade her not to engage with them. Again, he thought of the dead guard; had the rebel group killed him? Would they harm Maya if she resisted? He shook his head. After working with Gil for so long, he'd come to know these people, yet never wanted to become one of them. Another beep—this time from Alex.

'When you arrive, I need to meet.' The audio echoed.

Liam moistened his lips, his eyes darting between his device and the door. He rose to his feet and resolved to return to New Albion. Maya was mature enough to decide for herself. He had to stand by his own choice.

The government building was a rush of activity that no one seemed to even notice Liam wandering the halls. He glanced at his device, trying to track down the location Alex had sent him. He turned down corridors, passing the white clinical rooms, break rooms, and eventually the lush gardens, heading towards a wing he'd never been to before. Liam paused by a door, with a red-light flashing above it, and looked at his device again for more information. When the card reader flashed green, he pulled the door open, and Alex awaited him on the other side, waving him closer.

"What the hell is going on here?" asked Liam. "Why did you tell me to go home and then ask me to come back?"

Alex pulled Liam closer, so close his breath touched his skin. He dragged him into an empty office. "We don't have much time. They've told me to front a charge. It's way over my pay grade, but I couldn't say no."

"A charge? Is it the West Country? Has the war reached us?"

Liam clung onto Alex's arms; he didn't want to let go.

"No. It's No Man's Land. The rebellion group over there are stepping above their station. My team needs to push them back into line."

"Back into line?"

"Yeah. They do this sometimes. Every few years, they get a bit big for their boots. The government asks us to keep on top of it and push them back when things get bad."

"You mean kill them? Scare them? What exactly?"

Alex studied the floor. "They were placed there to die in the first place; they aren't officially citizens, anyway."

"They're *people*. They've made a life there. We passed through; you saw it for yourself firsthand."

Alex rubbed his chin. "I know. I don't agree with it, but there's no other way. I can't go against commands."

"My father asked me in as well. Am I going to be called to partake in the attack?"

"He did?" Alex's eyes grew wide. "Listen, the rebellion group is planning things. Word got around about a recording; they're threatening to expose it."

"So? Is it worth killing for?"

"The recording is of you, Liam," Alex said. "And your father. The capital hasn't allowed this to reach people at the top yet. We have some intel and know where it's being stored. If we get it back, it goes no further, the plans to overthrow the government vanish, and your name is kept out of it away from Granswick. Your father's too."

A recording? Liam didn't know what to say. Who would have done this? He remembered speaking openly to Granswick, who promised the room was safe. That no one would dare to record messages in the governor's office. Then again, it was public knowledge that Liam was Robert's son. Anyone with a grudge could have tried to catch them out.

Liam narrowed his brow, tightening his grip around Alex's arms. He let him go and stepped back, banging into the door behind him. "Me? How?"

"I don't know. It seems you know far more than I ever did. I thought we were sharing what information we found."

"Is now really the time for that?" Liam said; his device beeped again with another message from his father. Liam grabbed Alex's hand. "Should I hide? Leave New Albion? Will you come with me?" He didn't want to lose this little piece of life he'd created.

"No. This mission will go ahead, we will get the data back, and everything will return to normal." Alex held Liam firm, his eyes boring into his. "You must be careful. Watch who you speak to and what you speak about. We think you were bugged. Do you know who'd bug you?" Liam shook his head. "Anyone from the group you stayed close to? Anyone from our night out? What about that guy, Gary, who started the fight? Could he be part of them?"

Liam shook his head again. He didn't want to think about it, but things were adding up. "It doesn't matter who. It just matters what we do now. I don't want anyone to get hurt, Alex."

"I won't make a promise I can't keep. I'm new to this too."

Liam pulled Alex closer, wrapping his arms around him; his chest beat like a drum against his. "I need to go. I better check in with my father. Promise me you'll stay safe and out of danger."

"I said I won't promise you anything. Go on. Go. I need to get back to the briefing."

Before Alex could break away, Liam pulled him in, their lips meeting each other with a wet thud. It wasn't romantic, and the kiss wouldn't end up in a poem. It was fast, rushed, but was needed.

Liam found his father inside his office, his head deep in another set of computer chips and wires. Sweat dripped down his narrowed brow. The room was silent except for his father's groans. He didn't look up when Liam approached. "What's going to happen to us if the team fails today?" Liam asked.

"They won't."

"They might."

Robert slammed down his tools. "No Man's Land has nothing. They *are* nothing. New Albion is the richest nation left on this planet. The team won't fail."

"Do you still think this is the safest place for me to be?"

Liam watched his father, noting the clench of his jaw, and the rise and fall of his chest.

"There is no other option than here, boy. You know that. It isn't perfect—it's far from it—but when the other option is living like those do in No Man's Land, or on the outskirts, this place is paradise."

"But they'll kill the people out there, won't they?"

Robert grabbed Liam by the lapel and yanked him close. "If they do nothing, *they* will kill us, or worse. Let this happen; keep it from the governor and never mention it again."

"What about your files? All the things you had saved?"

"Gone. All of it. I don't want you to bring it up again. I should have never trusted you so quickly." Liam couldn't help but feel a stab of pain from the words. "Who bugged you?"

Liam had an idea. A name and face he couldn't believe would do it. He refused to say it aloud. No matter what, he wouldn't tell his father, so instead, Liam did nothing but shake his head and shrug.

"Whoever it was, you tell me, and I'll sort them out." Robert released Liam and brushed his hands along Liam's jacket. "Hopefully by tomorrow that group will learn to keep its head down until another leader shows up."

"Has this happened before?"

Alex had shared a few details with him, and he was desperate to know more, gathering information while he had the chance.

"It always happens. New Albion monitor that place, and every few years, a new person thinks they can play leader. We let them mess around, trading and going past the wall, and then when they get too ahead of themselves, we slap them back down. If it happens now, and gets me and you off the chopping block, then we close our eyes and pretend we knew nothing."

"What will the guards do?"

Robert gathered wires in his hands. "They will get the data, the files, the recording, and burn the place to the ground. They'll make them start again and give them a warning. Whatever it takes to get the items back to us," Robert said. "And you will be grateful for it, too."

Chapter Nineteen

Fire and Flame

The sun had set, a silvery moonlit trail lighting Maya's path as she approached The Serpent's Lounge. She clung to the letter, the intensity of her grip creasing the edges. She halted at the door, pensively biting her lower lip before descending the steps.

It had been an age since Maya last crossed this threshold, and the thought that the bartender might remember her stirred a flutter of unease in her stomach. Their previous encounter had been memorable. To put it mildly, with Maya leaving her with a bloody face.

She entered unnoticed, with the hum of conversations continuing without pause. Guided by the pulsating glow of neon strips, she navigated her way to the bar where the woman with dreadlocks studied her with a sardonic tilt of her lips. "Brave of you to show up here again, girl," she said, her eyes running a quick inventory of Maya. "No deliveries for me today?"

"Kong, right?" Maya asked. Kong responded with a firm nod, crossing her arms. "Look, about what happened before... I'm sorry. But you were going after my family, my brother."

"And what brings you here now?"

Maya drew in a deliberate breath, reigning in the impulse to lash out at Kong once again. "I need to find Nic."

Kong raised an eyebrow. "Nic? Never heard of her."

With a heavy sigh, Maya flattened the letter on the bar, glowing blue and purple beneath the neon lights. She knew this was the right place and person, but she had to play nice. "I assume you'll recognise this."

Kong dismissed the letter with a nonchalant glance before dousing it in her freshly poured drink. "Means nothing. Trust is a luxury, and you're bankrupt."

Maya's patience waned as a familiar throb pulsated in her temples. In a swift motion, she hoisted her leg onto the bar stool and hitched up her trousers, revealing the distinctive mark on her ankle. "Does this change your mind?" she challenged, locking eyes with Kong.

Kong's expression shifted as she nudged Maya's foot back to the ground and discarded the note. "Follow me," she said, leading the way from behind the bar.

Beyond the bar's deceptive charm lay a stark hallway, a graveyard of forgotten stock. Crates and bottles cluttered the space, and the concrete walls were cold to touch, seeming to absorb the damp air. Maya kept her eyes low, tracing the grimy floor. "Are we far enough back now? I'm sure you can give me the location so I can get out of here," Maya urged.

Kong's laughter, rich with mockery, bounced off the walls. "You don't have a clue, do you? Every time the routes close up, you gotta use the tunnels."

"Tunnels?" Maya echoed, a frown creasing her brow.

Kong smirked. "Yeah, those old smuggler tunnels from centuries ago. Used to bring in wine, beer, and stolen goods from the dock into town. Most been filled in now, but a few remain. They lead right through to No Man's Land, under the divide and beyond."

Maya's gaze lifted to the cavernous surroundings. "Let me guess, you happen to have one of those tunnels?"

Kong's nod came with a proud smile. "Sure do. Snug fit, one at a time. No good for trade these days, but just fine for the likes of you."

She heaved open an ancient wooden hatch, revealing a dark void below, where a rusty ladder disappeared into the shadows. "You not coming with me to show me the way?" Maya asked, peering into the darkness.

Kong shook her head, her dreadlocks reflecting the faint light in the narrow corridor. "I'm far too busy here. There's one way down; you can't get lost. Give Nic my love."

Kong's eyes lingered on the ladder. Maya, though tense, didn't let it show. Instead, she placed her foot on the first rung, the metal groaning in greeting. "Here, don't say I didn't do anything for ya." Kong's voice floated down the tunnel as she handed Maya a torch, lighting the world of shadows beneath her. With that, the hatch closed with a thud, leaving Maya alone in the darkness.

Maya tightened her grip on the ladder, but it groaned again, and sent her crashing down. The fall was brief, but the dust it kicked up was not. Coughing against the swarm of dry air now in her lungs, Maya steadied herself onto her knees. The torchlight revealed the singular, ominous tunnel ahead.

Maya's knees scraped the rough ground. The light showed no end, but only the turning, twisting way forward. Sweat dripped down her face as she marched onwards. Sections of the tunnel widened, with parts of the trek even allowing her to stand and walk for brief moments. It soon resulted in Maya crawling again. She gritted her teeth and continued, though for how long, she didn't know. Eventually, the torch in her hand granted her a glimpse of the destination.

Her knees ached, and a sheen of panic-induced sweat coated her skin as she emerged at the end of the tunnel before another ladder. She took a moment to stretch her limbs and realign her spine with a series of clicks.

But before she could start her ascent, the sharp crack of gunfire pierced the silence above. Maya froze as echoes clashed around the chamber, followed by screams and rapid footfall. Instinctively, she switched off the torch and hunkered down, closing her eyes to sharpen her other senses. Shouts tangled with the sound of more gunfire. Amidst them, a familiar voice cut through—Nic. Her tone was one of ferocity, not fear. A thud above dislodged dirt from the ceiling, and without hesitation, Maya felt for the ladder and ascended.

A few rungs up, she paused again to listen to the murmur of a man's voice hovering near the hatch. Gently, she nudged it, wincing at the dirt falling into her eyes. With a quiet puff, she cleared her vision enough to spy through the gap, taking in the flickering lamps and richly adorned walls. She knew the location instantly.

Nic, bloodied and beaten, held a blade in her hand. A soldier cornered her on the floor, gun aimed at her head. He gave a cruel laugh, though Maya didn't give herself a chance to be scared. Jaw clenched, she crawled out from the hatch, hopeful the soldier wouldn't turn around and end her life in seconds. She crept along the floor with Nic in view, her fingers poised on the blade. Then, Nic's eyes flicked to Maya, enough to make the man question if he was alone. He spun on his heel, his dark eyes finding Maya immediately. Without thinking, she rolled across the floor as he lunged. Maya reached out for Nic as the guard raised his gun again, redirecting his aim between Maya and Nic in confusion. Maya jumped to her feet as the guard pointed the gun at Nic once more, and before he pulled the trigger, Maya pounced, gripping the blade. She sliced it through his neck, and he tumbled to the ground with Maya still on top of him. His body trembled, and he tried to groan, but nothing came out. It wasn't long until he stilled entirely, a silver film veiling his eyes as the life left his body. Maya stepped back, leaving the blade lodged in his neck. Her legs felt light, and her stomach was in knots. She glanced at her blood-covered hands, and then at Nic to check she was alive.

Nic placed a finger on her lips and, stepping over the man's body toward the hatch, slowly closed it. "Don't look like that. It was him or me," she whispered. "I'm thankful you chose me. I won't forget that."

Maya froze. Blood spilled from the man's body, pooling around him. He was someone once. A person with a life and dreams. Now, he was nothing more than a shell. "What's going on here?" she stuttered out, unable to comprehend what she'd just done. "I got the note, but I didn't expect this kind of welcome."

"There are guards all around No Man's Land looking for this," Nic raised a small plastic chip. "They have come to warn us or kill us—whatever they choose, I suppose. They want to stop the rebellion from speaking out, but it won't work. We've distracted them for now, but they'll return when he doesn't report back." Nic nudged the guard's body with her foot and scrunched up her face. "This can't fall into their hands." She pressed the chip into Maya's palm.

Still reeling, Maya could only nod; the ground felt like quicksand beneath her feet. A terrible thirst parched her throat, a thirst only hard liquor could quench. She needed time to process the weight of what she'd done.

"You need to go. They're after me; they think I have the files." Nic wiped her brow. "They won't look twice at you amid all this chaos. Find Lucas for me, assuming he's still alive. Protect him and his device." Nic pointed Maya toward a narrow grate on the ground beside the wall. "Last I heard, Lucas was near the New Albion gate. If you can, confirm he's not been compromised, but above all, make sure the files are secure. They're more important and take precedence over any lives, including our own. Understand?"

The gravity of Nic's stare anchored Maya to the harsh reality, even as confusion swirled within her. The blood on Nic's face... was any of it her own?

"I'm relying on you," Nic continued, her grip on Maya's arms firm. "Without this, our cause is lost. Understand? Repeat to me: what do you need to do?"

Maya took a breath. She could hardly recall her name, let alone the instructions. "Take the chip." She spat out. "Match it with the device Lucas has and stay hidden."

Nic nodded and smiled, ushering Maya toward the wall. "Don't dwell on what's happened here. That guard made his choice. He picked a side and lost." She pointed to a small grate on the floor. "This will take you to the outside wall of the hideout."

Maya eyed the grate sceptically. "What is it?"

"It's a drainage system," Nic reassured her with a thin

smile. "You'll find a bike outside. Keep your head down, stay sharp and away from gunfire. There are a few guards in the main room outside, but I can deal with them. The rest would have moved on from this area now. You should be safe."

Maya took a last look around the room. The man's body. The blood. Nic's hard face. The grate. Finally, she nodded. She knew her task and what was required of her.

With a nudge from Nic, Maya squeezed into the space, barely able to fit inside. "There might be water at the bottom," Nic warned. "Hold your breath and push through until you reach the other side. Short, easy and quick."

Maya patted her pocket, feeling the shape of the chip that was so small yet carried such weight. She extended her arms above her head and felt Nic's grip on her ankles, guiding her down into the grate with unspoken insistence.

The rush of blood to Maya's head turned the world upside down, yet Nic's hands were unyielding, offering no pause for thought as Maya edged closer to the chill of the stagnant water below.

With a final push from Nic, Maya plunged into the icy depths, filling her lungs with a desperate breath before submersion. The water was like a shock to her system, urging her forward. She clawed at the walls; her nails like anchors propelling her through the narrow space.

She opened her eyes in its murky depths, craving for a sign of escape. Every one of her muscles strained, pulling her toward the promise of air and freedom. Then, sensing the solid ground beneath her, she summoned the last of her strength and surged upward.

Her hands found a grate above, the metal cold and unforgiving against her cheeks as she pressed her face between the gaps, gasping for air. Panic seized her mind—

visions of remaining trapped there, drowning, or guards closing in on the other side. She fought for focus, and with a last heave, the grate above gave way, and Maya pulled herself out into the safety of the night beyond the wall.

She relished the gritty earth beneath her and rolled in the dirt, desperately trying to rid the murky water from her clothes and hair. The night air felt surprisingly warm against her skin and wrapped around her like a shroud. Steam rose off her like a spectre in the moonlight.

Maya surveyed her surroundings. The coast was clear, with no sign of guards. Off in the distance, orange flames and curling tendrils of black smoke marred the skyline. With the immediate danger behind her, Maya refocused on the mission and located a lone bike nearby. She mounted it and sped off toward the checkpoint.

Maya searched the barren expanse in search of Lucas, her grip on the bike's throttle betraying her nervous twitch, a reminder of the life her hands had claimed. Casting the haunting image aside, she focused on the present.

As she approached the trading gate, the scene beyond her was one of utter chaos. Guards scrambled beneath floodlights; their movements were erratic and betrayed their lack of experience, akin to her own. She hid with her bike behind a barrier of rocks and debris, studying the frenzied clash of the guards in the near distance. They were no soldiers, she thought; they were as useless in this madness as anyone.

Movement at the entrance caught her eye—a solitary figure on a bike, hooded and goggled. Lucas. She fired up her bike and tore across the terrain toward him, the guards' gunfire trailing him like a relentless storm.

Their paths crossed in a fleeting moment, and Maya cranked the throttle, the bike's growl merging with the adrenaline pulsing through her veins. As she executed a skidding turn, a cloud of dust billowed around her, temporarily veiling them from the pursuers.

The dust cloud created a momentary shield as she caught up to Lucas, flattening herself against the bike as gunshots sounded in the distance. Maya waited for the impact of a bullet that never came. "None of them are hitting!" Lucas shouted over the chaos.

Maya couldn't help but notice the smile on his lips. "Can we get away? Do you have the device still?" she asked.

Lucas nodded as they manoeuvred through a graveyard of rusted diggers and skeletal cars, remnants of a world left behind. Their evasion tactics proved successful, and eventually, the gunshots ceased in the distance, slowing Maya's heartbeat.

Lucas signalled to Maya and eased off the throttle. "What's the situation at base camp?"

"Nic is alive, if that's what you mean. Some guards are dead too," Maya reported, glancing at the dried blood that remained on her clothes; something Lucas noticed, too. "I had no choice," she added, justifying the decision as much to herself as to Lucas.

"Of course. I'm not judging you. To be honest, I'm not sure I'd have the guts to do the same."

"I'm not proud of it. Can we move on? Talk about something else?" Maya pressed, eager to put it all behind her.

"I want to check on Lydia. They've been targeting homes out here," Lucas said.

Maya trailed behind Lucas through the desolate landscape, the humid air heavy and suffocating, laden with the scent of unrest and burning debris. As they neared the ominous plumes of smoke she had seen earlier, the image of what had transpired came into sharper focus. The government had scorched the settlements bordering No Man's Land. A structure stood, one that was once a home now nothing but burning ash. As if they were worthless, the guards set fire to a small pile of bodies laid out beside it.

Coming to a halt alongside Lucas, Maya dismounted her bike, her heart heavy as the flames flickered before them, tainting the sky. She thought of Lydia and the sanctuary she provided to so many—including Lucas, who had grown up under her care. The silent wish for their safety hung between them as they observed the devastation.

She placed a hand on his shoulder, which stiffened at her touch. "It isn't looking good, is it?" he whispered.

"Let's go closer; we might be able to help."

Lucas shook his head. "No. It's too dangerous. Lydia would never forgive me if I played the hero and wound up dead."

"But we could save them, some of them—"

"They're gone, Maya." Lucas pointed towards the settlement. "The guards seem in no rush to leave. Their job is done."

Maya took in the view. "It's all so pointless."

"Yeah, but at least the device is safe. Both pieces together now." Lucas handed Maya the device. "Will you look after it until lottery day? It'll be safer with you."

Maya snatched the device and tucked it in the pocket alongside the chip. She didn't want the burden of carrying it, but felt like she couldn't say no, not after what happened here tonight. "We won't let them win. We'll make people stand up and see the truth. That's what we're going to do on

Lottery Day." Maya patted Lucas on the back and turned back to her bike. "You know the best way back home? My usual route's blocked."

After parting ways with Lucas, Maya was alone, journeying through yet another tunnel. Unlike the previous passageways, this one mercifully allowed her to stand tall. The passage was one of chipped rock, allowing gusts of wind to sail through the dark cavern. A throbbing in her head served as a reminder of the night's toll, and her damp clothes, now tattered at the edges, clung to her like a second skin.

The cave seemed to stretch forever, draining what little energy she had left. But as she moved forward, the unmistakable sound of waves crashing against the shore seeped into her consciousness, the briny scent of sea air revitalising her senses. At last, a dim light heralded the path's end.

Emerging from the cramped confines, Maya clambered onto the edge of a secluded cove, its entrance a mere slit in the rock face. Sand and pebbles crunched underfoot as Maya left the seclusion; it had likely been a smuggler's haunt in a past life.

As Maya crossed the stone beach, the dock came into view, and Gil's solitary figure immediately caught her attention. He sat by a makeshift fire, containing its flames in an old, rusty metal drum. She hesitated, wanting to avoid all interaction, but he was completely unavoidable, positioned directly along her path. Maya wrapped her arms around herself, attempting to conceal the blood and grime marking her clothes. She approached the flickering flames.

Gill stood. "Maya, what on earth happened to you? Come

here, closer to the fire." Concern laced his voice as he scanned her from head to toe.

"I'm fine. I need to get home. It's been a rough night," Maya croaked, attempting to downplay the obvious distress written all over her body.

Gil's eyes sharpened. "You don't need to lie to me, girl. You've come from the old smuggler's tunnel. I saw you with my own eyes."

"You did?"

"Only one place that leads to nowadays." Gil's gaze moved pointedly to her torn clothing and the exposed mark on her ankle. "What have you gotten yourself into?" he whispered, his question dangling in the air between them.

"Nothing. I just want to go home." Maya's voice betrayed her growing impatience, desperate to escape the conversation. She didn't want to lie anymore, and Gil's questions would only invite more lies, or worse, the *truth*.

Gil firmly grasped her arms. "That mark. I know what it means. I'm no fool."

Maya glanced down towards her ankle, her trouser leg ripped, the scar displayed under the light of the flames. "You supply to them and help them continue their efforts. What's the difference?"

"Joining and sacrificing everything for them isn't a wise choice, Maya. They will make you do things you would never do in the real world. How long have you been a member?"

Maya saw the guard again. The flash of his face, the blade in his neck. The blood. "A while." Guilt muffled her words and constricted her breath. "They do good work, Gil; they fight for a better life."

Gil observed her closely, taking in the crimson and disarray marring her appearance. "You're covered in blood;

you look like a mess, and you're overworked. Is it truly better? Or are they using you?"

"I'm not being used," Maya snapped. She had never allowed herself to be used and lived her life by her own rules without restriction. She wouldn't allow herself to be exploited, not after the government had taken her freedom.

"No? So, you can stand there and say you're happy with every choice you've made since joining them?" Maya cast her gaze downward, seeking answers from the ground at her feet.

Gil continued, his voice carrying the weight of experience. "I've been around since they started Maya—I've heard it all. I know better. Know what it used to be, and how it's changed with each leader. Don't blindly follow their ideas. Question them, and then you'll see how controlling they can be."

Maya clenched her hands into fists, hands that had taken a life only hours ago. She'd allowed a man to die. Maya thought about the recording, bugging her brother, and the lies and secrets she'd kept from day one. She'd never felt used, but as she stood there now, drenched in another man's blood, she had to question if she had been.

She looked at Gil's weathered face and kind eyes, the man who'd been there for her and her family for as long as she could remember. Her heart raced at the thought; she wanted to confide in him and get a second opinion. "They're planning something for Lottery Day. Nic asked me to plant a bug on Liam, and they got information, overhearing a conversation about the vote and the government's plans." The truth spilled from Maya's lips surprisingly quickly.

"That's why New Albion closed down the routes, then." Gil wiped his brow. "They do this every so often. Things find a way to settle, unspoken rules get broken, but both sides allow it. Then, someone from there gets big ideas, and the whole thing comes to a close."

"Nic is a good leader. She wants better."

"Aye, while that may be, it isn't worth your life, Maya. You shouldn't be indebted to anyone. Trust me on that."

"Well, after she exposes all this on Lottery Day, things will change. Whether or not we agree with it, there's no stopping it. The cogs are in motion."

"You stay home with your mother, keep away from it, you hear me?" Maya nodded. "If what you're saying is true, then you can't be caught up in the chaos."

Chapter Twenty

Before the Storm

Maya knew she shouldn't do it, but that didn't stop her from bringing the bottle to her lips again. The bitter whisky stung her throat, but she'd put up with whatever liquor Carla could find. She'd made her way from the docks to Carla's home, hoping she hadn't revealed too much to Gil. She hated herself for revealing her secret, but the lifeless body haunted her more than anything else. Speaking to Gil had helped.

Waking Carla in the dead of night, Maya pleaded with her to take the device. She couldn't bear the idea of keeping it in her room with her brother in the next room. The panic of him discovering it was too much to endure, as was the thought of facing him. Carla agreed to accept it, but given the state Maya was in, she wasn't likely to refuse.

Maya approached her home, her torn clothes revealing her dirty, muddied skin. She swayed and took a moment to inhale the night air before stepping into the mould-ridden corridor. She wondered if her brother was home sleeping, or if he'd stayed over *there* in secret.

When Maya pushed the door open, she halted at the sight of her mother gazing out of the kitchen window, the sole portal to the outside world in their tiny flat. Emma rolled her eyes with a disappointment Maya was all too familiar with as she stumbled toward the table and placed the bottle down. "Up late," Maya slurred, taking a seat.

Emma turned, holding the lottery ticket. "Another successful night? What on earth happened to you?"

Maya studied her hands in the warm glow. They were worse than she thought. "This? It's the rewards of a hard day at work, Mother." She took another swig from the bottle, and this time the whisky went down without a sting. "Still hoping tomorrow brings you luck?"

Emma smiled, looking at the ticket once more before stashing it in the drawer. "We lost Carla's grandmother this evening," she whispered. "She lasted longer than any of us thought."

Maya lifted her face, her vision snapping into focus. She had just seen Carla. "Does she know? Carla, I mean."

Emma shook her head and took the bottle from Maya, placing it in one of the bottom cupboards. "No, I wanted to wait until you were home, to tell her together, but you were so late, and time got away from me and, well." Emma sighed. "We can let her know tomorrow. She was such a wonderful woman."

"Carla's going to be broken when she hears." Maya watched as Emma wiped the tears from her cheeks. For years, her mother had taken people in and cared for them, keeping them going when they had nothing left. Why did she still care? Why, after all these years, after so much loss and death, why did her mother still care and cry for those she lost?

Maya thought of the man she'd killed, the one who didn't have time to kill Nic. She thought of his partner, and if there was someone waiting for him to come home. Wondering if he was missing or dead, or plotting revenge against the person who took him away. Maya reached for the bottle, forgetting her mother had removed it.

"She gave me the ticket, though. She knew she would not make it to Lottery Day. I brought it to her today, you know," Emma said. "Thought I'd give it back, ready for tomorrow." Emma sat opposite Maya, though her eyes were empty.

Maya wanted to offer comforting words, but none came to mind. That was never her role in this family. "Liam back yet?"

Emma shook her head. "No. He works late most evenings now. Same as you, I guess."

Maya peered around the empty flat, which was their home in name only. She wondered how her mother felt, staying here with both kids away, busy with their own lives. "Do you ever feel lonely here? Without Dad?" Maya let the question linger, having broken an unspoken rule. They hadn't mentioned her father in years.

Emma laughed. "I miss him every day, but don't confuse that with forgiving him, though, because I haven't." Emma got up and pulled the bottle from the cupboard, along with two glasses. "The job of a parent is to raise your kids well enough that they no longer need you. That's what my mother always used to say." She poured two glasses and pushed one toward Maya. "I did that with you two. It was tricky in the world we ended up in, but I think I've done it well for you both, in different ways."

Maya raised her glass. "We couldn't have asked for a better parent. We didn't need him, Mum."

Emma smiled, yet the whisky seemed to catch in her throat as she said, "He was a good man. I didn't ever see bad in him. I'll never know why he chose what he did." Emma sipped the drink again. "I secretly hoped Liam would track him down over there, just to gain an answer or two. All these years, and not a single word. I wonder if maybe he was looking for a way out. I don't know." Emma finished her drink and poured another.

Maya cherished these rare moments when her mother let her guard down. It was refreshing to see her as a person, not just as a parent. But knowing Liam had tracked him down stung. Could Maya tell her mother the truth? How would she react, knowing he had been sitting on such a secret? She couldn't do that. Not now, not tonight. Maybe tomorrow, once everything was out in the open, they could talk about it. "If you saw him again and had the chance to ask him a question, what would you ask?"

Emma laughed. "Oh, I don't know. It's all fantasy. In my head, he died years ago. Makes it easier to deal with, I suppose."

Maya nodded and sipped her drink. "I'd ask why he didn't fight harder to come back or take us with him."

"You think us going over there would have been better?"

Maya shrugged. "Not better, but different. Maybe."

"I'd ask him why. Why he lied about his vote and didn't contact us after he left? I'd ask... if he loved me. That's all I want to know, really. Did he truly love me?"

Maya stood up; the stench of her own clothes lingered as a stark reminder of the images she wanted to avoid. She placed her hand on her mother's shoulder. If she ever got the chance, she made a promise to ask her father that question. "He loved you, it was obvious," Maya said, though she didn't know how true that was. He'd been in contact with Liam for ages now, yet still hadn't attempted to show his face.

Maya stumbled to the bathroom. They were out of hot water, but she needed to shower. She suppressed a scream at the ice-cold water rushing down her back. Sat beneath the icy stream, trying to prepare for what lay ahead tomorrow. She had done her duty; gotten the information from Liam, and now it was down to Nic to pull off the rest; storm the stage, pretend to win the lottery, bask in the crowd's cheers, and then *bang*. She'd hit the country with the truth. Nic would go down in history as the woman who changed the world. Maya smiled and pulled her knees up to her chin. She'd helped make this happen. Though people died, even the man tonight by her own hands. That still stung, Maya knew how precious life was and she'd taken someones, but this was war. Wasn't loss and death inevitable? She had to tell herself that repeatedly to keep her mind straight. Still, battle lines had formed, and threats arose. The group still didn't stop. They pushed through, and now a sea of change was on the horizon.

Tomorrow would change her life for the better.

Chapter Twenty-One

A Day of Change

The air buzzed with excitement and cheers erupted from the crowd as Liam stood proudly on stage, his hands clasped behind his back and shoulders squared. The enormity of the celebration overwhelmed him. Lottery Day was an annual spectacle in Old Albion, and it felt even more momentous this year. People gathered on both sides to witness the unveiling of the lottery winner.

Liam surveyed the crowd, searching for familiar faces—his mother, Alex, and Maya. He stood among other guards—some of which were hired from the Freedom Day initiative, like himself, and others who were more seasoned members, such as Alex. Liam couldn't help but feel a sense of pride. On this elevated stage, overlooking the place where he'd grown up, he finally felt special. Important.

His gaze traversed the sea of people, capturing the

dancing colours of their flags—purple and blue fabrics held aloft on poles. Alex caught his eye, positioned near the front in casual attire. He'd rolled up his sleeves and swept back his blonde, tousled hair. Alex returned his smile, and Liam's cheeks flushed, understanding he'd been watching him the entire time without realising it. They hadn't spoken or met up since the night before. Liam knew the mission wasn't a success, yet here he was, on stage and still in his station. He had to assume things would be okay.

He peered further into the crowd to spot his mother, but he couldn't find her. Liam wondered what she would do were his father to join him on stage.

The guard beside Liam tapped his shoulder. "You get lumped with this side too? Bet they're having a right jolly over there."

"This is where all the action is. Best place to be."

"More guards this side. More to keep an eye on. They've even planted some in the audience, out of uniform." Liam glanced at Alex again, regarding his casual outfit in a different light now. "Don't you think the tension is a little off this year?"

Liam surveyed the densely packed crowd, noting their cheers. He turned to glance at the other guards on stage; no smiles adorned their faces. Instead, they clenched their fists at their sides. The cheerful atmosphere he'd initially perceived evaporated before him.

He thought of the recent raid and the leaked information. This morning, his father had assured him that Governor Granswick was unaware of the matter; despite the mission's failure to reclaim the information, the warning was enough to prevent further action.

When Granswick began his speech, the crowd fell silent.

"Welcome to our annual Lottery Day," he declared, prompting further cheers from the crowd. A familiar thrill traced Liam's spine, akin to the sensation he felt on Freedom Day. Granswick continued, "I am here to host the special day and offer citizenship to one lucky member of Old Albion, welcoming them into our bustling country and introducing them to a new way of life." Granswick clasped his hands behind his back, his crisp suit gleaming in the morning sun. "We will draw the ticket at random. I wish you all luck! The winner will be rewarded within the hour. I look forward to welcoming you, but for now, I will leave you in the hands of Mayor Lewis." Granswick bowed, and then extended his arm for Mayor Lewis to take the stage.

The mayor slowly emerged from the lineup, his dishevelled suit and sunken eyes a stark contrast to the governor's polished appearance. The members of New Albion exited the stage, with each guard, including Liam, turning and walking off in synchronised steps until their boots met the ground. As the mayor continued his speech, Liam could hear the same rambling lines he'd heard countless times before. People seemed impatient, hungering for something to celebrate.

Once offstage, Liam had some freedom to mingle in the crowd while staying alert for any unusual activity. However, he had no intention of being cautious. Today was a day for celebration; besides, Liam had kept his job thus far. A little mingling wouldn't hurt. He wanted to break through the people, find Alex, and celebrate with him—perhaps introduce him to his mother. The idea of moving crossed his mind again, becoming more of a reality with each passing day.

A sweat-soaked stench rose from the crowd, with some standing and celebrating in piled-up litter. As the audience erupted, Liam spotted Alex in the distance, his face flushed; although his discomfort was clear, he was still willing to experience Liam's world. The mayor finished his speech, then the lottery officials drew the winning number. On stage, a woman climbed up to claim her prize, as the winning number flashed on the display screen. The screen changed then, as images flashed, overtaking the number displayed. It took Liam a moment to realise they were photos of him, the governor, and his father meeting the leader from the West Country. The lottery winner stood tall, her hair and braids secured in a thick ponytail that dangled behind her.

Nic.

Liam's heart sank, and he gripped the sword attached to his hip. He did not know how to use it, or if it worked like a real sword at all. But he braced himself, his body tight as he searched for people he knew in the crowd, those he loved and cared about. He couldn't see his mother, and Alex had vanished from the spot he was in moments before. Nic moved to the stand as the audio played, blasting through the crowd. His father's voice—it was unmistakable. Then Granswick's voice joined the noise, playing on devices around him he couldn't quite place.

The exposure of Liam's part in the lies overwhelmed him with guilt. Nic threw her hands up, and banners fell across the divide behind her—the perfect backdrop, revealing the true nature of New Albion to all. The recording rang throughout the crowd, compelling them to listen and open their eyes to the truth. Liam searched the crowd, but saw only their flushed, furious faces. Many eyed him in his uniform, a uniform that marked his clear alliance to the other side.

Nic stepped forward as guards rushed the stage. Should he intervene? Stomp up the wooden steps and silence the truth from her lips? He didn't need to. Before anyone could reach the stage to stop her, a gunshot rang out, shattering the stunned quiet that had stilled the crowd. Ringing echoed in Liam's ears, stopping his heart. His legs turned to jelly as he watched crimson blood splatter onto the banner as Nic fell to her knees. In that instant, the world changed.

People stormed past him, knocking others to the ground and trampling over their bodies. Bracing, Liam pulled himself to his feet, gasping for air. The chaos showed no order. Guards from New Albion hurried away, retreating behind the safety of their gates. Lottery Day, a time for celebration, was now one of chaos.

Although Liam wanted to mourn Nic's death, he couldn't afford the luxury. His priority was to find his mother and get her to safety. Liam pushed through the erupting crowd, the people wise about what would happen next. Refusing to be silenced, the crowd launched flaming bottles against the stage, setting it alight. Liam hated himself for falling for Freedom Day, allowing New Albion to deceive him; he'd dared to believe in something greater, something to better the two countries, not a scheme used to serve their own interests. He'd witnessed brutality: the prison cell, the orders to kill any and all citizens in No Man's Land, the bullet that had killed Nic only a moment ago. These atrocities came from New Albion. These were all things he knew were going on, but still turned a blind eye to it for the hope of a better life. He was no better than the guards on the other side.

He hoped Alex was different and truly meant something to him.

Liam struggled to the outskirts of the crowd, attempting to gain higher ground. There he spotted Carla being shoved against a makeshift wooden barrier, her face contorted in pain. Liam rushed toward her and pulled her from the crowds. "Are you okay? What the hell happened?"

Carla looked at him, pulling her arm away. Liam feared her hatred after what she'd heard on the screen. "Are you hurt?" she asked, examining his chest.

Liam glanced down at the dark stains on his jacket, unsure if the blood was his. "Is Maya here? Is she safe? Mum too?"

"I don't know. I've had a rough day, so I came to let off some steam, but it seems like that was everyone's idea."

Carla wiped her hair from her face, and Liam noticed her red eyes. He wanted to ask more, but he had his own fears to deal with. He removed his jacket and threw it to the floor to blend in.

The crowds dispersed and fled the chaos while the audio still blared. Guards had arrived in full force now, shoving people away from the platform and yelling for them to retreat. Their attempt to instil order worked for some, but not for all. The guards drew their guns, aiming them at the citizens of Old Albion. They broadcast Liam's voice alongside Granswick's, so he needed to stay out of sight. He had no place there anymore. His dreams from moments ago were gone.

With the space clearing, it became easier to search for familiar faces. Below, a small crowd circled someone on the ground. Liam spotted Alex, then, his shirt stained a deep red, his hair glinting beneath the pockets of sun. Liam rushed down and jumped from the small platform he'd climbed.

His boots hit the floor as he approached Alex, fear-ridden thoughts racing through his mind. He noticed his sister, then, standing with blood on her hands. Liam clenched his jaw, desperately hoping she wasn't behind Alex's pain.

Then, as he drew closer, he saw it. The small crowd

gathered around a body on the ground; blood seeped from a crushed figure, a victim of the scared and frenzied mob. His mother. His gentle, beautiful mother lay on the ground. Liam looked at Maya again and the blood on her hands. The crowd all tried to help, but their efforts were as useless as Liam had been over the years. His purpose, as the eldest child—the son—was to look after his mother. And he'd failed.

Liam and Maya didn't speak; they couldn't find the words, even if they wanted to. Workers packed bodies into makeshift coffins constructed from the rubble they found on the ground, then escorted the coffins from the crowd.

For the first time in a long while, Liam and Maya worked together. They helped lower their mother's body into a box and carried her through the district. Alex stayed to assist alongside Carla. All four of them walked through the street his mother had lived in. Nobody shed tears; death didn't hold the same grace anymore. People died in the district all the time. It didn't make this moment any easier, though—he'd lost the first person close to him. It seemed wrong, surreal, like it hadn't really happened.

They followed the line of mourners, who each carried a loved one of their own, before stopping outside the run-down church, the only place where it felt right to be. They lowered her box alongside the others who lost their lives today. Liam peered across the many caskets, wondering who else was dead and whose world had changed just like his. He gave Maya a half-smile, one she didn't reciprocate. Alex draped an arm around his shoulder, shuffling closer and closing the gap between them. "What do we do now?" Alex whispered, his voice quieter than the breeze.

Liam turned to him, studying his tired face, and the blood dried into his clothes. He shrugged. He didn't know what to do. In fact, he wasn't sure he even knew what day it was. He stared at the box with his mother inside, hoping she'd have the answers.

Maya strode towards him with rage burning in her eyes; her mind was clearly in another place than Liam's. "Sis. Do you think we should talk?"

"I think you should," Alex replied. "I was there with your mother when you arrived." He turned to Liam and aimed a finger at Maya. "She was part of this, Liam. Part of *that* group."

"Is this true?" Liam asked. How did Alex already know this about his sister? Why did he keep it from him? It made Liam wonder what else Alex had stored hidden.

"Don't start." Maya ran her hand through her hair. "Today has been a mess. Don't act all high and mighty when I heard Father's voice being blasted on the stage. You kept things from me, too."

Liam bowed his head until he watched his mother's casket once more.

"You have the mark on your ankle. I spotted it earlier. All this destruction is down to your group's plans," Alex spat.

Liam pulled Alex towards him; he'd do anything to shut him up. In a way, it felt good hearing him defend so fiercely, even though he found it hard to agree.

"We all lost today," Liam said to Alex. "None of us have come out of Lottery Day any better." Liam turned towards Maya to where Carla stood behind her. "I bet the rebellion is now wounded, with Nic going how she did." Liam glanced at the ground again, as if that's where he'd find the answers. "She was strong, a good leader. I'm sorry to see her go."

Carla's eyes burned red as she pointed at Alex. "It was your boss who did it," Carla said. "Your people carried out the shooting. If that had never happened, it wouldn't have spooked the crowd like it did."

Alex moved closer. "Hold on. It's nothing to do with the government. I, I mean, we wouldn't carry out orders like that."

Liam stepped between them when he noticed Maya curling her fingers into a fist. With the size of her arms lately, he didn't fancy Alex's chances. He gripped Alex's shoulders and brought him closer. He recalled the mission assigned to him last night; the guard killed at his post, and the man imprisoned without food or water. "We know what they're capable of, Alex. There's no need to pretend anymore."

Alex narrowed his brows, trying to fight the truth. "Either way. They wouldn't have agreed to that. They hide things. They wouldn't assassinate like that, not in plain sight."

"That makes it better, does it?" Carla asked. "No matter how you look at it, someone killed Nic, and now they'll hide the truth again from us all."

Alex rolled his eyes. "The truth is, both sides should have stayed apart. Then this would have never happened."

"And we would have never met," Liam replied simply, and the group fell silent again. More people arrived behind them, carrying more loved ones to their resting place. "Arguing will get us nowhere, sis. Mum's gone; we need to stick together. After that announcement, I can't exactly be seen in New Albion again." Though Liam wasn't sure he'd be safe in Old Albion, either. "We need to make a plan. What I learned from father and the governor was horrible, but there was more for me to learn and uncover—I'm sure of it."

Maya nodded. "We'll regroup. Nic played her most powerful move. It isn't over, Liam; it's just beginning."

Liam smiled, glancing at Carla and then Alex. He wanted to do right by them all; he wanted the life he had in mind to work for everyone's sake. "We can work together," he said. He reached for Alex's hand, noticing the dried blood under his fingernails. His mother's blood. Alex smiled at him. "You still work there. You can help; you can connect with Robert. Make a difference."

Alex tensed, and he averted his eyes. "Liam..."

Liam knew Alex. He'd seen the good in his eyes; knew Alex questioned the way of things, too. He could trust Alex; he just needed to let him know it would be safe to do so.

"Please. I know you. I know you want to do right. Isn't the death of my mother enough? Or the things they made you do in No Man's Land? Isn't it clear to you?"

Alex paused. Carla stared at him, and Maya held her fist poised and ready. Eventually, Alex nodded. "I'll do what I can. I didn't know your mother for long, but I was there with her during those last moments. She was kind, I'm sure of it. She loved both of you dearly." Alex faced Maya then. "As for Nic's death, I'm telling you that decision didn't come from higher up. Whoever decided that was the moment chose that on their own."

The orange sky was ablaze, a reflection of the tension permeating the district. Riots, lootings, and parties ensued, ensuring no one in Old Albion slept that night. Everyone's blood ran high, with the taste of possibility in the air. Liam spent time with his sister. They spoke of their mother, and how she moulded them into who they are today. Then they talked about their father, the rebellion, and what the next few days might bring. Over the past few months, they had fought different battles and kept secrets from one another. But now, as the fight came to a head, as the world changed in a flash, they had each other. They had hope, and as they sat on the church hill, looking towards the dividing wall, they both agreed that their next task was to bring it down.

Part Three

"Forge your path, push through the obstacles, and sculpt your own future with determination, knowing that every step forward is a brushstroke of your unique masterpiece."

Chapter Twenty-Two

Arise from the Fire

Maya lingered in her home, a place once warmed by her mother's presence, yet now felt cold and devoid of light. The world no longer seemed real, as though she lived in a stolen reality. Liam stood beside her. She tried not to blame him, but without her mother's guidance, she found it hard not to.

He retreated to their mother's bedroom, where boxes awaited to swallow the remnants of her life. The flaked paint on the walls remained unchanged and carried a lingering scent that, for a fleeting moment, made Maya feel like her mother was a mere step away. Sitting on the edge of the bed, she asked, "Have you heard from Dad?"

Liam shook his head and unfolded a flattened box. "No. No word from any of them, and I'm too scared to contact them and find out."

"Afraid of being taken captive?"

"Maybe."

"You should be. Carla and I saw them take protesters away by the gate a while ago. We never saw their faces again," Maya said. "Do you think he knows about Mum?"

"When Alex gets in contact, I'll find out more. Father might still help us."

Maya laughed and leaned on the door frame. "You still believe that? Mum talked about him the night before the lottery. Said he was a good man. I don't know if I can bring myself to believe it."

"Alex is good, and so am I. Why can't he be?"

"Can't he be both?"

"Stop being smart. He asked about you, and he wanted to help Mum. He was stuck there with no options. I truly believe that."

Maya tried not to laugh. Liam had been doing trade runs for years into No Man's Land, and then even risked escorting Alex across the border. She'd been back and forth between the two places, taking multiple routes in and out. Why couldn't her father do the same?

"We managed to get to the other side. He could have contacted us if he wanted to."

Liam sighed. "You've never been there; you don't know the control they have on people. They track and follow everything you do. He would have died if he'd tried. He told me they were even stricter in the beginning, more than they are now."

Maya patted Liam on the shoulder. Despite being the older sibling, he was too trusting and forgiving. It made her feel protective, like she needed to set up barriers around him to keep him safe. She couldn't help but think that if it were her children on the other side, she would have found a way to contact them, no matter the risk. Perhaps her father wasn't as brave, or maybe she was just foolish.

"I need to go do some work. The group has been wanting to meet up to sort out the next steps now that..." Maya paused before forcing herself to say it. "*Nic* is dead. We need to keep the momentum going."

Liam tucked a box away and pulled out another. "Is it safe to go over there?"

Maya nodded. "Carla said so. Apparently, New Albion is reducing the numbers of guards on our side, so we can still get through, but we've had to stop shipments and trades for now."

"You telling Gil? He might have some stuff to send through." Liam scratched the back of his neck. "Maybe I should grovel for my old job back."

"You need to focus and keep an ear out for any information from across the divide. We need all the contacts we can get, and Alex or... *father* will be the ones to provide it."

"If they call... you saying I should go back over?"

Maya shrugged. "They might take you away, or worse. Are you willing to risk that?"

"To see Alex again? Yeah."

Maya laughed; she relished this side of her brother, who'd always had his pick of men. Alex's name was the first to linger on his lips for longer than one night. She was jealous of him for finding a snippet of joy during a time when happiness was sparse. "Ensure it's safe. Make sure you come back to me, brother."

Liam smiled as Maya turned to leave. When she glanced back, he was packing their mother's life away, as though she never existed.

* * *

Packing her mother's life into boxes had drained her more than she expected. She peered into the windows of other apartments and homes as she journeyed towards the divide. Who was inside each home? How many boxes would their lives fill? Perhaps it would be more than her mother's. She wondered how many boxes her own life would contain when the day came.

Maya met Carla at the post, the same one she'd used when first arriving at No Man's Land. There were no guards on duty—no one to stop them going further into the outskirts if they wished. The eerie silence was unsettling, and the uncharacteristic privacy from New Albion was unusual. With tensions running high on both sides, perhaps the guards needed time to cool off.

"How are things in the district? Still tense?" Maya asked, pulling herself up onto the quad bike.

Carla settled in behind her. "Things are bad. There's non-stop fights at The Old Vic; the streets are filthy, and people are arguing at all hours of the day. I don't know when it will stop, but it's frightening."

"It's what happens when you push people too far. The message Nic wanted to spread worked, in a way. Got into the right ears. Now, people want to let out their anger."

Carla tucked her hair behind her ear as the wind picked up. "We need to keep the momentum. I don't want Nic to have died for no reason. New Albion must be planning things; they've gone silent."

Maya glanced in the bike mirror to the unguarded dividing wall behind them. "How are you getting on with your grandmother's things? Liam's packing away Mum's stuff now."

"It's weird, isn't it? I've done most of Gran's. I kept a few photos. Did you know there were photos of my mother in the West Country? Her family was enormous over there. I wonder how many of them are still around. I'm going to show them to Lucas and maybe try to build that bridge; perhaps we can visit them one day. Together."

"I don't blame you," Maya said. "At the moment, I'd grab any connection I could."

Maya saluted the skeleton of Theodore Lockhart as they entered the base camp. Although crowded, the room was silent. Nic's necklace lay on the table at the back and immediately snagged Maya's attention as she sought Lucas. Finding him in a booth, she slid in beside him, hoping the dim light hid her anxiety.

Lucas smiled at Carla. "Glad you could both make it."

"Of course. We heard about the meeting, though messages seem harder to come by at the moment," Maya said.

"Everything is. We've had no shipments since the attack. No help from anyone. Without a leader, progress tends to step back a few years, but hopefully, that'll change tonight."

Carla leaned over. "Are we getting a new leader?"

Maya glanced at the table where Nic so often sat. She wondered what a new leader would be like and the options and ideas they'd bring to the group.

Lucas nodded. "Yeah. It's been so tense around here; people are anxious, waiting to see what the future holds, and if they believe in the new one or not. There's a lot riding on this."

"Yeah, well. I've made my promise already. I won't let my mother's death be in vain. Whatever happens. We continue this fight."

Carla patted Maya on the back. "Maya, isn't that your mate by the table?"

Maya glanced at the wooden surface again. Holding Nic's necklace in her hands was Kong, her dreadlocks falling down her back, and her face stern and sharp. Maya held her breath, fearing a quick election of Kong as leader. What would that mean for her?

"We've waited enough," Kong announced. She clapped her palms like Nic used to. "We still go by Nic's words. Death happens. We do not mourn them, but we make their death count. Nic is now one of those numbers, another taken by the enemy for the cause."

Maya watched, surprised by the authority Kong held over the group, her voice resonating to even those at the back of the room. Although they hadn't gotten along on the occasions they'd met, Maya couldn't help but feel a sense of pride watching her now.

"Before Nic left us, she chose her next successor, like every leader before her. Open the envelope." A woman beside Nic held a white envelope, secured with a wax seal. "We are all in agreement. This is Nic's handwriting and seal." The woman beside her smiled as the crowd nodded, murmuring their agreement. Lucas banged the table with his fist. Kong gave a slight bow to the woman, letting her rip the letter open. Everyone watched, studying the woman's eyes as she read the note Nic left behind. Kong's eyes widened, and the woman spoke the name again and looked up at the crowd. She narrowed her eyes, scanning the room. Then she found Maya's table and passed the letter to Kong.

Maya looked at Lucas, who was unaware that the woman was staring at him. Maya nudged him on his side, and he straightened. The woman pointed at them again. "You! Come up here," she said. Maya looked at Lucas again, waiting for him to stand. "Girl. Come to the table!" The woman shouted this time, and Maya turned her head, her eyes widening as she realised the woman was pointing at her.

"Maya, what's going on?" Carla whispered as Maya slid out from the booth. Slowly, she stepped toward the table as if she was heading on stage. Was she being punished? Had Nic written about her in the letter? What on earth could be happening?

Maya stepped past Kong, who had put the letter down. "What's going on?"

"Maya. Nic has left us with the biggest burden No Man's Land has ever faced. Her sacrifice has propelled us into the next step, and it is you who she has chosen to take her place."

Maya didn't react; she couldn't register her words. Gasps and murmurs rippled around the tables, but no one cheered. No one celebrated. Maya's stomach tightened, trying to work out why Nic would impose this burden on her shoulders.

She turned to face the crowd, but no one moved. Instead, they waited for more information—the punch line of a joke that would never come. "This can't be right!" someone shouted from the audience.

"What does she know about us?" yelled another.

Maya turned to Kong, who slammed her fist onto the table, quelling the embers before they could ignite. "Enough. If any of you respected Nic, then you will respect her last wishes!" Kong bellowed. "I was with her when she wrote this. The name read is correct." Kong turned to face Maya then. "Nic was a special person to me. We shared years together; we battled hard to get the group to what it is today." Turning to address the crowd, she yelled, "We need a leader! Someone who is fierce; someone who will show no fear when facing the enemy. Nic wanted this to be the end, and Maya will be the bridge we need." Kong grabbed hold of Maya's arm and lifted it into the air. "Together, we can bring New Albion to its knees. Now, stand and cheer for our new leader! Allow Nic's memory to mean something!" Kong cheered, and half the room followed suit. Maya stayed silent alongside the other half, and when Kong turned to her again, there was a smile on her face, larger than Maya had ever seen. "Will you accept, Maya? Will you pledge your life to the group? Do what you can to take down the oppression and build a new future? Do you accept the role given to you by our previous leader?"

Maya scanned the room. Most of the crowd appeared to have come around to the idea after Kong's speech. She wanted to do right. The reason she joined this group and fought so hard to keep it going was to make a change. She thought back to her empty house and dead mother. Her father's broken promises. The moment her mother was trampled to death, her life in Old Albion ended. The rebellion gave Maya something to focus on, a way to hold off the drinking and to implement actual change, continuing what Nic had shown her.

Leaders died; they never survived for long. But Maya was okay with that. She had a chance to be something—to do something. Smiling, she nodded and accepted the role. She did not know how long it would last, or if she'd soon join Nic six feet under, but she didn't care. Maya needed this; she wanted this, even if she didn't believe she deserved it.

Maya was in the backroom, the same one where Nic had asked her to plant a bug on Liam. It was also this space where the tunnel led her, the room where she'd killed a man. Bloodstains adorned the rug, a haunting reminder of the choices she had made. A necklace lay on the surface before her, a symbol of Nic's legacy. The distant sounds of laughter and chatter seeped in from outside.

Maya pulled out a wooden chair and sat, contemplating Nic's last moments. She ran her fingers along the desk and over the blank papers, looking at the pen Nic left behind. Tears blurred her vision as footsteps approached from behind, and a heavy hand landed on her shoulder.

"You eyeing up her stuff already?" Kong remarked, pulling out a stool to sit beside Maya. She picked up the necklace and ran the chain through her fingers. "You ready for this?"

Maya, still fixated on Nic's belongings, said, "I don't know. You commanded that room out there. Why didn't she pick you?"

Kong laughed, tucking the necklace in her pocket. "Maybe she likes me too much to see me killed."

"Maybe," Maya conceded, with a smile. "I didn't know you two were close. I'm sorry again, for our first meeting... for punching you."

Kong stood, holding the pen. "Its old news. This is your place now. My job here is done."

"Wait," Maya said, reaching out to stop her. She needed guidance; needed all the help she could get. Experience meant everything in a role like this. "Tell me about how you started working here and how you knew Nic."

"I wanted change. I heard rumours about the rebellion years ago, and the tunnels in my bar that led to No Man's Land. Nic and I started an alliance to help trade."

"You said she was a special friend; you were with her when she wrote my name. That must have been one of the last things she did before..." Maya didn't finish the sentence.

"I was her confidant, here to guide and advise her and tell her when she was being stupid. She was stupid a lot. The silly, beautiful fool." Kong pulled the necklace from her pocket before gripping Maya's shoulder again. "Let me give you some parting advice. Find yourself someone who will be honest with you, who will stand by your side and do anything for the group. You'll need it in the times ahead, if you're going to lead us to the end."

"The end?" Maya interrupted. "She really believed that?"

"She died, didn't she? Went on stage, knowing what they would do to her. Don't let her death be in vain. We're so close now. I'm still a part of this; I'll help you, but you must find someone close—someone *you* trust." Kong turned to leave, and a shadow fell behind her a few moments after her departure.

It was Carla, clutching the photos from her grandmother's house, with Lucas following behind. "You doing okay in here, boss?" Lucas quipped, sitting on the stool Kong had used.

"I was showing Lucas the family photos. Well, until he almost spilt his drink on them," Carla added, glaring at her brother. "Has it settled in yet? Being the leader?"

Maya looked at her friend, and then at Lucas, battle-worn and keen. Maya didn't know if she was ready, or if she ever would be. But all eyes were on her now. So many people depended on *her* to make the right moves. She had no choice. Nic gave her life for this, and picked Maya for a reason—a reason she didn't know yet, but she needed to try until she did.

"We need to plan." Maya coughed, forcing her voice to sound steady. "First mission is to join No Man's Land with Old Albion. We need to unite the two while New Albion lowers their watch. Together is how we win this," Maya declared. "Kong will help set up a base. Carla, I want The Old Vic to be another base for when the time is right." Carla raised her eyebrows as Maya turned to Lucas. "I want you to take charge here whenever I'm not around. I'll speak to Gil; I'll set up trade again for the survivors to help them rebuild, but they must help us when the time comes. Can you do that?"

Lucas stood up, smiling. "I can. If we supply them with food and water, they'll help. While Lydia didn't make it from the fire, some of her kids did. Some people I count as brothers and sisters are still here, and they're willing to fight."

Maya leaned back in her chair. "Okay. When we hear from Alex and Liam, we can get intel on what New Albion is planning. We'll counter their attack and infiltrate their weaknesses, and eventually, we'll bring down the divide."

Maya heard her own words, spoken like an ageing captain of war. Whether she believed in them was another question altogether, and although it sounded right to say, she did not know if they held any weight.

"Taking to the job like a duck to water," Lucas chirped. "Nic would be proud."

A smile graced Maya's lips. She nodded. Nic would be proud, and she hoped her mother would be, too.

Chapter Twenty-Three

Confined

Liam kept his device on him and continuously checked for a message from Alex.

Home didn't feel like home any longer, though truthfully, it hadn't for a while, and his mother's absence made him want to stay even less. It had been a few days since he'd heard from Alex, and although no news was good news, that didn't stop his mind from jumping to worst-case scenarios. He needed to get out of his head and out of this place he once called home.

So, Liam took to the streets. The district was alive as the sun set; people gathered in groups outside the market, some leaning against entry ways into their homes and flats. Either-way, they turned their backs to him as he passed. He was now known as the one who turned against his own people, and although nothing had come of it yet, he expected to be attacked every time he left the house. In a way, he wanted a fight—anything to feel something.

As he turned a corner, footsteps sounded behind him—sure and steady, belonging to more than one person. He fancied a fight, a way to let off some steam, but he didn't want to be killed. He picked up his pace, hoping the steps would soon disappear.

They didn't.

Instead, the footfall increased, forcing Liam to burst into a sprint down a dark, litter-strewn alleyway. He rushed through it, jumping over waste and splashing through puddles as he gathered speed for freedom. They wouldn't relent. He wanted to look behind him, but he didn't dare risk it in case he lost his footing.

At the end of the alleyway, he saw the great grey wall reflecting the moon's glow. He looked around; this place was his home, a place he'd once known like the back of his hand. But things had changed. They had built additional barriers, and they had cornered off the places he once used as shortcuts. Liam found himself in the open with nowhere to run. He turned to find three guards in New Albion's uniform: crisp, fresh, and brand new, just like their faces. Recruits from Freedom Day, he realised. The men stopped a few strides away from him, peering at the divide behind him with a smile. Liam didn't put up a fight. He raised his hands, hoping they'd go soft on him; perhaps they'd let him die quickly. Clenching his jaw, he closed his eyes as one guard approached him, yanking his hands behind his back. One of the other men tapped something into his device, and a spotlight shone down from the top of the dividing wall. Liam struggled; he didn't want to make their job easy, but it didn't last long. A blow to the back of his neck brought him to his knees, and his vision blacked out as they lifted and carried him away.

He awoke in a damp, cold room, with moans sounding around him. Liam's eyes adjusted to his surroundings and the dim glow in the distance. Metal bars enclosed him in a sort of prison. Standing on wobbly legs, Liam stumbled up to the bars on the opposite and leaned his head between the gap to catch someone's attention. No guards were present. His heart pounded in his chest as he realised where he was. He found himself locked in the cells he'd come across before. He didn't bother to scream; doubted anyone would hear him, and even if they did, they wouldn't help.

Liam shuffled to the back of the cell and slumped to the floor, turning his head to the cell on his right. A man was inside, hunched over. All bones. Liam smiled, not knowing if the man could see him, or discern a smile from a frown. "You been here long?" Liam asked, studying the man's thin frame; he felt foolish for asking.

The man lifted his head, his expression mostly concealed by a lengthy white beard. "A boy your size won't hang around here for long," he groaned. "They'll give you work, no problem, but the ones like me," he bashed his chest with his fist. "We're left in here as punishment."

Liam couldn't help thinking of the man he'd spoken to in here before. He was a young, fresh-faced man, if you looked past the bruising. Where did they take him?

"Work? What do you mean?"

The man laughed again, followed by a cough. "Anyone sent here can either work on the outskirts or stay put and die. No other option."

Liam leaned closer to the railing. "The outskirts? They're forbidden, though. Mostly uncharted," Liam said, moving his head closer. "What work is possible out there? It's nothing but a wasteland."

"I'm not there, so I can't say. But I've been told I have the better deal; take that as you will."

Liam leant against the bars, the icy sting of metal burning through his top. His eyes weren't adjusting well to the darkness.

After what felt like hours, a guard appeared, the scent of warm soup wafting in with him. The man in the cell beside him leaned against the bars, pleading for food or water, but the guard did not react.

It was hard to tell the time of day, given the cells remained in eternal darkness. The guards' patrols ensued sporadically, which Liam assumed was a way to disorientate the prisoners' concept of time. Liam had slept for so long the back of his head was sore. All he wanted was to see Alex again.

Liam awoke once more at the sound of footsteps coming down the hallway, each one in sync—a mob of them.

Through the window in the door, Liam saw Governor Granswick, his dark crisp uniform vanishing with the shadows around him as he entered. "Liam, there seems to have been a mistake." Granswick clicked his fingers, and one guard unlocked the door. "They should have never taken you to this... place. Come, follow me. I have some pressing words to share with you."

The man in the neighbouring cell uncurled from the corner, clutching the bars with both hands. "You mean he's free? You're letting him out?" he shouted. "Let me out, sir. Please. I won't cause harm."

Liam approached Granswick, unsure of how much he trusted him. Were they about to send him to the outskirts?

"Deal with his request," Granswick whispered to a guard. "Follow beside me, boy." Liam did as he was told and strode beside Granswick, while his guards secured the rear. The dark hallways erupted with a burst of light as they reached a small set of stairs, circling up into the world, he remembered. The clean, white walls of New Albion. "I'm sorry you had to go down there. I told my men to collect you, and well, you were placed in the cells by mistake."

Liam scratched the back of his head, stroking the lump where someone had struck him. Was him being placed in a cell overnight truly a mistake, or a warning?

When they eventually reached Granswick's office, Liam went to take a seat, but the look in Granswick's eyes made him stay standing. "So, you wanted to speak to me? Sir."

Granswick's lips curled. "Yes. After the events of Lottery Day, well, things have been difficult. Robert told me about your mother." He paused. "I am truly sorry for your loss."

"Thank you, sir."

Sweat travelled in rivulets down Liam's back. What was Granswick thinking? He must know about the audio files and how they came from Liam, how he had caused all this trouble. Why had he released him from the cell? Liam had expected to be killed on the spot, yet here Granswick was, calm. Relaxed.

"Those recordings," Granswick began. "The rebellion group bugged and followed you. I suppose you want to seek revenge on them and see that they're punished for your mother's death?"

Liam looked up at the governor, unsure if he'd heard him correctly. Liam blamed no one but the man before him for his mother's death.

"I need to know where your loyalty stands, Liam. You

are a great asset to us—to me. A boy who has taken to a new world and reached the very top of it. You're a good one to have on side. You have impressed me, but when you didn't sign in for work... well, to say I was disappointed would be an understatement."

"My mother died, sir. I needed some time."

"Look at me when you address me." Granswick clicked his fingers, and Liam looked up. "I understand the feeling of loss. My mother was taken far too soon as well, but those recordings... we haven't been able to find the root of them. I know the bugging device came through to this side and passed across No Man's Land, but how did they attach it to you? Do you know?"

Liam kept eye contact, wanting to laugh at the thought of selling his sister out after just losing his mother. Liam shook his head. "No. I had no idea until I heard the recording myself, sir."

Granswick stepped across the room and opened the door. "Follow me." He turned on his heel and departed from the area, with Liam following close behind until they reached another set of stairs: steep, grey metal steps that lead to the building's rooftop. Liam had never been up there before; in fact, he'd never been so high up in his life. His stomach fell and his legs wobbled beneath him as he took in the view. "I care for all the people you see before you, Liam. Each one is under my rule, including those over there, in the district, and everywhere in-between. I care about each one of them, but I stop caring as soon as they lie to me."

Liam followed Granswick's hand to the blue painted rooftops of Old Albion before glancing back at Granswick, whose jacket flapped in the wind. He glared at Liam.

"Old Albion is separate, isn't it? Mayor Lewis has run it

ever since the divide."

Granswick's laughter carried on the air. "Mayor Lewis couldn't run a thing by himself. He hides in the family manor on the outskirts, away from all real responsibility." His smile vanished when his eyes found Liam's, and leaning closer, he whispered, "He does what he's told, and that works for the both of us. Never underestimate me."

Liam nodded. "I understand, sir."

"Your friend, Alexander." Granswick pulled his collar tight around his neck. "We sent him on a mission to retrieve those recordings before they were brought to anyone's attention. Did he not inform you of the intel before Lottery Day?"

Liam licked his dry lips. The wind made it hard to hear Granswick, but he understood the message he was trying to sell. Liam had lied to him, and Granswick was aware of it. He even knew about the mission. "You once said to me, sir, that nothing goes unnoticed. I'm sorry to have lied. I didn't realise you knew of the recording."

He let out a chuckle. "I know everything that goes on, Liam. I need you to have a think about where your loyalty lies. You and Alexander have grown close; you've broken a few rules, and even taken him across the divide, if I recall. All these acts are harmless and count towards the data gathered for the Freedom Day initiative. But I cannot allow people here to be working alongside the rebellion. It is too dangerous for our country and our future." He stepped forward, clasping his hands behind his back. "So, I'll ask again. Who bugged you?"

"I don't know, sir. I worked for the dock before this, and I know they've traded with the rebellion group in the past. It could have been anyone from the district. I'm sorry to have let you down, sir."

Granswick narrowed his eyes. "Fine. I'd still like you by my side." He paused and inhaled the fresh air. "Tell me, how much do you think you know about life outside these walls?"

Liam felt another lesson coming from Granswick, who seemed to enjoy dwelling on stories from the past. It reminded Liam of a father reading bedtime stories to a child, but if it kept Granswick calm—and Liam alive — he was willing to play along. "Only what I see in front of me. Like I told you before, I never really went to school or thought about anything beyond the walls around me."

Granswick smiled. "I'm somewhat jealous of your naïve ability to see the world through such a narrow lens." He crouched and closed one eye, pointing again into the distance. "This land changes. There is a reason the outskirts are kept from our maps, and why it is forbidden to travel across. Do you know why?"

"As kids, we were told stories about monsters, sir. All I know is that anyone who's gone has never come back."

"That's somewhat true. The weather ruined this world; it's changed countries, moved borders, and invited war. Now we face the same fate. Less land, frequent floods, grounds which change with each season: dry some years, drowning in others. There's nowhere safe out there, or at least that's what we thought."

"We heard stories at the docks that, under the water, lays old homes and land. We never knew how true it was."

"People say New Albion is the only future, and I believe that to be true. We can't take everyone with us. We left people behind in the past. Every remaining country fights for life—a future. I think we have found the answer to that here."

"But you're worried that it's now all at risk?"

"I don't blame the people for fighting. It's in our nature. But we are so close. We won't get a second chance at this. We are the pioneers, Liam. Another move from the rebellion could end us all. Do you understand?"

Liam peered out at Old Albion, tracing the dividing wall with his eyes. He understood; he knew what was right, and also who deserved the option of choice more. "The man in the cell. He mentioned prisoners going to the outskirts. Is it true?"

"The man said no return, did he not?" Liam nodded. "Then how can his tale be anything but a delirious story, if no one has ever lived to tell it?"

Liam wanted to question him more. He'd been caught in a lie and hated that Granswick was doing the same. But he said nothing. The outskirts meant nothing to Liam; his loyalty lied with Old Albion, the people who helped raise him, not the man who stood before him now. Granswick clearly trusted Liam, or at least wanted him around enough to keep him happy. That suggested Granswick might also keep Alex safe.

"Can you give me any guarantees? My father. Alex. Will they be safe if I stand beside you?"

"You test me, boy. The similarities are undeniable." Granswick rose to his feet again, chuckling. "Remember, I am the one in charge. It is a guarantee I want from *you*, not the other way around."

Liam narrowed his brows. Who was Granswick referring to? He'd mentioned in the past how Liam was familiar to him somehow.

"Put it this way, if you cause issues again, like the chaos seen on Lottery Day, then Alexander will see the force of the law first. Maybe then, you can both find out what happens to prisoners who go to the outskirts. Do I make myself clear?"

Liam nodded, blushing. He'd gotten too friendly, lured into a false sense of security by the openness of Granswick's conversation. He needed to take what he'd learnt and remain silent to prevent its ever being used against him.

Liam left the rooftop and made his way back to familiar ground until reaching his father's office, his feet naturally taking him there. He saw him inside and heard his groans of annoyance as he pushed open the door, finding his father surrounded by three screens, each displaying data and text Liam couldn't read and didn't care to.

When Robert looked up, he rushed toward his son. "Liam. Thank god," he said, wrapping his arms around him. Liam wasn't used to this, the hold of a loving parent. He thought such feelings had died with his mother, so he relaxed into the hug. "I heard about your mother." Robert hung his head. "I never had time to put things right."

"Few do. It's why you should try when you can."

"Are you back here for good?" Robert gripped Liam's arms. "Has Granswick allowed you to stay? Those recordings were almost the end of me. They got me working on old tech and all sorts of rubbish for punishment. The things I had to promise him to keep my job—my life. I hope it was worth it." Robert looked at the screen on his desk.

There was no time for pointless chatter. Robert was acting like nothing had happened. Maybe he'd always been a useless father, and Liam hadn't realised until now.

"Maya knows about you. She recognised your voice. I've told her everything."

"I see." Robert sank into his chair, and the previous bounce to his movements vanished. "How is she?"

"She's coping in her own way. She doesn't understand

why you left us."

Robert tapped the table with his fingers. "Would she meet me, do you think?"

Liam thought back to all the years Robert refused to see them, not even bothering to contact them with a letter. Why would he now risk his life when he hadn't before?

"Isn't that dangerous after everything you've gotten away with? They'll find out."

"Your mother is gone. I need to do something, offer *something*. I'll go to a trading post and meet her in the divide, away from prying eyes."

Liam raised his eyebrows. "You'll be killed. Eventually, they would find out."

"It's worth the risk. If you see her, tell her I want to meet."

Liam toyed with the idea of telling his father about the rebellion he was now a part of. But no secret was ever safe for long in these four walls. He'd said too much.

"Granswick had guards take me to a cell; he left me there for a bit to worry and then took me on a personal tour to the rooftop."

"He did?" Robert huffed. "Must be serious. We don't seem to have many guards left over here anymore. I see fresh faces every day, new recruits from Freedom Day, boys walking around with no experience. The roof top is his brief escape, no eyes or ears there. What did he say?"

"Told me to pick a side, and that there's a bigger picture to all this. He said I shouldn't worry about Mayor Lewis, then ended the tour with a threat that really got me thinking."

Liam thought of Alex and hoped he was safe.

"What did he say about the mayor?" Robert asked, a glint in his eye.

"Not much, why? What do you know?"

"They're old friends, who go back years, long before the divide. As far as I know, they used to work together. There have been... stories about the two of them, bonds that make little sense. They're supposed to be rivals, but Granswick is always loyal to him and protects him. I wondered if he'd let anything slip to you."

"If he did, I didn't clock it."

A knock at the door abruptly halted Liam and Robert's conversation.

Liam stood upright, looking up at Alex, who stepped in, his hair a tumble of blonde as he closed the door behind him. Liam went forward, reaching for Alex and kissing him. Alex stepped back, his eyes darting to Robert behind them. "I'm glad to find you both here. I heard you'd been called in and taken to the cells. I tried to get to you, but..."

Liam smiled at Alex, relishing every movement of his lips. "I'm safe. Granswick still wants me to work here beside him to show off the good work of the Freedom Day programme."

Alex looked past Liam at Robert once again, who was back on his desk, pretending not to eavesdrop. "What have you told him?" Alex whispered into Liam's ear. "Nothing about the rebellion, right?"

Liam shook his head, though he wanted to tell his father and explain where the recording came from, explain how far Maya had gone in the group, to tell him how proud he was of her, and how he should be, too. "I'm going to tell him. He needs to know; he might help."

Alex gripped Liam's hand. "Think before you do. We don't know who we can trust."

Robert coughed. "What are you two whispering about?"

Alex kept hold of Liam's hand as Liam stepped towards Robert. "There are things I need to tell you. Are we free to talk in here?"

Robert raised a brow, tapping something into his device before offering his hand for Liam's device, too. "Be quick. They'll notice if we are offline for too long. What is it?"

Alex turned to Liam, his eyes wide. Liam wiped his sweaty palms on his trousers and said, "The rebellion... the recording came from Maya. She joined up when Gil sent her to do some trade."

"Maya!" Robert slammed his fist onto the table. "My girl bugged your clothes and sold us down the river? No. I can't believe that. Nic was the leader. It would have been down to her."

"Maya has taken that burden too. She's been chosen to lead the group, and Alex and I are working with her, too."

Liam held his father's gaze. He was taking a risk, but he wanted to trust him. To use the power his father held, they had to win him around by telling him the whole truth. Perhaps the danger of losing Maya to the rebellion would be enough for Robert to fully switch sides, or so Liam hoped.

Robert bit his lip. "What? You can't be here, son. If that's true, then you must leave."

"Please. We need you to help us from the inside. It's all Maya wants—all she asks." Liam said.

Alex stood between them, raising his hands between them both. "Your father is right, Liam. Granswick is only using you; he wants you to agree to anything. I've found a few things out, and while it's nothing concrete, I've heard enough talk about it." Alex looked at Robert. "Can this information stay between us three?" Robert nodded, crossing his arms. "New Albion has people working and living in Old

Albion; they hide away and feed information back to us. The call for Nic to be killed didn't come from Granswick. A request was assigned to plants operating in Old Albion." Alex sighed. "I think there may be some in the rebellion group too, working alongside them. We need to be careful here, only speaking to those we trust."

Robert ran a finger along his chin. "Alex is right. You need to leave here, Liam. Get out, quit, do whatever you need to do. It's not safe for you here anymore. Alex and I can co-ordinate information between us and send it back to you."

Liam stood, helpless, as the two men in his life battled out strategies and tactics without him. He wanted to step in and offer advice, but he already felt so defeated.

"You want to help us?" Liam asked his father. "To work with us?"

"I've wanted to do something for years. The rebellion has had many forms, and though some have come close, they've never reached the finish line. If what you say about Maya is true, then now I must act, no matter what the outcome means for me. I can't lose her because of my mistakes."

"That's very noble of you, sir," Alex said. "But for now, we need more information, more members and people behind us."

"I can get access to stuff. I need to speak to Maya first. Meanwhile, you pay Mayor Lewis a visit. He's bitter and drunk enough to spill a secret or two. We need to get something on Granswick, something we can use against him. I'll bet Mayor Lewis holds some answers, if the rumours are true."

"Granswick mentioned the outskirts that Mayor Lewis could stay out there. Is that a possibility?" Liam asked.

Robert pursed his lips. "I've heard talk of a manor on the

outskirts for years. Granswick has spoken rarely about his life before the divide, but on occasions, he's mentioned a family home that had been left to ruin."

Alex smiled. "I can look through some of the old maps that are restricted. The manor must be on Old Albion's side, close enough to the district for the Mayor to use it. That should narrow it down for me to find something. Leave it with me."

Liam nodded as they switched their devices back on. He looked at his father's office, where he'd spent so many years alone. He wondered if he'd step foot in New Albion again once he left today. Recently, Liam planned to move his whole life here, and now his plans were to take it down. He just hoped he wouldn't lose anyone else by doing so.

Chapter Twenty-Four

Whispers Echo

Maya endured another sleepless night, the haunting responsibilities of No Man's Land keeping her awake. The room remained adorned with Nic's possessions, like a museum of life and death. Maya stood in the very space she'd taken a man's life, and though no blood lingered, it forever stained her mind.

With a heavy sigh, she rubbed her eyes. How many lives might she take while in charge?

The thought of home lingered, even if it held no allure now. Glancing up through the window in the ceiling at the still dark sky, Maya realised she had a few hours before daylight.

Straightening, she settled into Nic's desk, eager to absorb as much information about her newfound obligations as possible. She sifted through hastily scribbled notes and pieces of paper detailing recent deals and trades. In one of the desk drawers was a worn notebook, formed from an assortment of hastily gathered papers and off-cuts of card. Opening it, Maya was shocked to find it brimmed with details. It documented a historical record dating back to the first year the divide was erected.

As she turned the pages, the diary-like entries transitioned into more crisp, informative records. The first leader, who lasted only two years, chronicled a grim history of death, inflicted by fighting and the struggle for necessities. An internal tug warred inside Maya. A desire to pause, yet the need to understand her present compelled her to press on.

The notebook transformed, mirroring the evolution of leadership—from an idealistic beginning to the pragmatic management of a small country. Maya bowed her head, anxious about the legacy she had to live up to. At first, the people of No Man's Land had no contact or aid. Leaders battled against joining up with Old Albion, while the citizens refused to acknowledge New Albion's existence. Later, plans involved official pleas for aid, government rejections, and a bitter sting as Mayor Lewis, someone Maya had once held in high regard, signed agreements to withhold help.

Growing up, Maya believed her side of the country to be the heroes, the ones who offered help and refuge to those who needed it. Her mother was an obvious example of this, dedicating her life to aiding those in need. The notebook's pages painted a different reality.

As she learnt of the history and each failing leader, a pattern emerged. Each leader found the problem was the divide, though not the physical wall—through the nation's citizens. That was the rebellion's weakness. At the end of the scrapbook, Nic journaled her last thoughts and ideas. She noted that the previous leader hoarded explosives, passed them down, and stored them for the day the wall fell. Maya ran her finger along the dried ink as she read the last letter Nic wrote.

'The next leader needs to be a connection, a bridge between us and them. I have searched for months without success. The people of Old Albion are tired, working, struggling to stay alive. The people here mean well—they're strong—but it isn't enough. A new girl came to deliver for Gil recently and broke every rule in the book to do so. I liked that. Wasn't sure she was up to much at first, but she's shown she's willing and holds a certain power when it comes to connecting with the people. When I was looking down the barrel of a gun, she took the culprit's life to save mine. She didn't question risking her own for the good of the group. To protect our information. Not many would do that to go against their family. I asked a tremendous amount of her, and I was surprised by her success. She quickly formed bonds with a few of the members, even reuniting Lucas with his sister. At least I can go to my grave knowing their parents got their wish. What really sold me on Maya was her connections to Old Albion. Her mother is a beacon of the community. Maya has a face that people trust; she's someone the people want to please and listen to. It may be reckless, but I think she's the link to ending this and finally getting past the last hurdle. The bridge we have been searching for all these years.'

Maya stopped reading. Nic laid the groundwork, and now she knew her goal; following in the footsteps of past leaders, dismantling the wall, and opening the country's eyes to the harsh truth. As she thought through the list of past leaders, who each left behind a small legacy, uncertainty about her own future crept in. She understood the change she sought would live on through the people she survived, those who carried the torch long after she was gone. She needed to make her mark on history while she could and keep the momentum going while they had it. It wasn't something she was prepared to waste.

The sea air revived Maya's spirits. Despite the recent events in her life, the familiar routines of the men and women at the dock continued, seemingly unaffected by the change in recent times. A wave of conflicting emotions washed over her as she approached Gil's office. Quitting her job felt like an act of betrayal, though it was a choice she had to make to focus her time and limited energy solely on the group.

Inside Gil's office, she found him engrossed in paperwork, sitting before the backdrop of a rusted ship. "Gil, do you have a moment?" Maya asked.

He looked up, the lines on his face etched deeper than she'd noticed before. "Didn't expect to see you here so soon," he said, pushing against his knees to stand. "I've got all the time in the world, as long as you're quick. We have a few citizens wanting to get a boat over to West Country."

"To go back to the West? Are things really that bad here?"

"Well, with the riots starting, things can only get worse. We've seen it before; me and your mother know it all too well." Gill looked at the floor. "Sorry. I forget sometimes she's no longer with us. I was sorry to see her go."

Maya managed a smile. "It doesn't seem real that she's not here."

"I didn't book you any shifts, but if you need money or support, I'll give it to you. No labour needed."

There were things Maya wanted from Gil today, but for the first time, money wasn't one of them.

"I've been keeping busy, distracting myself with other things. I'm not here for work, Gil, and not for handouts either."

"I see." Gil settled back into his chair. "Then what brings you here?"

"It's No Man's Land. The supplies have been cut off since Nic's..."

Gil narrowed his eyes. "You ain't still part of that, are you? That group is heading in one direction, Maya. You need to use this opportunity to get out of it before they lure you any deeper. Don't think it'll be long before they choose another one and try to square up a deal with me again."

Maya felt the urge to reveal her new role, yet held back. "They need a trading agreement again. Getting in and out from this side is easy for one person, but anything larger is near impossible at the moment."

Gil nodded. "They've blocked off all routes, including those we need for larger shipments. There's nothing I can do, Maya. I've seen New Albion move things around, upping the shifts of guards in the busier areas. Most of them are around the main district now, watching the wall. I won't get my own men caught. Not now."

"Will you do it for me when it's safe? Just the basics, like water, some food?"

Gil bit his lip and scratched his white stubble. "I promised your family I'd keep an eye on you. I'm never one to let a promise go." He sighed. "I can't guarantee anything now, but if it's safe and I see an opening, I'll get something across. But you must promise me one thing."

Maya leaned on the door frame. "What?"

"You'll end all communication with that place. Don't step foot across the divide. Focus on your future, wherever or whatever that may be."

Maya felt the need to itch her scar, the branding on her

ankle. It was challenging to meet Gil's gaze as she agreed to his demands. She hated lying to him, but had no other choice. As the fledgling leader she was, making deals meant embracing uncomfortable compromises. If it ensured people got water and maintained their strength for what lay ahead, then it was a sacrifice worth making.

"Maya, before you go... will you update me when the new leader is picked? I don't want any surprises later on if I'm going to be doing trades again."

A further nod had Maya agreeing to another lie. Doubt lingered in the corners of her mind, but she couldn't afford the luxury of second-guessing herself. Swift decision-making was imperative and questioning her choices only hindered progress.

Maya was running late, the gathering crowds a testament to the urgency. The sun hung low on the horizon, casting a dusty glow around her feet as she turned the corner toward Mayor Lewis's residency in the district of Old Albion. Her mother had always tried to see the good in this man, vouching for his efforts on this side of the country. The rebellion group, however, held a different view. Mayor Lewis had been in power ever since the divide went up, his public appearances becoming less and less as the years rolled on. Now, with momentum building among the residents since Lottery Day, Maya had aimed to capitalise on the unrest. This meant projecting their message to the only man capable of legally implementing change.

She turned the corner and froze. The crowds had swelled beyond Maya's expectations. Standing atop a rusted van was Carla, her long blonde hair dancing in the wind. Her voice rang out, strong and determined. "We are here to make a change, to reveal the truth once and for all," she proclaimed, inciting cheers from the crowd. "We were lied to, all of us. Everyone we've lost results from their lies, and Mayor Lewis needs to answer." The crowd roared their agreement as people of all ages raised their arms in support. Towards Mayor Lewis's office, a few men rattled the iron gates, attempting to force them open. A palpable anger permeated the air, tipping dangerously close to rage. Maya hesitated to quell it. This country had remained stagnant for far too long. If there was ever a time to let rage run rampant, it was now.

Maya pushed through the crowd toward the van where Carla stood and pulled herself up onto the bonnet. She surveyed the surrounding faces, the countless expressions of support and passion. New spectators gathered in the back, their faces uncertain of what to believe. The recording played once again from the van, the same one that resulted in Nic's death and her mother's demise. It appeared to have a calming effect on the onlookers as they noted every word, every lie. Many shook their heads, a ripple of murmurs heard among the crowd. The group of men assaulting the gates redirected their attention to the newcomers. Rage boiled at the surface, and Maya knew she needed to act before the situation escalated. With the lack of guards patrolling Old Albion recently, there would be no stopping them. The men formed a barrier with clenched fists and knuckles white with tension.

Maya joined Carla and raised her hand, taking the megaphone from her. She positioned herself between the two opposing groups. "Please, before you air your doubts, I need you all to think and listen to what you heard on Lottery Day."

"It's nothing but lies! The recording is a fake!" someone yelled from the crowd.

"That rebellion group created it to force their way into

our homes," another added. Maya spotted the man shouting. It was George. He'd sold a kidney for a Lottery Day ticket, and now he was here, standing against the movement. Maya glanced at the men lined up opposite, readying to fight. She raised her hand to prevent their advance. They were on her side, and it was her responsibility to calm the brewing tension. Raising the megaphone, Maya declared, "The recording is real. It was created by my own hand; in fact, it was a recording of my brother, who worked on the other side for the Freedom Day initiative." She paused, letting the weight of her words settle. "They have been lying to us for years, pushing us into boxes for their own gain. Now's the time where we must see through the lies and work together."

The murmurs from the crowd heightened. "We can't trust people from No Man's Land; we can't trust a word they say."

"I am from here," Maya replied, keeping her voice steady. "I grew up here; I've lived in Old Albion my whole life." She glanced at George, a man she had spent countless evenings with drinking at The Old Vic. She wanted him to hear her; wanted to get through to him. "The divide tore my family apart. Lottery Day ended with my mother dying in the streets, yet I'm still here, standing witness to a change, one we can all prosper from."

The tension remained in the audience and among the men beside her. Panic crept into her mind, fearing a repeat of Lottery Day. "Wait!" a voice from the crowd yelled. The men halted. "It's Emma's girl. Maya, isn't it?"

Maya shielded her face to identify the speaker. A small woman in tattered clothing approached, her kind blue eyes meeting Maya's. "Your mother was a wonderful person. She spoke of her children with such delight." Maya recognised the accent. It was the woman from the West Country. "You both cared for me and reunited me with my family. Your mother found us a home, clothes, and food. You're her daughter, are you not?"

Maya nodded. She remembered Mithra from the day she and her mother helped to reunite her with her children. "That's right. I'm glad to see you're doing well, Mithra." Maya smiled. "I know my mother helped many people here. She taught me everything I know about the world, about life's injustices."

Mithra smiled and stepped past the men toward Maya. "I stand with you," she said. "The West Country is following in the footsteps of Albion. We see first-hand what the future holds if we let them take it from us." Behind her, more people followed; Mithra's children were first, and then there were others—kids and adults, some from the West Country, and others from the district. Each passed with a smile or nod, forming silent rows alongside Maya, who couldn't help but grin when George relaxed his stance and moved to stand beside Mithra.

As time passed and the sun descended, the crowd outside Mayor Lewis's home swelled. He hadn't shown his face, instead refusing to comment or join the movement, but Maya didn't need him. Her influence had already expanded, bridging the gap between No Man's Land and the place she called home. While her support might be small, it had the strength to grow stronger with time. She'd lit the embers, and that was all she needed to create a fire.

Maya looked up at the sky, thinking of her mother, and thanking her for all the good she'd done, and all the people she'd helped who had made this moment possible.

Carla tapped Maya on the shoulder before embracing her. "The message is getting out there, Maya. We're going to split the crowds soon before guards arrive. But we've done it.

We're one step closer."

"It'll be worth it, won't it?"

"Maya." A man leaned toward her. "We have a request for you in No Man's Land, on the side of New Albion, near the trading point."

"A request? From who?" Carla asked.

"No name, but they want to talk about a trading opportunity. Could be worth it." Maya glanced at Carla, hoping for an answer. "Lucas will meet you at the base camp; he'll be with you. It's all we could agree on."

In the darkness, wind lashed at Maya's cheeks as she picked up speed, riding alongside Lucas. They both enjoyed the calm and solitude their journey provided. Following his lead, they passed the base camp and traversed small settlements—snippets of the lives people had forged for themselves in this unforgiving place. Maya ventured deeper into No Man's Land, further than ever before. The more she distanced herself from the capital, the wider the divide became between each side. She observed the empty space of dust and dirt, a barren wasteland offering no chance for life to grow or survive. "How much further?" she shouted over the wind.

"Not far, though we're reaching the limits of where we should be. The message said to go northwest until we see the red light."

"Any idea who this is?"

Lucas shook his head. "No, but they must be worried about being caught. This is miles out from New Albion's city."

After a few more minutes, a red beacon became visible ahead, blazing bright atop the divide. Maya and Lucas parked beside the grey wall. "They wanted me to meet alone?"

"That's right. They said they would strike a trade deal if you did. We need anything we can get, Maya. Knowing there are still people on that side willing to go against Governor Granswick is good news. We need to spread the message on that side as much as we need to on the other."

They approached until reaching a ladder hanging against the wall, forged from metal chains. "I take it that's for me?" Maya asked, pulling on the ladder.

"If you want me to follow, I will."

Maya rested a hand on Lucas's shoulder. "No. I'll go alone. You're in charge if I don't come back."

Lucas laughed and brushed away her hand. "No thanks. I've just got my sister back. I don't want to risk that for a role I'll be no good at."

Maya smiled, thinking of Carla. They shared so many similarities. She placed her foot on the ladder's first rung and gripped the cold chain with both hands. "You'll be here when I come back, right?"

"Of course, boss."

Maya gritted her teeth as she climbed the unsteady ladder, feeling the light night breeze. Her arms tensed with each rung, and she refused to look down. Heights were not her usual domain; she had only ever gazed up at the wall, never down from it. Eventually, she reached the top. Up high, the air felt cooler, and the wind more powerful. She turned, peering down at Lucas, who was barely visible in the dark. As she did, she spotted a figure on the other side, close to the edge. Their long coat waved in the wind, and a trail of smoke escaped their lips, with Maya noting the dim glow of a cigarette.

"I'm here," Maya called toward the figure; her feet felt

unsteady at such a height.

The person stepped closer to the red beacon until the crimson glow illuminated their face. Maya saw her father for the first time in years. Hearing his voice had been unsettling, but nothing compared to seeing him in person, an arm's length away. Maya's heart raced, and she forced her legs to remain upright. She rested a hand on the beacon to prop herself up, taking in his face. He had aged, as everyone had, but the chiselled jaw that Liam inherited poked through the ravages of time.

Her father smiled and opened his arms. In a deep voice, he whispered, "Maya. My little Maya."

The wind picked up as he stepped closer, meeting Maya near the wall's edge. "You wanted to make a trade deal? With me?"

He laughed, glancing at the small concrete shack to the side of him—an old guard's watch room. "Shall we speak inside? These winds will be the death of us." He gestured for Maya to precede, but she remained rooted to the spot. She looked at the floor again, weak at the knees. She stumbled slightly, catching herself on the beacon before her father could reach her. Shrugging off his help, Maya strode forward and opened the door that groaned with years' worth of neglect.

Her father joined her inside, and the dim yellow light bulb flickered to life. It was enough to illuminate the small room, highlighting more details of her father's face. "So, was this a big ploy to meet me?" Maya asked, crossing her arms and leaning back on the cold concrete bench.

Smiling, he sat opposite her in his pristine uniform, and the long coat without a broken seam. "A lot of things have happened in a short time. I reconnected with Liam when he came over. I wanted the same with you."

"You may sway Liam, but you won't fool me so easily. I'm not the little girl you last knew."

"Of course. I knew Emma would have brought you up to be the woman I see before me. I am already proud."

Maya rolled her eyes. Liam had forgiven their father, but she hadn't. She couldn't. "What do you want from this? To play happy families now Mum is gone?"

He bowed his head, his eyes meeting the floor. "I regret so much—some choices were made for me, and others I made myself. Losing your mother that way awakened something in me. As the group did for you, I assume."

"Your corrupt country awakened me, *Father*. The one you work for."

"As did Liam, yet you found a way to forgive him."

"I had nothing to forgive. You're the one who vanished from our lives, lied about your vote, and disappeared overnight as soon as the divide went up. You had no contact with any of us, instead you used your time to climb the ladder of greed." Maya sighed, peering up at the flickering light bulb.

"I don't expect forgiveness, but I am here now. I want to help. Coming here and meeting you so soon after the recording... it's dangerous for me."

"No one asked you to risk your life."

"No, but I wanted to. Liam left his job; Granswick threatened him to make a choice, bringing Alex's safety into question. We can work on one side, while you work on the other."

Maya met Robert's eyes. "Liam told you then? Everything we have planned?" Robert nodded, though Maya didn't have the energy to be angry at her brother. He must trust their father to be so open. She wasn't sure she could do the same. "How do I know this isn't a trap? This entire setup?"

"I would never put you in danger. I've had to travel to the outskirts for this meeting. My every move is tracked and accounted for, Maya. I've left my device behind. It's just us here. I promise."

Maya stared into her father's eyes. She found them comforting, as if she were a little girl again. She had never imagined those eyes could lie to her, but they had in the past. "What are you willing to do?"

"I worked on things for years; it's what I showed Liam when that recording happened. There's more, though, more than even I know."

Maya leaned forward. "I spoke with a woman called Lydia. She was killed under New Albion's orders. She told me that the votes released back then were a lie; some high up, well-off people bought votes to choose where they went to live when they brought in the divide."

Robert nodded. "It's true. A handful of council members who voted the wrong way ended up stealing the votes off others."

"Carla's parents held two of those votes that were stolen. They ended up here, you know." Maya pointed down at No Man's Land. "They died in a place where they shouldn't have even been."

"There are lots of casualties." Robert sighed. "It's why I want to help."

"It'll be dangerous. Are you willing to risk everything now?" Robert nodded. "But you weren't before? What's changed?"

Robert ran his hands through his hair. "I was only trying

to survive. I did what I needed; Kept my head down and worked. I had no one and got caught up in the theatrics of it all. Now I can see what the divide has done to people, how it was tweaked and plotted for a certain result. New Albion and Old Albion isn't the end goal here, it's just the beginning. If I want to put a stop to it and help it come crashing down, then it needs to be done now. Before the government become too strong to stop." Robert leaned closer, reaching for Maya's hands. "Tell me what you need, and I'll work to get it done. Let me help you. Now I know you're the leader. It's only a matter of time before Granswick acts, and I cannot lose you, Maya. Not after Emma."

Maya stared at the lines running across his palms and his soft fingers. She glanced at her own hands, noting the cuts along her knuckles, the hard skin on her fingertips, and the dirt caked beneath her fingernails. "The next step you talk of is getting the people of New Albion on side with us. They need to know everything we do. We can't do this if we're fighting each other. Do people in New Albion know anything about what's truly going on?"

Robert shook his head. "No, they don't. People are kept on a tight leash there. They only interact with people in their zone; they all work and socialise with the same people. An echo chamber of opinions. It's what the government wanted."

"They all work the same job role, though, right? I remember Liam mentioning that."

"Mainly, yes. Data input to help improve AI. It's simple busy work."

"Then we use that. Once you have the information about whatever Granswick is working on, we'll spread it to every person's home and device to make sure they can't miss it."

Robert nodded, leaning back on the bench. "It could work; Granswick will know the source came from me, but it can be done."

"So, what do we do first? Any ideas?"

"No," Robert said. "Maybe something in the outskirts. There have been energy surges out there, but so much of our produce is grown there and brought in. Everything is so out of the way that anything else he's planning could be done in secret."

"What about trade for us in No Man's Land?"

Robert narrowed his eyes. "Maya, that was a ruse. I have no trading routes to offer."

"I need something to tell them."

"Ask Gil; he's the one with the connections, not me."

"I've sorted Gil. We need devices or equipment to sell to the West. That comes from you lot."

"Fine. I can get a few things, but not much. When we next touch base, I'll supply some tech to trade."

Maya smiled and stood. "It was good working with you, Father." She extended her hand to shake. "Hopefully next time we meet, we'll have enough to bring the country to its knees."

Chapter Twenty-Five

Outside

Darkness descended earlier with each passing day while the heat carried from the west faded, leaving the country in the grip of autumn. Stones crunched beneath Liam's boots as he trod along the dilapidated path leading toward the city's outskirts. The omnipresent divide loomed beside him.

Liam scratched absently at the back of his neck, noticing the outstations were eerily vacant for this time of day, the guards having abandoned their posts. His gaze refocused towards Old Albion, where smoke rose into the air from various locations. In recent days, the public had become restless; they clashed in the streets and broke into shops and homes, leaving them in more ruin than before. In this volatile environment, a tiny spark had the potential to ignite the entire country, a prospect that filled Liam with fear. He yearned for the naïve image of New Albion he once shared with Alex in those days when ignorance was bliss. Were people better off remaining oblivious, shielded by deception?

Liam slowed his pace as he neared the station, treading cautiously, despite the absence of guards. Standing beside the divide, he felt the coolness of the grey metal beneath his touch. He reached for the door handle and peered through the small window of the guard's shelter. Empty. He groaned, swung the door open, and found chaos inside: broken tables and chairs lay scattered. Someone must have ransacked the place. Liam stepped through and made his way toward the central door separating Old Albion from New. It was a formidable slab of metal with bolts the size of his hand. Locked. He knocked three times, the resonant thuds echoing, as if within the belly of a sleeping giant.

He sat on a stool, resting his head on his hands as he waited. On the outskirts of the district, this outpost felt desolate. Any further, and Liam would step into uncharted territory, a land from which no one had returned. Surveying the room, he speculated on the cause of such a mess, wondering if someone had fled the outskirts, seeking refuge from the terrors that lay there. There were no traces of animal marks. Human hands unmistakably worked this destruction.

After some time, three knocks prompted Liam to rise to his feet. He patted down his top and cleared his throat, his heart quickening as the door unlocked with a thud. The heavy metal groaned as someone slowly pushed it open. Alex peeked around the side of the door, his blue eyes scanning the room before a smile crept onto his lips. "We did it." He stepped in and closed the door behind him, brushing his hair from his face. "Your father was right; they left this route abandoned."

"Did you make it here, okay? You weren't followed?"

Alex shook his head, pulling a hood over his face. "Not that I know of. Lucas helped me to get across No Man's Land. We shouldn't dwell here, though. We have quite the trek ahead."

Liam followed Alex's gaze outside towards the outskirts. The wind had calmed, yet the bitter chill lingered. With careful steps, they strode side by side into an unknown world that opened before them, wild and overgrown. They passed a once-guarded watchtower, now abandoned. Alex pulled out a piece of paper, biting his lip.

"What's that?" Liam asked, peering over Alex's shoulder. "Is it a map?" He noticed a compass etched at the top. "I thought no one had the outskirts mapped?"

"They haven't," Alex replied. "But Mayor Lewis seems to have kept this place under wraps for most of his life, so I made a copy of the records I found dated before the divide."

"I see." Liam scratched the back of his head. "I can't believe he's got a home out here in the wild. All those years we were told to never set foot out here in case we never returned."

"We may not yet," Alex said, studying the map. "This manor was once a well-known home, no doubt partly lost to nature, or whatever else goes on out here."

"Did father help you get this information then? I hope he's keeping to his word."

"He is. He met with Maya; said it was frosty, but agreed to help her, too." Alex slowed until he walked beside Liam, holding his hand. "We need to trust him; we need to be able to trust someone. Do you know what you want from the mayor?"

Liam shrugged. He hadn't thought too far ahead. He wanted to pass the outskirts first, find the manor, and see if

Mayor Lewis was inside. Only when they succeeded would he allow himself to think of the next steps. "Hopefully, he'll tell us some stuff about Granswick and offer something useful. Maya wanted me to do this, probably to keep me busy now that I have so much free time."

After a short walk, they stopped at a rusted, ivy-covered gate that blocked their view. Liam wrapped his fingers around the iron bars, peering through at the manor before them. "Is this it?" he asked, examining the cracked windows, fallen roof tiles, and overgrown garden. "It's hard to tell in the dark, but surely no one could live here?"

Alex pushed open the large gate, which groaned on its hinges. "It used to be a family home of the governors. Clearly Granswick doesn't respect the mayor much if he left him to dwell in a place like this. Maybe we could use that to our advantage?"

Liam stepped across the threshold, lifting his knees high enough to make it through the long grass towards the entrance. "No guards here either, by the looks of it."

"Who needs guards when you have the tales of the outskirts to protect you?" Alex said, ascending the stone steps to the front door. "We truly have been taken for fools."

"Do you ever wonder..." Liam tugged Alex's hand to stop him from going any further. "Do you ever wonder what life is like... out here?"

Alex raised an eyebrow. "Deadly."

"We're alright, though, ain't we? Maybe it's the answer to our troubles. I can't live in your land, you can't in mine, so why not out here?"

A closed smile tilted up the corners of Alex's lips. "We could go on an adventure and take our pick of leftover land and homes."

"We could find a bigger place than this."

"Grow our own food."

"And have animals, pets, and all sorts." Liam stood so close to Alex now he felt the warmth emanating from his chest. Alex laughed. "Oh, you were just playing along."

"It's a nice idea, but a dream that's far beyond our reach," Alex replied. "Maybe we can save it for another day." Alex turned, gesturing to the doorway. "Shall we?"

Liam rolled his eyes and stepped into the building. He wanted Alex to promise that one day they'd find a way to be together, but he knew life wasn't that simple, especially in this world.

Inside the manor, Liam could barely make out a once grand staircase through the darkness and a flicker of orange from the room upstairs. The shadows danced to their own music as Alex and Liam walked through the entrance hallway. Alex leaned closer, whispering, "Shall we go for the surprise? Someone's here, right?"

Liam nodded. "He's got to be. No one has seen him in the district since Lottery Day."

They ascended, following the light leading them down the hallway. As they grew closer to a door, slightly ajar, they heard sounds from inside—moaning, followed by a slight giggle. Liam looked at Alex, confused. Inside the room was an immaculate child's bedroom; the blue paintwork was spotless, and toys and dolls lined the wall above a wooden trunk. To the side, Liam saw the lantern beside a freshly made bed. "Who did you say owned this place before?" Liam whispered, tiptoeing into the room's centre.

"I didn't get all the information. All I know is that Mayor Lewis has been living here ever since the divide and it was partly in Granswick's name."

On the floor, Liam picked up the giggling toy and placed it on a shelf. Beside the toy was a family photograph—an elderly mother and father, Liam presumed, standing beside two boys and a young woman with a pram. Liam drew closer to inspect it, recognising the young woman right away. He'd seen her photo before. Before he could pick it up for a closer look at the others, a gunshot rang through the house, deafening Liam, who held his hands to his ears. He stepped forward towards Alex to protect him.

"What are you doing in my home?" Mayor Lewis yelled, stepping from the shadows.

Liam shook his head and then checked Alex up and down. There was no blood; no one was hurt. He raised his hands and followed Alex's lead. "Sir, we're not here to harm you."

Mayor Lewis stumbled, collapsing onto the bed. "Get out of my bedroom! Get away from my home." He looked at Alex's long black cloak. "That's from New Albion; what on earth are you doing out here?"

Lewis slurred his words, his breath stinking of rum and rotten ash. He'd handled drunk men many times and knew how to calm them, no doubt better than Alex could.

"We've come to speak to you, sir," Liam said, trying to keep things respectful. "I am from the district; you've been my mayor for most of my life."

"Poor you," he slurred, wiping his mouth. His eyes seemed unable to focus. "Did my brother send you? Wanting to check up on me?"

"Brother?"

Liam smiled, lowering his hands. This was the odd relationship his father mentioned. The rumours about Lewis and Granswick... were they family? "Granswick?" he guessed. "No. He doesn't know we are here." Liam turned to the photo again, assessing the young men in the image. It was of them. "He's your older brother, isn't he? Was this your home?"

"It still is *my* home." Lewis licked his dry lips. "What are you? Part of that rebellion group? Here to take down the government. I've seen it all before."

Liam refrained from laughing. He didn't want to admit Mayor Lewis had guessed so correctly.

"We want to know a few things about your relationship with Granswick, although I suppose we know a bit already," Alex said. "It isn't public knowledge that you're related; I've never heard that before."

Lewis chuckled, falling back onto the mattress. "People never talked about me. Hand me that photograph you keep staring at," he said to Liam, whose eyes widened. Liam handed him the photo. Lewis began pointing at the people in the photograph. "We have Granswick's mother, his father, Granswick's precious wife, his child, and at the bottom of the pile, me."

"Granswick has a child?" Alex remarked.

"This is about *me*!" Lewis yelled. "Not him. I am here, you know; I'm still around! Those lot aren't." Lewis threw the photo to the ground.

Alex glanced at Liam, confused. Liam stepped forward and picked up the photo again, unsure of how to react or reply. He's seen his fair share of drunkards in the past, but Lewis behaved more like a spoiled child. He squinted at the woman standing beside the pram. That's when it clicked. He'd seen her photo before in Gil's office draw, hidden away.

"The woman there. Who is she?" Liam asked, pointing at her.

Lewis narrowed his eyes. "Katherine. My brother's wife to be at one time. She didn't last, though."

Alex took the photo from Liam.

"You said they were Granswick's parents. Were they not *your* parents, too?" Liam asked.

"No." Lewis sat up. "I was adopted. The younger brother, who Granswick always looked down on. But I've always been there—always did what I was told. Maybe I should tell him about you both."

"There's no need for that. Granswick has already given me an ultimatum about New Albion," Liam said, stepping towards the lantern. "Let's just say I don't think I gave him the answer he wanted."

"Ha!" Lewis laughed, nearing Liam's face. "I see it now. It's obvious really. Did you work for him? I remember seeing your photo when President Alma visited." Lewis stumbled to his feet, and Liam watched the gun tucked into his belt. "You're the spit of him." Lewis grabbed Liam's chin, jutting it towards the light. "His precious son. No wonder you've gotten away so lightly and with so much. He never could discipline that boy of his."

Liam shook his head from Lewis' grasp and straightened, towering over Lewis. "What do you mean?"

"His son was to be a strapping young thing, the image of his father. The brat died, though, during the beginning of the divide, when all the riots and fights were happening. Wasn't that strong, after all."

Alex narrowed his eyes. "The riots were on this side mainly. Did his son vote against AI?"

"I wouldn't take much notice of those votes; a load of them were bought off, anyway. A few clicks on the computer, and the vote was switched to another user," Lewis smirked.

"Nah, his son Damion was a rebel through and through," Lewis said. "I never crossed the line. Did what I was told; I gave my vote to some rich old man and given this worthless job as a reward."

"You mean the role as mayor?" Alex asked, tapping his foot on the ground.

"They give me protection and send me my instructions; I apply their laws through Old Albion. We were told the country was split into two and that we made our own rules, but it's all lies. They control us—*he* controls us. And all I have to do is get drunk and live here like I always did."

Liam's cheeks glowed, and the ringing in his ears still stung. All this time, Granswick had ruled the country. All the poverty and struggles put upon this place were purposeful. "Why are you telling us all this? Aren't you worried we'll expose it all?"

Lewis smiled. "Don't you know most of this already? People know all sorts, yet it never gets around."

"Quite the risk," Alex said. "Maybe you want the news to travel? Show your brother you aren't so useless after all."

Lewis broke out into another fit of laughter, rolling along the bed. "Please. We've seen this play out before. Do you think you're the first group of people to work this out and try to make a change? You always fail. It's written in the bloody stars."

"People can't be that predictable. There comes a time when they reach their limit," Alex replied, moving closer to Liam.

"It's too late, anyway; most of the job is done. Granswick is already onto the next step while you remain focused on the now. Why do you think I've been sent over here to wallow in this mansion by myself? The protection has gone. Even

Granswick has been left with a measly supply of guards to offer him protection. Why were so many recruits for Freedom Day were assigned guard duty, do you think? These kids run around and act like soldiers, but they don't know a thing. Why else would he be so reckless in his choices? He's growing desperate; he's scared he'll be left behind with all of us while the next stage is set without him in it."

Liam ran his hand along his forehead. Granswick had mentioned a plan to him on the rooftop. He'd practically invited Liam to forge the future alongside him. Knowing Liam resembled Granswick's son explained why Granswick was soft on him. Mayor Lewis had given them all the information they needed. He was delusional—an arrogant drunk. "Come on Alex, let's go."

"What? Why?" Alex whispered.

"He'll take you with him, Liam." Lewis spat. "With a face that looks so similar to Damion's, he'll want to keep you close. You could work him with such ease. Not like me or your friend here. We're to be left behind, but you... I think you could make it. If Granswick gets there on time."

Liam furrowed his brow. "Are you going to tell us what the next step is, seeing as you're so loose lipped already?"

Lewis smiled and rolled his eyes. "If I could, I would. Being out here, alone with my family, can be lonely. We have spirits and wine in the cellar to last us years. You're welcome to join me when you're left all alone." Lewis pointed at Alex.

"Come on, let's go," Liam said, turning towards the door.

"Wait, before we do," Alex knelt to Lewis's eye level. "The votes that were faked. How many are we talking? Do you know?"

"Not enough to make a difference, but enough that people who wanted to be part of the future could make sure they were, no matter the result. Quite the scandal, if you can get the word out, that is."

"We already have," Liam replied with venom. "Old Albion knows the truth, and before long, New Albion will, too. Your brother may have been able to keep one side at bay in the past, but he won't be able to stop both."

"I wish you luck. Like I say, there's no love lost between my brother and me. What do I care if he loses? Losing Damion was enough to send him over the edge all those years ago, so I've played my part."

Liam clenched his fists. Mayor Lewis was goading them, waiting for them to bite. "Come on, we need to get home," Liam said, pulling Alex from the room. "He's a nutter."

"Maybe, but he has a whole host of information." Alex turned back towards Lewis and handed him his device. "Write some names down on here, just the names of stolen votes. I can do the rest."

Lewis narrowed his eyes but began tapping away. Before long, Alex put the device back into his pocket and joined Liam outside. "Do you think he killed Damion? He seems quite proud of the fact his nephew is dead."

Liam rolled his eyes. "What do I care? Both brothers are mad in different ways, causing all this chaos for some family feud. Doesn't it all seem pointless?"

"I've never seen Granswick in such a state as Lewis was today, though. Maybe he's the saner of the two."

Liam wrapped an arm around Alex as they crossed the outskirts. "Madness has many faces. All we can do is make sure we kill them all."

Chapter Twenty-Six

Guilty Mind

Wild winds swept the coast, making the dockyard sway and creak. Maya steadied her footing, taking slower steps along the dock. Behind her, the district simmered, a pressure cooker on the brink of exploding. In every direction, groups of citizens had gathered—some fought for justice, while others exploited the chaos for their own gain. The untamed laws of No Man's Land had infiltrated Old Albion, turning every man into a self-serving combatant, desperate for imminent change.

Maya relished the chaos she had played a part in creating. Unburdened by her mother's death, she continued the work of past leaders, seeing it through to the end. She sensed her friend's weariness as she watched Carla struggle against the wind; her vibrant blue eyes had dulled in recent weeks. Maya draped an arm around her shoulder. "We won't be long. Gil just wants a quick word, and then we can return to base. Liam and Alex should be there tonight. I hope the outskirts were safe for them."

"Is anywhere safe anymore? Look around, Maya. Recently, people were fleeing from the West Country, and now they're fighting each other to board a boat back over there."

Maya glanced at the rusted ships, three that she could see anchored at the dock; a mixture of citizens from Old Albion and West Country hurriedly embarked, laden with luggage. She regarded Carla, whose long blonde hair whipped in the wind. Was she cut out for this life? "It's tough now, but it'll be worth it. For what we can bring to this country."

Carla nodded, gazing across the ocean as they approached Gil's shack. Maya scanned the area, which appeared mostly deserted, if not for a half-empty mug resting on the table where Gil usually stood watch.

They ventured toward the boats, reaching the cargo area beneath the main dock. The creaking floorboards overhead provided some relief from the wind. Maya felt her breath slow as the stinging faded, and the sensation finally returned to her ears.

"Where are we now?" Carla asked, peering into the darkness.

"Shipment area. It's empty most of the time during a shift. It's where we used to come for some quiet or a rest during our breaks."

"I thought I was the only one who knew that trick," Gil said, stepping out from behind a shipment box. He flicked his cigarette to the floor, which disappeared between the cracks into the sea. "Carla, nice to see you. Wasn't expecting company."

Maya smiled, walking toward Gil. "It's okay. Where I go, Carla goes. We have no secrets."

Gil raised a brow. "Quite. How are things in the district? Can't say I've wanted to go in for a while; I'd rather keep my legs in working order."

"Tensions are high. It seems Nic's death wasn't quite the cut-off New Albion had hoped for," Maya said.

"You know, I've lost three men in as many weeks from fights or stabbings. Some have even gone off to loot stuff themselves. This place can't withstand the chaos for much longer."

"The fight is real, yes," Maya said. "But it's going to be worth it."

"You truly believe that?" Maya nodded. Gil pointed at Carla. "And what about you?"

She looked down at her feet, where the waves crashed below. "I... I don't know. But we can't turn back now. We have little choice but to go on."

"Gil," Maya said, "Why did you want to meet me here? I haven't got much spare time at the moment."

Gil laughed. "You've turned down my shifts and quit your delivery job, and yet you're short of time."

Maya bit her bottom lip. While she was used to Gil's bluntness, his coy demeanour set her teeth on edge. He fumbled for something in his pocket.

"Listen. Things are tough here and they're only going to get worse," he said, turning toward the sea. The ocean danced in his eyes. "I made a few promises in my life, most of which I didn't keep. But your mother and father? Our friendship goes all the way back to our teenage years."

"Gil, I really..."

"Please, let me say my bit." Maya bowed her head, allowing Gil to continue. "When they took your father, I promised him I would watch over you all."

"I know, Gil, and you've kept your word," Maya said. She lifted her hand to reach for him, but he let it hang there. Gil wouldn't accept or appreciate the gesture.

"I tried my best. Now she's gone and, well, my cards have been dealt." He met Maya's gaze. "I need to save you, girl." He pulled out some papers from his pocket. "I've got you a place on the boat. It's leaving for the West Country in a few hours."

Maya narrowed her eyes, looking at the papers and then Gil's watery eyes. "Why would I want to leave? Now we're so close to ending this?"

Gil rubbed his nose, his eyes darting to Carla. "It's a fresh start. The war is only starting over there, but there are parts that are safe. You have a better chance there than here. Please. Take the tickets and go."

Carla stepped forward, grabbing the papers from Gil. "No name. It's blank."

"I run these shipments; I can put who I want on there."

Carla glanced between Maya and the papers. "You should take the offer. Get out safely and let this play out."

Maya looked at the papers in Carla's grip. It was a good offer, but running away? Abandoning the rebellion and the connections she'd made? It simply wasn't an option, not with so much momentum behind them, not after all the death and loss she'd endured. She had to see this through until the very end, no matter what fate awaited her.

Maya stepped back. "No. I won't leave."

Gil lowered his head and rubbed his chin. "Carla. You've got family out there, right?" Carla nodded. "A fresh start for you both?"

Carla's eyes widened as she turned to Maya. Carla clearly found new hope in Gil's offer, but Maya had decided. Did Carla want to leave? After all, she wasn't in as deep as Maya; if Carla went, she could almost guarantee her safety.

"My brother," Carla said. "If I go, can I take Lucas? We can meet our family and start again."

"Carla, no. What are you saying?" Maya asked, gripping her friend's arm. She knew she shouldn't think this way, but it hurt knowing that Carla wanted to escape. "We're a team."

"The seats are yours if you can get back in time with him," Gil replied gruffly.

"I have to try, Maya. We spent so long apart, but a chance to connect with family over there would mean so much."

Maya looked at Gil, who couldn't meet her eyes. Carla rushed off, running to collect Lucas with the offer of a new life. Maya knew how important family connections were. Maybe Carla had a point.

The waves crashed behind Gil, and Maya licked the saltwater from her lips as she waited. "Okay," Maya said, stepping towards him. "We're alone now. Carla's gone. What did you *really* want to say to me tonight?"

Gil scratched his beard again. "Will you take the ticket? Will you get on the boat and go?"

Maya shook her head. "I can't do that, Gil. You know that."

Gil sighed and shouted over the crashing sea. "I've done some things in the past, girl. Things that haunt me."

"You've done good too. Look at what you did for No Man's Land."

"No. It was all for self-gain—to stay hidden."

"Hidden?" Maya stiffened, clenching her fists. "What do

you mean?"

He met her eyes for the first time since they'd been alone. "Lottery Day was a total shambles. I was meant to keep you all safe." A tear trailed down his cheek. "I loved your mother, maybe more than I should have."

"Gil, what are you trying to say?"

The guilt written in the lines on his face told her most of the story. She didn't want to believe it. It couldn't be true.

"When Nic was shot, that was supposed to be it—the end of it all, like a reset. But they hadn't expected you. You always were overlooked."

Maya sucked in a breath. "You know?"

Gil nodded. "I hoped you weren't; you were new to the group. I never thought you would be picked to replace her."

"It is what it is. With Mum gone, I had little else to lose. If she was alive, well... maybe my answer would have been different. But she isn't, so this is the path I chose."

"I'm so sorry, Maya. If I had known the crowd's reaction, I never would have done it. I'd have found another way. Created a different outcome." Gil covered his face with his hands, weeping.

Maya stepped back; they were both so alone. Rushed footsteps sounded above them, mixing with the sound of crashing waves. If she screamed, no one would hear her. "Gil..." she said. "What did you do?"

Gil looked up at her, his eyes alive in the moonlight. "I had no choice. I put it off for as long as I could."

"Put what off? Spit it out! You've never been one to mince your words."

Anger swelled within her. She knew what he had done.

"They told me to end it, so I did it swiftly so she felt no pain." He rubbed at his knuckles. "I got rid of the leader to reset and calm things for a few more years. When you told me about the plan for Lottery Day, it seemed like the obvious way to correct everything." He wiped a fallen tear. "But the path it set you on... I can never forgive myself."

Maya stepped forward, her hands as white as the moon above them. "Say it," she spat. "Tell me what you did!"

"I killed her, alright!" he shouted. "I shot her on that stage to end things, yet all it did was cause chaos—chaos you found power and momentum in."

Maya laughed; she didn't know what else to do. Gil had been nothing but a trusted family friend. For her entire life, he had been there for them, and now… it didn't seem real. "Do you work for them? The government?"

"Yes. I have for years. I kept an eye on this side to keep things moving along."

"And when they tell you to kill, you kill? No matter who it is?"

"No, I… I never meant for your mother to get hurt, but if I didn't follow the orders, it wouldn't have turned out well for me."

"Well, you have blood on your hands, Gil." Maya looked at the paperwork crumpled in his pocket. "So, you want me to leave? Why?"

"New orders came in for the new leader."

"They want me dead? So soon?"

Gil nodded. "You scare them, girl. If you get on the boat, I can say you're gone. I won't have to…"

Maya peered around; they were alone. Gil had called the meeting, shocked to discover Carla by her side. Yet he swallowed her offer, willingly letting Carla go to find her brother, leaving them isolated. She bit her lip, refusing to look away from him.

"To kill me," Maya finished. "You've known me since I was born, Gil. How could you even think about doing this?"

"I don't want to; I would do anything to make sure I don't have to."

"If I turn around and walk away, will you let me go?" Maya turned her foot, ready to leave. Gil wouldn't hurt her; she was almost sure of it. Almost.

"Maya." Gil's voice was deep, more serious than she'd ever heard it. "I can't let you walk away. They have me in a hold here and I don't have any options."

Maya stepped towards the stairs, away from Gil. When his footsteps followed hers, she paused and slowly turned to see his face for one last time. In his hand was the glint of a blade.

Chapter Twenty-Seven

Dead of Night

Surprisingly, the stroll through the outskirts proved tranquillity in contrast to the foreboding tales that had circulated during Liam's upbringing. He questioned the authenticity of everything he'd ever learned about the country. Had his entire life been one intricate web of deception?

The soothing pulse of stones beneath their boots marked the beginnings of Old Albion as they passed the outposts. Liam turned to Alex, who remained engrossed by the device in his hands since they departed the manor.

"Anything intriguing?" Liam asked, fixated on the photograph that had captivated his thoughts. He contemplated making a detour to seek answers from Gil and ask about the woman in the photograph. When Alex seemed oblivious to his question, Liam raised his voice a notch.

"Hey!" he exclaimed, prompting Alex to redirect his attention. "Lewis mentioned that the woman in the photo was Granswick's wife, presumably the mother of his child."

Alex affirmed with a nod, tapping on the device. "Yeah, he glossed over it, but she might be significant. Strangely, I've never seen or heard of her before. Guess Granswick likes to keep his personal life secret."

"I have."

Alex halted in his tracks, his full attention on Liam now. "Really? You saw her in New Albion?"

Liam shook his head. "No, in an old photo at the docks. I stumbled upon it one day when I was poking around for things I probably shouldn't have, and I questioned Gil about her."

"Odd. Is she from Old Albion then? What does Gil have to do with any of this?" Alex lifted his device to his eyes, once again engrossed. "Who was she?"

"Gil didn't say. He lost his temper and told me to stay out of his business. I asked him about it again on my last day before joining the program; Thought he might open up, but he shut the question down just as quick."

"I made a copy of the photo. Now that we're closer, I can run a scan on her image to see if there are any details. Might be worth a go." Alex's tongue stuck out from his mouth as he tapped away.

Liam chuckled and ruffled Alex's hair. "Always thinking ahead, aren't you?"

"It shouldn't take much longer. Let's keep walking. We can head to No Man's Land through the tunnels and see if it picks up any signal."

They continued, leaving the solitude of the outskirts towards the district. The night air turned bitter, and the breeze picked up closer to the coast. "Any signal?" Liam asked, peering at Alex's screen.

"A bit, though we would have finished this in seconds if we were on the other side, but seeing as the signal's low—and I'm in private mode—it slows stuff down." Liam smiled. "Oh! It's found a match. Katherine Wilson. She's alive." Alex paused. "She's based in New Albion Medical Centre D."

"Medical? What's wrong with her? Does it mention any family, a husband—anything?"

Alex's eyes scanned the information, darting from left to right. He scratched his head and met Liam's gaze. "This isn't making sense. You said Gil had a photo of her, right?"

"Yeah. I haven't seen it since that day, but I remembered her face the second I saw the photo in Lewis's room."

"It says here that her emergency contact is Gil."

Liam stepped back. Gil had never mentioned having a woman in New Albion. She couldn't have been his wife or sister. She was too young, and besides, Gil had always been a loner. Liam's mother often said Gil's only love was for the sea, and how he let no one in. "You sure?"

"That's not all. She's been in a coma for years, a few months before the vote."

Liam lowered his head. Whoever she was to Gil, it must be hard knowing a loved one was in such a state for so long. "Damn. Poor Gil."

Alex froze and whirled to face Liam again, wide-eyed."You know what happened to people who didn't vote, right?"

"Of course; they were sent to No Man's Land, but she was in a coma. She couldn't vote."

Alex bit his lip. "Exactly, but people were still taken off life support when the wall went up. If they weren't in New

Albion, the hospitals over here..." Alex trailed off before looking around, the shame clear across his face. "They left people to die if they were on the wrong side. Those who didn't vote weren't viewed as citizens."

Liam took a moment to take in Alex's words. Was humanity truly that cruel? To give up on the vulnerable just because they couldn't vote? It didn't mean they deserved to die.

"It must have been Granswick. He must have made sure she was taken care of."

Alex shook his head, turning towards the dock. "There's no mention of Granswick on her forms. Gil's listed as her current carer. It looks like he supplies the funds to keep her bed in medical."

Liam probably should have asked Alex how he'd gotten all this information. Should someone so easily be able to access this level of detail? Liam had learnt that privacy wasn't exactly on the top of New Albion's agenda. "So?" Liam replied, turning towards the entrance of the tunnels. He wanted to go back and report what they learned from Mayor Lewis. He had no time for family drama.

"Liam." Alex gripped his hand. "This is going to sound crazy, but how much do you trust Gil?"

"With all my heart. Why?"

"Nic's death came from someone working on this side in the district. We know that much."

"That was your unconfirmed theory. What's that got to do with Gil?"

"He voted against the use of AI, right? He'd worked the docks and lived in Old Albion for years. Katherine was in a coma during the vote but is currently in New Albion receiving paid care." Liam nodded. Things were adding up, but could he really believe what Alex was trying to say? "I think he made a deal. When the chaos of the divide was happening, Gil kept her life support on to keep her alive."

Liam straightened, pulling his hand from Alex's. He shook his head and looked at Alex like he was a stranger. "No. He wouldn't. Gil helped the people of No Man's Land for years. He did trades and helped people get into the country for safety. He wouldn't have killed Nic. There's no way he'd have made any deals. No way."

Gil was a tough man, distant and closed off—a boss. He didn't allow anyone to take him for a fool. He'd scrapped plenty of times after a few drinks, but always made friends with his enemies by sunrise. There had to be another explanation. There had to be.

"But it's all here," Alex said, tapping the device. "None of these reports make sense otherwise. Isn't Maya meeting with him tonight?"

Liam shook his head and glanced at the sea, the docks visible in the distance. Then he saw a figure running towards them, her long blonde hair flowing with each step. "Carla?" Liam strode towards her. "Carla, what's the rush? Is Maya not with you?"

Carla doubled over, gasping for breath. "I'm on my way to get Lucas," she said, pushing the hair away from her face. "Gil gave us an offer—well, he offered it to Maya first, but now he's giving it to me and Lucas if he wants to join me. I need to find him."

Liam looked at Alex. "Offer?"

"He's got a new life for us in a safe part of West Country, probably towards the south of the island. He wanted Maya to get away from the rebellion group, but I wanted the offer too." Carla smiled, ready to set off again.

"Was Gil okay? Normal?"

"When is he ever normal? He was the same; a little flustered, perhaps, but there was a lot going on." Carla shrugged, brushing down her top. "New Albion has taken back a load of their guards from this side. There are no patrols here anymore. It's gone wild tonight. To be honest, it's one reason I want to leave."

"The watchtowers were empty too. I guess Granswick is taking all the protection for himself."

"They're in the cargo section if you want to see them. I need to speak to Lucas." Carla smiled and ran off towards the tunnel's entrance.

When Liam turned, Alex was on his device again. "What now?"

"Just running another check. Seeing if Gil had any transfers from New Albion into his account here. There should be a trail."

Liam crossed his arms. "Should I ask how you can easily access people's financial accounts or…?"

Alex rolled his eyes. "Ask your father. He's the one that showed me all these tricks. Ah, look. The same amount every year."

"That means nothing. We know he's paying for Katherine's care, so who can blame him for that?"

"But look. Last month, the payment was sent in full the day after Nic died." Alex's mouth hung open. "A year's payment of care for a job done. It's adding up."

"What about today? Look, there is another one." Liam pointed at the plus symbol beside a payment on the screen.

Alex licked his lips. "Does Gil know Maya is the new leader?"

"I don't know. Maybe. He ain't stupid, and he knows us

like we're his own kids."

Alex's eyes widened. "He sent Carla off to get Lucas, no questions asked."

"Maya's alone with him... right now." Liam suppressed the urge to empty his stomach and turned towards the docks. Alex moved into position beside him, and without a word to each other, they ran towards the dock.

Liam and Alex sprinted across the wooden dock, pushing past fleeing people trying to escape onto the anchored ships. Liam skidded to a halt at the storage area, squinting to see beyond the shadows. He struggled to hear over the crashing waves but eventually spotted two figures in the distance, and moonlight glinting off a blade's reflection. "Gil!" Liam shouted, stepping down towards them. "Wait, think about what you're about to do."

Gil stopped, the blade firm in his grip. Pain settled into the lines of his face. This was a man he'd looked up to for years and worked alongside day after day. He thought of the drinks they'd shared, and the love Gil claimed to hold for his family. Now, with a blade raised high above Maya's neck, Liam didn't recognise the man before him.

"You don't have to do this, Gil." Maya raised her hands, straightening. It was clear she refused to surrender. "We can work this out."

Gil glanced at Liam, his eyes moving to Alex behind him, and then back to Maya. Slowly, he shook his head. "No going back now. I can't risk losing her. I'm sorry."

Gil's tone was low, much rougher than Liam had ever heard it. Stepping forward, Liam raised his hands. "Tell us why. After all these years, we at least deserve that."

Gil looked at the floor. "Knowing won't do any good."

"It's only fair," Liam replied, taking a step forward. "We know about Katherine."

Gil froze. "Katherine..." the name lingered in the air like a ghost. "Suppose you deserve to know why I've fallen into this bloody trap. Might stop you doing the same thing."

Maya stepped back, but Gil followed her, keeping the blade near. Liam moved to stop him, but Alex held him back.

"She's my daughter," Gil said firmly. "When the divide happened, I thought they would take care of her over there. Little did I know how monstrous they were."

Beside Liam, Alex said, "They killed so many in the hospitals, people who just happened to be on the wrong side. It wasn't fair."

"None of that time was fair, lad," Gil said. "Everyone was desperate. Still are. It's what they thrive on. It gets people doing stupid things out of desperation." Gil's head sunk to the floor again.

"What happened to her?" Maya asked, her body stiff.

"She was a gentle soul; had a beautiful child and a nice family, or so she told me. She took ill one day—something on the brain, they said—and that was it. She was doing well in hospital, but then the vote happened, and eventually, the divide. It threw her future into the air."

"Did you make a deal to keep her alive?" Liam asked.

"I'm not proud of what I've done. I worked for the government and fed them information to ensure they kept her going, but I don't regret it. Nic knew her fate would come. I was just the one who pulled the trigger."

"But what about us?" Liam brushed Alex's grip aside and walked toward Gil. "You stepped in when our father left. Stood by Mother's side all these years, and gave me every opportunity to provide for my family. And now, here you are, with a blade to my sister's throat."

Gil looked at the blade, inches from Maya's neck. "It's a sad tale, but so many are. I wanted her to leave, but the orders were clear. You scare them, girl. They want you gone. Payment for another year is the offer." Gil watched Liam, tears in his eyes.

Liam had never seen Gil shed a tear. Even with the icy winds often lashing against their faces, his eyes had remained dry like stone.

"Don't do that!" Liam shouted. "If you want to kill her, then don't you dare cry for her."

Gil's hand trembled as he stepped forward, his arm around Maya's body, bringing her closer against his chest. "If I fail, Katherine will have no one. If you carry on and win your mission, the country will change, and she will die."

"New Albion is going down, Gil, whether I die now or not," Maya choked. "We won't back down. You know that. If you're going to do it, then *do it.* There will be another leader by tomorrow, another person to follow this through."

"Gil." Alex stepped forward. "Katherine's child, Damion. He was your grandchild, right? Granswick was the father."

"That's right. Never wanted much to do with me, but Katherine loved him, and that's all that mattered. I was happy to stay in the background, away from Granswick. If my girl was happy with him, then I was happy too."

Memories of better times seemed to haunt Gil's eyes, remembering the daughter he so fiercely protected, even now. "Mayor Lewis killed Damion, you know. He was behind his death. Pure jealousy." Liam let that hang in the air; while he didn't know this as fact, he hoped it was enough to make Gil second guess his next move.

Gil's eyes widened. He lowered the knife and loosened his

grip around Maya. "That bastard."

"Katherine's tests back when she was taken ill wouldn't have shown what happened to her," Alex said from behind Liam's shoulder.

Gil released Maya and strode toward Alex, pointing the blade at him instead. Liam moved to stand in the way, puffing his chest.

"You keep your nose out of her files, lad. That ain't no one's business but my daughter's," Gil said, swaying the blade.

Alex looked up. "There have been more tests since. AI has been checking everything on her for years. Did you know she was poisoned? Likelihood being 95.7%."

Gil's jaw dropped, his eyes darting between Liam and his sister. "By who? Why?"

"I can't say, but Mayor Lewis told us Granswick had a grand plan; he had everything in his head," Alex said. "Maybe he wanted a few blackmail options to bribe people on this side. People like you."

Gil narrowed his eyes. "You telling me Granswick poisoned her on purpose to use as a pawn? Don't be sick, lad. That was his wife and the mother of his child."

"She was the perfect dosage, enough not to kill her. It's all here. The fees they charge you are a fraction of what it should be. None of this seems like the truth, Gil. I think you've been played, like everyone else."

Gil stepped back toward the edge of the dock, his arms collapsing by his sides. The waves crashed behind him as tears fell down his cheeks. He looked at Liam and then Maya. "You two were such a gift to me," he said, peering at the blade in his hand. "I've done awful things; I've pushed back change with every order given to me."

"Gil." Maya stepped forward, reaching for him. "It's not too late to forgive."

Gil shook his head and lifted the blade. "No. Don't you take another step." The knife edge glimmered in the moonlight. "If you succeed, if my Katherine can't make it in the new world you create, make sure she has a peaceful send-off. She was too good for this world." Gil let out a cry and looked at Liam. "Sorry, kid. You've made me proud, you know. You never failed your mother. Never. And you," Gil turned back to Maya. "Are the strongest person I know." Half smiling, he wiped a tear from his cheek. He gave Liam one last look before raising the blade to his throat. Liam and Maya darted toward him, screaming for him to stop, but the blade slid across his neck, splattering the wooden boards in crimson. Gil fell backward into the sea; a pool of red water stained the waves as his body slowly sank as Liam looked over the edge.

"Gil, no!" Maya shrieked, collapsing to her knees to peer over the dock. She turned her head to look up at Liam, who offered his arm to pull her up. Gil was never a man to listen to the advice of others. He'd decided, and clearly the guilt of betraying them both was too much to live with. Liam wanted to cry for his friend and the trouble he'd carried alone for all these years. But he had to look forward to the people who were still here. The family he still had left. "Are you okay?"

Maya rubbed her hand along her neck and peered into the sea. "I'm fine. It's Gil I feel sorry for, the silly fool."

Liam wrapped his arm around her shoulder while his heart beat out of his chest. He'd just lost his mother, and finding Maya like that, seconds from death, was an image that would forever haunt him. He held her tighter, recalling the look in Gil's eyes before he died. His death couldn't be in vain.

Screams echoed out from above, followed by the sound of something crushing. Liam, Maya, and Alex, worried about people spotting Gil's blood, sprinted to the surface; however, the screams came from the district. Fires lit up the sky, accompanied by loud bangs, gunfire, and screams that emanated from Old Albion. Liam grabbed hold of Alex and brought him closer. "What do you think is happening?" he asked.

"It's New Albion; they're panicking and hoping I'm dead by now. They want to make the most of it," Maya said.

"What are we going to do?" asked Alex.

"We won't back down," Maya replied. "We need to match their speed. Get things in place and take them down. Now."

"Now?" Alex glared at Liam. "But we have so much more we need to do. We need the people of New Albion to be on our side; we have some information from Mayor Lewis, but we need time to send it through."

Liam smiled. "We have one thing on our side, though. The guards. Granswick's protection is lower than ever before." Maya stared at him, confused. "A few parting words by Mayor Lewis. Their numbers are down and experienced guards have moved on. One reason they employed so many of us from Freedom Day was to cover the slack, no doubt. It could be an advantage."

Maya nodded. "You head back and sort things with Robert—I mean, Father." Maya sighed, narrowing her eyes. "We need to group the district and No Man's Land together. It ends tonight."

Chapter Twenty-Eight

Motion

The sky faded into darkness, and the life and energy around her fell into silence. Shadows now cloaked the place she grew up in. Panic lined her face as she watched the world descend into chaos.

Screams echoed through the walls and buildings. Maya turned to the small group from No Man's Land, who had heard the plan had shifted to tonight. They, too, had wide eyes and faces etched with fear. Maya paused, taking a moment to think and reflect. Was she doing the right thing? So much blood had been shed. Was she truly ready to lead this?

Maya shook her head free of doubt. There was no time for it. They needed a firm leader. She called everyone over with a wave, with Carla and Lucas among the crowd. "Are you okay?" Carla ran towards Maya, wrapping an arm around her shoulder and assessing her red neck. "Did Gil do that? I can't believe I left you."

Maya nodded. She hated what Gil had done—not only to her, but to Nic—exploiting the trust they had built throughout her life. But she wanted to mourn for him, despite Nic's words. *'We don't dwell on the sorrow here.'* Maya needed to remember that going forward. "Let's focus on what's ahead. What's happened to the lights? Any idea?"

Lucas raised his hand. "Yeah. Seems New Albion has cut the power to the entire district. All the water is off too. It won't be long until people panic, even more than they already are."

"I see." Maya looked down at her worn boots, feeling as tired as they looked. "Mayor Lewis? Any sightings?"

Lucas shook his head. "No. He's been working with New Albion the entire time. Liam filled us in a bit before they headed towards our base camp."

"So, no water, electricity, and soon, no food. People from the west are running scared, and our own people are in the same boat. Literally." Maya sighed, and although she didn't want to, something had to give. "We need to make our move tonight. There's no other option. Lucas, can you rally the people of No Man's Land? Anyone willing to fight or can walk and carry a message, get them together."

"And go where?"

"You'll need to go through the divide. Gather them and make your way across No Man's Land, you can get into New Albion quicker. Liam and Alex are currently working on making the way safe for us. Once it is, you can meet us over there towards the government towers. Help increase our numbers once we make it over from our side."

"Our numbers are low. How certain are you that your

side will do their part?" Lucas asked.

Maya turned to Carla, who had tied her hair neatly to one side; even in the chaos, she was beautiful. "We can work on that. The Old Vic will be a meeting point. Gather everyone there and ask if anyone from the west will join us. There won't be many, but every hand will help."

Carla nodded, tucking a loose hair behind her ear. "Are we ready for this, Maya? We've only recently planted this idea in people's head. What if no one wants to help, or worse, ignore us? They've cut us off from everything. People might not want to risk losing more than they already have."

"It'll work." Maya hoped. "People here know things haven't been right. New Albion thinks cutting off our supplies will hinder us, but it won't. We will use this to push people up and get them moving. The divide comes down tonight, Carla. I want to make sure of that. Not just for us, or everyone suffering here, but for Nic and all the past leaders who pushed the crusade further with each sacrifice."

Carla turned to face the wall in the distance. Maya's eyes joined hers. Even with the lights off, the metal reflected the moonlight. "How do we take that down?" Carla whispered.

"We had a few things put aside by past leaders. Each one played their part in this, no matter how small." Maya turned to Lucas. "The supplies we've kept need to be spread out, enough for three groups: the people of No Man's Land, some for Kong at The Serpent's Lounge, and some for Carla at The Old Vic."

"When you say supplies…" Carla bit her lip.

"Guns, mainly," Maya replied. "Traded over the years. Some sold, and some were kept for days like this. There's also something bigger. Something I'll need you to be in charge of."

Maya knew Carla had more questions, but her lips didn't

move.

Maya followed Lucas towards the divide, past the unmanned wall, and into the dirt ridden No Man's Land, leaving Carla behind to arrange things in Old Albion. Riding with Lucas through the darkness always had a calming effect on Maya. The world seemed so much simpler and clearer in her mind now.

"I'll take you to the supply area, help share it out, and then I'll be fine on my own!" Lucas shouted above the roar of the throttle.

"Nic had been planning for this, you know. She left letters and journal entries from all the leaders before, but didn't get time to finish."

"We knew of notes and books, but they weren't our concern. That burden comes with being a leader, I suppose. How much are we talking about? Nic never let anyone see inside."

"I don't know. Enough to take down the wall, or at least that's what was promised."

"And the burden. How heavy does that feel to carry?"

"A mixture of guilt and pride, I suppose." Maya smiled, and Lucas raised an eyebrow. "Who am I to be the one to end this? I'm no one special. I don't come from No Man's Land. All I did was fall into this. It feels… unearned. Does that make sense?"

Lucas chuckled. "You know what Nic did before she was a leader?" Maya shook her head. She knew so little about the past leaders and only what she'd learnt from the journals. "She used to prepare the meat. Took it from the trade and prepared it. Nothing else. Nothing special. A leader before her was a girl who did nothing but read old books and posters she'd found on the floor in the wild. Never washed or combed her hair, but she was chosen as the leader. Why? I don't have that answer, but they were no more special than me or you, Maya."

"I see..."

"What they did after gaining power created their lasting legacy. If you're able to pull this off, unite the sides, and take down that wall, you might go down as the best one yet."

They stopped a mile from the base camp, where a battered shelter awaited them—totally unremarkable and unnoticeable to any passers-by. "What do you think this used to be?" Maya asked, jumping from the bike and brushing the dry dirt from her hands and cheeks.

"No idea. It's part of some building that was here when No Man's Land was part of the country. All kinds of work went on around here before it became a landfill for the building work for the divide." Lucas stepped closer. "Maybe when all this is over, we can start rebuilding what was once here."

"It's a nice thought," Maya said, approaching the metal gates. "There's a lock. Do you know the code?"

Lucas nodded and crouched beside it, flicking the numbers on the lock. After a few seconds, he pulled the doors open. In the distance, Maya saw dirt lifting into the air. "Help is on the way. At least we know our scouts got the message out and that people here are willing and ready to help."

Lucas laughed. "I had no doubt about the people here. It's the district I worry about. Come on; let's have a look inside."

Maya followed Lucas and stepped inside the building, instantly shivering. Another door blocked their way, this time with an electronic lock. "What's the deal with this?" she asked.

"Nic liked things to be secure down here for important stuff, I guess." Lucas tapped numbers into the keypad, and the door unlocked.

"Did Nic tell you all her codes, then? I'm starting to feel left out here."

"Getting jealous? Apparently, Nic was training me for this role for years. I never noticed it until you were chosen, and I had to step up. Kind of obvious now I look back on it all."

Maya and Lucas stepped further into the building. The room was freezing cold, with no windows or light entering from outside. To her right, a cord dangled, and she pulled it. A flicker of light came to life. "This might be the one place in the country with any power," Maya said as her eyes adjusted.

"Don't get too used to it. It runs on a generator; there's not much kick left in it now. Come on, we got to be quick." Lucas picked up a box and looked inside. "Guns, lots of ammo, torches, oil, lighters. We'll all be needing a bit of everything."

Maya marvelled at the range of equipment put by. Years of hard work, gathering, bargaining, trading. She thought back on all the leaders and all their selfish acts done for the aim of greater good. Her heart thudded. Was she really about to do this? After so much time and planning, was she really going to take this on?

"When the crew arrives, we can divide things up into three for everyone. Let's try to start this revolution off on equal stakes." Maya walked past the shelves of boxes. Another box stood on its own on a rear shelf. Maya peered inside and chuckled. Red sticks surrounded by hay and wood chippings. She turned to Lucas. "I have the stuff for

Carla here." She picked the box up in her arms and turned to walk past him. He leaned over to peek inside the box before following her back to the bikes. Maya placed the box in the hold at the back. The crew in the distance was getting closer now. Things felt real as her stomach tightened. She traced a finger along the fading red lines on her neck, thinking of Gil and how much she'd been through recently and what was still to come. The moonlight made Lucas's skin glow. He smiled at her, his eyes full of energy. "I should go. Are you happy with the plan?"

Lucas nodded. "Sure am, boss. I'll get the supplies set up here and then accompany Liam and Alex across the wall. I'll ready anyone willing to help, and if all goes well, I'll meet you in New Albion?"

Maya needed to leave, but it didn't feel right. She glanced at Lucas's hand and felt her own waver. Meeting his eyes, she laughed. "I feel like this is a goodbye. There's a chance one of us won't make it—hell, even a chance none of us will."

Lucas chuckled and rested his hand on the back of his neck. "I know what you mean. In times of war, people find each other and have sudden moments of passion in case there's nothing left for them in the morning. Isn't that what all the stories say?"

"Yeah, something like that," Maya whispered. "I don't want that, though. Is that strange?"

"Not at all."

"I feel like I should kiss you and prepare to face death, but that's not us, is it?"

Lucas shook his head and opened his arms to pull Maya in for a hug; he slapped his hand hard against her back and pulled away.

Chapter Twenty-Nine

A Thousand Feet

The winds sang a sweet tune as Maya rushed past, her temples throbbing from the chaos in the streets. Cloaked in shadows, and hidden within the alley, she sought refuge in The Serpent's Lounge.

Inside, Kong commanded the room from behind the bar, her stern face surveying the bustling scene as people ferried supplies back and forth. "You got the message, then?" Maya asked, fixing her gaze on the bottles behind Kong. Maya contemplated whether it would be wise to have a drink at a time like this.

"Rather suddenly and unexpectedly, but indeed, I received the message." Kong flashed her a stony stare. "Not sure you really have the hang of things yet, though. Brave move, striking so fast so soon."

"Maybe that's what we need. They think I'm dead in a

pool of my own blood, so when better to strike than now?"

Kong smiled before seizing a young boy by the scruff of his neck. "Make sure The Old Vic has the same number of people as us!" she shouted into his ear before glancing at Maya again. "You sure Carla is up to this?"

Maya nodded instinctively, though recalled how, only a few hours ago, Carla was on the brink of leaving everything behind. "She's ready," Maya said, taking a deep breath. "And we can count on you? I know we haven't always seen eye to eye..."

"I told Nic not to trust you so quickly and said there was a list of people a mile long who should be chosen instead of you, but she saw something in you; there's no doubt about that. I may not have agreed, but I'll stand here, rally the troops, and fight alongside you anyway. Don't worry about me." Kong poured a shot of vodka and downed it. "I've been waiting for this moment for too long. I'll be there, with Nic in my heart." She pounded her chest with her fist, and Maya met Kong's determined gaze, where the will to fight blazed in her eyes. Maya stood up, attempting a smile as a silent acknowledgement of Kong's commitment. Her legs wobbled and her head spun as the reality of the present surged through her. This was real. Never had it felt so tangible. Surveying the bar, the people, the placards, and the electric excitement, Maya knew the fight was ending. Regardless of the outcome, it ended tonight.

They marched through the streets as black smoke blanketed the sky above them. The sound of boots was heavy on the ground and moved in a synchronising rhythm. Maya no longer had to sneak around in the shadows. They passed The Old Vic, where more people spilled out from the old wooden doors to join their march. Maya spotted Carla, her face alight with energy, her eyes sparking in the night. She lifted her arm and shouted out to the cheering crowd. People around clasped torches; men and woman strode side by side, gripping guns while hoping no bullets would need to leave their chambers. Maya wasn't so hopeful about that.

She pushed through the crowd towards Carla before pulling her atop of the van that slowly drove towards the wall—the government building that divided their country for so long. Up high, she had a better view of the people; many faces were familiar, while others were total strangers. She held onto Carla's hand, squeezing it tight. Travellers from the West Country marched alongside them: children, adults, and the elderly all spilled out onto the streets with the same fighting spirit. "We're really doing this!" Carla shouted to Maya.

"We have to! This march, the rebellion. It doesn't just belong to us; doesn't just belong to No Man's Land anymore. It's broken through."

The march continued past the fires, the place Maya once called home. With each step, people gathered to watch outside their crowded homes; some joined and followed. New Albion's guards had retreated, causing chaos and leaving it all behind them. But as the rebellion marched closer to the capital building, guards appeared, decked out in the dark uniforms Maya knew all too well. Helmets covered the faces of scared men forced to carry out orders Maya was sure not all agreed with. She held herself tall. Hoped this moment wouldn't come; she'd hoped for total peace, but that wasn't a usual outcome of an uprising. Even her inexperienced mind knew that much. A cornered animal would fight, and Maya knew she had to kill.

She held onto Carla and dropped from the top of the van into the crowd. Kong was there, her face as stern as the first time Maya met her. Kong raised her hand, pointing towards the guards outside the capital building. People raised shields —some plastic, others metal, and some with no shield at all. It didn't stop them. Gunshots fired without warning, prompting smoke to fill the air. Maya's ears rang as she ducked, hiding behind any protection she had. A woman dropped beside her, dark blood running along her clothes and filling the cracks in the pavement. Maya winced. A body under her watch. As more gunfire rang out, Maya looked over the plastic shield; the guards were there still, some on the ground, and a few with shaking legs. As they fell to the floor, she thought of their families, their own lives. She hated the fact people had to die—innocent soldiers who were only following orders, but she needed change, and this was the only way it was going to happen.

After what felt like hours, the gunfire stopped, and the group marched forward again. Maya watched the floor as they proceeded, stepping past the bodies of those who gave their lives for this moment. Some stayed behind, desperately attempting to cure the wounded. She imagined her mother in this situation. She would have been among them, trying to heal the injured.

Approaching the formidable capital building, Maya felt the weight of history behind its imposing gates; gates her brother had walked through months ago. Determination surged through the crowd, and a spontaneous attempt to force open the doors begun. Maya peered up at the daunting divide, its dull metal blending into the night sky. Maya elevated above the united assembly.

"This wall will no longer divide us!" she declared fervently. "We have come together as one. We won't allow them to split us apart!" Cheers erupted, accompanied by men pounding against the doors while others attempted to scale the barrier. Maya continued rallying the crowd. "This group has broken through. In these last moments, remember that the people of New Albion will join us soon. We will spread the truth to them. Remember, the people are not our enemies. It's the men in the towers." Each word echoed, a reminder that the true adversary was in power, not amongst the people.

Maya turned toward the capital entrance, still locked, still standing. The need for more time pressed upon her. Maintaining morale and sustaining the crowd's energy was crucial to the cause. Her thoughts turned to Liam, and she hoped his part of the plan was under way.

Chapter Thirty

Exposed

Tension hung heavy in the night air as Alex brushed the dirt from Liam's uniform. Lucas stood beside them, preoccupied with the task ahead. "How does it feel to be back in it?" Alex asked, securing a rapier in Liam's belt.

Liam lowered his gaze to his boots, scuffed and dulled. Marks etched the leather as a sign of battles waged, and the uniform, a tight fit against his chest, held a weight of history in its design and colour. He hadn't expected donning the guard's attire again or venturing into New Albion. Yet, here he stood, aligned with the person he had chosen, preparing to return to the place he was now a wanted man.

Lucas placed a comforting hand on Liam's shoulder. "You can do this, mate. Robert's been in touch; he's waiting and ready for you both."

A fleeting smile crossed Lucas's face, then disappeared as

Alex returned, engrossed in his device. "Maya's given instructions to Carla, right? She's committed to this?"

"Yeah," Lucas affirmed, his smile replaced by a more sombre expression. "She's rallying people at The Old Vic. Maya's coordinating with Kong. We have supplies pouring in from both locations, stockpiled high from Nic." The weight of responsibility lingered in Lucas's words. "We have people ready to follow your lead. Once you get things in the open, we'll converge with Maya's group."

A lock of hair fell into Alex's face, who sighed. "No pressure, then." He turned to Liam. "Okay. You ready, big guy? Hopefully, Robert has everything sorted for us."

Liam nodded, yet his attention wandered to the surrounding chaos. The memory of Gil's last look before disappearing into the sea lingered. "I'm ready for whatever comes," Liam affirmed, following Lucas towards the deserted trading site along the divide. "There's a ladder. Climb to the top and walk along the divide until there's a signal. That's where Robert will meet you. Once things are clear and open, we'll join up."

As Alex climbed the ladder, Lucas met Liam's eyes. "Take care of him. I want to see both of you in the end. You got me?"

"Of course. We'll be fine," Liam reassured him, steadying his grip on the ladder. Emotions passed between them in the quietude.

"I mean it. Things are crazy on both sides. They won't go down without a fight. If we don't meet again, it's been a pleasure knowing you." Lucas pulled Liam into an embrace before pulling back and wiping his face. Lucas turned back towards base camp. "Go on. Get gone," he urged, as the night's uncertainties closed around them.

* * *

From their vantage point atop the wall, Liam surveyed the unfolding devastation in Old Albion, a place that was once home. He couldn't help but feel uncertain—he and Alex had traversed a path that blurred the definition of home. Black smoke cloaked the air, and the distant glow of fires painted a vivid illustration of the chaos below. Darkness obscured the once-familiar streets, the destruction confined to one side of the country. So far.

The weight of what was to come pressed on Liam as they neared the meeting point. He seized the opportunity to ask Alex questions he might not ask again. His words tumbled out. "What do you think the odds are?"

Alex arched an eyebrow. "Good, better than average. Maybe."

Liam's gaze shifted towards New Albion, its glittering lights a stark contrast to the opposing district. "Do you think we have enough time to get through to them all?"

"That's to be seen," Alex replied, his tone measured. "The people of New Albion aren't stupid. If we get the information to them, they'll see the truth. I'm sure of it."

The conditional nature of that *'if'* lingered as a reminder of their mission's precarious nature. He wanted to believe they would see and respond to the message by joining their cause, but the civilians of New Albion had a relatively good life. They were secure. What if security meant more to them than the truth? "What about after all this? What are your plans?" Liam halted before the red beacon.

"After? We will carry on together, no?" Alex's response was one of casual certainty.

Liam gazed into Alex's eyes. *Together.* What did that mean in this world, where their lives were miles apart? Could their hiding end by this time tomorrow? Liam had doubts. Even if they won this war, he didn't know what the world would look like after. "Where will be home when the wall is down?"

Alex's gaze shifted towards the ladder leading to New Albion. "Why don't we work that out later? We have to get there first." Liam tightened his grip on Alex's hand.

"But in case we don't make it to later. It would be nice to know now."

With a sigh, Alex said, "The wall will be down. Peace will be seen through the country—no more war, no division. We will have a home, jobs, friends. That's what I want the future to be. As long as you're there beside me."

Liam turned; his gaze stretched beyond Old Albion past the turmoil. "So much could be waiting out there for us. I'd like to see it, if we can."

"It's a deal," Alex said. "Now, shall we? I'd hate to keep your father waiting."

From the shadows, Robert emerged, his hood lowered as he greeted Liam and Alex. "You made it unseen?"

"We are fine, Father," Liam replied. "Maya is on course to start now. We need to open the way, spread the message to everyone we can."

Robert nodded, gesturing for them to follow him down a narrow alleyway, passing desolate gardens and silent bars. The city lay eerily still. "Where is everyone?" Liam asked.

"Locked down. They don't know what's going on, but even Granswick can't hide the fighting going on in Old Albion. People are spooked; it's a good time to act."

Their path led towards the tower, evoking memories of Liam's recent past here, where moments with Alex in the gardens and walkways felt like a lifetime ago. Robert guided them through a back entrance, using his device to bypass security measures. "My ID won't last for much longer, but if it's still working now, then we can take that as a win." He waved them both in, past the door. "Come on. I have everything set up to go in the office."

Huddled together, Liam and Alex followed Robert through the office hallways and upstairs, avoiding cameras and sensors at every turn. With the lights off inside the building, Liam had never seen the place in such darkness. Footsteps echoed, and Robert pressed a hand against Liam's chest. "There's two of them," he whispered, directing Liam with his eyes. Guards. Liam recognised them from his first day, lined up as comrades. They stood unsuspecting, guns in hand.

"You take the one on the right." Robert murmured as the three of them approached. Liam crouched, trying to hold his breath. None of this felt real, not until now, but seeing these men with their loaded guns… he didn't know if he had it in him to act.

Robert pounced on one guard before Liam seconded guessed himself. A heartbeat behind, Liam lunged at the other before he knew what was happening. He wrapped his arms around the man's neck, forcing him to drop his weapon. Mayor Lewis was right. These men lacked fighting skills, training, and experience. The man struggled in Liam's grip, but not for long. A snap came from Robert, and Liam spun as the man's body sunk from his father's grasp to the ground. Robert narrowed his eyes at Liam, his nostrils flared, willing for him to do the same. But he couldn't. Liam didn't want to kill this man. He had the strength; he knew that, but death was so final. Instead, he gripped the guard's throat until the man stopped struggling, hoping he'd fall unconscious. He didn't. He kicked and thrashed, the gun still clasped in his grip, his finger ready to pull the trigger. Robert crouched down with something in his hand, and then the man came to a standstill. Liam pushed himself up, wincing at the wetness on his uniform. Dark blood stained his chest. His father had already sheathed the blade and moved towards the office door.

"Are you okay?" Alex asked, turning Liam towards him to check him over.

Stained with blood, Liam hauled himself up to standing.

"I didn't want to..." Liam trailed off.

"I know," Alex said. "But it was him or us, and we need to do this. Everyone is counting on us. Try to remember the bigger picture tonight, when you need to make these hard choices."

Liam entered the office behind Alex. Robert already sat at the computer, tapping away at the keyboard. His father's ability to act like nothing happened amazed him. He'd just taken two lives—men he had passed in the hallway. Dead. Yet he's there, acting as if nothing occurred. Had his father done this before? Become hardened to death and killing? "I'm sorry, boy, but there was no other choice. We have been lucky it's only two so far." Liam nodded and accepted the answer. Now wasn't the time to argue.

"How are you going to do this, then?" Alex leaned on the back of Robert's chair. "There's no way of hiding that this information comes from you. You know that, right?"

Robert nodded, running his fingers along his chin in contemplation. "I'm aware of the risk, but blood is already on my hands. It's worth it, if we do it properly. We need to send all the documents, the voice recordings, everything to the devices logged in New Albion—every active user."

"I have created a file, a video that will play upon

opening," Alex explained. "That will be the fastest way to get the info out there. Then, if they wish, people can look through the details. But we need people to see what has gone on, so they can join Maya on the streets."

Alex placed his device onto Robert's computer, and Liam stood watch beside the door, hoping not to hear any more footsteps. "How long will it take? We need to give access to Maya as well," Liam said, tapping his foot. "We need the doors unlocked and scanners off if they are to get over to this side."

"Not long, boy. In a few seconds, every device will know the scale of the divide and the lies that filled this country. With them all locked up at home, it couldn't be more perfect." A confident smile played on Robert's lips. "Granswick will get this message too, you know, as will everyone who is around him right now, offering protection. It's now or never."

Alex tapped his device, and Liam walked over, watching the small progress bar fill the screen. "Is it happening? Right now?"

"Sure is," Robert chuckled. "I added in a little extra too."

"Oh?" Alex inquired.

"Every nation that is interested in implementing a divide of their own will receive this message, as will all the users in every country that have registered interest. Anyone who has a device, bought or traded, will see it."

Liam patted his father on the back. "Really? You've warned all those people?"

"It'll take a while. We'll deal with our lot first." Robert spun in his chair to another desk opposite him. "Now we need to give access to Maya." He clicked on a screen above him and flicked through the surveillance cameras until finding the government building. Outside, a riot of people waited, with Maya at the front. "Do you want to do the honours, son?"

Liam nodded, following his father's finger on the keypad. He pressed the button, and within seconds, the building came alive. The emergency lighting flashed on, and alarms rang out, the doors opening just before the screen flicked off. They'd done it. New Albion would soon have the wool pulled from their eyes and join the cause.

Granswick was the only one standing in their way.

Chapter Thirty-One

Confronting the Truth

Sirens wailed as the doors to the building surrendered with a resounding thud. The floodgates opened, and the crowds poured inside. Eager not to be left behind, Maya hurried alongside Carla as the rebellion crashed through the gates and scanners. For years, Maya had pondered the mysteries beyond the wall, and now the secrets of New Albion were about to unfold before her eyes.

Scanning machines flashed crimson within the building before casting the room in total darkness as the emergency lights extinguished. Amidst the chaos, hurried footsteps joined the sound of gunfire. More guards stood ahead, weapons aimed. Undeterred, Maya pushed forward with the crowd, overwhelming the guards in seconds until they were nothing more than casualties in the wake of a revolution.

"You keep going forward! Run until you're shot!" Kong

bellowed.

Deafening gunfire sounded again, but Maya and Carla remained unscathed as they pressed forward until reaching the desolate streets of New Albion, eerily silent amid such conflict. Appearing from behind, Kong rested a hand on Maya's shoulder, holding a gun with beads of sweat on her brow. "You sure you don't want one of these? Things are serious now," Kong said, panting.

Maya glanced at the tightly gripped gun in Kong's hand and shook her head.

The surrounding buildings transformed into shadows, illuminated only by the flaming torches held by her people. The streetlamps flickered. "Do you think Lucas is on his way?" Carla asked, matching the march's rhythmic pace.

Maya observed the towers ahead. Did the people believe in this cause as fervently as she did? Were the residents of the country on their way to join them, or fight them?

Draping her arm around Carla, Maya said, "If Lucas got through, he'll be waiting for us a few streets down." She mentally retraced the map she'd glimpsed at base camp.

The doors and windows of passing buildings opened, and Maya braced herself, anticipating the worst; gunfire or protests. Of course, some met her expectations, throwing objects to the ground with shouts of dissent. Yet, amidst the dissent, a few ventured out, holding their devices, with the sound of Granswick's voice emanating from their speakers. With each step, their numbers swelled. People arrived on foot from far outside the main city. Driver-less cars lined up as people left them to join the march. Maya forged ahead with Kong and Carla at her side.

They reached a crossroads, and Maya's eyes brightened as she saw them in the distance—the people from No Man's

Land, their torches ablaze, with Lucas leading them from the front. They seamlessly merged with the crowd, becoming a single force before the imposing tower that was completely shrouded in darkness, if not for the solitary light on the top floor.

Lucas joined them at the front and embraced his sister before turning to Maya with a reassuring pat on the back. "Knew it wasn't goodbye. You ready for this?" he asked. Uncertain of what awaited them, Maya turned to Kong, who silently handed her a gun.

"We focus on getting through those doors, no matter what. Liam did his job, and now we need to make sure we do ours," Kong said.

Guards encircled the tower in black uniforms, their weapons drawn and aimed at the crowd. She knew that life, including her own, could soon be lost. Maya clenched her fists as she pressed on. The guards held steady, awaiting orders. A man stepped forward, dressed in a uniform of deep royal blue. His eyes, alive with the reflections of the fires, bore into Maya. "This can end now before it's too late. Turn back!" he shouted. "The Governor is being kind. Take this as a warning and go."

The crowd booed, while others angrily denounced the officer's claims. "People of New Albion stand with us!" Maya yelled. "Will you shoot your own?"

People advanced until forming a human barrier with linked arms. "We have seen the truth!" a woman proclaimed, dressed in a suit unbefitting of such conflict.

The captain raised his hand, and the guards moved their fingers to the triggers while the crowd stared into the barrels of their guns. Maya refused to avert her gaze. One guard hesitated—arms shifting, feet subtly turning. He was unsure of himself. When the captain lowered his hand, they resisted the order. A few shots rang out, and people fell beside Maya. When the smoke from the gunfire cleared, it revealed the fallen captain on the ground, blood pooling around him. Conflict and confusion plagued the remaining guards. Maya knew these men were not all from here. Some were recruits from Freedom Day. Old Albion lived in their blood, and they had made their choice. She would be forever thankful for that.

In a panic, the guards turned to fire at each other. Kong swiftly responded, pushing Maya to the ground, as the guards on the wrong side of history killed one another on the steps.

After, the crowd stepped over the bodies, and then the fallen guards. Maya vowed to remember the face of each fallen officer. Even after all this time here in New Albion, they still sided with their home and were willing to die for it.

When she reached the tower entrance, Lucas joined her. "Go inside and take a few people with you. We'll keep things under control out here; there are more guards headed over. We already took down a few groups on our way to meet you, but there will be more." Lucas said.

Maya nodded, glancing back at Carla. "Do you have everything we need for when this is over?" she shouted.

Carla nodded, her expression one of unyielding resolve.

"Come on," Kong urged, pushing open the door. "I'll watch your back, take you to the end, for Nic. For the rebellion."

"I'll see you once this wall's demolished," Lucas declared, turning to join his sister.

Maya's desire to stay and ensure the safety of her friends clashed with Kong's insistence as they entered the empty tower block. That might have been the last moment she shared with her friends, in the world she once knew. If she never left this building again, at least she'd die knowing the world wouldn't be the same one she woke up in.

The doors closed behind them, muffling the alarms and spiralling red lights. A group of people emerged ahead, while other guards lay dead on the floor, a grim sight. Kong raised her gun, but Maya intervened, lowering her weapon.

"They're wearing the uniform," Kong whispered.

Liam raised his hands, locking his eyes onto Kong. "You made it then."

Maya rushed towards him, pulling her brother into an embrace, while ignoring the blood and sweat clinging to his uniform. Her attention shifted to her father, his face weary. Dark circles ringed his eyes. She smiled at him but refrained from stepping closer.

Footsteps approached from behind, and Kong braced herself, gun at the ready. "The elevator is over here, but it's off. We need to take the stairs," Alex said. "Maybe sooner rather than later."

"You guys go. If any get through from here, I'll hold them off." Kong declared. "Go now before I change my mind."

Maya nodded and tossed Kong the gun she had given her; she needed it more. She gave a closed smiled to Kong, a secret thank you for the guidance she'd given Nic, the time she had spared for Maya, and her harsh lessons from when they first met. Maya couldn't call Kong a friend, not truly, but she could thank her all the same for what she had done to help.

Maya pivoted and followed Robert toward a door, where a stairwell awaited beyond it, a dark concrete spiral stretching endlessly upwards. "Come on," Robert beckoned, already beginning the ascent.

Maya's calves burned by the time they reached the fourth floor. Sweat dripped down her forehead as she clung to the banister. Beside her, Alex moved effortlessly, his face determined. "Why are you so good at this?" Maya asked breathlessly.

"I always take the stairs."

Robert wiped his brow. "Have much trouble getting here?"

"People died, guards rebelled, but we got here. I was surprised by how little they had waiting for us. We need to make all this worth it." Maya said, wanting to put an end to the conversation.

"It seems they have re-positioned the guards. Good for us, I suppose." Robert said. "But where they've gone is anyone's guess."

Maya's breaths came heavy, yet the end of this trek felt far out of reach. Maya had sacrificed so much to arrive at this moment. She pondered her brother's courage, Nic's sacrifice, her mother's selflessness, and her father's return. Maya hated herself for allowing him back, but an undeniable love persisted, one she didn't have the strength to push away.

She sighed as they reached the top. She collapsed onto her knees. This was the end—only a single door stood between them and the culmination of their efforts. Pulling herself up, Maya gripped Liam for support. "This is it. There's no going back from this."

Maya pushed open the door that led into a narrow hallway. The opulence of the top floor was a stark contrast to the chaos below it, decorated with marble walls, lavish furnishings, and gold-framed paintings hanging on either side of the corridor. Through the large double glass doors,

Maya saw the powerful figures of New Albion, with their guards standing watch. Robert advanced yet raised his hands, confidently striding forward.

Maya wanted to stop and pull him back, but he escaped her.

"Granswick, I have brought them right to you," Robert declared. "Just as requested."

Maya felt a wave of nausea as the door behind them locked shut. Liam clenched his jaw in anger as Alex pressed against the glass, attempting to open it. She'd trusted her father after he'd looked into her eyes and promised so much. She felt a fool. Another failed leader. How could she let this happen, right at the final push?

Robert halted, and the two bodyguards lowered their guns at the sight of him. "It wasn't without risk and loss. I had to do many things I'm not proud of to gain their trust, but you'll agree it was all worth it for this." He opened his arms, directing Granswick's attention toward Maya, who spat towards the floor. She wished she'd kept Kong's gun now to put a bullet to the back of her father's head.

Smiling, Granswick stepped forward, looking beyond Maya to Liam. "Boy, I had such hope for you. You were to be the face of our future. And you, Alexander… you had a career; everything you could ever dream of was soon coming your way, yet you wasted it all for nothing."

Alex held Liam's hand and turned to meet Granswick. "Robert, what have you done?" he asked.

Robert faced them and a smile crept across his face. "What I had to do to reach this moment. I really had no other choice." In one swift motion, two shots rang out, and the bodyguards dropped to the ground. Robert lifted his gun, and Granswick's mouth fell open. He stepped back into the group of other officials towards the back wall.

"Robert. Why?" he shouted.

Maya advanced, though she was unsure of what had just happened. Had her father played Granswick all along? Liam and Alex stood beside her, joining Robert in a line. "I would never betray them, sir," Robert replied. "You, of all people, know the strength of family ties."

This was her chance. Maya needed to be the leader Nic wanted her to be and tell Granswick what he had done, to show him the hurt and pain he'd caused for this country. "We are ending this tonight, Granswick," Maya declared. "The divide is over; the wall is coming down, and to do that, we need to take you as well."

Granswick laughed, his eyes manic. He swiped back his hair and adjusted his jacket. "You can't stop this! Not now. It's too far gone. We're already a step ahead, as we so often are."

"We have shared the truth! Your people have joined us. We want change, and so do they."

"Stupid girl. This place isn't the end goal. *You* were the experiment. All you've done is rush it along and left your people in chaos."

"It's not true," Alex asserted. "Your governmental reign is over. There's nowhere else to run."

Behind Granswick, other members of the government seemed restless as gunfire reverberated from outside. Black smoke obscured the view from the windows. "They are right, Granswick," a woman stated, peering out the now open window. "We are finished."

"Stand down, and we can end this now," Maya urged, stepping forward with her father.

The woman laughed. "No. Failure wasn't an option. I

won't be sent off to the outskirts, not to those places." She pushed aside those around her and moved toward the open window, standing on the ledge. Arms raised, she turned her back to the window. And fell. Maya gasped, reaching for her, but it was too late.

Another man stuttered, "We know what you will do to us. We know what the savages in No Man's Land did to Theodore Lockhart. That is not a fate I will accept. We still control our lives." More followed suit, opting to jump to their deaths instead of facing the consequences. Granswick turned to face the only remaining individuals on his side.

The remaining man looked into Maya's eyes, his crisp suit tight along his shoulders and chest. "You can walk right past us," Maya said. "We will bring you no harm."

Wide-eyed, the man looked at Granswick, his face covered in sweat. He took a step forward as Granswick held out his hand. "If you want to go, you go through the window or you stand beside me. I will not let you run away from this. We are not cowards."

"Don't listen to him," Maya said as the man stepped back in line. "If there was any time to be free, it's now. Walk past us. I cannot say what will happen to you beyond that door. Living or dying is up to you. But you can take that step, make that choice."

The man looked between Maya and Granswick again. He wiped his brow and advanced forward slowly before his steps quickened into a run. He rushed past Maya towards the door and swiped his card to unlock it, and vanished without looking back. Maya stared into Granswick's eyes; he had nothing left.

"What's in the outskirts, Granswick? What are they so afraid of?" Robert asked.

Granswick laughed and swiped the fallen hair back from his face. "We built this as an experiment to test the limits of what people will comply with. Pushing AI to its limits, seeing how easily people could be moulded. How far we could take the control, and what would be too much. Safe to say, you all exceeded our expectations, but it seems we have reached the limit in research now."

"Then why open up the sides? Why create Freedom Day in the first place? Isn't that what allowed all this to happen?" Alex questioned.

Granswick nodded, and his eyes came alive. He was enjoying this in a weird, twisted way. The questions, all eyes on him. "Freedom Day was a necessity. We had all we needed from New Albion, but a world needs both sides to work. Our troops were low, having moved onto more... important work. When better to train up a fresh group of followers?"

Liam's voice came from behind Maya. "What about the outskirts? Mayor Lewis is out there, living in some crazed fantasy, but he's safe. Why were we blocked from going past the borders?"

Granswick looked at Liam before answering. "This world is fragile; it's breaking more and more each year. You all stand here and think you're fighting a noble cause. It's all for nothing; Albion is but a footnote in history. You are the pre-planning; the real future lies out there, out of sight. We needed to keep you under control. This land where Old and New Albion stands is doomed to flood and become unstable. It won't be long until this entire city is underwater, and we needed to guarantee a safe land for those we wanted, elsewhere, out of sight."

Maya listened, taking in every syllable. The smug look on his face made her sick. This was nothing but a game for him. An experiment.

"So, you're playing God? Is that what this comes down to? All this hate, death, war? It's men in tall towers wanting to shape the world to how they want it?" Maya clenched her fists.

"It's a future, is it not? Better that than no future at all."

"I'm not so sure," Maya spat.

"Then stay here. See how long you last," Granswick said, grinning. He was alone and cornered, with nowhere else to go.

Maya narrowed her eyes, watching his body tense. "Who do you report to? If what you say is true, who is above you?"

Granswick chuckled. "There are only a few countries left. Our lands and borders may have changed, but with so little left out there, we had to come together. There are one or two countries still independent, but they will be left behind too if they do not join us. One world is the only future. One government. That's what my role in history will be—pushing my people into having a future, selling our ideals and practices to the ones who remain." Granswick chuckled. "It's exactly why you're too late, Maya. You will be forgotten, and I will live on." Granswick glanced at Liam. "It's why I can't have you joining me now, boy. I won't allow you to stop me. Not after the choice you've made." Sighing, he added, "Under my wing, you could have had it all, but you chose the wrong path when it truly mattered."

Granswick opened up his jacket and pulled out a gun. All Maya could do was watch as he pointed it toward her, and a shot rang out. Smoke spiralled from the barrel, and Maya closed her eyes, preparing for the pain. It never came. When she opened her eyes again, she found Robert on the floor before her, blood soaking through his jacket as he gripped his arm. Liam rushed past her, his image a blur as he withdrew the thin sword from his belt. It was for display, and Maya was sure it would snap, but he plunged the end through Granswick's body. Liam dropped the end of the blade, so it remained lodged in Granswick's stomach. Blood spurted from his mouth, dripping onto the ground. He stumbled toward the open window, trying to find his footing. Maya watched him fall as a smile played on his lips. She rushed toward the window alongside Liam; they watched as Granswick plummet to the ground.

Outside, cheers erupted as Granswick's body hit the pavement with a thud. She turned back toward her father, who now sat up with Alex beside him, wrapping something around his bleeding arm. "You did it," he muttered.

Maya turned to Liam; sweat poured from his ashen face. The realisation had kicked in, Maya realised; she knew the feeling all too well. He'd taken a life. "You saved me," she whispered, lacking the energy to shout or be excited about the future they'd just created.

Maya reflected on Granswick's words as they walked down the stairs, through the corridor, and past the bodies of guards Kong had fought off. She studied them all, trying to discern if Kong had survived or not. Although she didn't find an answer. She hoped they had done the right thing, despite Granswick's warning echoing in her mind again and again. *'You are too late'* is all he offered. She prayed that wasn't true; she hoped the future wasn't so set in stone that it was unchangeable.

Outside, a growing crowd had gathered, circling Granswicks body. Blood and tears filled the streets. Carla stood beside Lucas, smiling, the anxiety and dread having faded from her eyes. Maya perched on the steps of the tower in a pool of dried blood. Raising her hand, a chorus of cheers ensued. Her brother stood by her, while her father joined her other side, still gripping his wounded arm.

Maya nodded at Carla, who pressed the button. A small explosion came from behind them, collapsing a part of the wall. Cheers rang out, and Maya stepped forward, standing tall. "Today marks the end of an era, and the dawn of a new future!" she shouted. "We stand here, united, having shattered the chains of oppression that bound us for far too long. The divide that sought to tear us apart has crumbled, and now we stand stronger than ever."

She turned to find Liam embracing Alex. "We have faced adversity and fought against the lies and manipulation that sought to keep us divided." Lucas jumped up and down beside his people: the children he grew up with, who were now men. She thought about Lydia, who gave these children so much when she had nothing. "But we have triumphed, and in our unity, we found strength. Today, we declare the end of totalitarian control, ensuring we can decide our destiny."

Maya paused, closing her eyes. She reflected on every leader before her, of Nic, who pulled Maya into this world and allowed her to believe change was possible. "As we stand amidst such change, let us not forget the sacrifices made, the lives lost, and the struggles endured. It is a testament to our resilience and undying spirit that we have overcome the darkest forces that sought to silence us."

More cheers rang out, and though Maya had more to say, she stopped. Tonight was a night of change, but she didn't want to disregard all the loss. She hoped Granswick was wrong, and it wasn't too late; hoped the country would be better from her actions.

She looked past the crowd toward the crumbling divide. It had existed for as long as she could remember, yet seeing a hole through its heart made her chest swell with pride. She'd done something; she only hoped the future would be better than the past.

Part Four

"The future unfolds, not as a precise masterpiece we envisioned but as a mosaic of unpredictable hues, each stroke a surprise, challenging the boundaries of our imagination."

Chapter Thirty-Two

United

Remnants of the wall stretched across the land like a gaping wound, a constant reminder of what once divided the country. Maya sped along the desolate expanse that was once No Man's Land, relishing the moment of respite with her eyes closed. She inhaled the dusty air before stopping and dismounting her bike. Her boots met the dry ground, where members of No Man's Land and the rebellion had united for the first time since that fateful night one month ago.

Earlier, Maya had visited the graveyard, where the recently added graves served as solemn markers for the lives they couldn't save. She ensured no one was forgotten. Beside the newly erected statue, Lucas stood with his hands in his pockets, worn goggles draped around his neck. Maya approached and ran a hand along his back. "Does it look okay to you?" she asked.

He smiled briefly at her before returning his gaze to the engraved names. "Found Mum and Dad. Look, right there." Kneeling, he traced his finger across the inscriptions. "It's hard to believe they stole and switched so many votes, isn't it?"

Maya nodded solemnly. "Cowards, the ones responsible for this."

"At least Carla and I found each other. I guess some good came from it." Lucas stood, brushing dirt from his knees. "How are things in the district? I've heard reports that things aren't too good."

Maya looked in the distance to where her home once was, near the docks. "It'll take time. People won't merge overnight."

"But the looting is still happening, right? Thieves moving into New Albion now. It's lawless out there. Everywhere."

Maya swallowed, unable to meet Lucas's gaze. Trouble hadn't vanished. In fact, it had grown. With no laws and no government, people were creating their own, with new factions and groups emerging each day. "Makes No Man's Land seem calm, doesn't it?" A bitter laugh escaped her lips, yet her stomach churned with guilt. Losing the divide had unleashed the best in some, but the worst in others. The country hadn't changed for the better instantly, like she'd hoped.

"Carla mentioned leaving The Old Vic," Maya said. "Is she coming to live here with you?"

Lucas nodded, scratching his palms. "That's right. We want to build and keep No Man's Land alive. It's home. She feels closer to family here, I guess."

"I should head back home sometime. I haven't been back

since Mum..."

Lucas wiped away the tear rolling down Maya's cheek. "You have family left, Maya. Spend time with them while you can. I don't know how much longer Alex and Liam will stay around here, but you're always welcome here. Carla said you're basically a sister to her."

Maya surveyed what remained of base camp, belonging to a group whom had no further use for her. She glanced at the branded scar on her ankle that marked her allegiance and pondered her place in the world she'd helped create.

"Remember Carla's offer. You can come here too, call it home. There's always room for my leader."

Traversing the district from No Man's Land felt surreal to Maya. She kept glancing over her shoulder, anticipating a guard to stop her at any moment and inspect her bag, yet each checkpoint remained empty. The streets of her home were still ablaze with fire, and while passion ran deep among the people of Old Albion, their sense of security felt fragile. Jobs were scarce, businesses had shuttered since the onset of looting and fighting. New Albion kept its technological prowess, but the same resilience didn't come easy to her hometown.

Maya sped through the markets, past the closed pubs and clubs, until reaching her block where Liam waited, leaning against the wall with a device in his hand. He pocketed it as she approached. "Not smoking?" she prodded.

"Not drinking?" he retorted, a smile playing on his lips. Maya laughed. Even with the stress, the fights, the riots, the guilt, Maya hadn't thought about drinking in weeks. She hadn't even noticed its absence. "Ready for this?" He led the way inside, up the concrete steps, and past the familiar flaking paint and flickering light.

The flat looked exactly as they'd left it. A collection of memories bundled up, with some items boxed away and others discarded. The air held a hint of dampness as Liam opened the window, and at the kitchen table sat Robert, his arm still in a sling. He smiled at them while Liam eyed a shirt on the floor. "Charity? Plenty of people in need."

"I suppose," Maya replied, lifting a crumpled shirt her mother had worn. "How does it feel being here, Father?"

"Strange. I can smell your mother's perfume, though it's faint. There are things here we bought together, and just as many items we didn't."

Maya turned to Liam. "How's Alex? Surprised he isn't here."

Liam scratched his neck. "He's settling his mother at home. She's been a bit spooked by the riots, so he wanted to spend some time with her."

Maya looked at Robert, wondering what he thought of how things had unfolded. "Any word of the government trying to rebuild?"

Robert shook his head. "No. I don't think that'll be anything to worry about for a while. I suppose whoever remains is busy on the project somewhere on the outskirts Granswick teased us about."

Maya wondered how much of what Granswick said before his death was true. Some people had left the city and ventured into the outskirts. None had yet returned, but that meant nothing. She still had things to finish up here before ideas of the outside world filled her mind. The thoughts of adventure and trips to unknown lands were best reserved for others.

"Would you meet me in New Albion later, Dad? There's

somewhere I need to visit." Robert gave a weary nod.

"Shall we sort this stuff out, then?" Liam suggested, picking up items from the kitchen. "Once Alex has settled his mum, it won't be long until we head off."

Maya glanced at the bag across Liam's shoulder. "Sure, let's get this place empty. I think I'll follow Carla for a bit and see what's left for me in No Man's Land once I've finished everything up here."

As she watched her father and brother pack away their life, Maya struggled to feel elated. The truth was, she hadn't thought about anything beyond taking down the divide. The world that emerged since wasn't simple, and she hadn't expected that not everyone would play by the same rules. She was glad Liam had found happiness and felt content leaving; it left Maya with no choice. She had to move on, too.

She walked to New Albion with her father by her side. It still felt odd, having him in her life, as if the past few years had never happened. She hoped her mother would understand Maya's need to forgive him and accept him again. He'd sacrificed a lot to do what he did with Granswick, and Maya had to give him points for that.

They stopped before a large, pristine building. "This is it? Medical Block D?" she asked.

Robert nodded, and they headed inside.

The walls were a sterile white, formed of reflective plastic; the smell of antiseptic invaded Maya's senses as she turned her head, passing each room. So many beds were empty. She wondered if this was usual, and the beds were always empty here, even while people in Old Albion died from a cough uncared for. "What are you trying to find here?" Robert asked.

Maya thought back to Gil and the last look on his face before he sliced his throat. He'd spent years protecting his daughter, keeping her alive. This was the least she could do for him.

"Doing something for Gil," she said, and Robert narrowed his eyes. "I know what he did was wrong, but he had his reasons, like we all did."

Robert lowered his head. "He was a great friend to me and your mother. I wish I knew he was working for New Albion; I could have warned you or maybe stopped him from…"

"He did what he thought was right. Gil wasn't one for feelings. It's best we remember him how he'd like to be remembered." Maya stopped at the reception. The desk wasn't manned; there was only a screen. She typed in Katherine's name, and it displayed a room number. "You know where this would be?"

Robert nodded and turned, walking down a hallway. "Who's Katherine?" he asked.

"Gil had a daughter. They placed her here when the divide happened. It's what Granswick used to blackmail him over all these years."

"A daughter? I never knew."

"No one seemed to. I don't know how he kept her so hidden away. I wish Mum was still here. She might have known something."

Robert nodded. "They were always close. She probably would have taken his secret to her grave."

Maya stopped outside the room and pushed open the door. Katherine lay on the bed, her chest softly rising and falling. A tube came from her nose and a plastic casing covered her mouth. "She's still here then. I don't know how much longer Gil had paid for. What will happen when the money runs out?"

"It's hard to say what the future holds for this entire place. Without a government in charge, the funding is gone. Places like this won't be able to function for long. I suppose everything will be shut off, eventually."

"There's no staff. Is that normal? Or have people already left?" Maya asked.

Robert shook his head, his eyes large. "I don't think there's much we can do. Groups are popping up all over. It won't be long until people come here and take supplies for themselves. Old Albion has been low on medical supplies for years. This will be like a gold mine for them."

Maya held Katherine's hand. She didn't know the woman and never would, but it felt right. She felt almost envious of her, sleeping and completely oblivious to the world around her. When the machines turned off, she would die without ever knowing what happened. Maya leaned towards her and whispered, "Your father loved you, and he did everything he could to keep you safe." She turned to her father. "This isn't right, you know that." Maya wished her mother was here. She would help these people and rally the community to keep things in order.

She looked at the machine built into the wall, wondering which button would turn it off and end Katherine's misery of an existence. But she couldn't do it. She wasn't here to play God, not like Granswick. So, she left Katherine and the medical block. Maya needed to focus on something other than drink and practice what her mother taught her. What was the point in coming this far and changing so much if she planned to sit back and do nothing? She turned around and thought of all the people who could do good, pondering the wasted talent in both the district and No Man's Land. It needed to be harnessed, and that was something she could create; something she could spend her life focusing on.

Chapter Thirty-Three

Onward

The dock was silent, except for the crashing waves that turned into foam upon reaching the shore. The weight of Liam's backpack settled on his shoulders as his hands clenched around the straps by his sides. He strolled along the dock that was devoid of the usual hustle and bustle; without Gil, the chaos that came with the shipments had ceased. No vessels arrived from the west, and none departed, leaving the waters still, aside from its natural flow. Liam couldn't help but wonder what effect Albion's uprising had on the world. Had others learned from their upheaval, or were they destined to repeat the same tragedies? Was Albion's warning enough to stop history from repeating itself?

Inside Gil's weathered shack, Liam claimed his familiar spot on the worn wooden stool. The desk, usually adorned with a few playing cards, now lay bare. A nostalgic pull led him to open the drawer in search of Katherine's photograph. However, he was only disappointed as he found the compartment empty, its contents pilfered by someone who had beaten him to the remnants of Gil's past. He hoped Gil had the photo on him and sunk to the ocean floor with the memory of his daughter by his side.

The soft sound of footsteps interrupted his thoughts, and Alex, his hair tousled by the sea breeze, appeared in the doorway. "Hiding from me?" he quipped. Liam pushed himself upright, tapping rhythmically on the desk.

They hadn't had many moments since the divide went down to sit and talk. Life had been so busy trying to adapt. But now, the sea air allowed time for quiet, so Liam could reflect on what happened. "How much do you reckon Father told Granswick all this time?" Liam mused.

"You mean his double bluff? Hard to say," Alex replied, running a finger along his chin. "Granswick always said they never missed a thing. He saw it as an experiment and let us think we were sneaking around, not being seen, but I guess we were seen more than we thought."

"And my father played along with it? Allowed us to get away with stuff under the guise of a test?"

Liam thought back to all the stolen moments they'd shared. The lunch breaks, the reading lessons in Alex's apartment, the trip across the divide, their first night in each other's arms. So many times, they believed they had beaten the system, strengthening their connection in secret. All along, Granswick was aware. Robert had allowed it all to happen by feeding information back under the guise of trapping them all when the time came.

"Exactly. Why'd you ask?"

Liam sighed, the weight of regret settling over him. "Just

thinking of Gil and the guilt in his eyes before he killed himself. I still feel bad about that; I think we could have saved him. Helped him."

"Gil was a man who did what he wanted. He couldn't live with the idea of killing Maya, so he took himself out of the picture. He knew Granswick couldn't control that and look at what happened. Without Gil pushing Maya like that, she might never have gone ahead with the plan early. It caught everyone off guard, and we won in the end."

Liam nodded. He hated how smart Alex was, how profound and rational he could be.

They strolled in companionable silence, the absence of the district's chaos providing a welcomed calmness. The city was volatile since the wall's demise, with law and order unravelling as leadership vanished overnight. "Shall our first stop be Mayor Lewis's manor?" Liam proposed, absent-mindlessly kicking a stone along the path.

"Be lucky if it's still standing. Think Mayor Lewis is long gone now. Been a few left-over members of New Albion government missing too, people who used to work in the offices, like me," Alex replied, tapping on his device.

"Missing by choice, do you think?"

"Maybe they found that place on the outskirts. The perfect city that Granswick alluded to." Alex shrugged, continuing to scroll through his device. "Lots of reports online from people who are still active. Some say they chose to leave. The prisons below were empty, you know. There wasn't a single person in there when they checked."

Liam couldn't shake the memories of the men he encountered in those deserted cells, and one man's warning of people being dispatched to work on the outskirts.

After they eventually passed the outposts and the track

they followed to visit Mayor Lewis, Liam pondered the unknown. "Think we'll find this stuff out when we get far enough out?"

"I don't know. For once, it's something I can't look up on here." Alex gestured to his device. "That's what's so exciting. Our own adventure out there."

Liam chuckled and playfully jabbed Alex's side. "Not scared of the monster stories, then?"

Alex adjusted his top and scowled. "Of course not. Nothing but fairy tales." He cleared his throat and moved closer to Liam. "Isn't it strange? How the only place we can see ourselves together is away from our homes?"

"Did you want to stay? We could try to work something out."

"No. I didn't mean it like that, and things in Albion are horrible, anyway. If you ask me, I think we're safer in the outskirts. We can find our own home out there, maybe."

"If they deployed guards and sent the prisoners to work, we might wish we'd stayed here." Liam chuckled. "Some government officials jumped from a window to avoid being sent out here. Doesn't that play on your mind?"

"It didn't," Alex replied, though his eyes shifted.

Liam wrapped his arm around Alex, pulling him closer. "Don't worry. I'll protect you from anything."

"You forgetting that right hook I landed on your friend? I can take care of myself."

They passed the manor, where they could hear music and laughter inside, as they continued their journey. By the time the sky turned orange, they stopped to rest atop a hill. The landscape had opened up, revealing miles of fields, lakes, and sunken buildings. Liam gazed ahead, wondering how different this land was before, while trying to ignore

Granswick's words about the changing, uninhabitable land. He hoped they would discover whatever it was they were working on out here. Turning to Alex, Liam leaned his head on his shoulder. "If we need to, we will come back, won't we?"

"Come back? For who?"

Liam shrugged. "Maya, my father, your mother. If the group needs us, we'll come back, right?"

"Of course, though I'm not sure how we'd know." Alex pulled out the device. "This thing is useless out here. But if we feel the need to return, we will."

"Where do you want to go first?" Liam asked.

Alex pointed forward, closing one eye. "Right there, the furthest point we can see. I heard rumours of a group of travellers making this same journey, you know. Could be paradise a few days walk away from here, where we can live off the land and grow our own food."

"Are you making fun of me again?" Liam playfully tapped Alex on the arm. "I'll turn around and head home."

Alex laughed, brushing his hair from his eyes. "Come on, let's set up camp for tonight." Alex got up and pulled open his bag, and Liam leaned back into the grass, relishing the gentle breeze on his face. He recalled his first day when he bumped into Alex, thankful for that moment of kindness. Turning around, he propped his chin onto his hands and watched Alex set up the tent, hoping there were many more days like this one ahead.

Chapter Thirty-Four

A New World

Maya stood atop the tower, watching tendrils of smoke rise from the destruction. The building lay ransacked, a desolate echo of the lies and schemes that had once unfolded within. With each step, she traced the paths her father, Liam, and Alex had walked.

The bitter wind whipped around her, tugging at her hair as they reached the top, overlooking the city below, now tainted by anger. Splinter groups had emerged, seeking to level the playing field between poverty and wealth. She couldn't condemn them; it wasn't her role; besides, the roles had become blurred in this new reality she'd helped create.

Robert stood beside her, his arm now free of the sling, and placed a comforting hand on her shoulder. She reciprocated, grazing the spot where he'd taken a bullet for her. "Enjoying the view?" he asked gently.

"I'm not sure. Chaos is spreading like wildfire. There's unrest everywhere. I didn't think it would become... this."

"Chaos is inherent, Maya. Peace follows. You have to believe that."

"Maybe." Maya's gaze drifted toward the outskirts, the uncharted territory where she hoped her brother had found happiness and safety. "What do you think happens next?"

Buildings spewed smoke, and homes were in ruin; the streets of New Albion bore the scars of upheaval.

"Next?" Robert tightened his grip. "The entire country will burn, my dear. Loss will touch everyone, if it hasn't already."

"I see," Maya replied flatly.

"You sought freedom and the power to shape your destiny, like many out there wanted."

Maya blinked away tears, the cold air stinging. "Freedom in exchange for this?"

"It may burn, but it's the survivors who'll rebuild," Robert said. "We learn; we correct. It's up to people like you to forge the world anew." Robert smiled. "It was the generations before you that created this path, like me, Gil, and your mother. We sat back and allowed all this to happen. Now it's yours to create."

"Rebuild," Maya repeated.

Robert turned to Maya and pulled up his sleeve. A red scar flashed on his skin, and Maya instantly knew what it was. "Thought I'd pledge my allegiance. On the right side, this time."

Maya smiled, running her finger along the raised skin that matched the brand on her ankle.

"So, do you think it was worth it? In the end?" Robert asked, letting the question linger.

Maya pondered the journey she'd been on, the losses, and also the challenges to come. It was an impossible question, but one she sought to answer. Biting her lip, she nodded. "I think it was. Despite the problems, the divisions, at least these are now our problems to solve moving forward. We have the choice, and that, for better or worse, makes it all worth it."

Robert pulled her close, his warmth intertwining with hers. "I hope you're right; I really do."

A Word From The Author

Thank you for reading Divided.

I spent so much time thinking, planning and trying to create a world that could feel true to the life we are living in at this moment, but also a story that shines a light on what our near future could become if we allow it.

Recent world events have helped narrow the make believe of dystopian fiction into reality, and I can understand why so many people are feeling fearful of what is happening. Myself included.

I ended this novel on an edge of hope for the future. Maya and Liam may not have found the absolute answer to fixing things, but I'm not sure anyone ever will. This novel is, of course, a piece of fiction, and the real world isn't this bleak, and hopefully never will be.

I wanted to create a fictional world exploring the potential impacts of politics and technological advancement, both positive and negative. I hope this story will stay as a part of fiction.

If you enjoyed the book, it would mean so much to me if you could post a review. Each review is paramount at getting the word out about Divided, and get as many eyes on this story as possible.

Again, thank you for spending the time reading this story. It truly means so much to me. I'd also like to thank my beta readers, especially Sharayu Marracino and Levi D Reynolds who were the first people to set eyes on this world and gave me wonderful feedback on the characters and the setting. Thank you to my ARC reviewers and anyone who has supported me on this journey. My editor Eden Northover at EdenEditorial, who helped shape this book into what it has become. I want to thank Tithi at Grandfailure for creating the artwork for the bookcover and Covers by John for creating the typography. Without you both, I don't think anyone would have picked this book up.

Also by Ben Andrews

SECRETS & LIES SERIES

Secrets, Lies & Revenge

Secrets, Lies & Sacrifice

Secrets, Lies &Obsession

THE GHOST MERCHANT SERIES

The Ghost Merchant

Alma's Story: A Ghost Merchant Novella

THE FRACTURED WORLD SERIES

* * *

Divided

Subtracted - coming soon

Find out more at benandrewsauthor.co.uk

www.ingramcontent.com/pod-product-compliance
Ingram Content Group UK Ltd.
Pitfield, Milton Keynes, MK11 3LW, UK
UKHW042016130126
466914UK00001B/3

9 781919 236704